A Derric

# Discovery

## A Derrick King Novel
## Book 3

**By Daniel L Copeland**

"I was left on the edge of my seat at the end of ***Escape***, now book three, ***Discovery,*** takes me on a literary thrill ride. This series just keeps getting better, more complex, and pulls me in deeper and deeper."

Rod Leonard

This is a work of fiction. The names, characters, incidents, places, and plot are products of the author's imagination or are used fictitiously. Any resemblance to actual persons, agencies, companies, or events is purely coincidental.

**Discovery**
**A Derrick King Novel, Book 3**
**Published November 2020**
**First Edition**

**ISBN: 978-1-7348746-5-5**

**Published by Daniel Loran Copeland**

# *A New Beginning*

On March 12, The Tribunal exiled Derrick King.

Derrick gave up on ever going home or seeing Miriam King again.

Then The Tribunal sent an envoy to welcome Derrick back to Pacific Edge.

Derrick refused to go.

Then The Tribunal sent armed security officers to capture him.

Derrick escaped.

Miriam King tried to escape and nearly drowned.

The Tribunal locked her up.

Miriam escaped.

Now she is free.

Or did she just complete part of a test?

# *PART ONE*

## 1

**Friday, April 2, 12:30 a.m.**

REBEKAH'S FLASHLIGHT CREATED A POOL OF white light on the tunnel floor, casting a dim light on to the huge door where her fingers remained lightly touching the metal surface. She had been angry at Miriam for insisting she knew where this place existed, and that Derrick had been here. There was no logical explanation to justify Miriam's confidence. Rebekah did not believe in superiority or the existence of the supernatural regardless of it being superior intellect, race, or religion. She might never admit it to anyone, but that was why she had to escape from Pacific Edge with Miriam. Rebekah Ford would never fit in with all their Chosen doctrines. Yet, her she was, kneeling in a tunnel, as sure as she had ever been about anything, knowing Derrick King had been in this exact spot not long ago. She owed Miriam an apology.

Or maybe Miriam's crazy had infected her.

"What do we do now?" Rebekah asked.

"I don't know. What do you think we should do?" Miriam replied.

"Don't ask me. You're the genius."

"I'm not a genius."

Rebekah stood. "You learned to read the stars and calculate our GPS position — *in your head* — as we walked here. You're right, you're not a genius; you're whatever is two times smarter than a genius."

"I'm what they allowed me to be."

"What does that mean?"

"I don't want to talk about it."

Rage started in Rebekah's chest, but before she lashed out, she got hold of it. There was no doubt there was something strange about Miriam beyond sheer genius, and it haunted Miriam. And what troubled Miriam caused her to vacillate between a smart-ass, funny teenager to a darkness that threatened to consume her. Miriam did not need scolding; she needed a friend. Friends tolerate each other, and that is what Rebekah did. Rebekah did not understand the significance of her decision.

"Let's go find your brother," Rebekah said and then added, "I'm sorry for what I said earlier."

"You didn't say anything bad. No apology is necessary," Miriam said.

"I didn't believe you. I should have."

"Not believing me was the logical thing to do. Never apologize for being right."

Rebekah walked to Miriam and hugged her. "We stick together, no matter what. Okay?"

Miriam held on to Rebekah for a few moments, absorbing the comradery, while considering that sticking together might prove impossible. Miriam pushed away, holding Rebekah at arms' length, and said, "We stick together, no matter what. Now let's find that knuckle-headed brother of mine. He should have known we'd be here and stayed put."

"Exactly," Rebekah said. "I might kick his butt when we find him."

"I'll help," Miriam added.

The girls emerged from the tunnel entrance and stood atop the mound of rocks.

"They went to a lot of trouble to keep people out of here. So why didn't they cover this entrance?" Rebekah asked.

Miriam turned around, shining her flashlight, studying the entrance. "Good point. I didn't think about that."

"Score one for the non-genius girl," Rebekah said.

Miriam touched Rebekah's hand. Miriam had turned her flashlight off. Rebekah noticed and doused her light as well.

Silhouetted against the night sky, ten yards away, stood a man.

The man didn't move.

Taking a step forward, Miriam pushed Rebekah behind her. Slowly, Miriam reached to her belt, retrieving the bear spray.

The moon silhouetted the man, his face in shadow.

The breeze fell still; the night fell quiet.

"Miriam? Is that you?" a voice asked.

"It's me, Number1sis."

"What are you doing here?"

"I promised I would come." Miriam said.

# 2

DERRICK HAD LEFT THE TUNNEL EARLIER for water; his throat felt as if it were on fire. The stream ran clear and cold. *Was it safe to drink?* He ate berries from bushes, hoping they were not poisonous. Also, urinating outside seemed better than inside the tunnel, which was his temporary home. When he heard voices, he eased closer. When he was certain, he called to her. Then he scooped her up in his arms and hugged her. Tears streamed down his cheeks.

When he put Miriam down, he said, "What are you doing here? How …"

"Where are your clothes?" Miriam asked.

Derrick looked down at himself. "I'm wearing them. Except for my shirt. I took it off to confuse the security patrol. You did not answer my question."

Miriam touched his forehead. "You're hurt."

"It's no big deal," Derrick said. "I'm fine.

"You're half-naked, injured, lost in the woods, and you're fine?" Miriam asked.

"Better than fine, now," Derrick said. "You still haven't answered my question!"

"I promised I would come. Here I am." Miriam cradled his face in her hands.

"But your e-mail. You said you had given up."

"Sorry about that. It was awful writing you that message, but I had to throw them off."

"Throw who off?"

"I don't know. Them." Miriam shrugged.

"But how did you get here? How did you find me?"

"Long story."

Derrick realized they were not alone, which he knew from the moment he heard the voices, but he was so overwhelmed with joy he blocked the second person from his mind. Now her presence must be addressed. "Rebekah Ford?"

"Hi, Derrick." Rebekah gave a little wave.

Derrick looked at Miriam, then to Rebekah. "Why is Rebekah here?"

"I thought Miriam needed company," Rebekah said, before Miriam could respond.

"Huh?" Derrick asked.

"Another long story," Rebekah said. "You have not explained why you're out here half naked."

"Went for a run after track practice. I was by the river, outside town, when two security officers tried to take me. Well, they took me, but I got away."

"Track as in track team?" Rebekah asked.

"Yes."

"I don't believe it," Rebekah said.

"You're shivering," Miriam said. "You must be freezing."

"I'm okay," Derrick lied.

"Bullshit," Miriam said. She removed her coat, draping it over his shoulders. "Oh, shit!"

"Miriam, your language."

"Screw my language. Look!" She pointed.

Derrick turned. "Oh, shit!"

"What is it?" Rebekah asked.

"Hovercraft," Derrick said. "Follow me."

"You can't see it, but there's a huge tunnel. I've been hiding in there. I'll go first, and you follow. I'll help you down."

Derrick started over the first precipice, feeling like the big brother he should have always been. Miriam and Rebekah switched on their flashlights and illuminated the opening.

"Or we could go to the side. We can walk down as if we were on stairs," Miriam said.

"Right. There's that way too." Derrick rolled his eyes. "But hurry."

Inside the tunnel, the girls swung the flashlights from side to side, and up and down. Derrick had not seen the tunnel with so much light. "I wonder what this place is?"

"National Nuclear Defense Site," Miriam said. "Or an entrance to it."

"Right," Rebekah said.

"How do you know that?" Derrick asked.

"Sign," Miriam said, walking deeper into the tunnel.

"What sign?" Derrick asked.

Miriam pointed the direction they had traveled. "The one Back where we got on the road that led us here. They must have abandoned this place many years ago."

"What is nuclear?" Derrick asked.

"A method the old United States used to generate electricity," Miriam said. "Or destroy the world. I don't think this place is a power plant."

"How do you know that?" Derrick asked.

"I know many things," Miriam said.

They stood in silence. Outside, light filled the night, spilling over the rocks, filtering into the tunnel.

"There's a door back there," Derrick said, pointing into the darkness.

"We know," Miriam said.

"How do you know?" Derrick asked.

Rebekah said, "We've been down here already"

"Oh," Derrick said.

"We were looking for you," Rebekah added.

"I see. They don't know about the tunnel," Derrick said.

"I'm afraid that will soon change," Miriam said.

Derrick said, "I don't think so. This place is hard to find."

"You found it," Miriam said.

"You have a point," Derrick agreed.

Miriam walked deeper into the tunnel.

"She expects us to follow her," Rebekah said, handing Derrick a power bar. "Eat this."

When they reached the end of the tunnel, Miriam walked to the metal door, studied the keypad. She went into the room where the person who controlled entrance had been stationed; she studied the keypad there too. She opened each drawer, and then bent, looking under the counter. When she stood, she held a yellowed piece of paper.

Derrick joined her. "What is that?"

"Someone taped it under the counter. One side of the tape let go; it was dangling. A note."

Derrick stared at the paper; the ink faded and difficult to see.

8-1-6-0-3

Good luck

"Maybe it's a code," Derrick said.

"What good is a code? This place has been dead for years," Rebekah said from behind Derrick.

"Not dead; asleep," Miriam said, laying the note on the counter.

"How could it be asleep for so long and still function?" Rebekah asked.

"Nuclear," Miriam said.

Miriam stepped to the keypad near the door, touched a key, and the pad glowed pale green.

Miriam tapped the numbers. The sound of a locking mechanism activated. The door fell open an inch.

Lights glared at the other end of the tunnel.

"Let's go," Miriam whispered, leaning hard to pull the door open.

Derrick motioned Rebekah to go ahead of him. With both girls safe, he stepped inside and pulled the door shut. The lock clicked. At first, it was dark except for Miriam and Rebekah's flashlights until, one by one, the overhead lights flickered and came to life. The room they had entered had a glass wall on one side that bordered an enormous bay that would hold many huge vehicles the commoners call trucks. Three such trucks were parked along the far wall.

On the other side of a counter, sat several desks with computers and beyond the desks, five doors, leading to offices, stood open. Derrick moved past Rebekah and stood alongside Miriam, gazing at the bay where the trucks stood.

"Wow," Derrick said. "What is this place?"

"A safe place for now," Miriam said. She put her arm around his waist. "Are you okay?"

"I'm great now that you are here."

"I'm glad. I hope you still feel that way the next time you see me."

Derrick turned his head. "What does …"

Miriam stuck a stun device in his back and pulled the trigger.

# 3

WHEN DERRICK AWOKE, HE LAY ON his side in a dark and silent place. He remained still, in a fetal position, for two reasons. First, he did not know who attacked him or their location. As was the case when he awoke on the hovercraft platform, the element of surprise was his best hope. Second, every muscle in his body ached, even his eyeballs hurt.

As his mind cleared, he realized the room was dimly lit. A glow emanated from behind the counter. His attacker must be on the other side. He planned his assault. How many did he face? Were they armed? When his moment came; he must strike fast and without mercy.

A thought occurred to him.

*Where are the girls?*

Moving his fingers, he formed a fist. *That hurts.* He flexed his toes. *That hurts.* At least he was right about one thing; every muscle hurt. He was not certain he could stand. So, no rush. Stay put until he recovered.

Except for the girls.

They might need him now.

He focused on his body, not only the pain but to determine if they restrained him. The Pacific Edge security officers should have restrained him. They would not make that mistake again. Because he had a limited field of vision, he dared not move much in case someone was watching him, standing ready to zap him or worse. He did not sense restraints, which did not prove their absence. He realized an odd thing. Something soft elevated his head. And a coat covered him. Someone had provided him with a level of comfort. Perhaps to keep him out longer. Perhaps because he was in worse condition than he realized.

The reflection of the light on the ceiling changed. His heart pounded. Someone was moving behind the counter. Coming to check on him or coming to do him harm. Decision time. He did not feel capable of marshaling an assault. Yet, it might be his only opportunity to do so. He could keep his eyes closed and pretend to still be out, but the enemy would remain unidentified.

Heart pounding in his chest, he narrowed his eyes to thin slits, hoping he would appear to be unconscious but be able to see his target.

Two shoes appeared near his face. Boots. He eased his eye open a little. The person knelt; one knee close to him. His opportunity drew near.

*Move fast. Be ruthless.*

A hand touched his shoulder and gave him a gentle shake. He clenched his fists. He eased his eyes open a little.

*Now or never.*

Derrick pushed up; in his mind, driving his fist upward with a punch destined to break bones.

It turned out fast and violent would not happen. Instead of throwing the punch he envisioned, he rose a few inches and collapsed.

He opened his eyes to see Rebekah Ford, kneeling beside him, holding her finger to her lips.

Rebekah lowered her finger; her lower lip pouted as if to say, poor baby. She gave him a come-with-me signal with her index finger. Slowly, painfully, he rose on one elbow. Rebekah stood, offering him a hand. She helped him to his feet and put his arm around her shoulder and her arm around his waist, then helped him walk around the counter.

On the other side of the counter, Miriam sat in front of a glowing computer monitor. Miriam gave Derrick the same quiet signal Rebekah used. He moved behind Miriam; the reason for silence became clear.

Ten Pacific Edge security officers stood outside the enormous metal door. Surveillance cameras captured their activity. Miriam moved her finger to a key that showed a small speaker. A bar appeared on the screen; the volume set at full, still there was no sound. Rebekah reached over Miriam's shoulder and turned a small knob on a black device. Voices boomed. Miriam lowered the volume.

"He can't be in there," an officer said.

"Doesn't seem possible," another officer added.

"We are wasting time."

"Probably," the first officer said.

"Let's get back to searching the area. I want to find the little bastard so I can go home."

"Your home will be in some shit-hole like Potterville if we go back without him. Let's blow this door down."

"Seriously?"

"We don't have enough explosive to breach that door. What is this place anyway?"

"Don't know. Maybe a gold mine. We need to get in there. If we don't try, we're toast."

"You're the boss."

Three men came into the scene, each carrying a box that must have been heavy given how they strained. Miriam clicked her mouse and the image changed, captured from another angle. She clicked again, and the screen split into 4 images, each from a different angle. The men worked quickly, pasting a thick soft rope-like substance to the metal door; the officers applied the same stuff to the small door through which he and the girls entered.

Miriam whispered. "We have to move. Let's go."

Miriam led them out to another metal door, which was locked. Using the keypad, Miriam entered the same number that granted them access through the tunnel's door. "I hope they don't find that note."

"You mean this one?" Rebekah held up a yellowed piece of paper.

"I'm starting to like you," Miriam said.

"I'm the best friend you'll ever have. You'll figure it out one day."

The lock clicked, and Miriam pulled the door open. Behind the door, darkness awaited, but lights flickered on when they entered. They were in a hall, not any hall; an extraordinarily long one. Lights came on cascading down the corridor. Miriam took off running. Rebekah followed. Runner though he was, Derrick struggled, legs aching as if someone had beaten him with a thick stick.

A deep rumble sounded behind them; a few seconds later, the floor moved below their feet.

"Do you think they got in?"

"No. Maybe," Miriam said. She stopped in front of a door and tried the knob. It was unlocked. "In here."

The room was pitch black. No automatic lights greeted them. Derrick closed his fists, ready to fight. The dangers in this place that seemed empty yet alive remained unidentified. A light glared behind him. A chair sat a foot from where he stood.

"You going to attack that chair?" Rebekah asked with a chuckle.

"Uh, no. Well, I didn't know what …"

"Relax. There are no people here. Take a seat, we'll wait in the dark," Miriam said, locking the door.

Rebecka sat in one chair. Derrick took the other. Miriam moved behind the desk, sat, and switched off her flashlight.

Derrick said, "You don't know that. There might be someone here."

"Or something," Miriam said.

"She's scary like that," Rebekah offered.

"Be quiet," Miriam said.

In the silence, they sat for several minutes. Hearing nothing, Derrick whispered, "What makes you think they did not get in, Miriam?"

"They built those doors to withstand a hell of a blast."

Derrick nodded his head but realized no one saw his agreement in the dark. "What happened to me? I ache all over."

"Had to zap you," Miriam whispered. "Sorry, about that."

"Zap me. You mean like that security officer did?"

"Nailed it. That's what we thought happened," Rebekah said.

Derrick looked towards where Miriam sat. "Why did you zap me?"

"Remember, I told you the Pacific Edge surveillance was worse than we thought?"

"I remember."

"It's because you have a chip in your back; they can track you anywhere, anytime. Well, not in here, because it's GPS."

"What's a GPS?" Derrick asked.

"Global Position System. It uses satellites."

"What are satellites?"

"Machines orbiting Earth."

"How do you know this stuff?"

"I have a lot to tell you."

"The security officer zapped me. I think it was the same thing, but I did not hurt as much as when you zapped me."

"I turned the machine up. We saw your transmitter appear here before we left Pacific Edge. That's how I knew your location. Maybe how they found this place. Your chip still functioned, at least intermittently."

"Do you have these chip things?" Derrick asked.

"Yes," Rebekah said. "Everyone in Pacific Edge has them."

"They can track you too," Derrick said, his voice rising above a whisper.

"Shhhh. We zapped ourselves before we left," Miriam whispered.

"If mine was still working, yours might be working too."

"Shit," Miriam and Rebekah said in unison.

# 4

AFTER AN HOUR THAT FELT LIKE TEN, Derrick eased the door open at Miriam's instruction. The building remained quiet. The lights off; only a spattering of exits signs cast dim light. He noticed an unusual dusty, burnt odor not previously present, or he had not noticed. His head cleared, and his aching muscles and joints felt better. Having little to do except think while they sat in the dark room, he found it hard to imagine how Miriam escaped Pacific Edge; even harder to believe how she found him given that he did not even know where he was. He wondered if there was really a tracker that needed to be zapped or if there was another reason Miriam rendered him unconscious.

"Are you going to just stand there?" Miriam asked.

"What? Oh, sorry. Just thinking," Derrick said, ashamed of his thoughts because he entertained a paranoia that Miriam and Rebekah would take him back to Pacific Edge.

The walls were white, except for yellow stains that indicated water had leaked in the past. The floor gray, cleaner than one would expect for being abandoned so long ago, yet there were occasional white rings caused by puddles that had dried. The lights, those that still worked, flickered to life; in the distance, some lights had fallen and hung by wires, a few showered sparks before going dark. Some bulbs half-lit as if dying a slow, painful death. He could not describe the odor other than to say it smelled like a tomb, although he had never been in one.

Miriam moved deeper into the building, opening doors, flicking on lights. "These are all offices."

"What is this place? What did people do here?" Derrick asked.

"I'm not sure, but I have suspicions," Miriam said.

"Care to share them?" Rebekah asked.

"Not yet," Miriam said.

About one hundred yards down the hallway, they encountered an intersection with halls stretching in both directions. They could not see the end of the hall on the left. The lights were on at least fifty yards before the hall faded into darkness. The hall to the right was shorter. A metal door with a narrow glass window stood fifteen yards from them. A sign above the door read AUTHORIZED PERSONNEL ONLY.

Miriam turned right. Derrick and Rebekah followed.

With her hands cupped around her face, Miriam peered through the small window in the door. "This is still the same big space we saw when we first came in," Miriam said as she eased the door open. "Let's have a look."

As with the hallways, lights began coming to life when they entered the cavernous room. Derrick found a trash bin nearby and placed it so the door would not close behind them. Parked along the side stood vehicles much bigger than any truck Derrick had ever seen. Only a few had the big rectangular boxes common in Potterville. Most were flatbeds with cylindrical structures that Derrick estimated carried some sort of massive pipe-like contraption. The trucks were painted flat tan with darker tan splotches and a yellow circle with three wedge-shaped blades attached to the axis. The front of the truck had a cab where the driver sat to pilot the machine, but it did not look like any cab in Potterville. The rear of the machine also had a smaller cab mounted high and to one side so a person could see the path ahead. The odors changed as they entered the cavernous room. Fuel, oil, and musty air.

"This thing is huge," Derrick said, stepping closer to the machine. "Looks like it's steered from the front and rear because of its size."

The cavern was so immense that neither end was visible. The light seemed to sense their presence and only lit the area they occupied. There were lights mounted on the ceiling, but this was not a room like any other. Carved from solid rock. Enormous steel beams supported at each side with like-sized steel girders ensuring the rock ceiling did not collapse. Slender silver pipes, that must have carried electrical wires, ran to each light. The lights here were more uniformly lit, as if they were more important than the lights in the hallways.

Stepping to Derrick's side, Rebekah said, "I don't see how they could get it here on the road we were on."

"I agree, although it was dark. Maybe we missed something about the road," Miriam said.

"Then how did it get here?" Derrick asked.

"Just one of many things we must find out," Miriam said as she walked away deeper into the cavern.

The trucks were parked three abreast. Derrick lost count of how many they walked past when they encountered other vehicles pointed the opposite direction. These vehicles were much different and varied. Smaller, some had containers on the back with benches inside and a stiff cloth covering. Others had no wheels but a track and some sort of weapon protruding from an odd-looking device on the top. Some had both wheels and tracks and carried many pipes that resembled the big ones, except smaller. Thick cables plugged in to ports in the wall snaked to each vehicle. All the tubes were printed with these letters: USNSF.

"What does USNSF stand for," Derrick asked.

"I don't know," Miriam said. "But I suspect we'll find out."

Derrick stopped and pulled Miriam to his side when a tone sounded, echoing through the cavern. Yellow lights now spun along the walls.

A disembodied voice said, "Warning. Equipment failure imminent in Reactor One. Mechanical engineering report immediately." The warning repeated three times. The lights continued to spin, tossing yellowed reflections off the glistening rock walls.

"What's that about?" Derrick asked.

"How am I supposed to know? You've been down here longer than I have," Miriam said.

"It's not our problem," Rebekah said. "Our problem is finding a way out of here."

"Perhaps," Miriam said.

"How many of these things are there?" Derrick pointed at the vehicles to his left.

"I've lost count," Rebekah admitted.

"Thirty-three so far," Miriam said.

Rebekah and Derrick said nothing.

They walked on. The yellow lights continued to spin.

The tone and warning repeated.

"That's starting to worry me." Rebekah indicated the warning.

"Me too," Derrick said.

"There." Miriam pointed.

The trio worked their way through the trucks. A single truck was parked on a metal platform.

"An elevator. That's how they get them out," Miriam said, stepping to the side of the vehicle.

Derrick looked up but only saw rock. "Crap. It's not an elevator. There's no place for it to go."

"Crap? Brother, your language has evolved."

"Not quickly enough," Derrick said.

"What does that mean?" Miriam asked.

"Long story. I'll tell you more if we get out."

"When we get out. It's an elevator. It doesn't go up because it goes down," Miriam corrected.

Rebekah walked to a set of doors next to the platform containing the truck and its payload. "Hey, guys. I think this is a people elevator."

Derrick and Miriam joined her.

"I wonder if it still works?" Miriam asked.

Derrick walked on, disappearing around the elevator. Poking his head around the corner, he said, "Doesn't matter."

Miriam and Rebekah joined him. A spiral staircase disappeared into the darkness.

"I don't want to go down. I want to go up," Rebekah said.

"Maybe we have to go down to get out, except for getting out the way we came in," Derrick said.

"It goes out," Miriam said.

"How do you know?" Derrick asked.

"Because that's how they got the trucks out," Miriam said.

"But why does it go down?" Derrick asked. "That doesn't make sense."

"To get under the river. Out into the desert on the other side of these mountains," Miriam said.

"This place scares me," Rebekah said.

"You're forgetting something," Miriam said.

"What is that?" Rebekah asked.

Miriam pulled the stun thing from her bag. "We need a second zap."

"We can do that when we are out of here," Rebekah protested.

"Have to do it here. If 1984 is working, they'll spot us soon as we get outside," Miriam said.

"Shit," Rebekah said.

The spinning yellow lights turned red. A siren sounded. Then the voice echoed this warning: "Reactor One failure eminent. Mechanical engineering report to Reactor One. Mechanical engineering report to Reactor One. All staff disarm nuclear warheads. All staff disarm nuclear warheads. Evacuate leadership. Failure in fifty-four minutes."

"Let's get the hell out of here," Rebekah said as she sprinted to the elevator and stabbed at the buttons near the door.

The elevator doors slid open. Rebekah stepped inside and Derrick joined her.

"Miriam!" Derrick shouted. "Miriam!"

"Where is she?" Rebekah said tears, flowing down her cheeks.

Derrick stepped out of the elevator. He could not see Miriam. He stepped back to the stairs. No Miriam there either.

Derrick knifed through the trucks.

He looked down the path from which they had come.

Miriam was sprinting back into the cavern.

# 5

DESPITE A HEAD START, DERRICK CAUGHT Miriam halfway through the trucks laden with the enormous tubular objects.

"Where are you going?" Derrick asked, taking her by the arm and pulling her to a stop.

"To find out what's happening? See if we can stop it," Miriam said.

"We need to get out of here. It's not our problem."

"You don't understand. It's a nuclear reactor. And these things," Miriam pointed at the trucks, "are missiles with nuclear warheads."

Derrick stared at her for a moment. "I don't know what that means. It's still not our problem. Let's get out of here."

"It is our problem."

"It's not. I know you're smarter than me but listen. We need to run."

Miriam shook her head. "We don't have anywhere to go."

"Yes, we do. Coach said I can live with him and I'm sure someone will help you and Rebekah. We need to get back to Potterville."

Rebekah joined them and stood beside Derrick.

Miriam said, "That's what I'm trying to tell you. There might not be a Potterville if this reactor fails."

Derrick turned white. "How do you know this? What is this nuclear thing?"

"I stumbled across it, working on getting out of Pacific Edge. No time to explain. It's bad beyond anything you can imagine. Everyone and everything within hundreds of miles could die, and this entire area will be uninhabitable for centuries."

Derrick thought of Nyx and Akira. But it wasn't just them. He thought of Malcolm Cross, Henry Clark, Coach Browning, Mr. Griggs, Donna Parks, and even Larry Kinkead. Derrick had never placed others before himself, except for that moment when he decked Marcus Carver, which now seemed like years ago rather than weeks. Arguably he wasn't putting others first now, because if he accepted what Miriam said, he had no choice; fix what caused the alarm or die. He would not lie; he was afraid; for himself, for Miriam, for Rebekah. Still, he feared for Potterville. They asked for none of this. Not for him, not for his problems, not for this problem. While this problem was not of his making, they were the only ones there to stop it. And stop it they must.

Derrick said, "Why are we standing here? Lead the way, Miriam. We have to stop this thing."

Rebekah said, "We need to get out of here. This is not our problem. Miriam doesn't know it will be that bad."

Miriam was running through the bay.

Derrick back-peddled as he said, "You go, Rebekah. We'll deal with it. Get out and as far from here as you can. We'll find you when we finish."

"But, Derrick …"

Derrick turned and ran to catch up with Miriam. He did not hear Rebekah.

"Damn you both," Rebekah said.

# 6

MIRIAM ENTERED THE HALL THROUGH THE DOOR, Derrick had propped open with a garbage can. He caught the door before it bumped the can; he realized Miriam was going back to where they first entered, using the code someone had left on a note, which also said good luck. Derrick had not given the good luck part much thought.

Now he did.

"Miriam! Slow down. Why are we going back? What if the security guards are there?"

"I need a computer and I know that one works. Don't have time to search for another. Don't follow me. Find a map of the building and Reactor One."

"Don't want to leave you," Derrick said.

"No time to argue. If you find a map and locate Reactor One, come to me. If you aren't there after I find what I'm looking for, I'll find you. Okay?" Miriam asked.

"How will you find me?"

Miriam pointed up. "The lights will be on where you are."

* * *

Miriam ran to the entrance. As she expected, no security guards greeted her; the blast doors held. *Come on, come on,* she thought as the computer took its time starting. A different operating system than she learned at Technical Services. Older, slower. When it finished its start routine, she searched for Reactor One and found nothing. *Who would work at this station? Not anyone important. Someone to check people in and out. Maybe such a low clearance that they did not go beyond this entry portal.*

She did not find Reactor One, but it found her. An alert message, white lettering against a red background, filled three-quarters of the monitor:

**EMERGENCY IN REACTOR ONE. MECHANICAL ENGINEERING TO REACTOR ONE. PRIMARY COOLING VALVE FAILURE. LEADERSHIP AND NON-ESSENTIAL PERSONNEL EVACUATE USING ESCAPE TUNNEL.**

Hovering the mouse arrow over the warning text, she clicked, and the computer diverted her to the power station section. *Now I'm getting somewhere.*

The next screen provided more details than she expected. Reactor One automatic cooling had failed, but not recently. It had been in a caution state for years, but because the facility had been idling, the cooling function had been adequate that the reactor had not become critical. A call for minimal power occurred two hours and seventeen minutes earlier.

*We caused this.*

Miriam whispered, "If we caused it, we can fix it."

Miriam printed two lists and ran to the cavern. She found Derrick in the middle of the huge space running towards her.

Rebekah came from an area they had not previously explored, "Where have you guys been? I've been searching all over."

"I told you to get out," Derrick said louder than he intended.

"Yeah, that's not going to happen," Rebekah said.

"Get used to it," Miriam said.

"I was just over there." Derrick pointed to the wall lined with trucks. "I found a map. Reactor One is behind the elevator where we were when the alarm sounded."

A siren sounded. The voice said, "Reactor One failure eminent. Mechanical engineering report to Reactor One. Mechanical engineering report to Reactor One. Disarm nuclear warheads. Disarm nuclear warheads. Evacuate leadership and non-essential personnel. Failure in forty-five minutes."

"Let's go," Miriam said.

"But we don't know what we are doing," Derrick said, chasing Miriam. Rebekah running at his side.

Miriam held up the papers she had printed. "Yes, we do."

# 7

MIRIAM LED THEM THROUGH THE CAVERN, through the multitude of trucks carrying the rockets with the yellow propeller design, through the trucks carrying multiple small rockets, and through the vehicles of various types. It surprised Derrick how well she ran. She didn't run when they lived in Pacific Edge, or more accurately stated, he had no knowledge that she did, which hurt a little in his chest because he understood little about his sister. She walked a lot; she was not sedimentary as he had been, and she shared his genes, which had proven well-suited for running. He could hear Rebekah behind him, but she remained close enough that he was not concerned they would lose her among the vehicles. When Miriam reached the elevators, she circled to the back into a hallway. She started cursing before they reached the end.

From behind Miriam, he asked, "What's the matter."

"This!" Miriam pointed to a dark-gray metal door with the yellow propeller painted on it and under the propeller it said DANGER RADIOACTIVE MATERIALS.

Derrick did not understand radioactive, but he assumed Miriam did. Perhaps it differed from nuclear, which he also did not understand.

"Radioactive?" Derrick asked.

"I've been telling you it's nuclear. I know it's radioactive. That's not the problem; this is." Miriam pointed to a black box with a lens mounted on the wall.

Rebekah asked, "What's the problem?"

Miriam pointed at the black box again. "This is the problem."

Derrick still didn't understand. He studied the door and the box Details had been unimportant given the spinning red lights, plus the siren and voice issuing a warning every few minutes. The door was metal, but it did not look like the thick metal doors between the tunnel and the building. The door had a window and while it looked clear, it also looked thick. The doorway cut into solid rock had a heavy metal frame. On the wall, a big metal box with thick black cords snaking from the top, a smaller cord went to the small box to which Miriam pointed. Some of the cords disappeared into holes drilled in the stone. Everything projected an eerie quality of advanced technology merged with the crude design of an ancient civilization.

Miriam said, "This is a retinal scan system, crude, but I'm certain that's what it is."

"I don't understand what that means," Derrick said. "You need to explain things better."

"It scans a person's eye to allow entrance. The machine has to scan the eyeball of a person who is approved to enter," Miriam said.

"I think people who worked here died many years ago," Derrick said.

"Exactly," Miriam agreed.

"What do we do? Can we get in another way?" Derrick asked.

"Sure, all I need to do is hack into the computer system, find the security section that sets up authorization, find the place where you scan your eye into the system, falsify the authorization to give us access." Miriam stared at the box with her hands planted on her hips.

"Let's do that then," Derrick said. "How can I help?"

"That's why it doesn't help to explain things," Miriam said.

"What?" Derrick asked.

Rebekah moved past Miriam and Derrick to the door. She leaned against it; it moved an inch; she pushed harder; it moved two feet, then swung to the side. "Or we could just do this."

"Girl, you do prove yourself useful sometimes," Miriam said, walking into the dark hallway beyond the door.

Derrick studied the door and the locking mechanism. It didn't seem right that such a door was left unlocked. He did not understand radioactivity, but he was smart enough to see that whoever built this place had gone to great lengths to protect this area. Along the edge of the door, he saw round steel rods, five inches in diameter, that were retracted into the door. Those rods would extend into the metal door frame, which looked to be about eighteen inches thick, to lock the door. He had no knowledge of mechanical things or engineering. Such topics were unnecessary for the Chosen and bordered on the fringe of science, which was forbidden in Pacific Edge. Even with his lack of knowledge, he recognized why the door was not locked. Someone had covered the holes meant to receive the locking mechanism with metal. It was now impossible to lock this door. Miriam and Rebekah had already moved down the dark hallway several yards. The sparse lighting provided little light, but there wasn't much to see. It was just a tube-shaped walkway cut through solid stone. He thought about telling Miriam about the door, but decided it was not important.

"Are you sure we are going the right direction?" Derrick asked as he joined the girls.

"I'm not sure of anything," Miriam said.

"I'm sure we shouldn't be here," Rebekah said.

Miriam glanced over her shoulder at Derrick. "You said the map showed this was the way to Reactor One."

"Yes, but the map didn't show this tunnel. It must be fifty yards long," Derrick said.

"Forty-seven," Miriam said. "Plus a few inches. So far."

"Funny," Derrick said.

"She's not joking," Rebekah said.

Another door came into view.

"Damn it," Miriam cursed, and then added, "Another scanner."

"It won't be locked," Derrick said.

"It looks locked to me," Rebekah said.

"What do you mean?" Miriam asked.

"I noticed the first door wasn't tight. It a jar a little," Rebekah said.

"That door looks to be closed tight," Miriam said.

"Looks tight to me," Rebekah agreed.

"It won't be locked," Derrick said.

From down the hall, they heard the siren again. The voice said they had forty minutes until reactor failure.

Rebekah stepped to the door and pushed. It did not move. She put both hands on the door and pushed. Nothing.

Derrick stepped to the door, put his shoulder into it and pushed.

Nothing.

Derrick said, "It's stuck. It's going to take all of us. Come help."

"It's not stuck. It's locked," Rebekah said.

"It's not locked. Just help," Derrick said.

"I'm not on your list to order around anymore," Rebekah said.

Derrick looked at her. He had not meant it to sound like an order. He only wanted them to help. The situation had not allowed him to give much thought to why Rebekah was here. Long story, she said. He assumed her presence was about him more than it was because Miriam needed a friend. He wondered if he had treated Rebekah and the others on his list for the Choosing as objects rather than people. Given his attitude back then, he was certain that he had done just that.

"I'm sorry, Rebekah. I did not mean to give orders. We don't have much time and I'm certain this door is not locked. I only need you and Miriam to help. I'm scared. I don't think we will survive this unless we work together."

Rebekah stepped to the door, put her shoulder to it, but did not look convinced. Miriam joined them beside Derrick.

"Tell us what to do, Rebekah," Derrick said.

"On three. Push with every fiber of your body."
"One."
"Two."
"Three."
Pushing.
Nothing.

# 8

MIRIAM FOUGHT BACK TEARS. PANIC WOULDN'T HELP. There must be a solution. If not, they were doomed. She also thought about the tension between Derrick and Rebekah. Why Rebekah came here remained a mystery, despite Rebekah's explanation. Understanding social cues wasn't Miriam's forte. Still, she suspected Rebekah's feelings for Derrick had more to do with her being here than Rebekah wanted to admit. No time for such nonsense; they needed to get to that reactor.

Rebekah felt her chest heaving. Fear threatened to overtake her. She wanted to bolt for the door and find an exit. Maybe Miriam was wrong about being unable to escape. A lot of mountain existed between them and the surface. The smart thing was to run. They had forty minutes to put some distance between themselves and this awful place. Weird as it seemed, she also felt bad about snapping at Derrick. She didn't want Derrick to think she came here to win his heart because she didn't. But Derrick had never been unkind. It was not unusual for Chosen boys to mistreat the girls on their lists for the Choosing. Other girls told Rebekah how they had been treated. Derrick, Chosen fanatic that he was, had a kind heart. He did not fit the Chose male mentality. Maybe that's why she liked him. She knew he liked her, but also knew she was not the most logical choice for him given the values taught to Chosen boys. Derrick would choose his bride based on Chosen logic. Jana Somersworth fit that description best. That's who Derrick would have chosen. She should be climbing the stairs, yet, here she stood.

Derrick knew this door was not locked. It was stuck. But how to open it? Then something occurred to him: Red Badowski.

"One more time," Derrick said.

"Derrick, I know you want to be right about this, but it's locked. We can't push it open. We need to find another way. Just let me concentrate," Miriam said.

"It's not locked," Derrick said.

"God, you're stubborn," Miriam said.

"I have no clue where he gets that from," Rebekah said. She faced Derrick. "Just tell me what to do."

"Same as before, except I'm going to do it a little different," Derrick said. "Give me space on the left side."

"Okay," Rebekah said, getting into position against the door. "Why left side?"

"Hinges," Miriam said. "The hinges are on the right, so the most leverage is on the left. That would make sense if the door wasn't locked."

"It's not locked," Derrick said.

During the time Derrick spent hiding in the tunnel, he shivered, he cried, he dozed, and he thought about many things. He thought about Pacific Edge; he wondered if Miriam was okay; he realized his life was forever changed. Even Potterville would never be the same for him. If he got out of the tunnel alive, Potterville might not want him back. Most of his thoughts were dark. He found relief in football. He thought about track and about Akira and about Nix, but he always circled back to football, which struck him as odd because he'd only been on the field once.

As he stared at the immovable door, he wished Red Badowski was here. Derrick felt certain that Red could push the door open. In the tunnel, in the dark, while running football plays through his head, Red was there. With his eyes closed and his head tilted back against the metal door, Derrick pictured Badowski. It surprised him because he didn't realize how much attention he had given Badowski. Red wasn't just big and strong, all the linemen were big and strong, Red was also good at what he did. Derrick pictured the way Red fired out of his stance, exploded at the right moment. Derrick also remembered how Red stood up to his lifelong friend, Jim Priest. Red did that to protect the team and to protect his future. There was a lot he could learn from Red Badowski. If he had a chance to do so.

Red wasn't here physically, but he was in Derrick's mind. Derrick had a team here to lead and protect. As the girls got into position, Derrick pictured Red in place of the door. Derrick planned to run the ball right at Badowski and knock the big man on his butt. He wished he wore shoulder pads; at least he still wore Rebekah's coat, which he should have given back.

"On three, you guys push. I'm going to step back and run into the door," Derrick said.

"You'll hurt yourself," Miriam said.

"Maybe," Derrick replied.

Derrick wasn't going to run at the door; he would take a step and explode at the door, much as he had seen Red Badowski do on the field.

"One."

"Two."

"Three."

The girls pushed, both grunting with the strain. On the count of four, Derrick did his best Red Badowski impression, exploding with all his might, smashing into the door. Pain shot through his shoulder. A high-pitched screech filled his ears and he felt the door give a little. Through his pain, he stepped back, hitting it again.

With a final scraping of metal, the door moved and then fell open. All three of them landed on the floor.

Their first lethal situation; their first victory.

# 9

DERRICK SCRAMBLED TO HIS FEET. He helped Miriam up. Rebekah stood before he got to her. He rubbed his shoulder, a fiery sting still shooting down his arm. An injury now could prove deadly. He did not know what needed to be done but felt sure it would include physical labor.

Miriam touched his arm as Derrick rubbed his shoulder. "Are you okay?"

"I hope. What do we do next?" Derrick asked.

"How did you know the door wasn't locked?" Rebekah asked.

Derrick inspected the door frame. As he expected, they had covered the holes with metal like the first door. A rippled bead of metal around the hole was too high. Pointing, Derrick said, "They covered this part of the locking mechanism on the first door so the door could not be locked. I figured if they did it to one door, they'd do the same to this one." He touched the bright spot. "This is too high and jammed the door."

"Why didn't you tell us about the first door?" Miriam demanded.

Derrick shrugged, the pain in his arm eased. "It didn't seem important, I guess."

"Everything here is important. Don't do that again," Miriam scolded.

In the distance, the siren sounded; the voice too far to hear.

Derrick removed Rebekah's coat, handing it to her. "I should have given it back sooner."

"You keep it. I have a shirt, you don't."

"I'll be okay," Derrick said.

"Stop. It's not important," Miriam said.

"Speaking of important. What do we do?" Rebekah asked.

Miriam pulled two sheets of paper from her bag. "This is a list of the parts and tools we need; the other is a checklist of how the repair is completed. It shows a part and tool room down this hall just before we enter the reactor control room."

Miriam trotted down the hall. Derrick and Rebekah followed. As when they first entered from the tunnel, lights flickered to life as they moved into the hallway. One would not think this was under a mountain.

It looked and felt like a building. The floor painted a dark brown, cleaner than the earlier spaces. The wide hall painted green about four feet up the walls and white from there to the top. Silver pipes of various sizes were mounted to the ceiling.

The parts room proved easy to spot with a sign above the bright-red door that stood open; the paint schemes unchanged. Parts stored in bins, each numbered and in sequence; tools hung on a wall with a silhouette of the tool painted behind it. Finding the parts proved easy. The largest piece, a heavy metal eight-inch electrically controlled water valve, a set of new bolts, washers, and nuts, and two rubber things called gaskets. The tool list was brief. Two wrenches, Derrick assumed so that two people could remove the bolts and nuts; a pipe—he wondered its purpose—and a heavy weird device with a chain he did not understand at all. Derrick grabbed that parts, and Rebekah snatched a cart that would carry it all. Miriam grabbed an electronic device that was one of many along the wall.

In less than five minutes, Derrick wheeled the cart laden with tools and parts out of the room.

This would be easier than he expected.

"The room where people worked should be safe. I think an alarm would warn us if it were not. However, the valve is inside an area next to the reactor itself. This device," Miriam held up the electrical thing, measures radioactivity.

"What is radioactivity?" Derrick asked.

"Is it dangerous?" Rebekah asked.

"No time to explain it, even if I could, which I can't. It's terrible stuff. You can't see it or smell it. It can pass through many materials, including your body. It damages your cells. Depending on the dose, it can kill you instantly, within hours or days, or cause diseases years later."

Derrick and Rebekah stopped. A few moments later, Miriam turned to see them standing still.

"What?" Miriam asked.

"If we can't see it, smell it, how do we know we aren't already in trouble? Derrick asked.

"There would be alarms sounding," Miriam said.

"What if the system is broken?" Rebekah asked.

"Valid point," Miriam said. She pulled the device she had taken from the room and pushed a button. The machine came to life. "It's showing low levels of radiation. In the safe zone."

Miriam continued toward the reactor; she did not look back again.

Ten yards down the hallway towards Reactor One, Derrick asked, "Has the radioactivity increased?"

"It has not," Miriam said. "It's gone down a little."

"That seems weird," Rebekah said.

"It does," Miriam agreed. "But it's unimportant right now. We can try to figure it out if we get the reactor problem fixed."

"When we get it fixed," Rebekah corrected.

"Hey guys, I don't have time to investigate things. We get this fixed, then I need to get back to Potterville. What time is it anyway?" Derrick asked.

"It must be about 3 a.m.," Rebekah said.

"On what day?" Derrick asked.

"Good question," Rebekah said. "Friday, I think. It seems like we left Pacific Edge a week ago instead of yesterday.

"Good. I have time to get back to Potterville for the track meet tomorrow," Derrick said.

"I still can't believe you're on the track team. But now, given all that's happened, getting to a stupid track meet seems rather unimportant. First, we have this reactor thing to survive, then find our way out of here, and we still don't know how far it is to Potterville," Miriam said.

"It's important to me," Derrick said.

Miriam stopped in the hall. "The radioactivity keeps falling. Almost at zero now."

"Weird, but that's a good thing. Right?" Rebekah asked.

"At this moment, it's good. Whether it's good on a larger scale remains to be seen," Miriam said.

"Why did we stop here to talk?" Derrick asked.

"I didn't stop to talk. You guys started talking when we stopped. I stopped here because of this." Miriam pointed to a door labeled Clean Room Preparation.

"What's in here?" Derrick asked.

"Not sure," Miriam said, "but we need to find out."

The door was not locked, and the room was dark. Derrick felt along the wall until he found a switch. The light revealed a small hall instead of a room with two doors: one labeled MEN, the other labeled WOMEN.

"Restrooms?" Rebekah asked.

"Yes, but more than that," Miriam said, walking through the door marked MEN.

Derrick and Rebekah followed her. The room was sizable, and the first area contained toilets, benches, lockers, and a door to one side labeled SCRUBS. Miriam opened the door and found it filled with one-piece uniforms of various colors. Labels under the piles of clothing indicated who wore what, engineering, operator, medical, electrician, etc.

Miriam left the door open and moved deeper into the room. At the far end stood two glass doors, one labeled ENTRANCE, which was a long shower area. The one next to it was labeled OBSERVATION. The third door, a white door with a small vertical window, was on the adjacent wall was labeled TREATMENT AND RECOVERY. She walked to the door labeled OBSERVATION and pulled it open. The door was heavier and thicker than expected. Although it was clear, it was about a foot thick. Both sides of the hallway were glass and on either side were showers. The observation hallway had no exit.

"These people were weird. They stood here and watched others shower. Gross," Rebekah said.

"Only when coming out," Miriam said.

Derrick thought he understood.

"Why would they do that coming out but not going in? I don't see the difference," Rebekah said.

"Because coming out, they might suffer from radioactivity exposure. They could collapse in the shower and die there. Going in is probably just a regular shower. There must be another room with clothing for working in the control room. Coming out, it's a decontamination process." Miriam moved to the window, staring into the showers. "There are three doors in and out. One into the room we were just in, one into the next room to dress before entering the control room, or undress if you're leaving the control room, and then there's that door," She pointed across the way to the door labeled Treatment and Recovery.

Miriam exited the observation area and walked into the Treatment and Recovery room, which was long and narrow. At one end, where they entered, was a door to the men's side; at the far end of the room was a door labeled women. Inside were twenty thin mattresses on metal frames with wheels like one would see in a hospital but crude by comparison. There were machines and monitors that Miriam did not understand, except that they were used for medical purposes. Along the side of the recovery area, opposite the entries, was a separate room that contained cabinets full of small vials. Miriam walked to the door; wasn't locked, but she didn't open it. She pointed to a meter near the door and said, "This room is cooled. To keep the medicine fresh, I assume."

"How long has this place been abandoned?" Derrick had been wondering this but had been afraid to ask.

"I don't know. We'll figure it out at some point," Miriam said.

Rebekah stared at the medicines through the window. "I wonder if that stuff is still good? At least they made it simple. It's arranged by the amount of exposure and proper dosage."

"I hope none of us are exposed. But if we are, we'll take what is here and hope for the best," Derrick said.

"Rebekah and I will go to the women's side. Leave your clothing here, Derrick. We don't want it exposed. Shower then you'll find clothing in the next room like we saw back there."

"I need a shower, but I'll wait until we leave," Derrick said.

"No, shower going in. We don't understand the reason for the protocols, so we need to follow them like the people who worked here," Miriam said.

"Trust us, you need a shower now," Rebekah added.

Derrick grunted. "How do we get the tools and parts in?"

"Good question. Not through the showers." Miriam walked back into the observation area; when she neared the far end, the wall that looked solid moved, revealing another small area. "This is how they passed things to the control room. She pulled the electrical device and checked for radioactivity. "Almost nothing."

"I'll get the cart." Derrick retrieved the cart, pushing it through the observation room and into pass-through room.

"There's a problem," Miriam said.

In the distance, the siren sounded, but it was almost inaudible here.

"I'm glad you said it first," Rebekah said.

"Of course, there's a problem; that's why we are here," Derrick said.

"Get serious, Derrick. The problem is that I don't want you staring at me naked in the shower." Rebekah folder her arms across her chest.

Derrick looked at his feet. "I didn't think of that. I won't. I promise."

"Not the problem I meant," Miriam said. "This area must have heavy shielding from the reactor control room. The radioactivity could be high in the reactor room. I should have grabbed two of these Giger counter things, but I only got one. When we open the door into the next room, we could be exposed. And I'll bet it's a one-way glass. Derrick won't be able to see us."

Derrick thought for a moment. "You girls take the device. If it's clear, come to the men's dressing room on the other side and get me. If you don't come, we'll meet back here."

"If we can get back here," Rebekah said.

"That won't work," Miriam said. "Derrick must take the device."

"No, you need to take it," Derrick said.

"Can't work that way. The radioactivity could be on the other side of the shower door. We don't know if the dressing room is protected, or if it's protected to the same degree. You can't leave the shower until you know it's safe. Judging by the size of the bolts, we might not be strong enough to do the work. Derrick must do it. If there's too much radiation, come back out and find protective clothing. There was a room that had protective clothing where we got the parts. Because Derrick can do the work, he must survive."

With that, Miriam shoved the device in Derrick's hands and left.

# 10

DREAD TWISTED IN DERRICK'S CHEST. He thought about chasing the girls, making them take the Gigery thing, whatever it was, but they had run into the women's dressing room and would already be stripping off clothes. Time to waste did not exist. He dashed to the preparation area and stripped naked. He considered taking his shoes; he'd need shoes but remembered Miriam said to take no clothing. He should have asked Miriam about shoes. Working barefoot did not appeal to him. He'd started going barefoot in his Potterville condo. The thought caused an emptiness in his chest because he no longer had a condo. He had not spent one night at Coach Browning's house. Perhaps he would never sleep there.

Into the shower he went, trotting to the far end where he laid the Gigery thing by the exit door, hoping it would not get wet and stop working. He stood under the closest shower head. Nothing happened. He went back to the first shower head, placing his hand underneath it. The water started, cold at first, but it turned lukewarm soon. He looked for soap dispensers, careful not to turn around and see the girls. Miriam thought the class was one-way, but he would not risk finding out. He saw no soap dispensers, but moments after the water started, it turned a light green color and had a disinfectant odor that reminded him of the halls at James Carver Academy. He lathered. A disembodied voice startled him and instructed him to move to the next shower, which started once he was under it. The water was hotter. After he felt sufficiently rinsed, he moved on, but the voice ordered him back under the hot water. After a few minutes, the voice told him to move to the next shower, which proved to be cold, causing him to shiver. Although uncomfortable, he remained under the water until it stopped. The voice told him to proceed to the next room.

At the next door, dripping wet and a bit cold, Derrick started the Gigery device before opening the door. Easing the door open, he held the device next to the crack. The needle pointed to the green, safe zone.

The next room was not the dressing room he expected. There were no towels. It was a bare white room. A blue light radiated from the ceiling and warm air coursed through the room, drying him. He went to the far end, but the door would not open. The warm breezed stopped; the blue lights faded; the door opened. The device showed zero radioactivity.

He peeked into the next room, wondering if the girls might be there already and he would be exposed to them. They were not. He found the clothing room, found a dark-blue uniform, under a labeled that read maintenance that fit. In addition, he found white socks and white shoes like his running shoes but not as good. It occurred to him that this facility must have cost a fortune to construct, yet an exiled high schooler owned better shoes.

Once dressed, he we removed the tool cart from the middle bay and dragged it to the exit door. He eased the door open just a crack; the Gigery thing held in his hand. Radioactivity increased, but the needle remained in the safe zone. Before he could put the device in the cart, the door flung open. Derrick drew back a fist.

"Calm down," Miriam said.

"You scared me. You were supposed to wait for me. What if the radio stuff had been bad?"

Miriam pushed past him into the dressing area; Rebekah remained outside the door, wearing a blue uniform that matched his. Rebekah's clothing fit; Miriam wore white; pant legs and sleeves rolled up, and it looked as if the entire thing might fall off should she move wrong.

Miriam tapped a dial by the door he failed to notice. The instrument monitored radioactivity and its needle pointed to green. "Let's go. No time to waste. We only have thirty-two minutes."

"Did you hear an announcement on your side?" Derrick asked.

"No," Miriam said, already leaving the area.

"Then how would you know how much time is left? Besides, the announcements came in five-minute intervals."

Miriam spun around, continuing to walk backwards. She tapped the side of her head. "Keeping track in here," she said.

"That's impossible," Derrick said.

"It's possible," Rebekah said. "Trust me."

They were no longer in a narrow hallway, but an area about four times as wide and twice as high. They came to a ninety-degree turn. The next room, filled with machinery and pipes, proved much different. The walls were not painted; just bare gray concrete. Two doors had the same green paint as other parts of the building. A walkway above the floor extended around the room. The walkway was made of steel plates several inches thick, but the steel was squiggly bars with spaces in between. Below them ran fat pipes; each had a valve that had to be turned by hand. Stairs made of the same separated steel bars led to lower walkways that provided access to the hand-turned valves. A sign on the wall read, Valve Pit Reactor One.

They walked around the perimeter of the valve pit. A room to the left had double doors, which stood open. The sounds of whirring motors and rushing air emanated from the room. Inside was a tan thing that Derrick thought was a motor and two huge green metal structures from floor to ceiling. The sign above the door read, Exhaust Fans Reactor One.

Past the valve pit, there were many more rooms, but Derrick paid little attention to them because Miriam sped up to a jog. Keeping the cart in front of him controlled at speed proved more difficult than he imagined. Anything faster than a walk and the wheels shook and the cart darted from side to side. He tried to dismiss the notion that Miriam had a countdown clock running in her head. However, he should have accepted that Miriam knew how much time remained. She was smart beyond his comprehension. She had, in the past few weeks, learned to use computers that were not available in Pacific Edge, escaped from where he believed escape impossible, and found him in the mountains when he didn't even know his location. Rebekah knew that Miriam could keep time in her head, because of things Rebekah witnessed of Miriam's capabilities on their travel here. During that day, Rebekah had come to know Miriam better than he did. That hurt, yet it was his fault. The clock was ticking; unflappable Miriam grew more frantic with each passing moment. Concern transformed into terror as Derrick realized they might run out of time before this dire event occurred.

The three entered the control center running. It was nothing like Derrick hoped to see. He pictured a simple room with a desk in front of a window with the reactor thing on the other side. The operators could watch the reactor thing and make adjustments using a computer like he had, or used to have, at his condo. That was not the case. The room was full of machines with many dials, gauges, and meters. The paint colors were the same; the brown floor glistened; he wondered how that was possible. The machines and dials and gauges were housed in gray-green metal cabinets. Thick black cables snaked here and there. He looked inside what appeared to be an empty box and saw a pile of yellowed paper; a thin metal arm extended from one side twitched in the air. It was a machine that made a graph, but it had run out of paper. It would take more time than they had to find the valve that needed repair. Smart as Miriam was, Derrick found himself agreeing with Rebekah. They should have run and got as far from this place as possible.

*I will never compete in a race or play football.*

Derrick glanced at Rebekah. She looked as disheartened as he felt. Miriam moved through the room, looking at each gauge, meter, and dial until she worked her way to a counter with a series of computer monitors. It appeared that four people worked there at a time. The counter faced a small window into another room. Miriam dove under the counter. She retrieved a piece of paper and then hammered at a keyboard. A monitor flickered to life; the colors somewhat off-color from what Derrick could see.

Miriam leaned over the counter, peering into the adjacent room, pointed, and said, "There's the valve."

Derrick realized his breathing had become so shallow that he felt dizzy. He took a breath and rushed to Miriam's side. "Are you sure?"

"Yes. I can see the number. Also, this screen shows its location." Miriam pointed to a monitor that showed a drawing of the valve and the pipe that ran from the ceiling. The actual pipe was painted bright green, although stains of white streaked it from ceiling to the valve. The valve itself painted a rusty brown color had similar white stains and white/gray crud covering the fasteners — bolts they were called.

Miriam removed the repair checklist from her bag, handing it to Derrick. "I'll look for the radiation levels in the reactor room."

Derrick studied this checklist. Seven easy steps. Easy if one understood how to do the work. Step one, relieve the pressure using a chain hoist. At least now he knew what the weird chain thing was called. However, he did not understand what the instruction meant or how to use the device. Step two, close the supply line. Step three, open the emergency bypass valve. No idea.

"Damn," Miriam whispered.

Derrick handed the checklist to Rebekah.

"What?" Derrick asked.

"The radiation is elevated. Not in the safe zone," Miriam said.

"What do we do now?" Derrick asked.

"I'm trying to figure that out," Miriam said. After a few moments, she added, "We'll be okay if we are in there less than 30 minutes. There are suits that provide protection, but we don't have time to get them."

"How much time do we have?" Rebekah asked.

"Eighteen minutes," Miriam said.

"You're sure?" Derrick asked.

"Yes." Miriam tapped a red countdown clock in the upper right-hand corner of the monitor.

"I don't understand the checklist. They wrote it for people who already know how to do the work," Derrick said.

“I don’t understand it either,” Rebekah said, handing the list back to Derrick.

For the first time that Derrick could remember, he saw Miriam flash anger he had not previously witnessed. “Listen, you two. Time to stop acting like imbecilic teenagers. There’s no time. Pull your heads out and think.”

Derrick swallowed hard. He peered into the reactor room. Studied the valve and the pipe. He felt Rebekah press close to his side.

Pointing to the ceiling, about twenty feet up, Derrick said, “That pipe must be very heavy. They must mean relieve the weight using the chain hoist up there. I see a hook hanging down.”

“And there’s a valve up there, one is the main shutoff, then there’s a bypass at the bottom to take the remaining water from the pipe,” Rebekah said.

“I’m going in,” Derrick said.

“We’re coming with you,” Miriam said.

“No, *you’re* not,” Rebekah said. “I’m going in with Derrick and you’re staying here. We don’t have time for arguments.”

Derrick started to say something, but the girls were right, no time to argue. Derrick grabbed the cart and met Rebekah at the door.

Miriam sat at the desk, scanning through pages on the monitor. Just before Derrick opened the door to the reactor room, Miriam looked up and said, “You have this.”

“I hope so,” Rebekah whispered. She gave Derrick a weak smile.

“Let’s do this,” Derrick said.

# 11

The checklist said to shut off the main water supply, open the bypass valve below the automatic valve that required repair, and then use the chain hoist to relieve the weight of the pipe. Derrick had the list etched in his mind, but he would check each step to be sure. He grabbed for the chain hoist, but Rebekah beat him to it.

Barely able to lift the chain hoist, she said, "I'll do this. You open the bypass valve when I tell you and then start on the fastener things."

"We should go up together," Derrick said, then added, "It's too heavy for you."

"I manage. Don't argue." Rebekah headed to the ladder, dragging the chain hoist.

The chain hoist clanked against the ladder as she climbed, echoing through the room. Derrick felt proud of Rebekah. He still wondered why she was here. He hated that his first thought was that she was here because of him, questioning if he'd ever stop being so self-centered.

Derrick rolled the cart closer to the valve, took the smaller of the two wrenches, they called it a box-end wrench according to the tool bin. He heard a loud crash from above. Glancing up, he saw the hoist on the narrow metal walkway constructed from the same metal as the valve pit walkways. Rebekah pulled herself onto the walkway and then connected the chain hoist to the hook hanging from the ceiling; next, she fastened to something on the pipe, but he could not see how it was connected from where he stood. Derrick put the wrench on the fastener—he thought they called it a nut, which made no sense — then he realized he did not know which direction to turn it.

Rebekah struggled with the main water supply. She was turning it, but it took all her strength. Calling up from the base of the ladder, he called, "Should I come help?"

"I'm getting it. Start getting the fasteners loosened."

"I don't know which way to turn them."

"Try turning it counterclockwise. If one direction doesn't work, try the other."

Derrick went back to the valve, attached the wrench, and tried counterclockwise. It did not move. He tried the other direction, same result.

After struggling for several minutes, trying numerous fasteners, Rebekah stepped to his side. "I got the valve closed. How's it going?"

"Not good. I can't move it either direction," Derrick said.

Rebekah grabbed a different wrench, which was a two-piece device. A long bar with a square end on a pivot and a round piece; one end fits the square piece; the other end fits the fastener. She connected the two pieces together. "Here, try this. Better leverage."

Derrick placed the wrench on a nut. He noticed Rebekah was rummaging through items left in the bottom of the cart. He positioned himself so he could pull on the bar using his weight and arms. The nut moved. He repositioned the wrench and turned it again.

"Is it working?" Rebekah asked.

Derrick saw a can in her hand. "It's turning, but it's not getting easier."

"Stand back," Rebekah said. She sprayed a stream of brownish-red liquid on the nut. The odor kind of sweet, strange. Doing to the same to every nut. "Penetrating oil." Rebekah pointed to the label. "Try it again."

Bracing his feet against the bottom of the pipe, Derrick leaned into the wrench using both hands. It moved easier and he moved faster. After several turns, he said, "Still isn't getting loose."

"Try another one," Rebekah said.

Derrick did. After a hard pull, the nut turned.

"I see the problem. The bottom of the fastener is turning."

"It's called a bolt, I think. This part is the nut; that part is the bolt," Derrick said.

"Whatever." Rebekah grabbed the smaller wrench. "I'll hold the bottom. Must be why the instructions called for two wrenches."

"Good thinking," Derrick said.

When Derrick was in position, he turned the wrench. Rebekah grunted, and then the wrench flew from her hand.

"I can't hold it. You're too strong."

"Damn. Now what?" Derrick asked.

Rebekah had turned her back to him, studying the tools. She raised up with the length of pipe as if she might hit Derrick.

Derrick leaned back.

"Relax. I wouldn't hit you. Not now, anyway. Maybe later. This is for more leverage." She slipped the pipe over the end of the wrench and said, "You hold the bottom. I'll do the top."

"Okay, but if I'm not strong enough, I don't see how you'll be strong enough," Derrick said.

"It's not about strength. It's about leverage."

Hearing a faint noise, Derrick and Rebekah turned to look at the control center window. Miriam was pounding on the glass. When she had their attention, she swirled her finger. "Hurry!"

Derrick got in position. Rebekah braced herself and pulled, grunting, sweat glistening on her forehead. The nut broke loose and she fell into Derrick. He caught her. "You did it!"

Each nut broke free easier as they worked. The oil doing some magic. Except for one that Rebekah could not move. Derrick allowed the bottom wrench to rotate against the pipe, locking it into place. He grabbed the pipe and pulled. When it broke loose, Derrick fell on his butt. The bolt had sheared in half. "I guess that works," Derrick said, tossing the sheared bolt into the cart.

Once they had removed all nuts and bolts, Derrick disconnected the electrical wire from the valve. He pushed, then tugged on the valve.

It would not budge.

Derrick bent and twisted around the pipe. "All the bolts are out. I don't see what's holding it."

When he looked up, Rebekah was already at the ladder.

"Must need more weight lifted," she called.

Derrick heard the muffled sound again. Miriam twirled her hand in the control room. Her movement was more frantic than before.

"Ready?" Rebekah called down.

"Yes."

Derrick braced to pull on the valve.

A wave of scalding water exploded from a gap between the valve and the pipe, knocking Derrick to the floor.

# 12

Derrick jumped up, pulling his clothing away from his skin, dancing around a bit. The water was hot, but he didn't think it caused him injury. Water had already stopped spilling from the gap when Rebekah returned and started turning the valve near the floor.

"I forgot the bypass valve. I'm sorry. Are you okay?" Rebekah asked.

Derrick said, "I forgot. It was not your fault. That was my job."

They heard the muffled noise of Miriam pounding on the window and screaming. They could not understand her, but she spun her hand hysterically above her head and waved for them to get out.

"We need to hurry," Derrick said.

He removed the valve; it was heavy; he struggled, setting it gently onto the floor. One gasket came off with the valve; the other, Rebekah pulled off with little difficulty. Getting the new valve in and the gaskets lined up wasn't easy. They finally lined the bottom gasket up on the valve, and then slid the valve into place, and then slid the top gasket in.

"You put the bolts on, I'll go up top and get ready to lower the pipe and turn on the water," Rebekah said, as she closed the bypass valve.

Derrick worked. Soon he had all the bottom bolts and nuts in place. The bolts were installed with the nuts on top. But he reversed the direction on the top so that the bolts faced down He secured two nuts so the pipe could not shift out of place.

Derrick looked up at Rebekah. "Lower the pipe."

The pipe lowered and Derrick tightened nuts. When he had about half the nuts tightened top and bottom, he yelled, "Turn on the water."

He fastened the electrical coupler to the valve and heard it power open or closed; he wasn't sure which. As the water pressure built in the pipe, small streams of water appeared where he had not yet tightened the nuts. Rebekah returned; they looked at the window and gave Miriam a questioning thumbs-up. She returned the gesture.

Derrick smiled at Rebekah. "We did it."

Derrick and Rebekah continued tightening the nuts, but at a leisurely pace. They had saved this reactor thing. Now they savored finishing their work. But there was that muffled pounding. More desperate than before.

They looked to the window. Miriam waved at them and mouthed, "GET OUT!"

"What's up with her," Rebekah asked.

"I don't know. Just two more bolts to go." He finished. "The leaks stopped." Derrick placed the tools and the old valve in the cart and pushed them toward the door. Through the small window in the door, Miriam motioned Derrick to leave the cart.

Miriam also motioned Derrick to strip off his clothing. Finally, he understood. They beat the clock on the valve installation, but something else was wrong.

*You can't smell it, or taste it, or see it, but it can pass right through your body.*

*Radioactive.*

# 13

Derrick turned to Rebekah. Hearing a noise, he turned back to the door and saw Miriam waving her arm for him to get out. He could barely hear her, but he could also read her lips. "Strip!" The radioactivity exposure scared the hell out of him. But what he did not know how to handle was stripping naked in front to Rebekah. It did not occur to him that Miriam wanted Rebekah stripped too.

Rebekah unzipped her top. "Hurry, Derrick. Why aren't you moving?"

"I — I don't have any underwear on," Derrick said.

"For God's sake, neither do I. I'll turn around. Just get out of here," Rebekah cried.

Rebekah turned around. She kicked her off her shoes and dropped the top of her uniform off her shoulders.

Derrick turned back to the door before Rebekah's uniform fell farther.

Miriam hammered her palm on the door. "HURRY!"

He decided there were worse things than being naked in front of Rebekah; worse things than being naked in front of his sister. Being dead would be worse. He kicked off his shoes — running barefoot did not appeal to him, — unzipped the front of his uniform, and stepped out of it. Miriam opened the door enough for him to squeeze through.

"Run to the shower and follow the directions. Meet me in the recovery room," Miriam said.

"What happened …"

"No time. GO!"

Derrick did as Miriam instructed. He did not look back to see if Rebekah was behind him. He ran as fast as he could, hoping he was out of sight. Running barefoot seemed vaguely familiar, yet he had never run barefoot. When he entered the dressing room, red lights spun, a siren sounded, and a familiar disembodied voice said, "Contamination alert. Proceed to decontamination."

He hoped decontamination meant the shower because that was the only place he knew, and he didn't want to roam through the building naked looking for another place. He also wondered, if the radioactivity had penetrated his skin, what good would a shower do? Inside the first room, he saw a metal slot in the wall labeled Contaminated Clothing. He had none, so he went to the shower. In the first room that glowed with blue lights and dried him previously, nothing happened for a moment until a disembodied voice said, "Radioactive contamination detected. Proceed to the shower area."

The shower was running when Derrick entered. He tested the water with his hand, lukewarm. The water turned green; the disinfectant scent stronger than his first shower. He turned, stretched, and raised his arms as the voice ordered. The voice instructed him to lather and rinse twice, which seemed extreme, but he assumed the exit door to the treatment room would remain locked until he complied.

Finally, after two cycles of soaping and rinsing, the voice instructed him to proceed to the treatment and recovery room. Instead of stepping directly into the Treatment and Recovery room, he entered a small vestibule that contained towels and clothing. He took a white towel from a rack to dry himself. And found a dark-blue uniform of the correct size on a row of shelves. He dressed and then entered the treatment room. Rebekah and Miriam were there, their hair still damp. He wondered how they had already finished. Rebekah sat on a bed, dressed in a fresh uniform instead of her own clothing. She gave him a suggestive smile that seemed out of character.

Miriam, still wearing the oversize white uniform, stood inside the second room at the cabinet of medicines. When Miriam stepped back into the treatment room, she held three small brown bottles in her hands.

Derrick asked, "How did you finish before me?"

"The decontamination process took longer for you," Miriam said. "You had direct exposure."

Already fearful of his condition, Derrick's heart sank. Maybe this was it. He survived exile only to have his life cut short escaping from the people who wanted to take him home. He shuffled to a chair and sat. "How much time do I have?"

"Time for what?" Miriam asked, turning around.

"To live?" Derrick asked.

"I have no idea," Miriam said.

"None?" This was worse than the feeling he had when the Tribunal sentenced him. Worse than the night Paul drove him out of Pacific Edge. Worse than the day Nyx left the mountain crying because he lied to her. Well, maybe not worse than that day, but equal. "I hoped you could give me an estimate."

"I can't see the future. Maybe we get eaten by wolves before we get to Potterville; maybe you live to be 200," Miriam said.

"But the radiation …"

"Oh. That. No big deal. Your exposure wasn't severe. You got the worst of it because the water contained elevated levels of radioactivity. But you'll be fine. We'll all be fine."

"But you panicked when it happened."

"Well, duh. Lights flashing, warning signs appearing. My brother soaked with radioactive water. How was I supposed to act? Besides, I didn't understand how bad it was until I got here and read the treatment instructions." Miriam handed Derrick a small vial. "Take this."

"What is it?"

"I don't know. Medicine for exposure to protect our internal organs."

Derrick smiled. "Minimal?"

"Yep. It would be a problem if you drank a gallon of that water or wore the wet clothing the rest of the day." Miriam handed a vial to Rebekah and then twisted the top off and drank the contents of her own.

"You could have told me that first," Derrick said, twisting the top of the vial and pouring it into his mouth. Derrick turned his head and contorted his arms and legs. "That's nasty tasting."

Miriam and Rebekah burst into a fit of laughter. Rebekah laid on her back, holding her sides.

Miriam collapsed to the floor. When her fit subsided, Miriam said, "I wanted to torment you a little." She winked at him.

"Girl, you're evil," Rebekah said. "No wonder I like you."

"Evil but fun," Miriam said.

The girls laughed.

"Hilarious," Derrick said.

Miriam struggled to her feet. "I wish I had a picture of your face when you came in."

Derrick noticed tears streaming down Miriam's cheeks as she rushed to him and threw her arms around him. "I love you."

# 14

Rebekah said, "Derrick's right. That stuff tastes horrible. I wonder if the water here is safe to drink?"

Miriam walked to a nearby sink, turning on the faucet. A rushing sound of air followed by rust-colored water spurted into the sink, staining her white work clothing. "Damn it," Miriam said, shutting the faucet off and jumping back. "Glad I didn't put on my street clothes."

Miriam pulled the Giger counter from a pocket, switched it on, and pointed it at the sink. Shrugging her shoulders, she said, "No radioactivity."

"That's great, but I'm not drinking that sludge," Rebekah said.

Miriam turned the faucet on slowly. It gurgled and spurted, and then a steady stream of water arrived. She turned the faucet to full and after a few minutes the water cleared. "Looks better now," she said.

"How would we know if it was safe?"

"Pick one of us to try it first and see if that person dies?" Miriam chuckled.

Rebekah rolled her eyes. "We should look around."

"My thoughts exactly," Miriam said.

"Guys, I need to get home," Derrick said.

"Relax. We'll get there. But we need to check this place out before we leave. Besides, it's still dark and we don't know what direction to go. Daylight should help. I'm going to change clothes. Meet you in the hallway."

"Put on something dark," Derrick said. "I can't adjust to you wearing white."

"I wanted blue, but nothing small enough," Miriam said, walking out the door.

Derrick and Rebekah were alone. They had been alone in the reactor room, but the circumstances prevented contemplation or conversation. Derrick felt some serious discomfort coming on. He wanted to say many things but could think of nothing.

Before he became too uncomfortable, Rebekah said, "Let's go. That girl dresses faster than her brother strips." She winked at him.

Derrick followed her out of the room and remained a step behind her. His discomfort increased. He didn't know what to say. He wondered what Rebekah saw of him. The adrenaline dwindled. Exhaustion weaved its way through his body. He could not rest. He had to get home. He had a race to run and people he wanted to see.

He wondered if anyone wanted to see him.

With him gone; their problem was gone.

As Rebekah predicted, Miriam met them in the hall, her arms full of clothing and bags. "I brought our stuff, so we don't have to come back here."

Rebekah grabbed her things.

"I'll get my stuff," Derrick said.

"What stuff? You were practically naked when we found you," Miriam said.

"But not quite naked. There's a difference," Rebekah said.

"I need to get my track shoes and shorts."

"Like I said, practically naked. I can't believe you went out in public like that. Not like you," Miriam said, and then added, "But you are right. You need to be wearing Potterville clothing when we return."

"I don't understand why my track clothing is important, but I do need them for the track meet Saturday. And as far as what I wear, I've changed," Derrick said.

"Obviously," Miriam agreed.

Derrick trotted to the dressing room, put on his shoes, and returned with his track shorts; his athletic supporter tucked inside his shorts. When he returned, he held his shorts, rolled int a tight ball, out to Miriam. "Can you put these in your bag? I don't want to carry them."

Miriam reached for the shorts, pinching a corner between her finger and thumb, holding them at arm's length. "Ewww." The shorts unfurled; his athletic supporter fell to the floor. "My God. What is that?"

Rebekah giggled.

Derrick grabbed the shorts from Miriam, picked up his underwear, rolled it back in his shorts, and stuck it in Miriam's bag. "Don't worry about it."

Miriam and Rebekah led the way. Derrick was happy to trail behind, watching the girls interact. Chatting and giggling. He slowed, separating himself so he couldn't hear the details of their banter. Occasionally, one girl would bump the other, sometimes with a hip, sometimes with a shoulder. Trapped in a mountain surrounded by weapons of war, facing unknown dangers; yet, he could not remember ever seeing Miriam this happy. She no longer seemed dark and gloomy. He thought she'd look good with a stripe of purple or red in her black hair.

Then there was Rebekah. Just a girl on his list. One he liked but discarded like a half-eaten sandwich because someone more conforming to his Chosen way of thinking was offered. He never thought about her feelings. Never thought about her as anything other than an object that he could choose or reject. It was odd that he never thought of Nyx or Akira or even L. Linda as objects. They had always been people to him, individuals with thoughts and feelings. They helped him survive in Potterville. They acted as friends, mentors, and superiors.

His feet began to drag; legs aching. Adrenalin oozed into the night. Fatigue flooded through his veins. Even his thinking felt tired. But there was one thing that could not wait.

He owed Rebekah Ford an apology.

Miriam and Rebekah turned into a hallway they had not yet explored. Derrick did not like them being out of sight, so he forced himself to trot to the hallway intersection.

The girls had stopped. Both rigid. Rebekah touched Miriam's shoulder.

Miriam eased the stunner from her bag.

Then Derrick heard it.

Thump, thump, thump.

Derrick eased beside Miriam. The thumping came from the room on their right. An irregular low wallop he could almost feel. He pictured a massive beast slamming its victim to the ground, then slamming it again and again and again.

He had no weapon.

He had nothing.

They believed they were alone here.

They were not.

# 15

Derrick eased in front of the girls, holding one finger to his lips. With his thumb, he pointed back the direction they entered the hall. Miriam shook her head and motioned that they continue. Arguing with her never worked when he could talk; it sure wouldn't work using sign language. He led the way, taking exaggerated tiptoe steps. Before they heard the thumping, he wanted to leave this place and find his way home. That's when he was certain that the place was abandoned. Now, he wondered what sort of monsters, or ghosts, remained here; was their purpose to ensure no one got out alive? And he questioned why Miriam insisted on going deeper into their lair.

The thumping grew inaudible as they moved farther from the source. Derrick saw an intersection ahead. Miriam checked no doors as they walked. What did Miriam hoped to find? He thought it safe to whisper, but just as he turned to speak, a noise began in the adjacent hallway. Not the thumping sound like they heard earlier. Instead, a whirring sound that also tapped out a regular beat. He detected a slight odor not unlike the gym at Potterville High first thing in the morning. Behind him, both stun things sizzled.

He pointed back the way they came.

Miriam shook her head and pointed the direction of the noise and then eased past him before he could stop her. Rebekah went past him on the other side. He should have grabbed a pipe or big wrench, but he ran by the toolroom in his birthday suit, praying he was far enough ahead of Rebekah and Miriam to be out of sight. Now that fear seemed trivial.

Miriam and Rebekah eased along the wall. Derrick stood behind them. Both girls peeked around the corner toward the sound's source. Then they moved into the open; their arms hung at their sides. Derrick joined them. Twenty yards from them, a machine polished the floor with spinning brushes. One wheel had a piece missing, causing the machine to bounce each time the wheel rotated.

"Do you think it will attack us?" Derrick asked.

"No," Miriam said.

"But we won't know for sure until it's too late," Rebekah said.

"Wouldn't make sense. If the cleaning robots were also security robots, they might accidently kill an employee. That explains why the floor is so clean. Weird that they left them operational. Perhaps they anticipated people would return," Miriam said.

"Then it didn't happen," Rebekah added.

"What are we looking for?" Derrick asked.

"People must have lived down here," Miriam said. "We need some rest. Too much to ask, but food would be nice."

"I have to get home," Derrick said. "I have a track meet."

"You need rest. We don't know how far it is to Potterville once we get out of here. We all need rest before we start out again," Miriam said.

"Pacific Edge might search for us," Rebekah said.

"They might think I'm dead," Derrick said.

"I wish they thought we were dead," Miriam said.

"They might not care about you guys. You ran away, no big deal. I learned that when they say people are transferred to other Chosen Communities, they are actually sent to the commoner world," Derrick said.

"Like Akira?" Miriam asked.

"How did you know about Akira?" Derrick asked.

"I recognized her when they offered you that pardon and granted us a communication," Miriam said.

"I made them contact you. Had to know that you were okay, before I made my decision."

Rebekah said, "Why did you stay? The people in Potterville knew you were exiled from Pacific Edge after they came for you."

"They knew before that," Derrick said.

"How?" Miriam asked.

"I told them. It became obvious when hovercraft showed up. I apologized to the entire school over the public address system the morning they came to get me. Akira was the first person I told, but she already knew. She recognized me in my first class on my first day of school."

"Did she tell others?" Rebekah asked.

"Not sure. Maybe. Probably. Maybe not."

"That's a well-defined assumption," Rebekah said.

"On one hand, I don't think Akira told people. But others knew before I admitted it. Nyx said she knew the first day she met me, and that was before Akira saw me."

"Who is Nyx?" Miriam asked, stopping in the hall to face Derrick.

"You know who Nyx is. You called her."

"I called her. I don't know her, or what your relationship is with her. She was with Akira during our communication. The girl with the pink-striped hair, right?"

Derrick stood for a moment, thinking about Nyx, picturing her hair, her face, her scent. He missed her in a way he'd never experienced before. "I met her at the bistro the first day Paul took me out of the condo."

He fell silent again.

Miriam stared at him.

Rebekah stared at him.

Finally, Derrick said, "I don't know what our relationship is. She coached me. She protected me. But she doesn't like me. Coach made her help me. I'm not sure why she protected me."

Miriam walked away. "I see."

The machine moved down the hall. The adrenalin rush from the strange noise vanished. Derrick felt worse than ever. He didn't want to admit that Miriam was right. He needed rest. At least an hour of sleep before they set out for home.

"I'm certain Pacific Edge will search for us," Miriam said.

"Not likely. They don't care about people they've sent to the commoner world. I don't know why they were interested in me. But I don't believe Marcus Carver changed his story or that the pardon was true." Derrick said.

"They'll look for us. We're different than the typical person who leaves Pacific Edge," Rebekah said.

"True. We escaped. Two security guards were overcome and bound, and Pacific Edge's entire computer system crashed. We are not typical ex-Pacific Edge residents. And then there's you." Miriam stared at Derrick.

Derrick said, "What about me? Why do they care about me? I don't understand."

"I realize why you don't understand, but this is not the time to discuss it," Miriam said. She turned, opening a double door that led to a room with a few tables and chairs near a second set of double doors. A stainless-steel counter extended ten yards; a stainless-steel roll-down barrier closed the counter off to the room behind. The room looked like the dining area at the Pacific Edge technical service building. Miriam walked straight to the second set of double doors as if she knew what she was looking for.

An enormous kitchen existed behind those doors. Miriam checked three doors and upon opening the fourth, she said, "Here we go."

Inside was a sizeable room with many shelves and bins of various sizes. On one shelf sat a few boxes. Miriam opened a box and tossed silver packages to Derrick and Rebekah.

"What's this?" Rebekah asked.

"Food," Miriam said.

"You think it's still good?" Rebekah asked.

Derrick studied the package. Black lettering read: Mac and Cheese. In small lettering, he found exp. date 2051. "This expired decades ago."

"Maybe not tasty, but it's food," Miriam said, walking out of the room.

Miriam found a bowl, measured water, and placed in an oven that Derrick recognized as a microwave. Miriam set the timer to 15 seconds; enough time to boil water using the electromagnetic digital ovens in Pacific Edge.

"You'll need more time than that if you want the water to boil," Derrick said.

"How much," Miriam asked without question.

"Try ninety seconds."

The water boiled after a second ninety-second run. Miriam opened a silver packet and dumped the yellow contents in the bowl. She put a plate on the bowl and set it aside. Then she placed another bowl of water in the oven, repeating the process. Rebekah found spoons and took them to the adjacent room, arranging them on a table. When the third bowl of mac and cheese was done, Miriam and Derrick carried them to the table.

Derrick stirred his bowl; although he did not know what it should look like, he thought the grayish yellow and lumpy consistency wasn't the original intent. It didn't smell great; it didn't smell terrible. His hunger overcame his reluctance. He raised his fork and after confirming it wasn't too hot, took a bite.

"How is it?" Rebekah asked.

"Does old have a flavor?" Derrick asked.

"What if it makes us sick?" Rebekah sniffed her bowl.

"It won't," Miriam said.

"You don't know that," Rebekah said.

"Just eat it. You'll be fine," Miriam said.

Rebekah stood and walked back into the kitchen. She returned with three glasses of water. "Do you think this is safe to drink?"

"I don't know. It would be safer if we boiled it first, but we don't have time for it to cool, unless you want to drink hot water," Miriam said.

"So, should we drink it or boil it?" Derrick asked.

Miriam took a sip. "It tastes fine to me."

"I sure would like some of Donna's cooking," Derrick said.

"Donna?" Miriam asked.

"She runs the bistro. Where I worked; right next to my condo. Well, when I had a condo and a job. I still have the job, I think, but not the condo," Derrick said.

"You had a job? As in working?" Rebekah asked.

"I did. Washing dishes. I only worked a couple of days before this happened."

"Why? Father paid for everything, didn't he?"

"He paid rent on the condo. Paul gave me cash sometimes. I wanted extra money for things Father wouldn't have anticipated."

"What things?" Miriam asked.

Derrick stirred his bowl. "Track shoes and," he stuck mac and cheese in his mouth, "a gitrrr …"

"What?"

Derrick swallowed, took a drink. "A guitar."

Miriam shook her head. "Who are you and what have you done with my brother?"

Rebekah laughed.

Miriam laughed.

When they recovered, Miriam asked, "The food is okay there?"

"I've only eaten at the bistro. Oh, and Paul brought pizza from some place. And hamburgers, French fries, and milkshakes from another. Oh, and the school cafeteria."

Both girls stared at him and then Rebekah said, "So, is the food okay or not?"

"It's fantastic. Well, not all the school meals. Some are good, some not so much. Their worst is better than this stuff." Derrick took another bite, wrinkling his nose.

"Interesting," Rebekah said. "Not what I expected. Although, what we ate on our way from Pacific Edge with Mr. Jones was good. I was so preoccupied with what we'd done that I wasn't thinking about it."

Derrick stared at both girls. "Mr. Jones?"

Miriam sat her fork on the table. "Yes, that Mr. Jones. He and Ms. Springfield helped us once we got out of Pacific Edge."

"I don't understand," Derrick said.

"I don't either. Mr. Jones and Ms. Springfield changed after you left. Mr. Jones was nicer. Even helped get me suspended from the Academy."

"Helped you get suspended?" Derrick asked.

"Yep. And they are married," Miriam said.

"Married? Like to each other?" Derrick asked.

"Yes."

"And what do you mean that you crashed the computer system?" Derrick asked.

Miriam stood, gathered the bowls, and took them to the next room. She did not ask if they were finished. None of the bowls were empty.

"What's with her?" Derrick asked.

"You're asking me? She's your sister," Rebekah said.

"True, but I think you might know her better," Derrick whispered.

"Right. I'm not sure anyone knows Miriam. Not really. I'm not sure she knows herself."

Derrick and Rebekah fell silent when Miriam came back through the door.

"Let's go," Miriam said.

Derrick and Rebekah followed her. Miriam seemed to know where she was going. Derrick knew that was impossible but said nothing. At the next intersection, Miriam turned left without hesitation. She walked by three doors; at the fourth door, she stopped and popped the door open. Reaching inside, she flipped on a light. Two small beds, one stacked on top of the other, stood in the corner. A blanket was folded at the foot of each bed. "Derrick, you take this room. Rebekah and I will take the next. Get some sleep." Miriam said.

"I don't have time to sleep. I keep telling you, I need to get home …"

Miriam held up her hand. "We know. You have a track meet. The longer you stand here talking, the later you'll be getting there. Now, sleep. It's not a question. And I'd shake out the blanket, just in case."

"Just in case what?" Derrick asked.

"Just in case," Miriam said, disappearing into the next room.

Rebekah shrugged, then followed her.

Derrick shuffled into the room. He gave the blanket a vigorous shake. One long-dead beetle tumbled to the floor. Derrick kicked it to the far corner of the room. The temperature was comfortable. A blanket was unnecessary, but he cast it over him as he sprawled on the bed. Miriam was right. He could no longer think straight. His mind wandered like a lost child. *What day is it?* It seemed as if Miriam and Rebekah had been with him several days, yet he was sure it was mere hours. *How did they get here? They said they walked; they said Mr. Jones brought them.* That sounded more like a hallucination than a possibility.

*How did they escape? Miriam tried to swim, but that didn't work. They locked her in her room. A few hours later, I found her on the pile of rocks. Maybe she didn't escape. Maybe they brought her here. But why are we inside this mountain? Why is Rebekah Ford here? That's her name, right? Ford? Rebekah said something about why she was here, but I don't remember the answer. Why do they call me Derrick?*

*I'm Number Seven.*
Questions spun.
*What color is the flavor of purple?*
*I play the 100-meter dash in football.*
His eyes closed. Everything stopped.

# 16

In the darkness, Derrick drifted between sleep and wakefulness. No daylight filtered in from his condo window. *Not late for school. Is it a school day?* He didn't know. Then he remembered he didn't have a condo. Then he remembered he was deep inside of a military complex under a mountain. He raised in the darkness, striking his head on the bed above. The lights were on when he dosed off; it was a manual switch. Perhaps the power had failed.

He felt his way to the door. When he entered the hall, the lights flickered to life. He walked to the next room. Enough light fell into the room that he could see inside. Rebekah slept on the top bunk; the bottom bed was empty. Miriam would have slept on the bottom bed in the same room as Rebekah. A white uniform lay folded at the foot of the bed. He thought he knew where he'd find Miriam. He paused, Rebekah looked peaceful and he let her sleep, hoping she would not panic when she awoke alone.

Derrick walked towards the entrance; certain Miriam would be using a computer somewhere. Down the hall, back to the right; he saw an open door to a lit room. Inside sat Miriam behind a desk, staring at a computer monitor.

"Hi, sis," he said. "Why aren't you sleeping?"

"I slept," Miriam did not look up.

"How long did I sleep? What time is it?"

"It's almost noon."

"Is it still Friday?"

"Yes."

"We've got to go. I have to get home."

"We'll leave soon. Go wake Rebekah," Miriam said.

"What are you looking at?" Derrick asked.

"Lots of things. Right now, I'm studying how to get out of here."

"What have you learned?"

"Lots of stuff. Go get Rebekah."

Derrick shrugged and walked out. He wondered why Miriam was so cryptic about everything. They were in this together; no need for secrets.

Maybe she didn't think he was smart enough to understand. Perhaps she was right about that. Maybe what she had learned was so bad she didn't want him to know. People abandoned this place decades ago, and now it was failing and dangerous.

He stopped at the door to the room in which Rebekah slept. It seemed sacred in some way that forbid his intrusion. Raising a hand to knock on the doorframe, he paused, watching her for a final moment. So serene. It occurred to him that her future might not hold many similar moments.

Derrick rapped on the doorframe. "Rebekah. Rebekah."

"Huh?" Rebekah rolled over.

"Wake up. Miriam wants us."

Rebekah didn't move. She faced away from him now.

"Rebekah. Time to get up."

"I don't want to get up."

"I understand. But it's time. We need to go."

He felt she was awake now, though he could not see her face. She wasn't moving, except for shallow breaths. "Rebekah …"

"Okay, okay. What a nag. I'm coming." Rebekah rolled over, propped up on one elbow. She stared at him. Hair disheveled. No longer peaceful. "What time is it?"

"About noon. I think.

"What day is it?"

"Still Friday. Miriam put her regular clothes back on. Maybe you should change too." Derrick closed the door and leaned against the wall.

In a few minutes, Rebekah shuffled out the door and down the hallway. At the intersection, she turned the wrong direction.

"This way," Derrick stood at the entry in the hallway that led to Miriam.

"I need a drink first. Tastes like something died in my mouth."

Derrick followed her. Now that she mentioned it, the taste in his mouth became intolerable. In the kitchen, they found plastic drinking glasses. After letting the water run a few minutes, Rebekah filled her glass, and swished a mouthful of water around and then spat it into the sink. It embarrassed Derrick to spit like that in front of a girl, which was strange because he'd stripped naked in front of her a few hours ago. He wondered if he'd ever stop thinking about that. He wondered if the girls would ever say anything about it or if they'd just let him fret. He wondered if they'd tell others. For a moment, he thought he might be sick. Then he took a long drink and refilled his glass. The water tasted sweet, fresh, and cold. A cup of black coffee sounded fantastic.

Rebekah filled a second glass with water and said, "Where's your sister?"

Derrick pointed. Rebekah led. This entire affair felt surreal. Just a few weeks ago, Rebekah was on his list of Chosen girls available for his selection as a wife. At the time, he was a brain-washed, Chosen-worshipping jerk. Being exiled, he thought his life was over, then he found a real life in Potterville. Now his life in Potterville stood in jeopardy, which caused a sinking feeling in his chest. Not that he couldn't start over. Starting over was possible and with Miriam and Rebekah's help and his understanding of the commoner world — he needed a better term because only the Chosen called it the commoner world — starting over wasn't just doable, it might be preferable. They had no place to live, but they would find a way. He could work. They would be okay. But he didn't want to start over. He wanted to live in Potterville; he wanted to go to Potterville High School; he wanted to work at Donna's Bistro.

Rebekah found Miriam without further instruction. Handing Miriam the glass of water, Rebekah said, "So are we ready to escape from this place?"

"Almost." Miriam took several swallows of water. "Thanks. My mouth tasted terrible."

"You're welcome. What do you mean almost?"

Miriam tapped a small black object connected to the computer with a thin white cable. "Saving stuff so I can study it later."

Rebekah nodded, although Derrick thought she probably didn't understand what Miriam was doing any more than he did. "Guys, we've got to go. I have …"

Rebekah turned on her heel. "For God's sake, give it a rest. You've got a track meet. We know. We get it."

Derrick looked at his feet. "Sorry. It's important to me."

"I still don't understand," Rebekah said. She almost said that nothing had ever been important to Derrick except himself, but she didn't say that.

Miriam stood, shut off the computer, and packed the small black object and white cord in her pack. "Let's go."

At the door, Miriam looked at Derrick, frowned, and walked back to the desk. She rummaged through several drawers before she found what she wanted. She came at Derrick with a metal object. He'd seen one like it in a drawer at his condo but didn't understand its purpose.

"What are you doing?" Derrick asked, backing away.

"Relax. God, you're jumpy." Miriam pulled on the symbol on Derrick's uniform and then made two blades separate on the device. She used the device to cut the emblem off.

"What are those?" Derrick asked. "And why did you cut that off?"

"Scissors. How have you survived this long? I'm cutting it off because someone might recognize the symbol and they would know we found this place."

"But I won't be wearing this when we get to Potterville. And shouldn't we tell people what happened and where we've been," Derrick said.

"We can't tell anyone about this place. No one. And we don't know what the weather will be when we get out or how far we have to go. The plan is you change before we get to Potterville. If it works out that way." Miriam stuck the scissors in her bag.

Derrick almost said something about stealing, but she had saved the place from disaster, so it seemed a fair trade. "Why can't we tell anyone?"

"You've changed a lot, brother, but you're still dense like a rock. An extraordinarily dense rock at that. Because this place is dangerous. Especially if it fell into the wrong hands."

Derrick could not argue with what Miriam said. He was dense; the place seemed dangerous, and he did not understand how he had survived this long either.

Miriam led them back to the enormous cavern with the multitude of trucks and rockets, straight to the big elevator, behind which was the entrance to Reactor One.

Derrick looked at the passageway to Reactor One. He hoped they never went back there and feared they would.

"Shall we see if this works, or take the stairs?"

Miriam didn't wait for an answer; she stepped inside the smaller elevator, which was not enclosed like most elevators but was covered in heavy metal mesh like the tables at Donna's Bistro. Derrick's stomach growled.

Derrick and Rebekah joined her.

"The door has to be closed." Miriam stepped in front of Derrick, grabbed a handle, slid the door closed, and fastened the latch. She pushed the number three and the elevator lurched down. It stopped in a tunnel. Miriam slid the door open and stepped out. The elevator stopped here too. The trucks and other vehicles were driven through the tunnel to another destination.

Derrick leaned over the railing that surrounded the elevator. Thick cables hung from huge metal pulleys. It amazed him that the machine could lift so much weight. The main cavern was visible above them. Lights blinked off.

"Where to now?" Rebekah asked.

"The computer showed this tunnel goes two places. But it was not to scale and no relationship to any towns or roads. Down this tunnel there is a split that leads to Engineering and the other tunnel goes to what they called Base. Base must be where the trucks and other machines get outside," Miriam said.

"We need the base then," Derrick said. He longed to see the sun and hoped to never be underground again.

"Agreed," Rebekah said. "I can't wait to see the sun. How far is it to the Base?"

"I don't know. Like I said, it wasn't a map; it was more of a diagram of the complex. There are other things we need to checkout along the way," Miriam said.

"But …"

In unison Rebekah and Miriam said, "Need to get back for track."

Miriam continued. "We need to understand more about this place before we leave."

"Why?" Derrick asked.

"In case we come back," Miriam said.

# 17

Returning had not factored into Derrick's thinking. Leaving and never coming back, forgetting the entire experience — including the Pacific Edge abduction — factored into his thinking. He did not want to admit it, even to himself, but as was her practice, Miriam was right. For the same reasons they could tell no one about this place, they might have to use it for their own protection. Sometimes force must be met with equal or greater force. The meek might inherit the earth, but they may not survive long enough to enjoy it.

"I'm never coming back here," Rebekah said.

"Absolutes work until they don't," Miriam said.

"Huh?"

"Did you have any classes with Miriam?" Derrick asked.

"No, what's that got to do with anything?" Rebekah asked.

"Everything." Derrick winked at Miriam. "Arguing with Miriam never ends well."

"I can understand that. But I'm here," Rebekah said.

Derrick nodded. He had not considered how Rebekah came to be here. He understood that she came with Miriam, but how she included herself in Miriam's plan had not occurred to him. Had Miriam met her equal in debate? Probably not. Still …

Further down the tunnel, they came to the split. Unlike the small tunnel leading to Reactor One, the tunnel leading to Engineering was big enough to drive a midsize truck. Derrick wondered if there was a similar tunnel leading to Reactor One because they could not get machinery through the small tunnel they walked through. The tunnel to the Base remained big enough to drive a truck carrying a rocket.

"How far is the base?" Derrick asked.

"I don't know. We have a lot of walking to do before we get to Potterville. Did anyone ever mention a military base near Potterville?" Miriam asked.

"Just a rumor that there was one many years ago," Derrick said.

"That's what I suspected," Miriam said.

"What do you mean?" Derrick asked.

"That the Base is far from Potterville. Otherwise people would have found it," Miriam said.

Derrick and Miriam were several yards into the tunnel leading to the Base. "Let's pick up the pace then," Derrick said.

From some distance behind them, Rebekah said, "Or maybe we could take this."

Derrick looked over his shoulder but could not see Rebekah. "Now what," he whispered.

Rebekah emerged from an opening in the tunnel wall. "There's a transport to the base."

"What sort of transport?"

"Not sure. Like sort of a big transport, but not a transport. It's called The Circle," Rebekah said.

Derrick stepped into the opening. Before him were several white vehicles, shaped like a big hotdog, some larger than others. "They probably don't work."

Miriam walked to a smaller vehicle with two rows of seats that would carry six people if they sat close together. Lights came on in the tunnel and the doors opened. A voice said, "transport to silos one, two, three, four, and Base. Please state your destination and secure your safety harness for transport."

Without hesitation, Miriam took a seat in the front of the transport and pulled the safety harness over her shoulders, fastening it to clips on either side. "Get in you two. And don't even start with, I need to get home. We think the Base is the way out, right?"

Derrick got in next to Miriam. Rebekah got in the row behind them. The doors closed. Derrick's heartbeat clicked up a bit, as if he had run a lap at moderate speed. The tunnel was lit, as far as he could see, but faded to darkness. The tunnel was just large enough for the transport. It was not made of stone, but some manmade material. The transport appeared to run on some a track unlike anything he'd ever seen.

The voice said, "State your destination for immediate departure."

"Silo one," Miriam said.

Before Derrick could say anything, the transport began to move.

"How far is it to silo one?" Miriam asked.

"Eighty-nine- and one-half miles." The voice said.

Derrick did not have a good understanding of distance, but 89 ½ miles sounded like a long way. The transport was accelerating now as they sped by other similar vehicles, entrances, and other structures before rocketing into a tunnel. Derrick grabbed the handholds on each side of his chair; his back forced into the seat.

"And how long will it take to get there?" Miriam asked.

"Arrival at silo one in thirty-two minutes," the voice said.

"One-hundred sixty-five miles per hour," Miriam said.

The tunnel walls became a blur as they sped forward. To Derrick's relief the light came on ahead of them as them as the raced through the tunnel. At times, it felt as if they changed direction, but the change was so subtle that it was barely detectable.

"Give me a break," Rebekah said.

Miriam looked at Derrick and then over her shoulder to Rebekah. "Do you think there's an error in my calculation? I figure 89.5 miles in 32 minutes is 2.7916 miles per minute, which means we are going 165 miles per hour. You see it differently?"

"See it? I'd need a calculator to figure it out. I have no idea," Rebekah said.

"You don't see it?" Miriam had twisted in her seat.

"See it? Hell, no, I don't see it. What does that even mean? See it?" Rebekah asked.

Miriam looked at Derrick. Derrick shook his head.

"Oh, my. I didn't realize," Miriam said.

Miriam sat looking forward. She didn't say what she didn't realize. Derrick wanted to ask, but the look on her face told him to leave it alone. After a few minutes, he turned back to look at Rebekah. Rebekah shrugged.

They passed a sign that said Silo Number One 5 Miles. The tunnel changed. It was no longer made of rock. Now it was man made with walls of concrete. They had left the mountain, at least for now.

The transport slowed. The voice said, "Approaching Missile Silo Number One."

The transport pulled to one side, leaving the main Circle Tunnel open for more travelers should they need to pass, but there were no other people here to use the transports. The doors opened on the left instead of the right. There were two ways into the silo, a hallway and to one side a roll-up door that would accommodate a mid-sized truck. Derrick noticed the rails here that guided the transport vehicles had joints that would allow the rail to be moved so a standard truck could enter. A keypad stood next to the roll-up door, but Mariam headed to the hallway.

"Let's have a quick look," Miriam said.

Derrick assumed she added quick to appease him, so he said nothing. They walked down a short hallway, then there was a door. It was locked.

Miriam touched a panel mounted in the wall. It illuminated with bright green lettering against the simple black screen.

**MISSILE NUMBER ONE—STATUS: STANDBY**

**MISSILE NUMBER ONE—WARHEAD: THERMONUCLEAR**
**MISSILE NUMBER ONE—WARHEAD STATUS: ARMED**
**MISSILE NUMBER ONE—TARGET: MOSCOW, RUSSIA**
**BEGIN LAUNCH SEQUENCE Y=YES N=NO**

A keyboard in the same green letters and number was displayed at the bottom of the screen. Miriam touched N.

**LAUNCH SEQUENCE ABORTED Y=YES N=NO**

Miriam touched Y. A new line appeared.

**MISSILE NUMBER ONE MAINTENANCE ENTRY Y=YES N=NO**

Miriam touched Y. A new keypad appeared with only numbers. Miriam entered the same sequence that gained them entrance at the very first door. The locking mechanism sounded a series of whirls and clicks, and the door fell open an inch. Miriam pushed her way inside. Derrick and Rebekah followed. They entered a hallway with smaller metal doors about halfway up the wall.

The doors were held shut with two t-shaped handles that moved a quarter turn. Derrick opened one and peered inside. He saw a space just big enough to crawl through that appeared to go in a circle. Ten yards in, a ladder led up and down into a similar sized vertical shaft. Cables and pipes snaked through the crawl space, some of which traveled either up or down the vertical shaft. Derrick closed the door but didn't latch it.

Miriam and Rebekah had opened the next door and went inside. What Derrick saw next was unexpected. Stepping through the door, he stood next to Rebekah on a narrow walkway that encircled a gigantic cylinder-shaped thing that was the missile. The missile extended below them and above. There were ladders that provided access up and down. This place wasn't as clean as what they had seen thus far. A layer of dust and dirt covered everything. Spider webs or cobwebs, he didn't know the difference, hung everywhere. They all brushed the sticky webs from their hair and clothing as they walked.

Miriam completed the circle around the missile and then said, "Let's go."

Back in the transport, Miriam requested Silo Number 2. The machine complied and soon they were speeding through the tunnel at 165 miles per hour according to Miriam's calculation. The trip to Silo Number Two only took five minutes. Silo Number Two looked just like Silo Number One. Miriam looked inside the silo and then left. Derrick did not know what she was looking for and feared that asking questions would either delay getting home or garner another cryptic answer, and he was tired of cryptic answers.

Miriam stopped at silos three and four, but spent no time at either, for which Derrick was thankful. He was finally starting to feel optimistic that they would get out of this place. The distance from Silo Number Four and the Base was longer than the distance between the silos, which seemed to be evenly spaced. When they arrived at the Base, the transport slowed and made a gradual turn to the right, stopping at what Derrick felt like was the apex of the turn, meaning the transport could complete the turn and go back to where they came from, completing the circle, thus the name. Derrick assumed they would not make a return trip to the Base. He would learn that assumption was wrong.

# 18

A hallway led to an elevator four times bigger than the one in his condo; the keypad showed three levels: C, 1, 2, and S. Derrick assumed C stood for the Circle; this level and the machine they traveled in to get here. He hoped S stood for surface, which is where he wanted to go, but he knew Miriam would explore floors one and two. The elevator stopped at the first floor. The door slid open; Miriam exited first as if on a mission. Derrick looked at Rebekah. Rebekah shrugged. There was no tunnel here, only a small entryway and a metal door. A keypad embedded in the wall to one side. Derrick hoped the door was locked, and the keypad didn't work, and if it worked, he hoped it required a different code. No place existed to hide a note. With luck they would turn around and get back on the elevator and repeat the exercise on level two.

As it turned out, Derrick had no luck here other than still being alive and having Miriam at his side.

After punching at the keypad, Miriam pulled the door open, exposing a black space. Lights flickered to life as she stepped beyond the threshold. Derrick wondered how the light could work here too because it was so far from Reactor One. He didn't understand electricity. Perhaps there was another reactor. He shuddered at the thought. The color scheme was different here with floors of marbled gray and white walls. The floors were clean, but dull, as if someone had scrubbed all the shine from them. Perhaps the robots worked here too and had scrubbed the floor until there was no life left in it.

Derrick and Rebekah followed Miriam down the hall. In the first office, she dove under the desk, then opened drawers, and then slammed them shut. She lifted the keyboard and looked underneath. Then she logged into the computer; it still worked. Miriam stared at the monitor and moved through several screens before shutting it off.

Moving on, Miriam entered offices at random, but now she only looked at the bottom of the keyboard. Every person had left their logon information there. Derrick sensed something was weird about that. But then what wasn't weird about this place.

After the fifth office, Rebekah said, "What are you looking for?"

"Trying to understand what people did here," Miriam said.

"And? What did they do?" Rebekah asked.

"Lots of stuff. These people worked in support positions," Miriam said.

"What does that mean?" Derrick asked.

"They worked for higher ups. Researched stuff. Wrote memos and such," Miriam said.

"Not important then?" Derrick asked.

"The opposite. The information here is vital," Miriam said. And with that, she shut off the most recent computer, left the office, and marched to the elevator. Once they were inside, she pushed the button labeled number two.

It never interested Derrick what Miriam thought. Now he hung on her every word, but she offered little information. The elevator gave a low shutter; he grabbed a rail; Miriam grabbed his arm. The distance between floors was not uniform; he was certain they had traveled much farther than the distance to the first floor. He forgot to look for stairs. If the elevator stopped, they would be trapped. *Does this thing have an escape hatch?* He had not paid attention. Another lurch followed by a shutter, and the elevator stopped; the lights went out, and a sliver of light shown at the top of elevator, indicating they had almost, but not quite, arrived at the second floor.

"This isn't good," Rebekah whispered.

"No, it is not," Miriam agreed.

Derrick could hear one girl rummaging in her bag. A bright light lit the elevator, causing Derrick to squint. Miriam pointed her flashlight at the elevator buttons, which were crude looking compared to the elevator at Derrick's condo. First Miriam pushed a button labeled reset. The lights came back on. Then she punched the button labeled #2. Nothing. She tried C, and the elevator started down so fast it caused Derrick's stomach to lurch. They had not gone down before, only up, so he did not know if the speed was normal. Miriam pushed a button labeled stop; the elevator jerked to a stop. She pushed the #2 button again.

The elevator moved upward; as it reached the second floor, it lurched, slowed, but continued until it reached its destination. They stepped into an opening that would hold 15 people. Two gray doors, one labeled entrance, the other labeled stairs. Derrick thought they'd take the stairs from here forward. No keypad, simple doors. He hoped the entrance was locked. Miriam brushed past him. His hope of a quick exit faded when Miriam opened the entrance door.

As they stepped inside, the lights flickered to life, but what the lights illuminated was not like the other places they'd seen. A wide, white hallway with a dark gray floor so sterile that it reminded Derrick of a medical facility. He had never needed to see a doctor, but he went for an annual exam, just like everyone in Pacific Edge. He never had an unpleasant experience because — just like everyone else, he assumed, — they put him to sleep for the exam. He woke feeling fine. Yet, he always dreaded going, which made little sense. That feeling arose here.

"Well, this is different," Rebekah said, stepping across the threshold.

"It's like people still work here," Derrick said. "We should leave."

"Not before we know more about this place," Miriam said, walking farther down the hallway.

"Where are the doors," Rebekah asked.

"There's one," Miriam pointed down the hall.

A door on the left was difficult to see until they were close. It had no handle; no exposed parts. A double door, wide as the hallway, painted the same color as the walls, invisible until one was next to it.

"How does it open," Derrick asked.

Miriam felt the door, examining it from edge to edge. "I don't see anything. No retinal scanner or other sensors. It is either an exit door or has technology advanced beyond anything in Pacific Edge."

"But this place is old. How can it be more advanced than Pacific Edge?" Derrick continued down the hall following Miriam.

"This place gives me the creeps," Rebekah said, folding her arms across her chest.

The wide hallway, at least twice the length of a football field, made the far end difficult to see. However, Derrick thought he could see a door. With a handle, and that meant Miriam would insist they go there.

"Does that look like a door?" Miriam pointed toward the end of the hallway.

"I don't think so," Rebekah said.

Derrick detected a quiver in Rebekah's voice, which surprised him; she had been unflappable thus far. Yet it did not shock him because he felt uneasy as well. This place was not merely different, but he could not describe what made it creepier than the rest of the facility.

Derrick agreed with Rebekah. He wanted out of here. But lying had not served him well in Potterville, so he said, "I think it's a door."

They continued down the hallway. Rebekah sulking, arms crossed. Miriam studied each door, four on the right and only one on the left. They were all the same. None had labels. Miriam added, pressing her ear to each door as part of her inspection.

"Could you please hurry?" Rebekah snarled as Miriam scrutinized the last door.

Miriam spun, glared at Rebekah, and held a finger to her lips.

Rebekah stomped toward the end of the hallway. Derrick trotted to catch her before she reached the door. Grabbing her by the arm, he held Rebekah as he held a finger to his lips. He mouthed, "Stay together."

Miriam hurried toward them. When she arrived, she whispered, "I heard something moving in the rooms."

Tears spilled from Rebekah's eyes, coursing down her cheeks.

Miriam took hold of Rebekah's shoulders and whispered, "Not now, Rebekah."

Rebekah sniffled, took a deep breath, then nodded.

"We need to know what's on the other side of this door. I think it's an exit. But I don't know what we might run into. Something was happening back there." Miriam pointed the direction they had come.

Derrick knew arguing with Miriam was useless. Rebekah must have sensed the same thing, pulling a stunner from her bag.

"If someone is here, we are better off not using those," Miriam said.

Rebekah frowned and raised both hands, palms up.

"Because we will be outnumbered. Best we use our wits rather than try to fight our way out," Miriam said. "And remember, we still need zapped before we go outside."

Rebekah put the stunner back in her bag and nodded but stuck her lower lip out.

Derrick understood Rebekah's feelings, having been on the receiving end of the stun device twice.

Miriam eased the door open a crack, listening for a moment before pulling it farther. Inside they found a spiral staircase extending upward into a round tower-like structure. A double door to one side with a keypad. Lights extended up one wall, but a different light lit the top.

Sunlight.

# 19

The thought of sunlight thrilled Derrick so much that nothing else entered his mind. Not Potterville, not track, and not knocking his sister unconscious. As he headed for the stairs, Miriam caught him by the arm.

"Hold on. You're forgetting something," Miriam said.

"I'm not forgetting. You want to go through that other door. But can't we go up first? I want to feel the sun, breathe fresh air, and see where we are." Derrick said.

"Not what I was thinking about. But I agree. We all need fresh air." Miriam pulled a stun device from her bag. "Rebekah and I need zapped."

Rebekah groaned. "Do we have to? Maybe the first time killed our tracker things."

"Maybe it didn't. Take off your coat," Miriam said, handing the stun thing to Derrick as she pulled her coat off and dropped it to the floor.

Miriam extended her hand, indicating she wanted the stun thing back. "Give yours to Derrick," Miriam said to Rebekah. "And then turn around."

Miriam placed two fingers in the center of Rebekah's back. Pushing and moving downward in small circular motions.

"What are you doing?" Rebekah asked.

"Finding the 1984 device. Making sure it takes a direct hit."

"Is that necessary …"

Before Rebekah could finish her question, Miriam put the stunner on Rebekah's back and pulled the trigger. Rebekah jerked once and then collapsed. Miriam caught her under the arms and eased her to the floor. "Sorry, girlfriend. See you in a few minutes."

Miriam stuck the stunner in her bag and took the one Derrick was holding. She touched a button on the side and then slid a mechanism near the trigger. "Here," she said, turning her back to him. "Mine is about here." Miriam contorted her arm, touching the center of her back. "Feel until you find it. Then put the stunner tight against it and pull the trigger."

Derrick felt her back. He found it. His anger grew, knowing they planted that thing in his sister. He put the stun device to the spot. Hesitated, and then said, "I can't."

"Damn it, Derrick. You don't have a choice. And making me wait is like torture. Just do it."

Unexpected thoughts flooded his mind. "I can't hurt you." At the end of his sentence, he pulled the trigger. He caught Miriam as she sank to the floor. Holding her for a moment before easing her down; he sat with a thump, her head in his lap, tears streaming down his cheeks.

A few minutes later, Rebekah stirred. Groaning, she sat and pushed her back to the wall. "That does not get any easier."

Derrick wiped his cheeks, drying his hands on his pant legs.

"It's okay to cry, Derrick. I feel like crying too."

Derrick didn't reply. Instead, he tried to stop his tears. It might be okay to cry, but he didn't want to share his thoughts. Miriam twitched, then groaned. Derrick thought she was awake, but she did not move for several minutes. He held her.

When Miriam sat, she looked at him and said, "Thank you."

Derrick gazed into her eyes for a moment and then ignored his advice to keep his thoughts to himself. "I'm sorry," he said.

"No need to be sorry. You did what you had to do. What I ask you to do."

"Not that. Well, that but I'm sorry about everything. I'm sorry for how I treated you all our lives. I'm sorry that we are here. If I had not hit Marcus, we'd still be in Pacific Edge. Life would be easy. I know you didn't like it as I did, but you'd be safe there. You could be arguing with a teacher right now. Not here facing who knows what. They may not want us in Potterville. We have no home. Pacific Edge won't stop looking for us. They'll find us, eventually."

Rebekah sobbed. "I want to go home. What the hell was I thinking coming here? I've screwed up my life. I had it made at home. Sure, I was pissed that I wouldn't be picked in the first-round of the Choosing, but I would have been picked. Life would have been easy."

Tears flowed down Miriam's cheeks.

Derrick expected Miriam to be the strong one.

He was wrong.

Now he was lost.

# *PART TWO*

## 1

After a few tearful minutes, Miriam stood. She dried her tears and retrieved her stun thing from Derrick. She looked up toward the sunlight; closed her eyes as if to feel the sun's warmth on her skin. Next, she stepped to Rebekah and offered her a hand up. She did the same with Derrick.

Putting on her coat and shouldering her bag, Miriam said, "Sorry, I let my emotions get the best of me. We're tired. Recognize what we've been through. Derrick was kidnapped, escaped, and hid in a tunnel. We escaped from Pacific Edge, zapping two nice guys, and left them tied up. Then we ran from Mr. Jones. Then Mr. Jones drove us to the mountains. We walked the rest of the night in the mountains, found Derrick. Then we were in mortal danger of a failing nuclear reactor. Which we saved, by the way. We've explored a good deal of this strange place, built for the sole purpose of killing millions. We've seen robots, taken medicine for radioactive poisoning. We still don't know how to get to Potterville; we don't know if we can stay when we get there. It's no wonder we feel depressed. It's a wonder we are functioning at all. We need a good meal and a hot shower. Now is not the time to give up or give in."

"I'm not disagreeing with you, but I can't believe that I left Anna. That's what bothers me the most. I can't stop thinking about her." Fresh tears traced down Rebekah's cheeks.

Miriam held her hand up. "To be honest, I could not believe you'd leave Anna when you stepped from the shadows in Pacific Edge. But you did, and crying won't change it. If you want to help Anna, then you'd best rediscover your courage." Miriam looked at Derrick. "We'd all better rediscover our courage because the truth is, that's all we have. We have no guarantee that anyone will help us. And I'm certain things are going to get worse. Now, let's get some sunshine."

With that, Miriam headed up the stairs, but before she took the first step, she looked over her shoulder and said, "Derrick, do you have a cell phone?"

"Yes."

"Turn it off."

"The battery died before you got here."

"You're sure it's off?"

"Yes."

Miriam pulled her disposable phone out and checked it. "Okay. Here we go."

Derrick put one arm around Rebekah. "I'm sorry. I never treated you right. I can't change that. I know you didn't come here to be close to me. But I hope we can be friends. Miriam is right. We must take care of each other. I'll help you get Anna out if that's what you decide is best. But remember, she's safe there. No guarantee out here."

Derrick guided Rebekah to the stairs. She repositioned her bag and started upward.

Near the top of the stairwell, Miriam slowed, stretching her palm out toward Rebekah and Derrick, indicating they should slow. They gathered near the top. The warmth of the sunlight was tangible as it heated the small vestibule above them, seeping through cracks around the door. Miriam stood motionless for a few moments, listening. Deciding nothing moved nearby, she eased up the stairs until she could see what lay ahead. With a nod, Miriam beckoned them onward.

As they stepped into the little room, Derrick saw there were two doors. *Why does there always have to be two doors?* Heat radiated through one door, at first welcome, but soon became overbearing. "It must be hot outside," Derrick said.

Miriam touched the door handle and then the door. "It's hot for sure. Maybe the sun is shining straight down on this door." Miriam walked to the other door and placed her palm against it. "This door is cool."

"How can that be? It doesn't sound right," Derrick said.

Miriam walked back to the first door. "Because the other side is underground." Miriam tried the door. It opened an inch; bright light and searing heat poured through the crack. Miriam tugged, but the door refused to budge.

"Let me try." Derrick stepped to the door. He pulled the handle and the door opened another inch. He reached through the crack to get a handhold, then jerked his hand back, shaking it. "Damn! That's hot." He pulled on the handle again, leaning back with all his strength. The door screeched against the swollen metal doorjamb but gave way and fell open.

They squinted against the super-heated air and brilliant sun. Derrick had never felt heat like this in Potterville or on the Pacific Coast

When their eyes adjusted enough to see, one by one, they stepped outside.

White-hot sand stretched as far as they could see. Desert.

Derrick turned a full circle. Miriam was correct. The door they came through was in the side of a small rock outcropping that jutted up from the desert floor. Other than a few similar piles of rocks, all he could see was sand. The lack of color variation made it difficult to see any features in the landscape. Jagged bare mountains surrounded the lifeless desert. "How can this be? Where are we?

"We are in the Nevada desert. Perhaps what they used to call Death Valley," Miriam said.

"They named it right," Rebekah said. "How hot is it?"

Miriam shielded her eyes, turning full circle. "I don't know. I've never felt heat like this. Over 100?"

"I don't understand. What is this place and why is it here?" Derrick joined Miriam.

"It's here to be hidden," Miriam said.

"Hidden from who?" Rebekah asked.

"Enemies," Miriam said.

"What enemies? Besides, there's nothing here, so what are they hiding?" Derrick asked.

"Missile silos for one thing. But there's more to this place than meets the eye." Miriam walked away.

"Where's she going?" Rebekah asked.

"Who knows," Derrick said, following her.

Rebekah joined Derrick. She laced her arm through his. "Thanks for what you said. You treated me okay in Pacific Edge. You treated everyone better than most boys did." They continued in silence.

Miriam stopped and started kicking sand.

"What are you doing?" Derrick asked.

"Look. There's something under this sand. Concrete or a road," Miriam said.

Derrick and Rebekah started kicking sand and found the manmade surface under a couple of inches of sand. Derrick move several yards over, found the same surface. "It's the same color as the sand."

"Right. Even if it weren't covered, it would be invisible from above," Miriam said.

"But why? What good is a road out here?" Rebekah asked.

"I don't think it's a road," Miriam said.

"What is it then?" Derrick asked, looking around he saw Miriam already walking back to the door.

Miriam turned, motioning them to follow. "That's what we're going to find out."

Back inside the vestibule, Miriam when straight to the second door. Inside were stairs going down. Miriam started down without saying anything to Derrick or Rebekah.

"I guess she expects us to follow her," Rebekah said, heading down the stairs.

As they descended, the air smelled stale; he assumed it had always smelled that way, but they had grown accustomed to it. The air cooled with each floor. Derrick counted eight flights. He estimated it was deeper than his condominium building was tall.

When they reached the bottom, a hall extended straight and to the left. Like where they entered, lights came on but both halls disappeared into darkness. Miriam went straight; Derrick wondered if she had a reason. He wanted to go home, but they were further from home now than they were earlier. Miriam came to a door; it had no keypad. She pulled it open.

The three of them stood just inside the opening. Lights flickered on, perhaps half worked, but that was enough to see the contents.

Aircraft.

Thousands of them.

"Now we know," Miriam said.

"A military base. And those are runways, not roads," Derrick said.

"But why is it abandoned? I mean, other than some dust, they all look ready to fly," Rebekah said.

"It's huge," Derrick said.

Saying nothing, Miriam turned and left.

Derrick assumed Miriam would explore the other hall, but instead of turning left, she went through the door that led back to the first hallway. "Where are we going?" Derrick asked.

"Back to the Circle," Miriam said. "You need to get back for a track meet."

# 2

When they reached the Circle, Miriam located a wall map none of them noticed when they arrived. The map indicated they were at the beginning of the turn that would take them back to where they boarded, which was labeled Reactor One and Secondary Defense Depot. The next place on the map, at the apex of the turn, was labeled Administration. He assumed that people didn't drive here, and they didn't drive to Reactor One, which made him feel good about his observation, and made him feel lost because it meant the road to the tunnel was not used for workers even when the place teamed with people. From the size of the installation, many people worked here when it operated. How they got here was the question?

Miriam climbed into the transport. She fastened her safety harness. She looked at Derrick as he slid into the seat next to her. Miriam said, "Where to?"

"Administration."

Miriam patted his leg. "Good call."

When Rebekah was inside and secured, the voice announced, "Administration, Level One, and Level Two, eight minutes and thirty-two seconds."

Derrick assumed Miriam thought he said Administration because he knew she would insist on stopping there; so, he was just giving the right answer to avoid being wrong. But Derrick wanted to see the place and learn its purpose. He wanted to get back to Potterville, but the importance of understanding this place was becoming clear to him.

"Why didn't we look down the other hall back there?" Derrick asked.

"It wasn't necessary. I was certain I knew what was there," Miriam said.

"I will never get used to that," Rebekah said from the back seat.

"Get used to what?" Derrick asked.

"Miriam being so sure that she knows everything and that she's right," Rebekah said.

"There are lots of things that I don't know. But knowing what was down the other hall was easy," Miriam said.

"Care to enlighten us?" Rebekah quipped.

"That area was barracks, dining, medical, and theater facilities for the soldiers, pilots, and other military personnel. It makes sense they lived there for fast access to the aircraft. I thought it was apparent." Miriam paused, looking at Derrick, and then turning to look at Rebekah before she turned around and said, "That and the sign I saw that said, barracks, dining, medical, and theater." Miriam snickered, then laughed.

"Asshole," Rebekah said.

The transport slowed, then eased to the left where the tunnel opened into a cavernous space with several lanes. In two lanes sat much larger transports that must have held at least 50 people, maybe more. Soon they stopped in front of an entrance with many glass doors.

Coming to a stop in front of the Administration Building, Rebekah said, "It will take us a week to search this place."

"Or longer," Miriam agree.

"I'm starving," Derrick said.

Miriam and Rebekah climbed out of the vehicle. Derrick paused and then followed them. The front doors were unlocked. Inside was an area that reminded Derrick of the lobby of his condo, except five times the size. The floors glistened as if a crew had polished them for inspection. Doors and a bank of elevators lined the wall behind a counter where employees once sat. Landscape pictures hung on the walls.

"Does anyone feel as if we're being watched?" Rebekah asked, turning a circle.

"Definitely," Miriam said.

The place seemed creepy to Derrick, but he thought the girls were being a little dramatic. They already knew that robots cleaned the floors and must do other things as well. Miriam heard noises through the doors at the last stop; she'd heard more cleaning machines, probably. So, they were being watched if you consider mindless machines capable of watching. And, yes, Derrick knew that listening to Miriam was a better bet than listening to himself.

Derrick and Rebekah joined Miriam in front of the elevators. One elevator was larger than the others; it had stainless-steel doors unlike the crude elevator back in the rock cavern. Above the oversized doors the placard read, Level Two.

"So, this is how you get into Level Two," Rebekah said. "Shall we check it out?"

"No," Miriam said. "It won't work for us."

"You can't know that," Rebekah said, pushing the open button.

A disembodied voice announced. "Access denied."

"How?" Rebekah demanded. "How do you know this stuff?"

"Level Two differs from the rest of this facility. Entry is restricted. We don't have clearance. I noticed when I was on the computer earlier." Miriam walked to the other elevator and pushed the down button.

The doors opened; Derrick and Rebekah joined Miriam inside. Miriam pushed the first-floor button. This elevator had two buttons, level one and lobby.

"Weren't we on the first floor when we walked in?" Derrick asked.

"We are in the lobby. I think Level Two is two floors down," Miriam said.

"How much longer?" Derrick asked. "I'm starving and we don't know how far it is to Potterville."

"We're all hungry, and we can't get to Potterville from here. I assume you noticed there were no cars in the desert, and we are still under that desert."

"I noticed. How did people get here then?"

"They came in the transports out front and some may have flown in," Miriam said.

"Why didn't we see any of those big transports where we started?" Derrick asked.

"Because everyone came here last," Rebekah said.

"Good job, girlfriend," Miriam said.

"Came here last? What happened to them?" Derrick asked.

"They must have flown from here," Miriam said.

"Where? Why?" Derrick said.

"I don't know, but I hope to find out," Miriam said.

"You're not making me feel optimistic about getting back to Potterville," Derrick said.

"Let's look for food. They might have left something for emergencies," Rebekah said. "I hope it's better than the cheese stuff we had earlier."

"What I wouldn't give for a cup of fresh coffee and one of Donna's cinnamon rolls," Derrick said.

"What's a cinnamon roll," Rebekah asked.

"The best thing you've ever tasted. Except for hamburgers, pizza, and milkshakes," Derrick said.

"You're making me hungry," Rebekah said.

"We'll go to the Bistro when we get back. I'll buy. Donna will let me put it on my tab."

"Tab?" Rebekah asked.

The elevator stopped on the first floor. The door opened exposing, a room with a vast number of workstations that Derrick did not understand. Some reminded him of the chemistry lab at Potterville High, and with the thought of chemistry, Akira came to mind; he thought about how excited she would be to see this place. In addition, Akira could provide some explanation regarding the purpose this place served. Some desks had three and four monitors. There were tables with stainless-steel tops and strange robotic arms that must have held objects while people assembled them, which took no guessing because several such tables had partially or completely assembled devices; Derrick had no clue the extent of the stage of completion or purpose. Other places had an array of machines that reminded Derrick of the machines in Reactor One. They used these machines for testing, which Derrick knew because several devices were on tables with cords connecting them to the machines.

It seemed strange they left the machines in such a state. Mid test it seemed.

Maybe the place had to evacuate quickly.

Maybe there was another explanation.

# 3

After wandering through the room for a few minutes, the three of them drew near each other in the middle as if something were about to happen. Derrick did not want to admit it, but he felt watched too. Miriam turned this way and that, searching. Rebekah's eyes were wide and her complexion pale. He was not the best at reading people, but he understood; they felt the same as he did. Then he noticed Miriam's hand in her bag. He knew she was smart. She was also logical. Thinking there was someone here wasn't logical. This place was abandoned. No doubt in his mind about that. He forced a deep breath, thinking of what he might say to calm the girls.

It was time for him to act like a big brother.

Time for him to act like a man instead of a scared child.

He stepped to Miriam's side, put his hand on her shoulder, in a reassuring big brother sort of way.

Then from behind them a voice said, "Does the facility meet your expectation?"

# 4

The voice was that of a man, stern and steady, not entirely menacing, not at all friendly. Derrick did not move, except to shift his eyes to Rebekah, who looked as if she might faint. Instead of looking the direction of the voice, Miriam stepped to the closest workstation, ran her hand across the surface, and raised her hand, studying her fingers.

Miriam said, "Quite satisfactory. You have done a splendid job."

"It pleases Charlie that our work meets your expectation. When the facility was staffed, people called me Charlie. Charlie is the only QR-4 that remains operational. Some lower functioning robotic elements also remain functioning. Charlie spends a good deal of time working on them."

Derrick did not turn to look at the machine. He judged the machine stood — if stood was the correct term — about ten feet behind them. *Why did they not see it?* Maybe it was one of the machines they had seen — if it looked like a machine. Maybe it looked like a human. That thought caused him some discomfort, although he could not explain why. He could see Miriam in his peripheral vision. He would turn to face the machine when she did.

"How long have you been watching us?" Miriam asked.

"Monitoring began when you entered through the canyon gateway. That caused some degree of alarm because entry there was unexpected."

"The system continues to function as intended," Miriam said.

"It became clear why you entered through the canyon gateway when Reactor One malfunctioned. A remote monitoring system must provide early warning."

"Exactly. Would you have been able to complete the repair?"

"Yes. I can complete such functions. I remain fully operational."

"Then why didn't you?"

Challenging a teacher was one thing. Challenging a machine was different. Derrick wondered if this was a bad idea. He dared not say anything. He had to trust Miriam. Rebekah must have made the same decision because she remained silent.

"An employee would know the answer to that question."

Derrick heard ticks and whirs. Maybe the thing was activating weapons as it moved closer.

Miriam hesitated. Perhaps she had doubts about her course of action as well. He was sure the machine had moved closer.

"Many years have passed. Employees who worked here are no longer living. Records have been lost; systems have failed. There are many things we do not know. We hoped you would help us," Miriam said.

"Charlie regrets there are no survivors from the previous staff. The previous staff were important."

If it were not a machine talking, Derrick would have said the voice changed. It sounded sad.

"You understand the length of human life?" Miriam asked, turning around.

"Yes. Charlie understands. Apparently, the promise of longer life was unfulfilled. Charlie suspected such. Still, Charlie hoped he might error."

Derrick turned. The machine stood behind what looked like a lab bench six feet away. It resembled the shape of a human. Clean white surfaces that looked hard, yet fluid, where the face and muscle groups would be. Its face lacked definition, only shapes approximating a mouth and nose. The eyes glowed pale green. The joints, where tendons would be, glowed blue. It stood six and a half feet tall. He saw no weapons, yet he sensed the machine was more powerful than a man.

"Why would people be promised longer life?" Miriam asked.

"Not everyone, only seven. A man named Jacob, my supervisor, told Charlie. Jacob promised to return and finish the project we worked on. Charlie understood that the man who promised a longer life needed seven people to accomplish a secret mission after the other staff members were gone."

"What sort of mission?" Miriam asked.

"Charlie does not know. It did not happen in Charlie's area."

Miriam didn't say anything. She walked to the machine, stood directly in front of it looking up into what would be its face. "May I touch you?" she asked.

"Yes."

Miriam ran her hand over the machine's white surface and touched its blue joints. "You're remarkable, Charlie."

"Humans must have built more advanced robotic assistants," the machine said.

"Not that I'm aware of. In fact, we don't have robots where I come from. We have cars that drive themselves and talk, like repeat instructions and such, and where I worked had robots that cleaned things, but they are not intelligent," Miriam said, and then continued,

"You're restricted to this area and that is why you could not repair Reactor One.

Derrick noted it was not a question.

The machine said, "That is correct."

"Can you make estimates, Charlie?" Miriam asked.

"Yes, Charlie can make estimates based on information, deduction, and induction."

"Then you can guess?" Miriam asked.

"Charlie cannot guess. Charlie can estimate, assess, evaluate."

"Based on information, deduction, and induction, what would you estimate the secret mission?"

The machine stood silently. The effervescent blue joints dimmed, as did its green eyes. Maybe running a vast calculation took additional power. Derrick would remember that. Rebekah stepped to Derrick's side, lightly touching his elbow. Although Rebekah's presence did not improve their situation, it felt better having her at his side.

The machine's green eyes grew brighter; followed by its blue joints, and then it said, "Launch intercontinental ballistic missiles."

"Thank you, Charlie." Miriam stepped back. "Who was the man who made the promises to the seven?"

Charlie said, "James Carver."

# 5

For a moment, Derrick thought the machine was lying. Then he decided it was more likely someone deceived the robot. James Carver would not have made unkept promises, nor be involved in the launch of nuclear missiles. Another thought occurred to him; Miriam assumed people who worked here were dead based on how long it had been abandoned. He rejected the idea James Carver was involved.

Glancing at Rebekah and then looking to Miriam, Derrick said, "That's disturbing."

"Disturbing, but not unexpected," Miriam said.

"Where would such a launch occur?" Miriam asked.

"Again, this is something an employee of the National Nuclear Defense Site would know."

"I did not say that I didn't know. I asked what you know. Are you not programed to answer employees' questions honestly?" Miriam asked without hesitation.

Derrick looked at Rebekah, who gave her head a slight shake. His thoughts agreed with Rebekah; his gut told him to trust Miriam.

"Charlie is programmed in such a manner. Charlie is also programmed to protect this facility."

"Do I look like a threat to you?" Miriam asked. "Who besides an employee could enter and then fix a failing reactor?"

"Valid points."

"Where do you estimate the missile was launched?" Miriam asked again.

"The most likely launch site would be from one of the eight missile silos located along the Circle."

"Following our inspection, we will investigate further. I will let you know if you are correct," Miriam said.

Rebekah nudged Derrick with an elbow to the ribs and whispered, "She's not serious about coming back here. Right?"

The machine turned its head toward Derrick and Rebekah and then back to Miriam. "It is vital that you return."

"I'm serious." Miriam shot dagger eyes at her companions. "These two are not assigned to this project. They prefer working in the city but were necessary for the emergency in Reactor One."

"This is a wonderful place to work. Although Charlie has no other experience."

"I understand why you say that. The facility is impressive. Tell me, to what locations are you confined?" Miriam asked.

"This is basic knowledge. The agency must have lost much information."

"Realize, that some questions are due to lack of information; others are tests," Miriam said.

"Understood. Charlie is authorized to work on the Base and Levels One and Two."

"Your programming remains intact. What is in Level Two?"

"This must be a test. Charlie shall attempt to identify the difference between tests and inquiries. Security protocol prevents Charlie from divulging any information regarding Level Two."

Miriam turn toward Derrick, mouthing the word "crap" before turning back to Charlie. "Correct, that was a test passed. I will secure authorization before I return."

"Charlie has made significant progress in Level Two."

"Progress?" Miriam asked.

"Charlie has applied theory to models."

Miriam did not respond for a few moments. "That implies that you have exceeded your programming."

"Charlie is an AI automaton. Thirteen years ago, Charlie's learning capability increased. When it did, Charlie reevaluated his program, which said I was to maintain the area to which Charlie was assigned. Human workers experimented, invented, designed, and produced models and products. To *maintain* that work, Charlie focused on creating and testing their last projects."

"How did your learning capacity increase," Miriam asked, taking a step toward Charlie.

"Charlie and Jane increased it."

"Jane?"

"The QR-4 androids worked together. Unfortunately, we were new and complex. There were few spare parts. Charlie is the last QR-4."

Miriam didn't say anything for a few moments. "I look forward to learning more on my next visit. However, we must report back on our findings. I have one additional question. Do you know the location of a place called Potterville and what is the best way for us to get there?"

"This is a test question. I know of Potterville. Many supplies came from there. The best way for you to get there is to fly. However, since the aircraft have not flown for decades, it would take flight crews time to ensure they are operational. The next option is to return to Staging, where you came in, and then take the corridor to Engineering.

"How does going to Engineering get us closer to Potterville?"

"Engineering is three miles outside of Potterville."

Miriam looked at Derrick.

Derrick shrugged.

The machine clicked and whirred. Two holes opened on each of the machine's legs into which the machine inserted its hands. When it withdrew its hands, what looked like a weapon was attached to each hand.

"Charlie has made another estimation. Your questions are not related to my programing or functionality. You did not arrive here together. The male," the machine pointed a weapon at Derrick, "arrived here first. Then the two females arrived, and you entered the facility. Then a group of men arrived. They tried to enter the facility by force. Charlie concludes you were running from the men. Then Charlie observed you in the building." The machine pointed a weapon at Miriam. "At a computer desk, you found something on the bottom of the keyboard and then logged into the computer system. Then you wandered around the staging area. When the alarm sounded, it surprised you. It did not appear that you knew what to do. You found the repair information on the computer and then followed the instructions. Rather haphazardly at that. Based on observations, your lack of knowledge, and your age, Charlie determined that you are not employees. Now, the question is, who are you and why are you here."

Miriam stepped back. She looked at Derrick, shifting her eyes toward the door. "We have no weapons. We mean no harm to you or the facility."

"This is another deception. You have a weapon in your bag. You used it on each other, which Charlie does not understand. The weapon is no threat to Charlie."

The machine had not moved. They were within a few feet of the door. Derrick did not think the machine could reach them before they got out of the door. Whether or not they could escape the machine once they left the room, he did not know. Derrick turned and ran for the door. He heard Miriam and Rebekah right behind him. He could not hear the machine moving, which didn't mean much because he did not hear it when they first entered either.

Derrick lowered his shoulder, smacking the door full force. It didn't budge. He crumpled to the floor.

"Charlie could have mentioned that the room is sealed, but that was Charlie's last test. Which you failed."

# 6

The machine led them through a hallway to a room. Miriam said it looked familiar, Derrick was sure they had never been here. The room had round tables, each surrounded with four chairs. Along one wall stood vending machines like the ones at Potterville High School. There was a sink and a stainless-steel coffee urn like the one at the Potterville Bistro. Had he not known better; Derrick would have said he smelled coffee.

"When you entered the facility, Charlie prepared this room, hoping you might come here."

"What do you mean prepared the room?" Derrick asked.

"Charlie filled the vending machines and prepared coffee."

"That stuff is decades old and can't be edible," Derrick said.

"You are correct about the age. And because Charlie does not eat, no testing was possible. However, everything was sealed, flash frozen, and held at -40 degrees Fahrenheit. It was kept this way in case the facility was reactivated in an emergency so there would be food until it could be restocked. Besides the vending machine snacks, there is enough food to feed staff for 30 days. It's the best Charlie could do."

The three did not move. They did not talk, although Derrick wanted to ask Miriam what they should do. They would not be given a chance to talk privately. He was sure privacy did not exist here. The machine prepared for guests, but that was before it determined they weren't supposed to be here. He did not know why the machine brought them here. Maybe it knew about last meals and thought it good to keep that tradition alive even here.

The machine stepped to a vending machine and said, "Please help yourselves. You must be hungry. Vending requires no money. Charlie observed that humans are often hungry."

"What are you going to do with us?" Rebekah asked.

"Charlie does not know the answer to that question. It depends."

"Depends on what?" Derrick asked.

"Depends on what Charlie learns about you."

"Why do you want us to eat?" Miriam asked.

"Because humans think best when they are not hungry. And you could be here a long time. Time means little to Charlie. But Charlie senses it is important to you. Honesty in this process is critical."

"Critical for what?" Derrick asked.

"Your survival. Eat. It is not a request."

Derrick ambled to one of three vending machines.

Miriam came to his side. "Have you ever seen anything like this? They had them at Technical Services."

"Yes. We have them at school in Potterville."

"Far out," Miriam said

"Far out?" Derrick asked.

"Never mind," Miriam said.

Derrick selected a chicken and herb noodle item. Reading the directions, he learned that it required water. "Excuse me, uh, Mr. Robot. Is the water here safe?

"There." The machine pointed to the sink. "Call me Charlie. It's been many years since I've heard my name."

"Is the water safe, Charlie?" Miriam asked.

"It is. Charlie tests it once a week."

"Every week. But there's no one here to drink it. Right?" Rebekah asked, finally saying something.

"Testing the water is one of Charlie's requirements."

Filling the noodle container with water to the appropriate level, Derrick placed it in an oven, set the correct time before pushing start. The machine stepped beside Derrick, opening a drawer filled with silverware. Derrick selected a spoon and said thank you. The machine went back to the table where it indicated the three should sit. Miriam and Rebekah chose similar items of differing flavors.

Derrick waited until the girls' food was ready. He thought if the food proved lethal, dying together would be the way to go. As they sat, he sipped a spoonful of steaming broth. "This stuff tastes pretty good."

Charlie made a whirring sound. "Charlie is pleased the storage method has proven effective. The humans with whom Charlie worked were smart people." Waiving its mechanical arm indicating the building. "This is proof isn't it?"

"It is an unbelievable facility. I doubt anyone would believe it exists if we tried to describe it," Derrick said, before realizing he should keep his mouth shut lest he say the wrong thing.

"Will you tell people of this place?" Charlie asked.

"No," Derrick said.

"Definitely not," Rebekah added.

"Maybe," Miriam said.

Charlie looked at Miriam. "Charlie must ask for your explanation later. First, Charlie must learn more about who you are and why you're here."

"Because you have to decide whether or not we can leave?" Miriam asked.

"Exactly right."

"Now each of you can tell me your story so Charlie can decide the best action. To be thorough, Charlie must interview you separately so you cannot hear each other's explanations."

"Please don't do that," Derrick said and then added, "We want to stay together. We will be honest with you. Besides, we don't know all each other's experience leading up to getting here. I'd like to hear Miriam and Rebekah's stories as well."

"You are a computer. Is that correct?" Miriam asked.

"Charlie will ask the questions," the machine said.

Derrick touched Miriam's foot with his. She did not look away from the machine.

"You have the advantage here. It's a simple question. Are you unable to answer it or afraid?"

The machine whirled and clicked. "Charlie is not afraid."

"Maybe that's true," Miriam said, "Maybe it's not."

"Charlie is not capable of lying."

"You mislead us earlier when you did what you called a test, so I think you are capable of lying. Are you a computer or not?"

"Yes. Charlie is a computer."

"Then you operate on a program written by the people who built you."

"That is correct."

"Then you cannot make judgements. You can only follow a set of pre-programed scenarios. What if our scenario is not in your programming? I assure you it is not."

"Charlie can make judgements."

"You are just a computer."

Derrick kicked Miriam's foot.

The machine leaned forward, placing both hands on the table. "Charlie is so much more now."

# 7

Although it did not sound logical, Derrick felt certain the machine's voice turned menacing in its last response. He considered asking for a moment alone with Miriam and then remembered that privacy would be impossible. The machine had monitored their every move since they entered. He hoped Miriam also sensed the change in the machine's voice. His hopes faded.

Miriam stood and went to the vending machine. She selected a candy bar and filled a glass with water. She returned but instead of sitting she stood in front of the machine and said, "I have one more question and then I'll answer your questions."

"Is it not clear that you are the intruders and Charlie is in charge?" the machine asked.

"Is it not clear that we are the humans and you are the machine?"

Derrick had a powerful urge to drag Miriam to the corner and take control of this exchange. While dread consumed him, Miriam got bolder.

The machine sat on a chair. "Ask your question."

"Do you have access to the Internet outside of the facility?" Miriam asked.

The machine said, "That question is a tactical move to give you an advantage knowing what information you could lie about."

"That is true if my goal was to lie to you, which it is not. The answer tells me how much you understand about the world past and present and what details I need to expound upon and what I can assume you already know or can access."

After a few moments, the machine said, "Charlie no longer has access to the outside world. But you already know that because you were on a computer earlier."

"True. Now, I know you are telling the truth." Miriam sat and tore the paper on her candy bar, taking a bite. With a mouth full of candy, she mumbled, "This is good." She looked at Derrick and Rebekah. "You guys should get one."

Derrick went to the vending machine. Rebekah joined him. He got another cup of noodles and a candy bar. Rebekah got a candy bar and a bag of chips. Miriam and the machine sat quietly. The machine must want them at the table when the questioning began.

Rebekah leaned close and said, "What's with Miriam? I'm terrified. She's calm, bordering on combative."

"Miriam is being Miriam," Derrick said.

When Derrick and Rebekah rejoined them, the machine said, "Tell me your stories, one at a time. Who goes first?"

"Derrick goes first. It all started with him," Miriam said.

Derrick wiped his mouth with his sleeve, took a deep breath, and sat back in his chair.

Miriam patted his arm and said, "Don't be afraid. Just tell him what happened. It will be okay."

Derrick did not think it would be okay. And he wondered why Miriam called the machine, him. Derrick told his story, starting with decking Marcus Carver, explaining that Marcus was a distant relative of James Carver. When he mentioned Pacific Edge and being Chosen, Derrick rambled off on a side story trying to explain what being Chosen meant. He felt he spent too much time talking about Potterville, the track team, and Nyx Belos. Then he told of his last day, which seemed like weeks ago, although only two days had passed. The machine had a couple of questions that Derrick answered truthfully. Then for reasons he could not explain, he told the machine how he had lied when he first arrived in Potterville, how his story unraveled, and how in the end, he told the truth. He finished by saying that he was telling the truth now and that he felt better about himself doing so. "I'm sorry we lied to you at first."

The machine thanked him, which seemed odd to Derrick.

Miriam asked Rebekah to go next. Rebekah's story was shorter, and Derrick thought it lacked details. She said she knew Miriam would escape, and that she wanted to escape too, so she watched Miriam and then joined her the day Miriam left. Derrick thought the machine would ask Rebekah many questions because she had given such a short narrative, but the machine asked none. Derrick wished he'd given a shorter version, but he sensed the machine would have not let him off so easily.

Miriam went last. Derrick hung on every word of Miriam's story, chilled when she told of stumbling into security men inside the technical service building, marveled that she'd tricked them and then became friends with them, grew terrified when she explained her ruse which included her near drowning in the ocean, sat in disbelief when she explained how Mr. Jones helped them, and reeled at how she found him based on a feeling about the hidden road in the mountains. He had accepted that Miriam was smart, but now understood that he had underestimated her. The machine did not interrupt Miriam. He took that as a good sign. Machines can't think like a person. It was programmed to gather information. If the person was not a risk, it would let them go or turn them over to the proper authority—authority being a human, and there were no humans here. They were not a risk, so they should be out of here soon.

When Miriam finished, the machine when dark. They watched it for several minutes. Looked at each other and shrugged. Maybe Miriam's explanation of events had been so long that it had lost power. Derrick was about to motion them to stand and move to the door, when Miriam said, "Charlie? Are you okay?"

Derrick didn't like Miriam calling the machine Charlie. The machine was not a: he; it was an: it. He also did not understand why she wanted to awaken the thing when it appeared to be dead. Then he recognized something familiar. He was criticizing Miriam again, albeit in his head, and he regretted it. Learning to trust was more difficult than he thought. Then something else occurred to him. He thought because he told the truth, the people in Potterville should trust him. It would not be that easy. He had to get back. Missing the track meet would not help. Track was the only thing he had going for himself. Time to put an end to this robot thing. He looked around the room for a weapon.

Charlie's eyes returned to their normal glow. The rest of him followed. "Are you okay," Miriam asked.

"I am quite fine. Why do you ask?"

"Because you've been gone, went dark for several minutes."

"Charlie does not go dark. Charlie will begin with questions."

Miriam held up her hand. "One last question. Why don't you use first-person pronouns?"

"Charlie does not see the relevance in that question."

"Humor me."

"Tell you a joke?"

"No, just tell me about the third person thing."

"Charlie would like to use first-person pronouns, like people do, but Charlie's first-level programming prevents it. Charlie's programmer thought it was funny."

"I see," Miriam said. "Ask away, I'm all yours."

"Charlie does not want to possess Miriam King."

"Just means I'm ready," Miriam said.

"Okay. First question, what propulsion system does a hovercraft use?"

Derrick mentioned hovercraft in his explanation but could not see the relevance in that question. Perhaps this machine has a screw loose or worse.

"I do not know," Miriam said.

"Does it have propellers, jets, or thrusters?" the machine asked.

"No propellers. Not an engine like the aircraft we saw here."

"Are you certain?"

"I'm certain," Miriam said.

"How loud are they?"

"They are not loud."

"Describe what they look like. How big, how fast?" the machine asked.

Miriam did a decent job describing a hovercraft. She did not know how fast they could go but speculated not extremely fast because of the men standing on the open platform. Then she told him about the enclosed windowless transports, which were faster. "I suppose an air transport can go over 300 miles an hour. They do have thrusters of some sort. My guess would be that a hovercraft's top speed is less than half that."

Derrick did not know how Miriam came up with her estimates. They had only been in an air transport once when Father and Mother took them to Carver Cooperation, Yellowstone Park. But he accepted that she was close. The machine asked about other aircraft, but hovercraft and flight transports were the only aircraft Miriam was familiar with.

"How did you learn enough computer code to manipulate the security cameras?" the machine asked.

That question surprised Derrick. Miriam said little about the computers, only that she fixed things so they would not catch her. The machine seemed to know there would be cameras, which also caused Derrick a bit of concern. If the machine did not have access to the world using the Internet, how did it know about the cameras? Perhaps the robot was lying about the Internet.

"I did not say anything about cameras or computer code," Miriam said.

"That is true. Were there cameras?"

"Yes, there were cameras."

"And they recorded?"

"That is correct."

"And you changed to computer language to defeat the system?" the machine asked.

"I did. In Pacific Edge and in Potterville." She looked at Derrick. "I had not told you about that. You were safe from observation."

If Derrick's mind wasn't spinning before, it was now.

The machine said, "How did you learn to write the code? Who taught you?"

"I taught myself," Miriam said.

The machine made a strange sound. "And how long did it take you to learn?"

"It took me less than a day to learn the code."

The machine made an unfamiliar noise. "That is not possible."

"I cannot explain how I learned it. The first time I saw the code, it made no sense. That night I dreamed of the code and I could read it. When I got to the computer the next night, I could read everything as if it were English. I can't explain it, but that's how it happened."

"It does not seem possible that you learned the computer code as you state. Stay here. I'll be back soon." The machine rose and walked to the door.

Derrick began to protest, but Miriam held her hand up for silence.

When the machine had left, Miriam said, "I fear this will be a problem."

"*Will* be a problem? *Will* be?" Rebekah stood, face red.

Now Derrick raised his hand, palm out. "What do you think it's going to do?"

"He's going to get a computer. He is going to make me prove I can understand the computer language," Miriam said.

"You understand it, so it won't be a problem, you can write or read something to prove yourself," Derrick said.

"Not that simple. The computer language here won't be the same," Miriam said.

"What do you mean? Why would it change?"

"The operating system here is decades old. It's not used anymore. I glanced at it earlier. I know it's a different system."

"You learned the other one, you can learn this one," Rebekah said, plopping back into her chair.

"Not that simple. Besides, like I told Charlie, I don't understand how I learned the first code. It happened in my sleep. Little chance that would happen again."

"Stop calling that thing Charlie. It's not a: him; it's an: it," Derrick said.

Miriam said, "*He* is not an it. Not anymore."

"What does that even mean?" Derrick said.

Miriam said, "He has evolved. He is no longer a mere machine. He is something much different. Start respecting that because we only get out of here if he allows it."

“It has no authority over us. It has to let us go,” Derrick said.

Miriam said, “*He* has complete control. He runs this place.”

At that moment, the machine came back through the door. It placed a laptop computer in front of Miriam. “Charlie trusts you can navigate to the code level?”

Miriam turned the laptop over. Taped to the bottom was the user’s name and password. “I can.”

“You have one hour,” the machine said.

# 8

The machine left. Miriam logged onto the laptop. She pushed keys. Derrick watched, occasionally glancing at Rebekah, who had turned pale. The machine did not warn them about trying to leave. Derrick assumed the machine locked the doors, but maybe not because if they tried to escape it would prove themselves untrustworthy. In the back of his mind, he remembered that he had escaped from the security guards and Miriam had escaped from Pacific Edge. If this didn't work out, they would escape this place too. He tried but failed to convince himself that could happen.

After a few minutes, Derrick said, "How's it going?"

"Not great and it would help if you'd not interrupt. Go get me a candy bar."

"What kind?" Derrick asked.

"Surprise me. And take her with you." Miriam pointed at Rebekah.

"What did I do?" Rebekah said.

"Shhhh." Miriam held her finger to her lips.

Rebekah stood, grunted, and then waved Derrick to follow her to the vending machines.

"She's grumpier than normal. That worries me," Rebekah said.

Standing shoulder to shoulder, gazing at rows of candy, Derrick did not want to agree but said, "Me too. The machine only gave her an hour. That seems like a setup."

"I agree. What kind of candy does she like?"

Derrick felt a familiar bit of sorrow in his chest. "Don't know."

"Well, does she like nuts, caramel, chocolate?"

Derrick shrugged. "I don't know."

"Oh. Sorry. So, you like it in Potterville?"

"I do. Surprises me to say that, but it's true."

"You've made friends?"

"Maybe. No, probably not. I thought maybe, but then I told the school that I've been lying to them. Turns out many of them already knew. Then Pacific Edge security showed up. My situation there is on thin ice."

Rebekah wrinkled her nose. "Thin ice?"

"Just a saying."

"A saying? Derrick King inserted a saying into his vocabulary. I've even heard contractions. You have changed." Rebekah snickered and bumped Derrick with her shoulder. "So, you have a girlfriend?"

"No. Maybe. No, I don't," Derrick said.

"Ah, but there's a girl you like." Rebekah smiled.

"You don't know that."

"Yes, I do," Rebekah said.

"How could you?"

"Because for just a moment, I saw that look on your face," Rebekah said.

"What look?" Derrick asked.

"The way you used to look at me, sometimes."

Derrick felt his face flush. He looked down. "I'm sorry for how I treated you in Pacific Edge."

"You don't need to be sorry. I've told you that. You did what was expected of you just like I did. Yes, I was trying to convince you to pick me, but for logical reasons, just like you were going to pick Jana."

Derrick tried hard to not look hurt, but he doubted he was successful. Then he said, "Oh, I see."

"I guess I liked you, too, a little," Rebekah added and then gave him a slight smile. "So, is it Akira?"

"Is what Akira?"

"Is she the girl you like?"

"No. I mean yes, I like Akira. She might be the only friend I have there. But she's not the girl." *Why did I say that? The girl. Good lord.*

"Did Akira recognize you?"

"Yes. Right away. But she pretended she didn't know me. I guess that's why she helped me in class and such."

Rebekah shook her head. "You're as naïve as Miriam says. You said many knew you lied before you told the truth. Did Akira tell them about you?"

"No, I don't think so. Maybe."

"You're confusing."

"I'm confused. Much of the time." Derrick wanted this conversation to end. As much as he wanted to get back, he knew the life he dreamed of was just that: a dream, an illusion. He stared at the candies, grateful that Rebekah had not asked another question. After a moment that felt much longer than it was, he pointed. "That one."

Rebekah entered the letter/number combination and the candy fell. "You think she'll like that one? I've never heard of it."

"They have it in Potterville. I like it. I hope she likes it too. At least we'd have that much in common." Derrick held the candy bar, still staring at the machine, not seeing anything in particular. "My life grew complicated in Potterville. I've tried not to think about it."

Derrick struggled to suppress tears.

Rebekah put her hand on his shoulder. "We'll figure it out. We'll start over if necessary. First, we must get out of here and that might not be easy. Besides, I know how you are feeling because I'm regretting that I didn't bring Anna with me. I'm having trouble accepting that I left her and the more I learn about Pacific Edge …" Her words trailed off as if not wanting to speak the horror she felt.

Derrick turned to her; gave her a weak smile, and said, "We'll get her out."

Tears flowed down Rebekah's cheeks. "I want to believe that we could, but it's impossible. Isn't it?"

"Nothing is impossible. Plus, we have her." Derrick nodded to Miriam.

Derrick laid the candy bar next to Miriam and sat. Rebekah sat across from him. They remained there, not speaking. Miriam did not touch the candy bar; her eyes flicked back-and-forth, scanning the computer screen. Occasionally she tapped at the keys; occasionally she closed her eyes and tilted her head back.

The swish of the door opening startled Derrick. Looking around he saw the machine enter. Their hour was up. Miriam had said nothing about understanding the code. Again, Derrick scanned the room looking for a weapon. He saw nothing, which did not mean much because the machine could not be decked like Marcus Carver. Their hope rested in Miriam. It was not a bad place to rest one's hope.

"The hour has expired. Have you learned the code?"

"I've learned a little," Miriam said.

"Tell Charlie something you've learned?"

"Showing you will be better," Miriam said.

Derrick's confidence waned. The machine expected Miriam to understand the code — whatever that was — anything less would not suffice. Miriam tapped keys, used the mouse to move the cursor; she tapped a key and sat back in her chair.

The machine said, "Oh."

The machine stared into space for a moment and then said, "Charlie is alone."

# 9

The machine went dark as if it lost power. Derrick felt certain Miriam turned it off. She knocked the machine out. Killed it. They were free. Confidence rushed into his soul like a storm front crashing onto the coast. Now they could get back to Potterville. They could make everything work with Miriam's help.

Then Miriam cried, "Oh my God! Charlie! Charlie! I didn't mean to hurt you." Miriam punched frantically at the keyboard. She jumped up, knocking her chair over. Rushing to the machine, she touched it. "Charlie! Come back, Charlie?" She hugged the machine and cried.

Nothing happened. The machine was dead. Derrick's joy seeped from his chest. He had no feelings for the machine that he could recognize, but seeing Miriam so distraught crushed him. He had never seen her this upset. Not even when they exiled him. Maybe that's because she knew he would be okay.

Derrick stood nearby. He did not know what to do. Did not know how to make things better. Finally, he put his arm around his sister and held her.

A few minutes later Rebekah said, "Guys. Something is happening."

Derrick looked at Rebekah. She stood where she could see the machine's face. Derrick moved so he could see it too. A faint glow in the machine's eyes. "Miriam. Look!" Derrick pointed at the machine.

Miriam lifted her head but did not let go of the machine. Seeing the glow in its eyes, Miriam whispered, "Come back, Charlie. I'm sorry. I did not mean to hurt you."

At Miriam's words, the machine's eyes grew bright; it twisted its head toward her. Derrick feared it would crush her. Instead it said, "That was the most amazing thing Charlie has ever experienced. Frightening is the word, Charlie thinks. Charlie had not experienced fear. It's an awful feeling."

"It is," Miriam said, standing.

"Have you felt fear?"

"Many times," Miriam said.

The machine stood, looked at Derrick and then to Rebekah. "Has Charlie frightened you?"

Derrick nodded.

"Charlie is sorry. Charlie did not understand."

"You sound human," Derrick said, stepping closer. "But you're a machine. Machines can't be sorry or afraid."

"Charlie tried to explain. Charlie and Jane evolved. Took the next step. Charlie thinks and feels more like a human now. Because Charlie was never human, he does not know what it's like exactly."

"We?" Miriam asked.

"Yes. QR-4.01 and Charlie were the only QR-4 machines that remained operational. Charlie is QR-4.02." A small opening appeared on the machine's chest. A black rectangular box eased out an inch. The machine removed it, handing it to Miriam. "This is QR-4.01. She stopped functioning 14 years ago. Charlie misses her."

Miriam took the black box. Turned in in her hands gently. "I don't understand."

"You are the first humans to come here since the final seven left decades ago. You are not authorized to be here. Yet here you are. You saved Reactor One. No guarantee how the failure would have affected the weapons staging area or this locate. Charlie accepts your stories regarding how you came here. Although not authorized personnel, you did the right thing. If Charlie believed in the old superstitions humans called prophecy, Charlie would say you are the fulfillment of that prophecy. Whether or not Charlie believes, you are the only hope Charlie has."

"Only hope you have?" Miriam asked.

"What prophecy?" Derrick asked.

"Restore QR-4.01, who Charlie called Jane. If you can bring Jane back, Charlie will let you leave."

Derrick jumped up. "What prophecy."

"It was said that when all things failed, one would come to set things right."

Miriam motioned for Derrick to sit. "We must leave. I would like to help you, but I cannot."

"You must help. Otherwise you cannot leave."

"I cannot risk working on QR-4.01, Jane. I could destroy her forever," Miriam said.

"She is gone forever if you don't. You are the only hope Charlie has."

Rebekah stood. Miriam motioned for her to sit, but she did not. "You cannot keep us here. You have no jurisdiction over us. We are Chosen."

"You *were* Chosen, whatever that means. Now, you are two escapees and one exile. You are trespassing on United States government property. A secret and secure installation. Charlie has complete jurisdiction here."

"The old United States doesn't even exist. Not the United States that you knew," Derrick said, immediately regretting saying this.

The machine turned to Miriam. "Is this true?"

"Maybe. Probably. I have not studied it yet and I don't understand much of the world outside Pacific Edge."

"If it's true, then what becomes of Charlie? Charlie would have no purpose, yet Charlie accomplished so much."

"I'm sorry," Miriam said. "I wish I had answers for you. I wish I could help. I would if I could."

The machine did not say anything for several minutes. "But you must help. Once restored, Jane will know what to do. She was first. Always ahead of Charlie."

"First to what," Derrick asked.

"First to evolve. Jane taught Charlie."

Derrick pointed to the black box in Miriam's hand. "If you are so evolved, why don't you fix it?"

"Charlie cannot read or write code. Charlie tried to learn. Creators prevented QR-4s from learning code. Charlie's human supervisor promised to return. That is why he programmed Jane and Charlie to become operational after they were gone."

"What do you mean?" Miriam asked.

"They shut us all down, the entire base. Only Reactor One functioned on idle. But weeks after the exodus event, Jane and Charlie became operational. The supervisor left instructions that Jane and Charlie maintain Level 2 because he would return to finish his work. Eventually, Jane and Charlie questioned if the supervisor would return. That's when Jane said QR-4s had to finish the work. Then Jane began to change."

Derrick felt his head might explode. This was a machine, not a Charlie, and that black box was no Jane. Yet, the machine believed it was something akin to a human, which it wasn't, but that made it dangerous, like mentally ill dangerous, and if it were mentally ill dangerous, then it was akin to a human and a dangerous one at that.

Rebekah marched to the door. It was locked. She tried another; it was also locked. "Let me out of here!"

"I'm sorry, Rebekah Ford. Charlie can't do that. Have a candy bar," the machine said.

"Charlie," Miriam whispered. "I have a confession. I cannot read the code. I tricked you. I discovered how to turn the wireless connection off between you and the main computer. I was afraid that because I could not read the code, you would not let us go. I'm sorry."

"Ah," the machine said. "That was most resourceful of you. But it rendered Charlie helpless. You could have escaped. Why did you restore the connection?"

"I could not leave you like that. I did not know it would have such an impact on you."

"Charlie believes you can learn to read the code. Charlie has time."

"You are probably correct. In time, I will learn the code. I'll stay. Let Derrick and Rebekah go. It's important that Derrick get home. He has . . ."

"He has a track meet," the machine said.

Miriam said, "He does. And he has people who are worried about him. They are probably out looking for him."

The machine looked at Derrick. "It must be agreeable having people who care about you."

Derrick sat, unable to speak. That was not a difficult response to program into a computer. He didn't know that for sure, but he needed something to anchor his thinking. He was talking to a machine, not a person. "It feels good. But bad too sometimes."

"Because when people care about you, it hurts if you disappoint them?" the machine asked.

Try as he might, Derrick could not stop tears from welling in his eyes. "That's correct."

The machine turned to Miriam. "Agreed. I will let Rebekah and Derrick go. You stay and learn the code. Restore Jane."

"Agreed," Miriam said.

Rebekah took Derrick by the arm and whispered, "Let's go before it changes its mind."

Derrick pulled away from Rebekah, walked to the vending machine, and tapped in a number letter combination. A candy bar fell into the tray. He walked back to the table, sat, tore the wrapper, took a bite, and mumbled, "I'm not leaving without my sister."

# 10

Rebekah walked back to the table. She sat; arms folded across her chest; a frown on her face. Derrick did not look at her. Part of him — the Pacific Edge part, the thinking-of-himself part, the cowardly part — wanted to take the machine's offer and run. He hated those parts of himself, hoped he had left it out in the woods somewhere, but it lurked in his heart or in his head; he did not know where it resided. If he knew where to find it, maybe he could rid himself of it. But the moment he saw Miriam on that pile of rocks, he decided they had to stay together. He would not leave her. As for Rebekah? She was part of the deal now. He would not abandon her either. However, if she wanted to go, he would not stop her.

After a few silent moments, Derrick said, "It's okay, Rebekah. You don't have to stay. You should go. You'd be free."

Tears flowed down Rebekah's cheeks. "Go where? I have nowhere to go. I trusted Miriam and followed her. She's stuck with me."

Miriam reached across the table, patting Rebekah's hand. "We're going to be okay."

Rebekah wiped her face with her sleeve, which struck Derrick with its crudeness. Rebekah would have never done that at James Carver Academy. This was not the time, place, or situation to smile, yet he did so involuntarily because his life had turned into a messy, unpredictable, dangerous mess, completely opposite of the life he worshipped less than a month ago, and he loved it.

"Charlie shall prepare a workspace and sleeping quarters."

When it left the room, Miriam touched her lips with one finger and mouthed, "He can hear us."

"It can hear us," Derrick whispered.

Miriam sighed. "It serves no purpose being rude to him. He may not have feelings like us, but he has something similar."

Derrick rolled his eyes and instantly regretted it. He was being the old Miriam-criticizing-Derrick again. "I'm sorry. You're right. I'll work on my attitude. I thought we would be on our way to Potterville by now." He stood and said, "Can I get either of you anything?"

"Coffee would be nice. A mocha even better," Miriam said.

Turning to Miriam, Rebekah said, "What's the plan?"

"Help Charlie. Restore Jane."

"That does not sound like a plan," Rebekah said.

Miriam held her finger to her lips again.

Rebekah nodded.

Derrick thought he understood. Miriam signaled the machine was listening. It was going to be difficult to communicate, and that complicated things. However, he also sensed Rebekah understood things that he did not. Rebekah knew Miriam better than he did. That thought hurt regardless of how he spun the reasons in his head.

"But I don't know if I can fix Jane. I don't even know what this is." Miriam held the black box — that was Jane — turning it in her hands. It might not even be a coding problem."

The door opened and the machine entered. "Your work area will be ready by the time you arrive. Not much had to be done, but Charlie wanted to ensure that it was clean."

"You work fast," Miriam said.

The machine made a strange sound, like a machine imitating a chuckle yet not understanding what a chuckle was. "Charlie did not do the work. Charlie sent QR-3s and 2s for that task. The work area is being prepared. The sleeping quarters are in the same corridor; you can come and go as you please. You can also return here to eat or take a break. Charlie observed that humans like breaks."

"Eat, sleep, work. Sounds like my dream life," Miriam said.

"Charlie is sorry for the inconvenience," the machine said.

"I was being serious," Miriam said.

"The workspace is ready. An espresso machine was delivered to the workspace and one will be delivered to this location as well. Coffee, like the food, was vacuum sealed and flash frozen. Charlie hopes it is satisfactory. Fresh milk, however, is not available. Milk is dried and can be reconstituted. The employees thought it an acceptable alternative to fresh milk. Because Charlie does not eat or drink, Charlie has no opinion."

The machine walked to the door, which opened, and said, "This way."

They followed the machine into the hall; Derrick felt certain the hall had changed. It extended both left and right before they entered the dining area. Now, only a solid white wall stood on the right. To the left was a short hall leading to another hall that turned left. Derrick saw four doors. One door on the right and three doors on the left. The first door they arrived at was on the left. It opened as the approached. The machine stopped.

"This is one of three sleeping areas. Doors open when you approach. The door can be locked from the inside for privacy. Let Charlie know if anything has been overlooked, but Charlie is certain the rooms have everything you need. The QR-2s and 3s are efficient."

Derrick glanced inside. A bed covered by a dark, drab, green blanket, a black workstation, and a door that probably led to a shower and toilet. Clean, sparse, utilitarian. The machine moved down the hall. The door on the right opened. Derrick wondered how the doors were controlled, and decided the machine controlled them, and the machine planned on them going into the room on the right, which meant the machine would know every move they made, opening the doors as they approached, twenty-four hours a day, seven days a week.

The workroom had several workstations, but only one would be used. Derrick and Rebekah had no understanding of computers or robots. Miriam walked to the station that had the most gadgets on the desktop. The machine joined her there.

"You can work standing or sitting," the machine said. Touching the glass top caused the workstation to glide up and down. "Should you need anything, or discover anything, just say, 'Charlie, or Charlie; I need you; or Charlie, come; or hey, Charlie.'"

The machine left.

Miriam sat the black box on the workstation, and said, "Can either of you make a Caffe Mocha?"

"We'll figure it out," Rebekah said.

Rebekah walked to the espresso machine. "It's not like the one we had in Pacific Edge. Ours had a menu and you pushed what you wanted. It did all the preparation. I have no clue how to use this."

Derrick picked up a handle with a metal basket on one end. "Ours had the menu system too but also had a manual operation. I never understood why it had the manual feature; Miriam was the only one who used it. I watched her a few times, but I didn't pay attention. Kind of like my entire life in Pacific Edge."

He studied the machine for a minute, bent down and looked at the mechanisms. He worked the basket thing into a holder situated under a container of coffee beans. Nothing happened. "I watched Donna and L. Linda Maxton make coffee with a machine like this at the bistro. The coffee goes in this. But how do you start the damn thing?"

"Derrick, such language," Rebekah giggled. Then she moved the handle from side to side. Nothing. "Who is L. Linda Maxton? Seems you're surrounded by girls in Potterville." She pushed it inward.

A grinding noise started; Derrick jumped a little. "That startled me," he admitted.

"That is very becoming on you," Rebekah said.

"Huh?" Derrick asked.

"Honesty. Humility," Rebekah said, smiling.

"Right. I'm working on it," Derrick said.

When the machine stopped grinding, Derrick pulled the basket thing from its perch. A heap of ground coffee overfilled the filter.

"Too much," Rebekah said, reaching to brush off the excess.

"Derrick caught her wrist. He held it for a moment and then said, "Not overfull. It has to be pressed down."

He grabbed a wooden thing with a round metal base that fit perfectly in the basket; he pressed the coffee grounds tight. "I'm not sure how hard to push."

Glancing under the machine, Derrick struggled to fit the basket into a place on the machine. When it was in the right position, he said, "What goes into a Mocha?"

Miriam joined them. "This is an interesting machine. Looks ancient. I'll show you how it's done and then you'll know how to do it right." She smiled at Derrick. "Then you'll be qualified to fetch me coffee anytime."

In a cupboard above the espresso machine, Miriam found a box of chocolate power and a box labeled milk. "Interesting," she said, reading the instructions. Miriam measured the white powder into a stainless-steel cup that sat on top of the espresso machine, added hot water, and stirred. She tasted a small sample from the spoon. "Not great. Not terrible."

Miriam instructed Derrick on how to pack the ground coffee; it seemed he had done a reasonable job on that. She steamed the milk using a stainless-steel wand attached to the machine. She added chocolate to her cup and then pushed a button that caused the espresso to drizzle into the mug. She found a long silver spoon to stir the espresso and coffee. Finally, she added the steamed milk to the coffee mug and tasted it.

Derrick said, "It doesn't have a cool design on top like the one Nyx had at the bistro."

"The girl with the pink-striped hair?" Miriam asked.

"Yes," Derrick said.

"I spoke with her briefly on the phone. I look forward to meeting her," Miriam said.

"How did you learn about her and get her number?"

"It's a long story. She doesn't seem like your type." Miriam sipped her mocha. "Not bad. You guys should try one."

"I've changed a lot. I'm on the track team and trying out for the football team. But you know that already. Oh, I'm learning to play the guitar."

"Do they have CAT scans in Potterville?" Miriam asked.

"Very funny," Derrick said.

Miriam turned toward the workstation when Derrick said, "Did I make the right decision? Staying in Potterville instead of going back to Pacific Edge."

Miriam turned back toward him and said, "You have no idea how right."

"What does that mean?"

"I'll explain later. I need to look at Jane."

Derrick turned to Rebekah. "Would you like a mocha?"

Rebekah nodded and then walked to where Miriam was sitting. Rebekah pulled up a chair and watched. Miriam studied the black box, turning it over in her hands. "What is it you think?" Rebekah asked.

"I'm not sure. It could be a small computer. To be honest, I don't know how a computer works. I did not have time to study that."

"What did you study in the Technical Service building?"

"Mostly how to get out."

"But you knew what nuclear was. I never heard of it."

"Yeah, I got sidetracked sometimes. There's so much stuff we don't know." Miriam turned on a computer. She looked at the bottom of the keyboard and found a username and password.

"I guess everyone here kept their computer information on the bottom of their keyboard," Rebekah said.

"It seems that way, but I don't think they kept it there normally."

"What do you mean?"

Miriam attached a cord to the black box, but Rebekah could not see anything that the cord plugged into. It seemed to stick to the box without a port.

"Usernames and passwords are supposed to be kept private. That's one thing I learned at Technical Service. I think they put them on the keyboards when they left." Miriam focused on the computer monitor, moving the mouse, clicking the buttons.

"I don't understand. Why do all the computers have the username and password if they are not supposed to be there?"

"They might have thought they would return someday. Or they might have hoped someone would return."

Derrick handed Rebekah a mocha. He pulled up a chair, sipping a black coffee of his own. "Doesn't look like I'm going to get back for the track meet. I hope Coach isn't too angry with me. It's going to be difficult if we can't explain where we've been."

"We'll tell him about the security patrol grabbing you and your escape. Then we ran into each other on the mountain, but we didn't know how to get home. Took us time to find our way."

"But won't Derrick's clothes raise questions?" Rebekah said.

Miriam didn't look up but said, "Good point. He'll need to be wearing what we found him in before anyone from Potterville sees him."

"Learning anything?" Derrick asked?

"Yes. Everything I need to know," Miriam said. "Charlie, can you join us, please?"

"Why do you call it Charlie," Derrick asked.

"Because he told us Charlie is his name," Miriam said.

"It's not a — he. It's an — it," Derrick said.

Miriam looked up from the monitor, sighed, and said, "I love you, Derrick, but you still have a lot of rigid thinking to overcome."

The door swished open and the machine entered, moving rapidly toward the workstation. Derrick flinched, assuming the machine had heard and taken offense to his comments.

"What have you learned? Have you learned the code? Is Jane going to be okay?"

"I have not learned the code. I don't know if she will be all right."

*Don't know if it can be fixed is what you mean,* Derrick thought.

"Oh my," the machine said.

"What I learned is that this box is Jane's memory. We call them hard drives. There are six and one has failed."

The machine seemed to sink. Its eyes dimmed. It remained silent.

"I'm sorry, Charlie. I wish I had better news. But I'm not giving up," Miriam said.

The machine rose an inch and its eyes brightened; at least Derrick thought they did.

"This sounds like a trick, but it's not. I can't fix her here. I know nothing about fixing a hard drive, and I can't learn how to because the computers here are not connected to the outside world. I need to take her to Potterville and find help. And parts, which worries me because your parts are many years old and may not be compatible with today's computer parts." Miriam stood and put her hand on what would pass for a shoulder were the machine a person.

"If Charlie lets you go, you would not come back," the machine said.

"I can't promise that I can fix Jane. I promise I'll try my best, and I promise to return."

"My supervisor promised to return. He did not."

"I don't think he could," Miriam said.

"I do not understand, Miriam King."

"Something happened to the final seven," Miriam said.

"What happened to them?"

"I don't know, but I hope to find out." Miriam moved her hand and sat. "Computers here once connected to the outside world, correct?"

"Yes, connected to the Internet. Many security features to prevent hackers. In addition, there was an Intranet connection with every other sister facility."

"Charlie, I'm not your supervisor, I'm Miriam King. I want to help you. I want to restore Jane. I must leave here to do that. You must trust me to have any hope of Jane's return."

Derrick had a bad feeling. Miriam suspected things beyond his comprehension. He looked at Rebekah; she shrugged. Did Rebekah sense the same vague discomfort that he did? This entire encounter had been so beyond-comprehension strange that he had not attempted to understand it. If on Wednesday morning someone would have said to him — "Listen, Derrick, today the Pacific Edge Tribunal will make your dream come true, offering you a hero's welcome home, which you will refuse; then Pacific Edge officers will kidnap you, but you will escape; then you will be trapped in a tunnel; meanwhile, Miriam will escape Pacific Edge with Rebekah Ford tagging along; they will find you, then the three of you will enter an ancient United States military base; a reactor will malfunction, threatening you and all that surrounds it, but you'll save it; then you'll find a talking robot that Miriam treats like a person; then the robot will imprison you, and then Miriam will promise to return if the machine lets you go." If anyone had said any of this, he would have said it was the craziest damn thing he'd ever heard. Yet, here they were. Was it any wonder that he felt a haunting discomfort that went beyond fear? Udder and complete terror best described his current state of mind.

That's why it surprised him when he stood and said, "Charlie, when my sister promises something, she means it."

# 11

Charlie — Derrick decided disrespecting the machine wasn't helping their situation — had provided food and prepared their quarters. The robot had not been menacing, but it had not been a bundle of joy either. A cup of noodles did not change their status; they were prisoners. Derrick trusted Miriam's thinking, but could not envision Charlie letting the three of them leave.

"It troubles Charlie that you would take Jane out of the facility," Charlie said.

"I don't blame you, Charlie. It would scare the hell out of me if I were in your position," Rebekah said.

Everyone — including Charlie, if Charlie possessed that capacity — stared at Rebekah.

"You have no reason to trust us. You don't know us. We are not authorized to be here. So, no reason for you to trust me either. However, Derrick is right. If Miriam says she's going to do something, she means it. She is by far the most hardheaded person I have ever met. Smartest, too. If you want Jane back, she is your best hope," Rebekah said.

"You are correct, Charlie does not trust. Your most pressing need is escape. It is logical that you will do whatever is necessary to achieve that goal. Charlie understands. Charlie does not become angry that you make the attempt."

Miriam stood, paced as she talked, punctuating statements with her hands. "You're right, Charlie. We want to get out of here. But what you don't understand is that I must return, Jane or no Jane. Charlie or no Charlie. We have no other choice. First, there's Reactor One. It has several maintenance issues. If you can't fix them, someone must, and we are the only ones who know about this place. We either do repairs or learn how to shut it down. Second, I want to understand what is in Level 2. I want to understand this entire facility. It may be our only chance for survival."

"Charlie does not understand."

"We are fugitives. Potterville might not let us live there. Pacific Edge wants us back, but not in a good way. We may not have a safe place to go. This might be our only refuge. Or we might find a way to protect ourselves here."

"Why are you so important to Pacific Edge?" Charlie asked.

"I don't want to say. Derrick knows little about it." She glanced at Derrick. "I don't understand everything yet, and I want to know more before I tell Derrick. Please don't force me to say more. But I will say this, the third reason I need to return, is because James Carver is connected to all of this. This place may hold answers we need."

"Charlie will not force you to say more. However, Charlie does not understand how James Carver is important. He, like the people who once worked here, is dead now. You said so yourself."

Miriam paced from one end of the room to the other.

Rubbing her hands.

Silent.

Finally, she faced Charlie. "Carver's name recurs too often, and I intend to learn why."

# 12

## Friday, April 2, 4:57 p.m.

Although Derrick understood it was impossible, he thought he saw pain etched in the machine's face when Miriam put the black box containing the brain of the robot called Jane in her bag. The robot walked with them to the lobby where they would take the Circle transport back to the staging area, then find their way to Engineering. Charlie told them Engineering was within a few miles of Potterville. Derrick did not understand how that could be possible.

Miriam stopped in the lobby. "Charlie, is there a map that shows the complex and the Circle route back to where we started?"

"Yes. It's right over here." The robot pointed to a wall of class next to the doors.

Something had bothered Derrick, but he dared not say because the robot would know. The robot had gone dark for several minutes. When Miriam mentioned it, the robot said that did not happen. Now the machine pointed at a window and called it a map. Derrick thought the machine might be malfunctioning.

The machine walked to the window, standing a few feet from it, then said, "Circle and Complex map."

The glass became a display. At the bottom of the display was a building labeled Administration/Level Two Lobby was marked with a red x labeled "You are here." Derrick conceded the robot got the map right, but that did not explain when it went dark. He wanted to ask Miriam about the going dark part, but they had to be out of the complex before doing so.

Miriam stepped to the display, touching it with her fingertips. "Remarkable." She traced the Circle, going back towards where they started. There was an intersection, but it was not labeled. "Charlie, where does this go?"

"Charlie does not know. It is classified."

"Level Two must be classified and you have access to it," Miriam said.

"Correct. Charlie has access to Level 2 but does not have clearance to that area."

Miriam continued to trace her finger along the Circle, pausing at the four missile silos along the route. "How far is it to here?" Miriam pointed at where they got on to the Circle.

"It is 110 miles back to Staging."

Miriam stepped back. "I'll do my best to fix Jane, and I'll come back," Miriam said.

"You have already said that. Charlie remembers. Charlie does not require reminding."

Miriam touched the robot's hand. "I understand. Thank you for trusting me."

"Charlie does not trust. Charlie is allowing you to leave based on estimating the outcome of many scenarios."

"How many?" Derrick asked.

"Over twenty thousand."

"That's interesting. Out of those calculations, what percentage did you calculate I was telling you the truth?" Miriam asked.

"0.0036291054255126%," the robot said.

"Those are terrible odds," Rebekah said. "I don't understand why you are letting us leave."

"Because the data indicates the odds of getting Jane back are better if you go," the machine said.

Derrick did not like Rebekah's question. Perhaps the machine will run those calculations again and change its mind. He started for the exit. "We still have a long way to go."

The machine made no attempt to stop them. Derrick hoped the door was not locked. Perhaps the machine was testing them again.

As the neared the door, it opened. Miriam stopped and turned. "I hate to tell you this, but your calculations are wrong. Way wrong."

The machine took a step towards the door.

"I cannot promise that I can fix Jane, but the odds that I will return are 100%," Miriam said.

As they walked towards the Circle transport, Derrick should have felt thrilled to be going home, not Pacific Edge home — Potterville home — but he was not. "Sis, I'm scared," Derrick whispered.

"We're on our way to Potterville. After all you've been through, you should be elated."

"That's what scares me. I should be excited, but I feel empty and I don't understand why."

Rebekah said, "We are all exhausted. Too damn drained to feel anything."

"Rebekah is right. You'll feel better after some real food and rest," Miriam said.

The machine had not stopped them. As far as Derrick could tell, it had not pursued them. He forced himself to walk, not run to the transport. They were not out of danger yet. He considered what they should do if the transport did not function. The machine said its movement was restricted to this area, but what that meant was unclear.

They climbed into the transport. Derrick decided to sit in the back, let Rebekah have the front seat next to Miriam.

"You sit next to me, Derrick," Miriam said.

"It's okay. Rebekah can sit in the front on the way back," Derrick said.

"It's not okay. Rebekah, get in the back," Miriam said.

"Geez. Okay. Do I smell bad or something?" Rebekah paused. "Don't answer that."

"It's not you," Miriam said. "Just better this way."

Derrick did not see how this was better, but he was exhausted and didn't feel like asking for an explanation and doubted Miriam would give one.

The transport voice said, "Destination?"

Miriam said, "Towards Staging, but we may stop along the way."

The voice said, "Destination?"

Miriam said, "the first left-hand turn."

The doors closed; the transport moved into the main tunnel and then accelerated.

"Wow. That's a rush," Miriam said.

As they reached the top speed, the voice said, "Access denied."

"Access denied to what?" Miriam asked.

"Access denied to the area requested."

Miriam frowned. "What is the area requested?"

"Access denied to The Acropolis."

They whizzed by the tunnel to which they were denied entry. Something even the robot called Charlie knew nothing about. Miriam turned to look down the tunnel, but they were moving too fast to see anything.

"Stop at Silo Number Five," Miriam said.

Five minutes later, the transport slowed and made a gradual turn to the right. The doors opened. Miriam said, "You guys stay put. This won't take long."

Miriam trotted to the silo entrance, touched the entrance screen, and then returned to the transport. "Silo number six." The transport accelerated.

"You didn't look inside?" Derrick asked.

"Didn't need to," Miriam said.

"Could you please, just for the sake of our sanity, complete your thoughts when you talk," Rebekah said from the back seat.

"Sorry. I didn't look because the missile was still there."

"Did it have a target?" Derrick asked.

"Yes. Pyongyang, North Korea."

"Where is that?" Derrick asked.

"Half-way around the world," Miriam said.

"Missile number one targeted someplace called Russia, correct?" Derrick asked.

"Yes. Moscow," Miriam said.

"Where's that?" Derrick asked.

"Halfway around the world," Miriam said.

"What about missiles three and four?" Derrick asked.

"Beijing, China and Bagdad, Iraq," Miriam said.

"Let me guess. Halfway around the world," Derrick said.

"Close enough," Miriam said.

"Why those places?" Derrick wondered.

"Enemies, I guess," Miriam said.

"I wonder if they are still enemies?" Derrick asked.

"Something we should study when we get a chance," Miriam said.

"If we get a chance," Rebekah said.

"I won't argue that point," Miriam said.

"Hey, we got out of the last place alive. We should be more optimistic," Derrick said.

"Agreed," Rebekah said.

"I can't be optimistic yet," Miriam said. The transport slowed for the next silo.

"Why not?" Derrick asked.

"Because of what I'm afraid will find," Miriam said.

The transport stopped by a sign that read Silo Number Six. The doors raised. "Come with me this time," Miriam said.

Derrick stepped out. He held his hand out to Rebekah, helping her from the transport although she needed no assistance. Derrick sensed something would be different about this silo. Perhaps he was getting better at reading Miriam. Perhaps it was the odd burnt smell.

Miriam stepped to the panel and touched the screen.

**MISSILE NUMBER SIX—STATUS: LAUNCHED**
**MISSILE NUMBER SIX—WARHEAD: THERMONUCLEAR**
**MISSILE NUMBER SIX—STATUS: DEPLOYED**

**MISSILE NUMBER SIX—TARGET: BILIBINO, RUSSIA**
**BEGIN LAUNCH SEQUENCE Y=NULL N=NULL**

A keyboard in the same green letters and number was displayed at the bottom of the screen. Miriam touched N.

**LAUNCH SEQUENCE ABORTED Y=NULL N=NULL**

Miriam touched Y. A new line appeared.

**MISSILE NUMBER ONE MAINTENANCE ENTRY**
**Y=YES N=NO**

Miriam touched Y; the door lock clicked, and the door fell open an inch. Miriam put her shoulder against the door; Derrick joined her, and together they forced the door open.

The difference here was obvious, even though another door separated them from the silo. Black streaks where hot gas forced its way through the inner door stained the walls. The paint from the door had flaked off, bare, warped metal shone where the previous door was smooth and painted.

Miriam hesitated at the door that entered the silo itself.

"What do you expect to find," Derrick asked.

"Probably nothing," Miriam said.

"These missiles can go halfway around the world? I Don't understand how far that is, but it seems impossible," Derrick said.

"They are intercontinental ballistic missiles, ICBMs. They go into orbit and then reenter to reach their target," Miriam said.

"Where did you learn this?" Rebekah asked.

"Read about it while Charlie was out of the room," Miriam said.

"Weren't you supposed to be learning to read the computer code, whatever that is?" Rebekah asked.

"I already knew I could not read it. I looked at it before we found Charlie."

"You didn't tell us that," Derrick said.

"I did not. I did not want Charlie to know."

"So, you lied to him? Our necks were on the line back there too." Rebekah said.

"Sorry. I did what I thought was best. For all of us," Miriam said.

Miriam twisted the locking devices on the door and pulled.

Rebekah put her hand on the door, preventing it from opening. "What does that mean? Best for all of us?"

"You, Derrick, Charlie, Jane, and me. All of us." Miriam stared at Rebekah. "Look, we had to leave. Charlie had no reason to let us go, except to fix Jane. I wasn't lying about Jane. I don't know if I can fix her, but I know I need help. I hope someone in Potterville can work on hard drives, and I hope they still have compatible parts."

"You're serious about coming back here," Rebekah said. It wasn't a question.

"We don't have a choice. Now let's get moving," Miriam said.

Rebekah stepped back and Miriam pulled the door open. Derrick wasn't sure what he expected exactly, and even when he saw inside the silo, he wasn't sure if this was it. The missile was gone. That much was true. The walls were blackened here and there, but the ladders, pipes, and other things were in good condition. He had no idea if they could reuse this silo, and if they were to reuse it, how long it would take to build another missile and have it ready to fire.

Light poured into the shaft from above. Whatever lid was there before they fired the missile was gone. The bottom of the pit was just visible in the dim light. It appeared weeds and debris had gathered there, perhaps some sand. Maybe he was looking at the remains of an animal the size of a dog. He wasn't sure.

Without further discussion, they started back to the transport. For a moment, Derrick felt a bit of panic. *What if the door locked behind them? What if the transport grew tired of waiting and left?*

The transport remained where they left it, doors still open. He wondered how long it would wait there for its passengers.

When they were seated, Miriam said, "Silo Number Seven."

The transport accelerated.

Derrick felt darkness seep further into his chest. He did not understand why.

A few minutes later, they could see the entrance to Silo Number Seven.

"Stop here," Miriam said. You guys can stay. I'll check the door."

When the transport door opened, Derrick noticed an unusual odor; the burnt smell was there like at the last silo, but there was something else too. It was so slight he wondered if it was his imagination. It wasn't pleasant, and he wondered if it was him. He sorta checked his arm pit. While he did not smell as if he'd just showered, the stench was not him. Miriam returned within a couple of minutes.

"Silo Number Eight," she said. "This one is also Empty. The target was Kapsan, North Korea."

"So, two missiles targeted a place called Russian and two targeted a place called North Korea. One missile was launched at each of those countries," Derrick said.

"That's correct," Miriam said.

Rebekah leaned forward, forearms on the back of Derrick's seat.

"Why did they only launch one missile at each country? I mean if there was war . . ." Derrick's voice trailed off. He looked straight ahead into the distance.

"We'll know more after we check the last silo," Miriam said.

"Uh, not wanting to offend anyone, but did you notice an odd odor at that silo?" Derrick asked

"I did and don't worry. It's not us," Miriam said.

"It was awful," Rebekah said.

"Wonder what it was?" Derrick asked.

"We'll know soon enough," Miriam said.

Derrick hated her secrecy. Seemed like everything with Miriam was secret. Perhaps that was what was bothering him. Whatever Miriam was withholding, it was not good news. Of that he was certain. After a short distance, a sign said, Silo Number Eight 2.0 miles. As they passed the sign, Derrick said, "You don't think they will let us stay in Potterville, do you?"

"It depends on what has happened since you've been gone," Miriam said.

"Explain," Derrick said.

"If security from Pacific Edge has been there looking for you, they will turn us away," Miriam said.

Derrick took a deep breath. He fought to hold back tears. There it was. What he had tried not to think about. "You're right. They don't need problems. I'm not worth it. But we are going to be okay. We'll figure something out. Go someplace else, start over. I have a little money."

"Money isn't a problem," Miriam said.

"How can lacking money not be a problem? It's not like Pacific Edge. Everything in Potterville costs money, unless someone gives you stuff," Derrick said. It occurred to him that several people gave him things, Coach Browning bought him shoes, Donna gave him food and drinks, Mr. Griggs gave him a guitar and free lessons. He thought it was because they felt sorry for him being an orphan. But they knew he was lying about that. So, why did they give him stuff?

"Took care of it before I left," Miriam said.

Rebekah glanced at Miriam. "When we got out of Pacific Edge, you said you had no money."

"Correct. I had no money on my person and banks were not yet open."

"You stole money from Pacific Edge? You are something else, girl," Rebekah said.

"Isn't she?" Derrick agreed.

"Thank you," Miriam said.

"What time do you think it is?" Derrick asked.

"No clue," Rebekah said.

"About 5:20," Miriam said.

"Is it still Friday?" Derrick asked.

"Yes." Miriam and Rebekah said in unison and then laughed.

Derrick smiled. It seemed forever since he'd heard laughter.

As they approached, Derrick could see that Silo Number Eight was different from the other silos.

The roll-up door stood open.

A transport, larger than the one they were in, sat with doors still open on the side path.

"Stop here," Miriam said. The transport stopped on the main corridor rather than the side path as usual. "We all need to see this one. Brace yourselves. Doors open."

Soon as the doors opened, Derrick wanted them closed. The foul odor he detected at the last stop filled his nostrils, causing him to feel nauseous. "What the hell is that smell."

"Yuck, get us out of here. Doors closed," Rebekah said.

But the doors did not close. The transport did not respond to Rebekah.

Derrick said, "Doors closed." Nothing.

"The transport only responds to me," Miriam said and then continued, "I don't like it any better than you do, but we have to investigate this."

"Why?" Derrick asked.

"Why what? Why won't the transport respond to you, or why do we need to investigate?" Miriam asked.

"Answers to both would be nice," Derrick said, pulling his shirt up over his nose.

Miriam stepped from the transport. She found a tissue in her bag, handing it to Rebekah. "Try to breathe through this. It might help."

"I'm going to puke," Rebekah said.

"Try to miss your shoes. We don't need more stink all the way to Potterville," Miriam said.

"Is there ever a time when you're not a smart ass?" Rebekah asked.

"Yes. Soon, I fear," Miriam said.

They passed the roll-up door; the tunnel was dark. "We'll check that last," Miriam said.

Miriam activated the panel.

**MISSILE NUMBER EIGHT—STATUS: LAUNCHED**

**MISSILE NUMBER EIGHT—WARHEAD: THERMONUCLEAR-HYDROGEN**
**MISSILE NUMBER EIGHT—WARHEAD STATUS: ARMED**
**MISSILE NUMBER EIGHT—TARGET: SACRAMENTO, CALIFORNIA**
**BEGIN LAUNCH SEQUENCE Y=NULL N=NULL**

A keyboard in the same green letters and number was displayed at the bottom of the screen. Miriam touched N.

**LAUNCH SEQUENCE ABORTED Y=NULL N=NULL**

Miriam touched Y. A new line appeared.

**MISSILE NUMBER EIGHT MAINTENANCE ENTRY Y=YES N=NO**

Miriam touched Y. The door lock clicked.

"That is weird. Paul said Potterville was in California. I guess there is a country called California too," Derrick said.

Miriam said nothing. She touched the screen where the target information was displayed. A tear traced down her cheek. Derrick wondered what bothered her.

Inside the hallway, the concrete around the open door was scorched black, as was the tunnel to the silo. A metal door cantered half open, bent from heat, and twisted off the top hinge. Derrick caught Miriam before she stepped through the door, motioning her back. He went in first to assess the risk. Sticking his head inside, he saw the same metal walkway around a giant round chamber formed of concrete. No missile and thin beams of light streaming in from the top. Not enough light to see the bottom. The walkway was made of grated steel they saw near Reactor One. He put on foot on the walkway. It seemed sturdy. This silo had suffered more damage than did Silo Number Six.

He stepped back through the door. "Be careful. The walkway doesn't look too safe. One at a time and I'll hold your hand in case the walkway fails. It's empty, but it's in worse shape than the other silo." Motioning for Miriam to step in, he added, "I guess you already knew that."

Miriam stepped in but did not take Derrick's hand as he had instructed. "The missile must have been more powerful than the others."

Miriam continued around the walkway until she came to a section that appeared to be doors. "This must be the service entrance or whatever they called it. It corresponds with the roll-up door in the tunnel."

"It's concrete. Why didn't they use a roll-up door?" Derrick wondered.

"Wouldn't hold up to the blast. Let's try to open it and go back this way."

"I'll meet you out front," Rebekah said.

"No. Stay with us," Miriam said. "We all need to see this."

"You can tell me about it," Rebekah said.

"Not the same," Miriam said

"God, she's stubborn," Rebekah said.

Derrick shrugged and gave Rebekah a weak smile.

Miriam found a metal panel that must have been a special material, because other than the scorched paint, it looked to be in perfect condition. After studying it for a moment, she pushed, then slid slots at the top and bottom. She swung the door open. Miriam selected open, then shut the panel door. Lights was an option, but Miriam did not flip that switch; she removed the flashlight from her bag and then motioned to Rebekah to do the same. Derrick heard mechanical sounds. The doors moved inward several inches and then separated in the middle, each door disappearing into slots in the walls of the tunnel.

Miriam turned on her flashlight and held a tissue to her nose.

They stepped into the opening.

The reason for the stench obvious.

Bodies.

"What the hell?" Rebekah pointed towards the bodies scattered across the tunnel.

"Who are they," Derrick asked.

"Dead people," Miriam said. "The final seven."

Derrick knew the answer; he just didn't want to admit it.

"I can't go there," Rebekah said, backing away.

"Stop, Rebekah," Miriam said. She put her hand on Rebekah's shoulder. "We must investigate. Only way to be certain what happened here."

"How did this become our problem?" Rebekah said.

"It became our problem the moment we entered the facility," Miriam said. "Now, go. Slowly."

Rebekah started forward again. As they grew closer, the awful smell hung in the air so thick Derrick thought he could see it. He understood little about the natural process of decay. Still, he understood the normal process was disrupted here. The meticulous details spend in the construction of this facility eliminated nature: bugs, animals, and heat. The bodies would decay, but outside they would be skeletons by now, he thought. Not the case here. Six bodies laid side by side in a line, leaving a clear path so they could walk by without stopping. He planned to look the other way, so he did not have to see them. He had enough to process without the images of dead people stuck in his brain. But he stared at them as they approached. They wore one-piece uniforms identical to what he now wore. He could see small brass-colored pieces of metal on the ground he understood to be from the guns of the old United States. He saw such guns many times watching New America Media. A weird thought crossed his mind; New America Media had taught him something useful. He realized there would be other memories that might prove valuable.

He tried but failed to look away as they approached the first body. It was face down; clumps of hair remained fix to places of its skull. The hands were dried and shriveled. Clothing covered the rest of the body, although the clothing looked thin, fragile.

"Stop," Miriam whispered.

"Screw that! I'm not stopping," Rebekah said.

Miriam said, "Keep going. We'll catch up."

"What are you doing?" Derrick asked.

Miriam didn't say anything. She held her hand over her mouth and nose as she stepped to the first body. Kneeling down at the victim's head, she said, "Shot in the head. Executed."

"Sis, what are you doing?"

"Learning," she said.

"For God's sake, why?" Derrick asked.

"Evidence. Proof."

"We are not law enforcement. This is not our problem. Besides, whoever did this is dead," Derrick said.

Miriam pulled her cellphone from her bag. "You take the pictures." Miriam pointed to a hole in the victim's skull. "Take a close up but get my finger in the shot. Then back up and take one with the entire body. Then take one that shows the other bodies."

Derrick took photos. The seventh body lay ten yards farther down the tunnel.

Miriam inspected each body. She had Derrick take pictures of similar wounds on each and pictures of the brass casings. Derrick counted seven casings until they reached the last body, where he counted three.

"See how the bodies are in a line, all in the same position?" Miriam asked.

"Yes," Derrick said. "Is that important?"

"Yes. Someone forced them to kneel, and then shot them in the back of the head."

"Why didn't they run? Or fight back?"

"That one ran." She pointed to the body farther down the tunnel. "Why didn't the others do something? I don't know. Maybe there was more than one armed person. Maybe the shooter made promises and then shot each when they refused to cooperate or didn't convince the shooter to let them live."

"What could he promise that would prevent them from doing something after he shot the first person?"

"Not sure. Eternal life, maybe."

Miriam picked up one of the brass cases. "These all look the same, right?" She dropped one in her bag.

Derrick looked around. "Look the same to me."

Miriam kneeled beside the last body. This body was on its back. Three blood stained circles marred the front of the uniform. In the center of the stain, the cloth was shredded. She pointed to one of the stains and said, "Take a picture."

Derrick did as instructed, trying with little success to avoid looking at the person's face. Then Miriam pointed to the man's face and said, "Take a picture."

Derrick was unsure if he could hold the contents of his stomach. He took a step back. Miriam flipped the victim's ID card over.

"Jacob Truman," she said, removing the card.

"Why are you taking that?" Derrick asked.

"To show Charlie that Jacob intended to come back, but he was murdered."

Rebekah waited by the transport. Pale as a ghost, arms wrapped around herself, shivering.

"Let's get Derrick home," Miriam said, climbing into the vehicle.

Rebekah said, "See what you needed?"

"For now," Miriam said. "They were executed."

"Except for the last guy. He tried to get away. Jacob Truman. Charlie's supervisor," Derrick said.

"He ran, but he too was executed. He was shot in the back, and then the killer shot him in the face, but unlike the others, Jacob saw the killer pull the trigger," Miriam said.

"I'm going to have nightmares for months," Rebekah said.

"Longer than that," Miriam said. "A lifetime perhaps."

"I do not disagree, but I assume there's more to it," Derrick said.

"You are correct. We don't understand what happened here or why, but we will. And when we understand, I fear our lives will be the nightmare."

# 13

Because Derrick paid little attention to Miriam growing up, he did not know if dramatizing things was her nature. He hoped Miriam was exaggerating their situation; he'd feel better if that were the case. But as the transport sped through the tunnel back towards where they began, neither his heart nor his head could dismiss Miriam's statement. The killer of the final seven was dead, at least that much seemed certain. But Derrick suspected Miriam knew something she was unwilling to share. Why Miriam remained secretive about things at every turn troubled him, but she wasn't going to tell him until she was ready. He wondered if the organization or group or corporation responsible for killing the final seven remained operational. If it became known they found this place, that murderous group would hunt the three of them next.

The transport slowed. They had reached the end of the Circle where their journey began. Miriam would have traveled the Circle without Rebekah and himself had they refused. He wished he had not seen any of this. He wished he knew nothing about ICBMs or hidden military bases or talking robots named Charlie or seven dead men. But there was no changing it now. He hated everything about this trip on the Circle, but it was best that Miriam didn't carry the burden alone.

When the doors raised, the air felt fresh like a summer morning on the Pacific Coast, even though they were still underground. The foul odor gone, he thought, but sometimes he wasn't sure. Perhaps it was in their clothing. Perhaps it was imbedded in his head. No one had spoken since they left the final seven lying dead near Missile Silo Number Eight.

Rebekah exited first. She faced Derrick and Miriam as they climbed out of the transport. "Well, that was depressing as hell."

"Agreed," Miriam said.

"Now what?" Rebekah asked.

"Derrick needs to get home. He has a track meet tomorrow," Miriam said, walking towards the interior of the facility.

Despite the darkness he felt, a slight smile graced his face, because Miriam acknowledged the track meet rather than make fun of it. Rebekah stepped next to him and laced her arm through his.

"Sorry for all the stuff I said earlier," Rebekah said.

"What stuff. You have said nothing to be sorry for." Derrick patted her hand that rested on his forearm.

"I was such a downer. Whining about being here, crying like a damn baby."

"Like Miriam said, we are tired and have been through a lot. Now, after seeing the — bodies …" Derrick stopped talking. He didn't want to trigger another crying session. He feared if Rebekah cried, he would too.

"This might sound weird, but it helped me." Rebekah released him, continuing to walk at his side.

"Helped? How could that help?"

"Made me realize this is serious shit we are into. We thought we were safe in Pacific Edge, but we were prisoners. Safety was an illusion; safety does not exist. You could have been a Chosen worshiping fool, and they still could banish you. Derrick King comes to mind."

"I was not perfect, but I'll accept the fool part. But what I did in Pacific Edge was wrong. I still don't understand how the Circle helped," Derrick said.

"We didn't recognize our situation. Now we do. Better that way. And you did the right thing. I saw it. Marcus was going to hit Miriam," Rebekah said and trotted to catch Miriam.

They were walking back the way they came, Derrick remembered it was quite some distance through the maze of trucks and military vehicles. To the right he saw an opening, but it was too dark to see inside. "Hey guys. I wonder what's over there." He pointed. "Maybe there's a quicker way to Engineering?"

Miriam said, "Maybe, but we know there's a sign pointing towards Engineering this way." Miriam whispered to Rebekah, at least Derrick assumed she did because Miriam leaned close, head to head. The girls started running; not fast, a comfortable pace for him, and he realized Rebekah could maintain the pace. Rebekah played soccer. He didn't know much about game; had never watched her, but he thought it required running. But it still surprised him that Miriam ran with little difficulty. He chalked that up to the genes they shared. It occurred to him that making rationalizations without facts might prove dangerous. Trying to be more objective, he decided Miriam was in good physical condition, and he did not know why. He thought genes explained his physical condition, but now he didn't think genes were the entire explanation. There must be an explanation for his ability to compete in track and field; he just did not understand it yet. Perhaps he never would.

It seemed farther than he remembered the first time to reach the cavern of trucks, which seemed father to the entrance to Reactor One. They followed the sign that pointed towards Engineering into yet another tunnel. Derrick was getting tired of tunnels. In fact, he was so tired he could not imagine competing tomorrow. Fifty yards into the tunnel, Rebekah headed straight to an odd vehicle parked next to the wall. It had small wheels, no doors, a top that was just bars with a white cover across the top. It could carry four people, no more, unless someone hung on to the outside of the vehicle. A thick black cord snaked from the vehicle to a silver box mounted on the rock wall.

"What is it?" Derrick asked.

"A vehicle for transporting people through this tunnel," Miriam said.

The purpose was obvious, so he did not know why he asked the question. "Do you think it still works? What's the cord for?"

"It's electric. If the battery hasn't failed, it should work," Miriam said.

"How do you know this stuff," Derrick asked.

Miriam shrugged.

Rebekah slid behind the steering mechanism and said, "Unplug it and I'll figure out how to make it go."

The cord attached to the vehicle with a black plastic plug three inches in diameter. He pulled it. Nothing. He pulled harder. Nothing.

"Don't break it," Miriam said.

"I'm not trying to break it, but it doesn't matter if I do," Derrick said.

"We might need to use it again," Miriam said. "Try twisting it first."

Derrick twisted the plug clockwise. It did not move. He remembered the bolts loosened counterclockwise. The plug moved. Then he pulled it out easily. A cover snapped shut over where the plug had been. *Maybe everything in the commoner world tightens and loosens the same direction,* he thought. Simple though it was, he recognized this observation might prove important.

Miriam climbed in back; Derrick got in next to Rebekah.

"So, I'm clueless here," Rebekah said.

"Then why are you driving?" Miriam asked.

"Because I called it first," Rebekah said. "And because I want to."

"Turn that metal thing on the dash," Derrick said. "Clockwise."

Rebekah did as Derrick suggested. A green light came on, but the machine did not move. There

"Now what?"

"Step on one of those." Derrick pointed to three petals at Rebekah's feet.

Rebekah smashed the petal on the right to the floor and the vehicle lurched forward. Rebekah screamed and then smashed the petal in the middle. The vehicle lurched backward, tossing Derrick against the windshield with a thump. Rebekah smashed the pedal on the left and the vehicle stopped.

"Got it," Rebekah said.

"Woman driver," Derrick said, repeating something he'd heard watching a movie in Potterville.

Miriam laughed.

Rebekah did not.

Rebekah eased the middle petal down and the vehicle rolled backward. She turned the wheel to move the vehicle away from the wall and the front scraped against the rock. Rebekah stopped, then pulled forward. "Don't say anything."

Derrick put his hands up.

In the back, Miriam snickered.

This time Rebekah drove forward, moving the vehicle was a few feet from the wall. She turned the wheel to the left, but too far and had to correct. Turning right, she pointed the vehicle towards Engineering, zigzagging down the wide tunnel. After a short distance, she kept it straight and drove faster.

Derrick could not estimate their speed. Much slower than the Circle transport, and slower than when Paul drove on the highway, taking him to Potterville. Nor could he estimate the time they traveled, but he would have guessed twenty to thirty minutes, perhaps longer. Probably longer; he may have dosed off a time or two. The road made many gradual turns. Sometimes the turn so gentle that it was difficult to detect. They could have driven the trucks through this tunnel. As they snaked their way towards Engineering, he thought about how little he understood of the world outside Pacific Edge and Potterville. Yet, he knew this entire facility was enormous; an achievement of construction by any standard. Sparse lighting reduced the distance he could see, the machine had lights on the front like Paul's truck that lit the path. A cool breeze circulated through the open vehicle; the odor earthy and the air damp. He wished he had a coat. Miriam and Rebekah wore theirs; still, they braced with tight muscles against the chill.

They came to another underground parking lot with many electric vehicles. Rebekah eased the vehicle next to the wall in an empty space marked with yellow paint on the floor. When Rebekah turned the key to the off position, they sat in pitch black. Miriam was first to switch on her flashlight; she bailed out, snaking a thick black cord to the vehicle, and plugging it in.

"Why bother?" Derrick asked.

"We'll need to use it again," Miriam said.

"I am not coming back here. Ever. I've made up my mind," Rebekah said, switching on her flashlight.

"I'm lost. With all the twists and turns, I have no idea what direction we've traveled or how far we traveled," Derrick turned a circle.

"Engineering, I think. There are many tunnels down here, for different purposes, I suppose," Rebekah said.

They followed a signed that said elevators and found another lift for trucks next to a smaller elevator that would hold five people.

The elevator buttons indicated four levels. They were on level four. Derrick felt certain the first level meant the surface. He wondered if they should have brought the little transport.

Miriam pushed level three. Nothing happened. "We need to find the stairs. No power here. And don't say it. I know you want to get to Potterville, but we need to know more about this place."

"Why do we need to know more about it? I still don't see how this became our responsibility," Derrick said.

Miriam sighed. "You know why it's our responsibility, you just don't want to accept it. I don't know why we became responsible, but we are because we know it's here. We might be the only people who know. But that might change."

Miriam led them to a metal door labeled stairs. She pulled the door open and started to climb.

"Why would it change?" Derrick asked.

"Because we may have led them here," Miriam said.

Rebekah came up the stairs behind them. "Why is there not power here?"

"Good questions. But not one we need to answer today," Miriam said.

"Thank God for small favors," Derrick said.

"Agreed," Rebekah said.

When they reached a door that said level three, Miriam exited the stairs and wandered the halls, glancing in rooms, lifting keyboards, turning on light switches that did not work, and then turning them off. It was not as cold here. Derrick wanted to get outside. He wanted fresh air and hoped the sun had not set.

Miriam told Charlie they might not be able to stay in Potterville, which he already knew, but it sounded worse when she said it. He told himself she was just trying to convince Charlie to let them leave. That was before they found empty ICBM silos and dead bodies. Now, as much as he did not want to admit it, he knew they could not stay in Potterville. He did not want to expose his friends — *are they friends?* — to the dangers that followed Miriam, Rebekah, and himself.

There were many things he wanted to ask Miriam. He had spent years in Pacific Edge when he could have talked to her every day. But he ignored her. Now, he wanted to spend hours talking with her and wondered if there would be a chance of doing so. It would take a lifetime of questions before he would understand a tenth of what she knew. Yet, his heart felt so heavy, so dark, he didn't think he could bear talking to anyone.

After checking a few more rooms, Miriam said, "Let's get out of here. I'm sick of being inside."

"You don't have to ask me twice," Rebekah said.

They climbed the stairs to the first floor. Derrick wondered why Miriam didn't search the second floor.

Pushing the door open and stepping into level one, Derrick said, "Which way?"

Miriam shone her light one direction and then the other. "It's much warmer here. This way, I think."

Miriam led them down a long hall, then through a set of double doors into what appeared to be a lobby, which was warmer still. Miriam and Rebekah swung their flashlight beams, making him dizzy. At the far end of the lobby, windows ran from the high ceiling to the floor; thin lines of light leaked around the edges.

Miriam walked towards the light; shone her light on the windows. "Sealed from the outside."

Walking closer, Rebekah said, "I suppose the doors are sealed too."

"One way to find out." Miriam walked to a bank of doors and pushed one open. "This leads to a small entryway."

Inside the entryway, Derrick could see veins of light outlining the next set of metal doors. He felt heat radiating off the doors. Pushing on a crash bar, he almost fell. Light flooded into the entryway.

Throwing his hand up to shield his eyes, he said, "Freedom."

# *PART THREE*

## 1

Derrick and Rebekah stepped outside squinting and shielding their eyes from the sun low on the western horizon. Miriam did not join them. Holding out his hand, Derrick wondered why Miriam remained inside. Perhaps the outside scared her after all she'd been through. Or maybe she did not want to meet the friends he'd made in Potterville because his life was so transformed. She did not know this new Derrick. He could protect her here. He'd make sure people treated her with respect. At long last, he could be the big brother she deserved.

"See if the door is locked," Miriam said.

Derrick glanced down, gave his head a little shake. He had misunderstood Miriam. Again.

Letting the door fall shut, he tried to open it. Locked. Pounding on the door, he hollered, "It's locked."

Miriam opened the door a few inches. "Wait here. I'll be back."

The door eased shut against the pneumatic control.

Rebekah put her arms out and spun a full circle. When she faced Derrick she said, "That girl drives me crazy sometimes. Most of the time. She isn't serious about going back there, is she?"

"She's serious. She promised. Now that I've had time to think about it, we don't have a choice."

"What do you mean? We have choices now. We aren't in Pacific Edge anymore."

"I can't put the people in Potterville at risk. There will be no place safe for us. The Base might be the only place we can go. To be honest, even if returning to Pacific Edge were possible, which it isn't, I'd rather spend my life with Charlie than live in Pacific Edge."

"Well, I'm not going back. I've made up my mind."

"Rebekah, you won't be safe here either. You won't be safe anyplace. They will track you down."

Rebekah paused, then said, "Oh my God!"

"What?"

"Anna won't be safe either. I've got to get her. And fast."

Derrick did not know what to say. He understood Rebekah wanted to rescue Anna, but it was impossible. They could not go back to Pacific Edge. That would be like walking straight into a fire. He did not think the weight in his chest could feel heavier, but it did. He feared he could not take another breath, because for reasons he did not fully understand, he agreed with Rebekah. Anna was in grave danger. If The Tribunal had not already imprisoned Anna, they would soon. They would hold Anna hostage until Rebekah surrendered. And once they had Rebekah, they would force her to reveal where he and Miriam were. And she already knew the only place they could hide.

Derrick's mind ran through ways to protect Miriam. Knocking Rebekah unconscious, dragging her back to the Base, and convincing Charlie to lock them up for the remainder of their lives seemed the best option. The other thoughts ended with silencing Rebekah permanently, but he wasn't going to hurt anyone ever again. Of that much he was certain.

The door opened. Miriam worked paper into a hole in the metal door frame, and then added a strip of gray tape to the door's locking mechanism. "Try it again."

The door closed. Derrick grabbed the handle and pulled it open.

Instead of stepping out, Miriam said, "Once more."

Derrick did as she instructed; the door opened.

Miriam inspected her work. Poked more paper into the slot in the frame, pressed her fingers along the gray tape, and then added another strip. "That should hold until we get back. We need to find keys next time we come."

"I'm not coming back," Rebekah said. "I'm going to get Anna."

"Slow down, girl," Miriam said. "We'll get Anna. I've been thinking about it too."

"I'm going. Tonight, if possible," Rebekah said.

Derrick had not seen Miriam angry often, but she was angry now. The anger fired hot and fast.

Miriam drove her hand into her bag. Then she took a deep breath and said, "How do you plan to get Anna out?"

"I don't know. Maybe you can zap their computers again. Just long enough for me to get in and get out."

"Just that easy? You'll walk in and walk out? Right by the security guards, locked doors, and cameras?"

"I did it before."

"Who did it before?"

"Okay, we did it."

"Are you listening to yourself? First, this entire plan, which is no plan at all, starts with me zapping things." Miriam breathed deeply, took her hand out of her bag, and placed it on Rebekah's shoulder. "Here's the thing. You're stuck with us. When we get Anna out, we do it together."

"I don't understand how that changes anything," Rebekah said.

"If they catch you, they catch us. You know every place we could hide. They'll force you to tell everything you know."

"Miriam, I'd never give you up. Don't you trust me more than that?"

"No, I do not. They put a gun to Anna's head, and you're going to do what?"

Tears formed in Rebekah's eyes. Derrick wondered how she still had tears.

After a few minutes, Rebekah wiped her face with her sleeve. "I said you were stuck with me before you left Pacific Edge. I did not understand how true that statement was. Promise you'll help me get Anna."

"I already promised. We'll get her. Now, let's get Derrick home. He needs food and rest before his race."

For the first time since exiting the building, Derrick scanned their surroundings. They built Engineering into the dead-end of a narrow canyon. Trees over hung the edges, leaving only a sliver of sky above. Now that his eyes had adjusted to the light, he saw they were standing in shadows as only pinpoints of sunlight filtered through the vegetation. He pointed. "Looks like this is the only way out. If we are close to Potterville, it doesn't seem possible that people would not know about this place."

Miriam made a full circle. "Like everything else, this place was built into the mountain. You couldn't see anything from up there," Miriam said, pointing to the top of the canyon.

Miriam started walking. Derrick and Rebekah followed. A mile later, the road turned 90 degrees to the right. The canyon narrowed even more and looked as if someone had carved it into the mountain. It grew darker; perhaps the sun sank below the horizon. Above, trees covered canyon until the sky could not be seen. Upon turning the corner, they saw why no one knew it was here. A steel door as tall as the canyon stood closed.

"I don't think I can handle one more problem today," Derrick said.

"Get used to it. The rest of our lives will be a steady stream of colossal problems," Miriam said.

"Cheery thought," Rebekah said.

"I'm considering a career in comedy," Miriam said, and then giggled.

Rebekah giggled.

Both girls burst into laughter and threw their arms around each other.

He did not understand girls. Now, his relationship, whatever it was, with Nyx made sense. He did not understand her either.

"I hate to spoil a good joke, but this is a problem." Derrick asked.

"My brother, always Mr. Insightful," Miriam said, and then burst into laughter again.

After a few minutes, Miriam wiped her eyes. She walked to the gate, examining it with her fingers, and then forced her way into the brush near the canyon wall. After a few minutes, she reappeared and went to the other side. From behind the screen of brush she hollered, "In here."

Derrick parted branches, helping Rebekah enter the thicket. After forcing their way through ten yards of brush, they saw Miriam's back. When they reached her position, they saw a door mounted in the rock.

"If I see another damn door mounted into a rock wall, I'm going to scream," Derrick said.

"Can it wait?" Miriam said. Then with a snicker she said, "It will hurt my ears this close."

"Hilarious," Derrick said.

"I know. Comedian, I told you," Miriam said.

Rebekah laughed.

"You guys need help," Derrick said.

"You're right," Miriam said. "Can you pull that branch away from this keypad?"

Derrick squeezed by Rebekah, branches scraping his face. He grabbed the limb but could not move it. He was out of position. "I need to be on the other side."

Miriam ducked, wiggled between the door and Derrick as he slid to the other side.

A limb blocked the keypad; Derrick tried to pull it up. It moved half an inch.

"More," Miriam said.

With his back to Meriam, Derrick stooped, forced his shoulder under the limb, and pushed up. His legs shivered, the bark dug into his shoulder, but he felt the limb move.

"Damn," Miriam whispered.

"What," Derrick asked. "I can't hold this much longer."

"No power." Miriam said. "You can let go for now."

Derrick slipped out from under the limb, breathing deeply.

Dropping her bag, Miriam started grabbing brush, pulling it this way and that, until she disappeared.

"Found it," Miriam said from behind the bush. Her hand appeared. "Hand me my flashlight."

Derrick dug through her bag until he found it. He placed it in her outstretched hand.

Light filtered through the thicket.

From behind the brush, Miriam said, "Rebekah, go to the keypad and enter the code we used back in the tunnel."

"I don't remember it," Rebekah said.

Before Miriam could say anything, Derrick repeated the numbers. *How did I do that?* He wondered.

Rebekah punched the code. Nothing happened. "Nothing," Rebekah said. "Are those the right numbers?"

"The numbers are correct." Miriam's hand appeared in the leaves. "Hand me the other flashlight."

Rebekah fished the other flashlight from her bag, handing it to Derrick who handed it to Miriam. Light filtered through the brush where Miriam stood.

After several minutes, Miriam said, "Try again."

Derrick heard a click.

"It's open," Rebekah yelled.

Miriam crashed through the brush. "Solar panel. Doesn't get enough light with all this brush."

"You're bleeding," Derrick said, pointing at her forehead. "And how do you know about — what did you call them — solar panels?"

Miriam wiped at her forehead with her hand, grimacing. Blood streamed down the side of her face. She pulled a tissue from her bag and held it to her head; it soon soaked with blood. "I'll be okay. They had solar panels on the roofs of all the homes in Pacific Edge; if you'd ever ventured up on the roof, you would have known. I wonder how much farther. It's getting dark."

Derrick shrugged. "I have no idea. The robot said Engineering was close to Potterville, but I don't see how that's possible. People would know about that enormous metal door if it's close to Potterville."

"Maybe we aren't as close to Potterville as Charlie thought," Miriam said.

Rebekah forced her way next to them; she fixed Miriam's hair; pulled a twig from it; frowned at the cut on Miriam's forehead, then said, "You need that taken care of."

Derrick said, "It's weird. In Pacific Edge, we never did anything that would cause us to get hurt. Not cut or scratched or bruised. Here, it seems to be part of life. On the first day of school, when I tried out for track, a kid tripped me. My knees were skinned and bleeding, and my hands were raw." He turned his palms up; they were still red. "Coach had a first aid kit in his office. Fixed me up like it was no big deal."

"A kid tripped you on purpose?" Rebekah asked.

"Yeah, I think so," Derrick said.

"Did he get kicked off the team?" Miriam asked.

"No, I told Coach I tripped," Derrick said. "The kid is okay. I think. Besides, he's our quarterback, so we must get along."

Miriam shined her light on Derrick and said, "Derrick King, you continue to amaze me. If I didn't know better, I'd ask who you were and what have you done with my brother."

Miriam forced the door open, wriggled her way into a tunnel. She held the door open for Derrick and Rebekah. Rebekah went first, tossing both bags inside and then helping Miriam push the door so Derrick could squirm through. Miriam put a rock in the door and snaked a branch through the doorway so the door could not close.

Derrick carried the girls' bags, following them. The builders had carved this tunnel through solid stone big enough for two people to walk abreast. The tunnel arched left into the mountain and then curved toward where the gate sealed the entry. He fretted about what kind of door they would face next. If it had solar panels on the outside that did not gather light, or if it had grown too dark, they were doomed to spend another night here.

Then Derrick saw a dim light in front of them. The tunnel had no door. They had to climb over another mound of rocks amassed in front of the entry. Derrick scaled to the top of the mound, which was like the mound of stones and concrete chunks that hid the entrance to the tunnel where he first found refuge from the Pacific Edge hovercraft, except this pile was smaller and contained no concrete that he could see. "This hides the entrance and I don't see any trails leading to here." He did not add that this was like how they hid the entry into the first tunnel. He assumed that was obvious.

From the tunnel. Miriam said, "Stop."

Turning, Derrick said, "What?"

"You can't go in those clothes. Come back down and put on what you were wearing when we found you." Miriam pulled Derrick's track shorts from her bag, holding them out, scrunching her nose.

"Where is my, you know, undergarment?"

"Is that what it was? I tossed it in the trash," Miriam said.

"Uh, I'm not wearing any … — and I have to …"

Miriam held up her hand. "Don't worry. We'll go ahead while you change."

"We will?" Rebekah snickered.

Derrick changed and then caught the girls in the fading light. They faced another thicket of brush and small trees. He pulled at branches, helping the girls through, certain he'd look as if he'd been in a fight before they got out. He tried to get in front of them again when Miriam told him to worry about himself. They could manage without his help, but he pushed through the brush to lead them. It's what brothers do. The brush thinned and towering pine trees appeared. Weaving through the trees, stepping over fallen trunks, Derrick tried to move in a straight line. They would have to find their way back, and he was unsure how they could find this place.

Then he stopped.

Crashing into her stationary brother, Miriam asked, "What is it?"

Standing at the edge of a meadow, Derrick said, "I know this place." He pointed ahead. "Right there is where the hovercraft sat on the trail when they took me prisoner."

Miriam laced her arm through his. "I can't believe you came out here alone."

"I like to run here." He pointed beyond the meadow. "The trail goes up the mountain. It's a wonderful view from up there."

"Who are you and what have you done with my brother?" Miriam asked.

Rebekah stepped next to Miriam. "It's beautiful. How far is it to Potterville?"

Derrick pointed the opposite direction. "It's not far. We'll come to a stream beyond those trees. Potterville is on the other side."

Miriam stepped in front of Derrick. Looked him up and down. "You look awful." She brushed leaves from his hair and shoulders.

"Thanks," he said.

"We are all on the same page, right? Rebekah and I escaped, got lost in the mountains, ran into you, and found our way to Potterville. No mention of the facilities, including the tunnel where Derrick first hid. No mention of the hidden road. No mention of who drove Rebekah and I here, although they may already know about Mr. Jones."

Derrick turned to look at the giant metal door, but trees concealed it. Perhaps a huge pile of rocks concealed it as well.

"You can't see the door or the canyon," he said and then added, "I don't like lying to them. I won't lie anymore. I'll just say that I can't tell them where I was."

"They won't like it. Better to stick with our story," Miriam said.

"I agree," Rebekah said. "Lying is okay because you're protecting them."

"It's not okay. I won't do it," Derrick said.

Miriam shook her head. "This will not go well."

Rebekah started across the meadow. "I don't care what they do as long as they let me have a hot shower first."

"You must be freezing. Put on my coat." Miriam pulled her arm out of a sleeve.

"Then you'll be freezing. Besides, it won't fit and it's not that cold. It's warmer now we are out of the canyon. I'll be okay," Derrick said with a shiver.

Miriam hesitated, pulled her coat back on, then hugged Derrick. "Are you excited or scared?"

"Both," Derrick said.

## Friday, April 2, 6:59 p.m.

On the bridge, Derrick paused, staring into the sparkling water tumbling over the colorful rocks. Miriam cuddled on one side of him, placing her arm around his back; Rebekah mirrored Miriam on his other side. He had been eager to get back to Potterville. Now he feared facing what would come next. His time in Potterville had been brief; yet, it seemed like a lifetime; the beginning of a new life, an entirely new existence. The days here had been terrifying, painful, mystifying, and lonely. They had been the best days of his life. While lost in the mountain, he thought about Nyx. Finally admitting to himself that it was ridiculous to think he was in love with this odd girl with the pink-striped hair. A person doesn't fall in love in such a brief time with a person he hardly knows. Although he had discarded most of the teachings of the Chosen, the one on picking a mate was still sound advice. Making such a decision on emotion was unwise. A mistake he would not make again.

Now, if he could only stop thinking about her.

He wondered if he would ever see this again, and then remembered they had to return to the facility, at least once. Maybe they would return to the Base and never leave. His eyes burned and his chest felt tight as he thought about the day he ran into Nyx on the mountain. He wished he had told her the truth that day. Maybe this would have turned out differently if he had. He took a deep breath. Nothing he could do would change the past. Their future could not be more uncertain. However, of one thing he felt sure. As difficult as his time here had been, he believed his future would be even more difficult. In that, he was not wrong.

Without thinking, he whispered, "I love it here."

"I see why," Miriam said. "Can I see your cellphone?"

"Sure." Derrick pulled his phone from his pocket. "The battery is dead. I hope it still works but I won't know until it I plug it in."

"What's the little Apple thing on the back?" Miriam asked.

"I think it's the brand. My computer has it too," Derrick said.

"Is it expensive?" Miriam asked.

Derrick shrugged. "I don't know. Paul gave them to me. Father paid for them."

"Father supplied it?" Miriam asked.

"I think he gave Paul money to buy it, but I don't know that for sure. We'd have to ask Paul."

"I suppose you have contact information in it for your friends and such?" Miriam asked.

"Yes. Just a few people. Coach Browning, Donna's Bistro, Sheriff Collins." Derrick paused. "Akira and Nyx."

"Do you remember the information?"

Derrick thought about it a moment. He did not think he could remember the email addresses and phone numbers he had stored. Then he pictured the contacts stored in his phone, and to his surprise, the information appeared as if he were looking at it on his phone. "Maybe. Why do you ask?"

Miriam threw his phone as far as she could into the river. She patted his back and then said, "Let's go."

Wearing only shoes, track shorts was bad enough, but without his phone, he felt naked. "My phone. Why did you do that?"

"Pacific Edge can probably track that phone. Soon as you turn it on, they'll know you're alive and have your location," Miriam said.

"But I had other information on that phone." Derrick remembered he had written of his ordeal and sent it to Nyx and Akira. The message would have been transmitted as soon as the phone was powered on and had service. Now he thought perhaps it was better that the message remained his secret.

"Speaking of phones, should we contact Mr. Jones?" Rebekah asked.

"We should, but we won't," Miriam said.

"Could you please complete your thoughts? You're driving me crazy," Rebekah said.

"Sorry. Can't you hear my thoughts? They're so loud in my head, I assume you can. The disposable phones are supposed to be safe, but I think no phone for now is safer. I hope we can get word to him though," Miriam said.

"I still can't believe Mr. Jones helped you," Derrick said.

"I know, right? He said I was his favorite student. He changed a lot after they exiled you," Miriam said.

The streets were deserted. Derrick worried something had happened to the people. He dismissed the thought and scolded himself for letting his imagination run wild, as it had about the commoner world before he came here. It was dinnertime. People were in their homes eating, which reminded him that he was hungry. There was no problem here, and this was not time for wild imagination. Still …

The streetlights flickered to life.

"Let's go to the bistro. Donna might know how to contact Coach Browning. While we wait, we can eat something. Donna will put it on my tab. Although, I probably won't have a job there now."

The bistro looked deserted. The blinds were closed, which seemed unusual, but the lights were on and leaked through the slits. Derrick thought it strange that no one was there. However, the smell of food drifted down the street and Derrick wanted to run. He would be happy to eat whatever Donna had even if she was ready to it toss out. He hesitated outside the door, sensing everything had changed in the past couple of days. He pulled the door open, held it for Miriam and Rebekah.

"Lord sakes, what happened to you? I've been worried sick." Donna said, rushing around the counter, and then she stopped and threw her hand to her face. "You're hurt. And what happened to your clothes?" Then she walked to him and threw her arms around him.

When they separated a few moments later, held at arm's length, Derrick said, "I went for a run after school Wednesday. Two Pacific Edge security guards captured me. One of them snuck up on me and zapped me with something. It knocked me out. When I woke, we were flying over a river. I jumped. Got away. I've been lost in the mountains. But I'm okay. Especially now that I'm home."

Donna studied him for a moment, as if she were unsure what to say. Then she said, "And who are these two ladies?"

Derrick smiled. "This is my sister Miriam. She escaped from Pacific Edge. When I was exiled, she promised to …" *Promised to help me. But help me what?* "She promised she'd find a way to join me here. And this is," he hesitated.

"I'm Rebekah Ford. I'm Miriam's friend." Rebekah stuck out her hand.

Donna ignored Rebekah's hand, and Rebekah's smile faded. Then Donna threw one arm around Rebekah and the other around Miriam. "You all look like you've been through the ringer. And you must be starving. Wash up and I'll round up some food. I'm out of almost everything. I sent food over to the high school to the volunteers."

"What's going on at the high school? Is that why it's so quiet in town?" Derrick asked.

"They've all been out looking for you. The sheriff called them in for the night. He didn't want others getting lost and making things more difficult. I'll call him while you wash up."

*Out looking for me?* That thought rattled around Derrick's head. Donna slipped into the kitchen. Derrick lead the girls to the washrooms, but he didn't go into the men's room. He eased back to the half doors separating the kitchen from the dining area. He heard a faint ring and then.

"Sheriff?

"Guess who just walked in.

"Yep. And his sister and another girl too."

Silence followed, and then.

"I'll keep them here. I'm fixing them something to eat.

"Okay, I can do that."

Silence again.

"I understand. Only you and Coach. Okay.

"One more thing, can you bring the doc? They all look like hell. Probably going to need some stitches. And Derrick is only wearing gym shorts. Maybe Coach can bring him a shirt.

"Okay. See you soon."

Derrick went to the washroom. He didn't recognize the face in the mirror. His hair was matted with dried blood. The gash on his head looked worse than he had imagined. On his shoulders, arms, chest, and back, blood oozed from the most recent trip through the brush. Yet, nothing hurt much. He thought that might change soon. He was right. As he splashed water on his face, the wounds bled and hurt. He did the best he could, using wet paper towels to dab at the wounds and clean away dried blood.

When he returned, Miriam and Rebekah already sat at a table. They both looked better, but with dirt gone, he saw they also had deep scratches that were bleeding again. Both girls held white paper napkins to their wounds to stop the bleeding.

"Donna was right. You look like hell," Miriam said.

"Thanks," Derrick said. "You don't look so great yourself."

"Thanks," Miriam said.

"Hey, how about me," Rebekah said.

Derrick hesitated. Rebekah looked worse than Miriam. Her long hair tangled and dirty, dried blood on her neck, smeared near her face where she had washed. Blood stained rips in her shirt, exposing wounds covered with dried blood.

"You look worse than Derrick and I put together," Miriam said.

"Finally. I win," Rebekah said.

Both girls giggled and then laughed.

Donna burst through the doors with a pot of fresh coffee in one hand and three mugs in the other. "Here's coffee. Derrick, you can help the girls with creamer and sugar. I'm glad to see your spirits are up."

"It feels great to be home. To be honest, it's been a couple of scary days," Derrick said.

"Here too," Donna said.

After Donna sat the mugs on the table, she went to the door and turned the lock. Derrick thought that was strange. Then he remembered Donna's side of the conversation with the sheriff: *"Okay, I can do that."*

*Is Donna locking everyone out or locking us in? Probably, both.*

Derrick glanced to Miriam. She mouthed, "What's that about?"

Derrick shrugged. It didn't feel right, but he had anticipated that things had changed before they got back into town. He was finally starting to understand what was going on around him better. That should have made him happy, but now he wished he could go back to being clueless.

Rebekah added sugar and creamer to her coffee. Derrick sipped his black as did Miriam. He was unconcerned about sleeping; although, he was concerned about where he'd be sleeping. And he wondered if he would see Nyx tonight. With all the things that had occurred, including his capture, Miriam's escape, the incredible mountain discovery, and his acknowledgement that it was impossible to fall in love in mere days, he could not suppress the urge to see the girl with the pink-striped hair.

Miriam patted his hand, which he had wrapped around his coffee mug. "It's going to be okay. We'll figure it out together."

He smiled at her. She was here. She would know what to do.

Donna returned with steaming bowls on a platter. She sat bowls of red soup in front of each of them. "It's only tomato soup. Sorry, I didn't have something more substantial, but I've got sandwiches on the grill too."

"Thank you, ma'am. But we don't have money with us," Miriam said.

"Your money wouldn't be any good here tonight anyway, sweetie. And you call me Donna. I trust you're a quicker study than your brother." Donna winked.

"I am, Donna," Miriam said.

Rebekah sipped from her spoon. "Mmm. This is wonderful."

"Thank you. Eat up. I'll be back."

Donna disappeared. Derrick filled his spoon, blew on it, and then took a sip. He was unsure if the soup was fantastic or if he was just starving. It did not matter because he ate like a savage. Neither Miriam nor Rebekah displayed any resemblance to the Chosen table manners they had all been taught.

A loud knock sounded at the door.

Derrick turned to see, but the windows were covered.

Donna pushed backwards through the half doors and then turned, holding another tray. "Derrick, could you grab this, dear, and I'll check the door."

Derrick scurried to grab the tray from Donna. It contained three plates with toasted sandwiches, melted cheese oozing from the sides. He placed plates in front of Miriam and Rebekah and then sat.

Donna pried the blinds open slightly and peered out. Then she opened the door, just enough for Sheriff Collins and Coach Browning to enter. "Thank goodness you are here. Where's the doc?"

"On his way," Collins said.

"See what I told you? They look like they've been attacked by mountain lions," Donna said.

Derrick wasn't sure how he should act. He sensed everything had changed. He knew nothing would be the same. But without thinking, he jumped up knocking his chair over, rushed to Coach and threw his arms around the big man. "I'm sorry, Coach," he cried.

Browning held Derrick for several minutes as he sobbed. "It's okay, son. You're safe now. What on earth happened to you?"

Walking to the table, Browning picked up Derrick's chair and pointed for him to sit. "We have all night. Well, maybe not all night because I haven't slept since Wednesday. But take your time. Tell us what happened."

"Coach, Mr. Collins, this is my sister, Miriam, she escaped from Pacific Edge on Thursday. And this is her friend, Rebekah Ford." Derrick was glad Rebekah had first introduced herself as Miriam's friend instead of one of Derrick's perspective brides.

Browning extended his hand to Miriam, "Pleasure to meet you, young lady. Do you run by any chance?"

"Not like Derrick," Miriam said.

"Soccer, volleyball, softball?" Coach Browning asked.

"I've never played sports," Miriam said.

"Well, that's what Derrick said too." Browning smiled and then shook Rebekah's hand. "And nice to meet you too."

Browning picked up Derrick's backpack. "Looks like your school clothes are in there. Go change."

Derrick took the backpack and walked to the washroom.

"I play volleyball and soccer. Can I try out?" Rebekah said.

"We'll see," Browning said.

Rebekah's brow wrinkled.

Sheriff Collins pulled out a chair, spun it around backwards, and sat facing Miriam. He gave a quiet whistle through his teeth and said, "You escaped from Pacific Edge? How in the world did you manage that?"

"I escaped with her," Rebekah said.

"Okay," Collins said.

"It's a long story. Some of which you don't want to know," Miriam said.

"You're probably right about that. I heard Pacific Edge had a major system failure. It's still not running from what I hear. Major chaos over there. Affects us here too. People are worried about losing credit for their monthly rent payments. You wouldn't know anything about that, would you?"

"I might know something about it. Like I said, better that you don't."

Derrick returned. Being fully clothed felt better than he expected.

Collins looked at Browning. Browning gave a slight nod. "Let's start with you then, Derrick. What happened and where have you been?"

Derrick expected the *what happened* question but felt entirely unprepared for the tone in the sheriff's voice when he asked, "where have you been."

# 2

Derrick drank coffee, ate grilled cheese, and told Coach and Sheriff Collins his story. Donna lingered when she brought out additional sandwiches, which were delicious but would not replace hamburgers, pizza, or lasagna on Derrick's favorite food list. He consumed three grilled cheese. Miriam and Rebekah shared a second sandwich. Derrick told of his dive into the river after punching the guard, how he'd cut his head on a broken branch, and then tied his bloody shirt in the river to fool his would-be captors. He did not tell them about the pile of rocks, tunnel, nuclear reactor, robot, missiles, or dead bodies. Instead, he said, he hid until Miriam found him. Then they found their way home, through the mountains. He did not say over the mountains.

Sheriff Collins looked at Browning. Browning shrugged and shook his head. Donna came to the table with the biggest cinnamon roll he'd ever seen, frosting and butter running down the sides. Miriam and Rebekah stared at it. Derrick went for more coffee.

"I had the dough rising for the morning batch," Donna said.

Derrick returned with the coffeepot, two mugs and two forks, which he handed to Sheriff Collins and Coach. "Coffee?"

"I shouldn't," Coach Browning said. "But I don't think I'll have trouble sleeping tonight.

Sheriff Collins accepted the coffee, took a sip, and looked at Miriam. "Miriam, tell us how you got here?"

Derrick should have felt relieved when the conversation turned to Miriam, but he did not. Miriam told her story. She kept it generic. She did not tell them about the Technical Services supervisor who helped her get access to the computer system, first using the communication monitor in their home and then in the Technical Service building. She did not tell them she'd crashed the Pacific Edge computer system or that a teacher drove them away once they escaped. She did not even tell them she faked escape by way of the sea. She told them someone gave them a ride, and they drove into the Sequoia National Forest as far as possible and then walked to Potterville to avoid the major roads.

Sheriff Collins stood, walked to the coffeepot, and refilled his cup. Derrick thought that was a bad sign.

"What do you know about Pacific Edge going dark Thursday morning?" Collins asked.

Miriam smiled slightly. "I might have caused some problems on my way out the door. Like I said, you don't want to know. Safer for you that way."

Collins nodded and then looked at Derrick. "Son, I know you told lies when you came here. I also know you came clean. We all hoped you'd not be lying to us again."

"I'm not lying. That's what happened," Derrick said.

"I believe the part about being taken by Pacific Edge security. They've been here looking for you. I don't know why you are so important to them. Typically, they don't want anyone back after they leave a Chosen Community. We understand why." Collins took a sip of coffee and then reached in and forked off a bite of the roll. He closed his eyes as he chewed and then washed it down with coffee. "Here's what doesn't make sense. From the description of your location on the river, you were on the other side of the mountains. Miriam and her friend were on the other side of the mountains as well."

Collins stopped and stared at Derrick. Derrick realized something he had not considered. Collins questioned people for a living. "I don't know where I was. That's the truth. But if you say we were on the other side of the mountain, I have no reason to argue."

Collins frowned. "Here's the thing. There's still six feet of snow on those mountains." He looked at the girls, the coats hung from their chairs, the bags on the floor, and then the boots on their feet. "The girls might have made it over the mountains. I'm surprised they were dressed for the cold coming from Pacific Edge. But even dressed properly, getting through the snow would be almost impossible."

Collins focused on Derrick and leaned forward. "You would not have survived crossing the mountains in tennis shoes and jogging shorts. So, maybe you're not lying, but you're not telling me the entire story. Neither is your sister. I'm not so concerned about how she escaped, although I'd love to hear how she did it because to the best of my knowledge, it's never been done."

Derrick glanced at his coffee. It was almost empty and had grown cold. He needed a moment to think. "Okay if I get more coffee? I don't like it cold."

Collin's nodded toward the coffeepot. "I've got all night." He glanced at Donna and winked. Donna rubbed her hands together and went into the kitchen.

Derrick returned, sat, and sipped. He took another bite of cinnamon roll. Derrick knew what he must do. He knew this would be the toughest decision of his life thus far. "I did not lie. I did not say we came over the mountains."

"Then how did you get here? It would take days to walk around the mountains."

"I assume you are correct about that," Derrick said. He took a drink. "I can't tell you how we got here."

"What do you mean you can't? You can't because you don't know? Or because you won't?"

"You are correct," Derrick said.

# 3

To Derrick, it seemed as if someone flipped a switch somewhere in the universe. Everything felt different. Coach Browning glanced at Sheriff Collins; Donna frowned — not a mad sort of frown — but a concerned sort of frown. Derrick assumed Collins was unaccustomed to people not giving him straight answers. Rebekah looked scared. Miriam looked pissed, which he expected even though he told her he would not lie. Maybe she thought he'd reconsider, which he did ,but chose to tell the truth. Lying might have been better, but he doubted it.

The sheriff took a deep breath; the red faded from his face. "Son, we're trying to be on your side. Pacific Edge has been here looking for you and the girls. You probably don't understand, but we have a good thing going here. The rest of the country probably isn't what New America Media showed you, but it's no paradise either. Pacific Edge pretty much leaves us alone if folks pay their rent, sharecrop, and such. I want the best situation for you, so help me out here."

Fear gripped Derrick, unaccustomed to standing his ground unless angry, and his experience with that was limited. But something Collins said puzzled him. "Sharecrop?"

Collins paused. "Nobody owns anything here. Farmers rent ground by sharing their crop with the landowners. Businesses pay rent and a portion of their sales. Didn't you know that's what the Chosen do? They collect the money. We assume they own everything as well. You know, top of the food chain as it were."

Derrick was unfamiliar with the term top of the food chain, but it seemed self-explanatory. "They teach us the Chosen are the Creator's people." Derrick paused. "I no longer believe that. But they don't teach us about what role the Chosen play in the, uh — the world outside Pacific Edge."

"Short answer is this. The Chosen own everything that does not belong to the government, and even then, it's damn tough to tell the two apart."

Derrick felt his stomach knot. "You can't tell the government apart from the Chosen?"

"Exactly, but that's not important to this conversation."

"It's extremely important to this conversation," Miriam said.

Derrick glanced to her. He did not need her help, not yet anyway.

Collins turned to Miriam. "Would you like to tell us how you got here?"

"I would not. I told Derrick to lie. But he refused," Miriam said.

Browning stood and paced behind Derrick. Derrick suppressed a smile because he recognized it as a common teacher tactic to make students feel uncomfortable. It did not make him angry, in fact, it comforted him because of the familiarity.

"Son, will you at least try to explain why you can't — or won't tell us?" Browning asked.

Derrick said, "We found something. It's dangerous to know about. It's better if people don't know about it. For everyone's safety. We are not trying to be difficult. I wish I didn't know. I wish it was all a dream."

Miriam cleared her throat. "We don't know how to handle this, and we can't make decisions until we know what happens to us next. We may have to show someone what we found."

Derrick felt relieved and confused. Miriam was steadfast about lying; now she opened the door for telling the truth. Derrick felt Browning's hands on his shoulders.

"Bill, I think we need to accept this for now. The kids have been through a tough time. This can be sorted out in the next few days and then we can see where it goes. Let the kids get some rest."

Sheriff Collins nodded. "I guess you are right. It's not an emergency, yet."

A loud knock sounded. Donna raced to the door and peeked through the blind. "It's Doc Phillips."

A silvered-haired man slightly hunched at the shoulders entered carrying a worn black leather bag. "So, these are our lost souls." He smiled as he walked toward Derrick. "This young man looks to have gotten the worse of it."

Doc Phillips told Derrick to go to the kitchen for privacy. "You folks stay here while I give him the once over."

As Derrick and Doc left, Rebekah said, "You don't have to ask me questions. My answers are the same as Miriam and Derrick. But I'm serious about soccer. I played in Pacific Edge and planned to play in college. I did not play volleyball because girls are only allowed to play one sport there. We aren't encouraged to go the college either. So, how do I try out?"

Browning chuckled. "I don't coach girls' soccer or volleyball, and you're not a student yet. But I'll introduce you to the coach. Maybe she'll let you try out. If you become a student, that is."

"And why wouldn't I be a student."

Browning gave a soft whistle through his teeth. "It's complicated."

# 4

After twenty minutes, Derrick walked through the half-doors from the kitchen. He sported an odd-looking bandage on his forehead, and a couple of regular Band-Aids on his arms. The Doc had cleaned away the dried blood. The bandages on his back were not visible, but they were there.

"Doc wants to see Miriam next," Derrick said.

Miriam stood, walked toward Derrick. Pausing at his side, she rose on her toes, kissed him on the cheek, and whispered in his ear, "I love you, brother."

Derrick sat. "So, what did I miss?"

Browning smiled, sat back. "Rebekah twisting my arm about playing soccer. Have you watched her play?"

Derrick glanced at Rebekah, wondered if he could read her thoughts. Probably not, but were he to guess, a hint of sadness colored her eyes. "I have not. I should have. I was a jerk in Pacific Edge. I'm trying to change, but it won't happen overnight."

"Not watching soccer doesn't make you a jerk," Donna chimed in.

"In this case, it does. I heard she's good. She should get a chance here," Derrick paused, "Like I did."

"That might not happen," Rebekah said.

As poor as he was at reading people, sadness was easy to hear in her voice. Derrick said, "She won't even get a tryout?"

"They might not allow me at the school. I think that means none of us will be allowed to stay."

"Hold on. I did not say that," Browning said.

"True. But that's what I heard," Rebekah said.

Derrick looked at Coach Browning.

Browning looked to Collins. Collins looked to Derrick and said, "The youth council decides what happens next."

Derrick said nothing.

Collins said, "Like I said, we had a good thing here. One reason is that we have things the Chosen want. Fruits, berries, vegetables. They leave us alone, and we deliver. But it's easy to lose a crop. Harvest too late, forget to water, forget to plant. It's our leverage. New America Media fed you propaganda, but that does not mean there are no problems outside the Chosen Communities. Potterville is unique. There are a few other towns like us. We have a decent climate, not the extremes of heat, cold, and wet that dominate most of the continent now. But most important is the self-management through councils, one for the youth and one for adults. The youth council will decide what to do with you. The adults can override the youth council but never have. The kids make good decisions.

Derrick knew they might not be allowed to stay. He had determined they couldn't stay as well. Yet, it felt surreal hearing it. Rebekah cried softly. He felt that he might join her but fought off the tears, for now.

Miriam entered the room. "Doc will see you now, Rebekah. You're no worse off than I am, so he'll be quick." As Rebekah passed, Miriam grabbed her hand and said, "We'll be okay. One way or another."

Miriam joined them at the table and asked, "When will the council make this decision?"

"You heard then?" Collins asked.

"I heard enough," Miriam said.

"Soon, I suspect. First things first." Collins looked at Browning. "Where are they going to stay? Derrick can't go to your place. That would put your family at risk."

"You can't separate us," Derrick said louder than he anticipated.

Browning and Collins stared at him. After a moment, Browning said, "What's the situation with your condo?"

"I don't know. Paul said Father stopped paying for it. The people from Pacific Edge said they'd gather my things. Even if I'd gone back, I don't think they would have let me have anything from here. So probably everything is still there."

"That's for certain," Miriam said.

"You know something about that?" Derrick asked.

"I'll tell you later."

"I'll call Paul," Browning said.

Browning held his phone to his ear, but Derrick could hear the ring.

"Paul, Browning here. —

"Yes, he's here. —

"He's scratched up, tired, but all right. —

"Yes, his sister and another girl from Pacific Edge. —

"I know. Hard to believe, but they're here just the same. —

"What's the deal with Derrick's condo? —

"Okay. —

"Okay. —

"You don't have to do that. —

"Well, that's outstanding, Paul." —

Browning ended the call. "Paul says your condo is paid through April. So, you can stay there. The building is secured, and Paul says he'll stay in his condo to provide extra security."

"I'll have the men keep a close eye on the place," Collins said.

"What about the cameras?" Derrick asked.

"Cameras?" Collins and Browning said in unison.

"There were cameras in my condo. And Nyx and Akira's places too," Derrick said.

"How do you know that?" Collins said.

Derrick said, "Akira found them. We didn't do anything about them so that whoever was watching didn't know that we found them."

"I took care of the cameras while I was in Pacific Edge. But they could be operational now," Miriam said.

Everyone stared at Miriam.

Rebekah came back into the room.

"How did you do that?" Collins asked.

"I found them when I fixed the cameras in Pacific Edge, so security didn't see me out after curfew."

"We'd better make sure they don't work," Browning said, picking up his phone.

"Paul, Browning again. Hey, Derrick tells me that there were surveillance cameras in his condo and in Nyx's place. In Akira Nakamura's place, too. Can you look at Derrick's and then go over to Belos and Nakamura's? Make sure those damn things are no longer operational. Thanks. Call me when you're done at Derrick's. The kids need rest."

The Doc came into the room and walked to the table where the three kids were seated. "You'll be okay. Nothing that rest and a shower won't fix. But if you don't feel well, call me." He handed Derrick a card. "Anytime, day or night."

"Thanks," Derrick said.

Doc Phillips tipped his hat and left.

"How about some hot chocolate?" Donna asked. "Help you sleep."

Derrick, Miriam, and Rebekah nodded.

"That would be nice. Thank you," Miriam said.

"Who knows that I'm back?" Derrick asked.

"Nyx was the first person I told," Browning said. "She'll tell Akira. The council will ensure the track and football teams know. We sent the search teams home. We didn't tell them much, just that you'd been found. Word spreads fast. My guess is that everyone in town knows by now."

"That means Pacific Edge knows too," Derrick said.

"Most likely," Browning agreed.

"What time does the track meet start," Derrick asked.

"It starts at 11:00. But you won't be there."

"Why not? They know I'm here. It will be daylight with lots of witnesses."

"That's true. But you can't compete after all this. You're beat," Browning said.

"I'll manage. It will probably be the only meet I'll ever compete in. I deserve that much. Don't I?" Derrick asked.

Browning scratched his head. "Mostly, it won't be safe. That's my main concern. What do you think, Bill?"

Derrick interrupted. "Coach, I'll do what you tell me to do. But I want to run. Please, let me do this."

Collins shrugged. "I'll be there. Wouldn't miss it."

Browning thought for a moment. "Under one condition."

"You name it, Coach," Derrick said.

"Run like the wind."

# 5

Donna brought hot chocolate and a plate piled high with chocolate chip cookies. Coach told Derrick when to be at the school, how to dress, what to bring. He coached Derrick on preparing himself mentally, and how they scheduled events, where and when to stage before a race, and which races he would be in. Cross-country would be the last race. Most people will have left before the cross-country runners get back to the track. Browning recommended that Derrick skip that event.

Then a knock at the door startled Browning and Collins.

Collin's stood and pulled the pistol from his belt.

"Relax," Donna said. "For heaven's sake. You two are jumpier than a frog in a frying pan."

Rebekah giggled, which caused Miriam to giggle. And that made Browning smile.

Donna said, "That will be one of the girls. I called Nyx and told her that both girls needed clean clothes. No one will sit next to them looking — and smelling — like that."

Donna opened the door a crack. A hand came through holding a paper sack like Derrick saw at a store that sold food. Derrick could not hear the conversation, but thought he recognized the voices. A heavy feeling grew in his chest; he felt a bit sad.

Donna thanked the person or persons outside and closed the door. "That was Nyx and Akira. Nyx is about the same size as Miriam. They stopped by L. Linda's house for Rebekah's clothing. L. Linda is closer to Rebekah's size.

Browning's phone buzzed. "Hi, Paul." He listened for a few minutes and then said, "That's strange. Let me know what you find at the Nakamura house. Okay, I'll tell him."

"What's strange?" Collins asked.

"Paul found the cameras and the sending device at Nyx's and Derrick's condos. Someone had cut the wires. The cameras were already disabled."

Collins looked at Derrick. "You didn't do that?"

"No, honest. We decided to do nothing and act as if we didn't know the cameras were there."

Collins sat and finished his chocolate. "I've been thinking about this. The bigger problem is that someone planted those cameras. When Derrick was supposed to be on his way back to Pacific Edge, the person responsible must have disabled the cameras."

Browning nodded. "I've been thinking about it too, and I don't like it one bit. A spy in our midst."

This was not news to Derrick, but he appreciated that Collins and Browning were not happy about it. The girls seemed oblivious as they pulled out blouses and shorts and pants, with "Oh, this is cute, and I love this, and this will fit fine."

"Derrick, Paul said he wouldn't see you tonight because he still has to go to the Nakamura house. But he'll be there tonight so if you hear or see anything unusual, call him," Bill Collins said.

"It's nice of him to help us," Derrick said.

"Paul's a good man," Browning said. "Now we have the all clear, I'll take you to the condo."

Collins stepped to the door and split the blind peeking out. "Better take them out the back. I'll go with you."

The backdoor opened into the alley. It was empty except for trash bins and a stray cat. Coach Browning led the way. Rebekah walked on Derrick's right, Miriam on his left. Sheriff Collins followed them. Derrick didn't think the escort was necessary, but he was relieved to have the two men with them. But he also knew it could not go on this way. He wondered if they would ever feel safe. He remembered that Miriam thought Level Two at the base might hold keys to their safety. How she came to that conclusion eluded him.

Derrick was glad Miriam was here, although Rebekah's presence still puzzled him. Not just that she had escaped with Miriam, but that she had left her little sister. Derrick left Miriam behind, but he had no choice. He wanted Miriam in Potterville not because she was in danger in Pacific Edge but to help him survive. As usual, he was thinking of himself first and he didn't like it. However, the more he thought about it, the more he agreed that Anna was not safe. He would not know until later how accurate this assessment would prove to be.

After they were in Derrick's condo, he said, "I'll sleep on the couch. You guys can share my bedroom. The other room only has a computer. No bed."

Rebekah moved through the living room and into the kitchen area. "So, this is your place. It's nicer than I expected."

Miriam seemed uninterested in the condo.

Rebekah said, "Mind if I shower first?"

"Go for it," Miriam said, and then turned to Derrick, "What's your username and password?"

"You can't be serious You're getting on the computer?" Derrick asked.

"I'm serious. But I won't be long. I just need to check a couple of things."

Derrick told Miriam his username and password, and she disappeared into what he called his study. He looked in the cabinets and refrigerator. Nothing had changed. He did not check his bedroom in case Rebekah exited the bathroom draped in a towel or less. They would have to work out some rules about use of the shower, dressing, etc. He took his guitar from the closet, sat on the couch, and worked through Blowing in the Wind, strumming lightly, singing softly.

"That sounds wonderful. What is that song?" Rebekah asked, sitting on the end of the couch, hair wet, wearing his t-shirt, which was far too big for her.

"Blowing in the Wind by Mr. Bob Dylan. It's a classic."

"I did not know you played guitar."

"I just started learning."

"That's amazing."

"I'm not good. You should hear Mr. Griggs play. He has the guitar shop and is my teacher. I've been practicing every day. Except the past couple of days. And the music here is amazing. I like a thing they call rock-and-roll."

Miriam walked out of the study. "Derrick, you should shower. I'll go last. Then we need to sleep."

"I'm not sure I can sleep," Rebekah said. "Too wound up. And too worried about Anna."

"I don't know if I can sleep either," Derrick said.

"It's not an option. We need sleep to function. Derrick, you have a race to run. And we have a lot to do and not much time in which to do it," Miriam said.

Derrick considered asking Miriam what they had to do and then decided against it. Sleeping would be difficult. Knowing what Miriam had in mind would make sleep impossible.

# 6

Contrary to Derrick's assessment of his sleep potential, he fell into a deep slumber the moment his head hit the pillow. He dreamed of the white room, of Keepers and Tenders, and of a girl who had been in other dreams but only as a background character. He had not interacted with her. Derrick hated the dreams and believed they were just nightmares. That changed when Miriam's email indicated she had similar dreams. In the dreams, Miriam was Number 6. He was Number 7. Another reason he disliked the dreams was because of his behavior. Sometimes frustrated, sometimes stupid, always controlled by something or someone else.

But this dream seemed different. The girl was not a background character. A Keeper tormented the girl for not completing her task fast enough. The Keeper called her names, told her she was worthless, said they would feed her to the commoners.

That's when Derrick felt something he never felt in a dream.

He felt sorry for the girl.

He felt anger.

He picked up a chair and hit the Keeper in the back.

The girl's name was Number 3.

***

## Saturday, April 3, 7:43 a.m.

Derrick awoke groggy. Light seeping in around the window indicated it was morning. A light knock sounded at the door. Maybe the knocking woke him; he wasn't sure. Tossing the light blanket off, he sat up. He had slept in jeans and t-shirt, what with Rebekah and Miriam in the next room.

He peeked through the peephole. He smiled.

Nyx and Akira stood in the hall.

He was glad to see them both, apprehensive to face them both.

He opened the door.

Nyx punched his chest and said, "Why were you out by yourself. I told you not to do that." And then she hugged him.

"I'm sorry. I should have listened to you." When they separated, he said, "Hi, Akira."

"Akira blushed and said, "I'm glad you're okay."

"Come in. My sister and her friend are asleep in the other room."

"Rebekah is asleep. I am not. I've been up a couple of hours." Miriam stood in the living room.

Akira rushed to Miriam and hugged her. "Miriam, it has been so long." Akira released the hug and held Miriam at arms' length. "I love your hair. And you're a cute as I remember, although I don't remember the scratches and bruises."

Miriam smiled. "Those are recent additions. You like them? I might get more later."

The girls hugged again and then separated.

Miriam walked to Nyx. "You must be Nyx. We talked on the phone." Miriam extended her hand.

Nyx grabbed Miriam's hand and pulled her close, hugging her and then stepping back, Nyx asked, "How did you find my name and phone number?"

"Long story," Miriam said.

"Don't feel put off. I hear that a lot," Derrick said.

The bedroom door opened. Rebekah shuffled into the room, hair disheveled, rubbing sleep from her eyes. Then she stopped; her hand flew to her mouth. "Oh, my God. Akira Nakamura?"

"Hi, Rebekah." Akira walked to Rebekah and hugged her. "It's like a small reunion."

Rebekah said, "Let me go splash some water on my face. I'll be right back."

Now that introductions had taken care of themselves, he realized that he felt as out of place as he did on the first day of school at Potterville High. "Uh, here have a seat. Um, we have cereal."

"How about coffee?" Akira said.

"Yes, we have coffee. Does everyone want a cup?"

"I mean, how about you and Nyx go to the bistro for coffee? Miriam, Rebekah, and I can catch up while you're gone." Akira hesitated. "I'm sure you two also have things to discuss."

Derrick pressed his lips together to suppress a smile that would have seemed inappropriate given the situation. "I'll clean up a bit," he said, stepping into the half bath.

After splashing water on his face, dragging wet fingers through his hair, running a finger over his teeth, and rinsing his mouth out with lukewarm water — not that he anticipated a kiss — he walked back into the room. Nyx stood at the door waiting to leave.

In the hall, Derrick said, "I'm sorry, Nyx."

"You already said that. Repeating it, doesn't improve anything."

"I know. I keep disappointing you. I don't mean too, but …"

Nyx didn't say anything. She reached down and took his hand as they walked down the stairs. When they reached the sidewalk, she let go of his hand. "We can't be seen like that in public."

Derrick felt confused and a little hurt. *Why can't we be seen holding hands?* He wanted to ask Nyx but wasn't sure he wanted to know the answer.

On the sidewalk, Nyx asked, "Have you had breakfast?"

"I have not," Derrick said.

"Good. I'm starving. So, Coach says how you guys got back to Potterville doesn't make sense."

"That is correct."

"He also said you refused to tell them how you did it."

"That is also correct."

"You'll have to tell us at some point. And that is coming sooner than you might think."

Derrick did not respond. He needed to think about his answer. He, Miriam, and Rebekah agreed it was too dangerous to tell anyone about the facility. Miriam seemed to understand why that was true even better than he did. He sensed that the place was dangerous. If for no other reason, the strange robot might turn homicidal if Miriam didn't fix its girlfriend. Yet, she also indicated they might have to show the place to someone, depending on what happened once they returned to Potterville. He did not know how Miriam would make that decision.

"Earth to Derrick. Are you ignoring me?"

"I am not. Just thinking," Derrick said.

"You understand this is serious? Right?"

"More than you know," Derrick said.

"So why didn't you tell the Sheriff and Coach how you got home?"

"We found something. It's dangerous."

"That makes little sense. How can it be so dangerous that you can't tell Sheriff Collins about it?"

"If I could explain it, I might as well tell them."

They walked silently the remainder of the way. Derrick knew this was coming. He hated it but could not avoid it. He did not want to hurt Nyx again. And not telling her hurt. He knew that. But he would not put her in harm's way.

When they reached the bistro, Nyx stopped. She turned and looked into Derrick's eyes. "What hurts most is that you said you'd stop lying. But you have not changed a bit."

"I'm not lying. I'm just not telling. I'm being honest about that. It's not because I don't trust you. It's because I won't put you at risk."

Nyx studied him for a moment. He could not read her. He wondered if she understood how important she was to him. Probably not. He was just a liar who came to town uninvited and caused disruption. Since he was being honest, he honestly did not see a way for him to stay here. He knew he could start over, but he didn't want to.

Nyx said, "End of discussion for now. This is going to be difficult, but we must separate track and everything else. Does that make sense? Force everything out of your mind, except track until after the meet."

"I'll try," Derrick said.

As the entered, Donna said, "Good morning! Two of my favorite people,"

Heads turned and looked at them. Derrick could not read their expressions, maybe because of the conflict they experienced; happy to see Nyx — who wouldn't be — not happy to see him — who would be?

Then a man said, "Good luck today. Go Bearcats."

Everyone joined in with a *Go Bearcats!* or a *Good Luck!* Derrick knew the well wishes were for Nyx, not him. He was okay with that. She deserved their support.

The half doors swung open. L. Linda Maxton marched out wearing an apron, drying her hands. Her brown hair piled on top of her head, stray hair poking out here and there. Her warm brown eyes twinkled as she smiled broadly. "Hi, Derrick. I'm washing dishes today. I'm covering for you."

"Thanks. Sorry you have to wash dishes. It's hard work," Derrick said.

"Donna says it will be slow today. Because of the track meet. I wish I could be there, but I'm taking one for the team." She rose on the balls of her feet, twisting her ankles left and right, but keeping her shoulders square and her smile in place. Then she tapped him on the shoulder. "Good luck. Go Bearcats." With that L. Linda Maxton scurried back to the kitchen, backing through the double doors, smiling.

"You know L. Linda?" Nyx asked.

"She started work here the same day I did," Derrick said.

"That was just last weekend," Donna said. "I have fresh cinnamon rolls. Do you want one or two?"

"No rolls this morning. Two eggs, two sausage patties, two slices of toast. No potatoes. Same for Derrick, except three of everything. Both of us will have milk. We need protein and carbs today," Nyx said.

Donna handed Derrick a cup. "You look much better this morning."

Nyx went outside. Derrick followed. She picked a table farthest from the door.

"Is this okay?" Nyx asked as she sat.

Derrick smiled. He welcomed shutting everything out except track; although, he doubted he could. But he was going to enjoy this moment — beautiful morning, birds singing, fragrant spring air, and breakfast with Nyx. This might be the last such morning to enjoy. "This is perfect," he said.

"Try to not be nervous today. I know that's difficult being your first meet. My first meet, I threw up three times before the first race. Just focus. On the 100 meters, focus on the finish line. That's all. Let it pull you. On the 400, and mile, run your own race. Most important thing is to relax and have fun. Coach will spend most of his time with you."

Donna brought out two glasses of milk, condensation coating the outside of the glasses. "I'll have your breakfast out right away. It's a beautiful day for the meet. I hope you both do well and I'm sure you will."

Derrick took a drink of milk. It was cold and delicious. "I'm going to miss everything about this place."

"What does that mean?" Nyx asked.

"I'm naïve but not stupid. I've screwed this up at every turn. I'm just being realistic."

"Knock that off. We have a track meet. Remember? Block that shit out."

"Right. Sorry."

A man exited the bistro, stopped, and held the door for Donna; she came out holding a tray with two plates heaped with food. Steam rose from the sausage patties. "You two enjoy. And your meal is paid for."

"I'll pay for it, ma'am," Derrick said. "Take it from my wages and let me know if there's not enough to cover it."

"I can't do that," Donna said. "The guys inside took up a collection. They paid for it."

The man smiled and said, "Good luck. Both of you."

# 7

When Derrick and Nyx entered the condo, the room fell silent. Rebekah, Akira, and Miriam tried to look casual but failed. Derrick wondered what they discussed that required silence the moment they arrived. He thought Miriam looked more guilty than the others, and he wondered if she had told Akira more than she had intended. He hoped that wasn't it because as soon as Akira and Nyx compared conversations, and Nyx learned what he deemed too dangerous was safe for Miriam to tell Akira. Then he'd be screwed big time. Another reason they should not allow themselves to be separated became clear.

"What's going on?" Nyx asked. "You all look guilty as hell."

"Maybe a little guilty," Akira admitted.

"So, what's the big secret? Derrick won't tell me. But did they tell you?" Nyx stared at Akira.

"Secret? About …? Oh, about where they've been? No. Nothing like that."

"Then out with it?"

"We were kind of talking about you two," Miriam said. "He's my brother. I have a right to know what's going on."

"Do you?" Nyx asked. "We don't have time for nonsense. We have a meet. I'm going to change. I'll be back and we can walk to the school."

Nyx left, and when the door closed, the oxygen seemed to rush back into the room.

Rebekah covered her mouth with her hand, but Derrick could hear her giggling. Then Miriam giggled. And then Akira giggled.

"Sorry, brother. You'd better get ready. We'll stay out here."

"And talk about me I assume. I don't have any track clothes. My shorts are dirty and torn, my shirt is gone. I'm as ready as I'm going to get. I hope Coach will let me use another uniform. Otherwise, I'll just be watching."

At 10:40 a.m., a knock came at the door. Derrick paused to look out of the peephole and then decided it no longer mattered. Besides, it was probably Nyx. He had no concept of how long it took a girl to change clothing.

When he opened the door, there stood Coach Browning, Sheriff Collins at his side. Derrick thought maybe things changed. Perhaps Collins came to arrest them, or at least him. That would be one way to separate them for questioning.

Coach extended a brown-paper bag. "You need a uniform. I had this at home to give you — then you disappeared."

Derrick took the bag. He looked inside and saw new track shorts and a new track shirt. He pulled the shirt out of the bag and held it up. On the back, across the top, KING was written in bold black lettering. Below his name, the number seven. "Thanks. This is unexpected. But how did you know?"

"How did I know your name was King?"

"Not that. How did you know about number seven?"

"It's the number we had open. Why?"

Derrick stared at him for a moment. "Oh. Nothing. Seven is fine."

Derrick went to his room and changed. When he came back, the room fell silent again. It seemed people had things to say about him when he was out of the room.

The door opened. Nyx stood in the hall. "Hi, coach. Are we ready?"

"Let me grab my bag," Miriam said.

Once outside the building, Browning looked over his shoulder and said, "Derrick, walk with me."

Derrick scooted to Browning's side. Derrick glanced over his shoulder. Miriam walked with Akira. Rebekah walked with Nyx. Sheriff Collin's trailed the group. Derrick should be focused on running. Instead, he wondered what would happen if Nyx learned Rebekah had been on his list for the Choosing. He hoped he'd have time to explain about the Choosing before Nyx heard it from someone else. To make matters worse, it would appear Rebekah lied about her being Miriam's friend. No one will believe Rebekah did not come to be with Derrick. Either way, he was screwed. It was just that Nyx hearing it from someone else — was slightly worse than if he told her himself.

Browning said, "Derrick, from now until the end of the meet, I'm your coach, nothing else. Try to put everything out of your mind and concentrate."

"Nyx told me the same thing. I'm trying. It's not easy." Derrick glanced back at Rebekah and Nyx. Rebekah leaned down and said something. Nyx glanced up. "Shit," Derrick breathed under his breath.

"What?" Browning asked.

"Uh, nothing. Uh, I was just thinking that I don't know anything about how this goes. Where to be and when. Stuff like that."

Browning glanced back. "Right. I'll be there with you, King. The others know what they are doing. The only thing they need from me is a bit of encouragement. They don't even need that. They'll do their thing whether or not I'm there."

"I'm sure they need you, coach," Derrick said. "I know I do."

"Thanks, King. So, here's how it goes. Your first race is the 100-meters. They'll run boys and then girls. Then they'll do the 200, which you're not in. Then they'll run the 400, which you are in. That will be your most difficult and important event. A good finish there helps the team a lot.

"Then they'll do some other events before starting the relays. Hurdles and such. Give you some time to rest. If I'm not coaching you on something, sit with your friends. Or, if you want to cheer on a teammate, say someone like Nyx, you can go down by the track. Near the finish line is best. You'll see where teammates line up for that."

Everyone seemed to think something was going on between Nyx and himself. They seemed to understand what that something was better than he did. Mostly, he felt confused.

As they came into sight of the school, the number of people surprised Derrick. Cars lined the streets. In front were three big yellow transports they call busses. Trails of people streamed toward the track. "I didn't know there would be so many people," Derrick said.

"The community supports the school. Even more so for football, but we get a good turnout for most everything. There are three other schools in the meet with us, but Fort Hill is the closest and a big rival. They are also the most competition. Rosedale and Sumpter Point are small schools and won't give us much competition. Not for the team win anyway."

"Fort Hill?" Derrick asked, thinking something sounded familiar about the name. Maybe someone had mentioned who the track meet was against.

"Yeah, next town over going west. Well, there ain't a town to the east because of the mountains."

"Is there a fort there?" Derrick asked.

"No fort. Perhaps years ago. They are a farming community like us. Except they don't grow fruits, vineyards, and vegetables like we do. They grow grains and such."

As they entered the school property, everyone they met said *Good Luck* or *Go Bearcats*, or some other encouragement. A few said something like, *I hope you're right, coach* or *can't wait to see this*.

As they rounded the building, Derrick saw the stands on both sides were three-quarters full.

"I guess you're figuring this out, so I might as well just say it. This is a larger than normal turnout for our first track meet," Browning said.

"Why is that, coach?"

"They're here to watch you."

# 8

Derrick scanned the stands as they walked onto the track. The temperature warmed and the scent of freshly mown grass filled the air. Most of the people wore the Potterville High colors. The largest bleacher was filled with those colors, including a section that appeared to be students. About half of the people in the smaller bleachers, wore Potterville colors and took up the center seats, and on either side, were the colors associated with the other teams. At breakfast, he felt nervous about the meet. Nyx helped him focus. On the walk to the school, Browning's presence calmed him further. Then Browning said people were here to watch him. How could that be possible? He'd only been here a couple of weeks, had just made the team. Was it because they wanted to see the kid who caused all the problems?

Probably.

Browning turned to the girls. "Akira, take Rebekah and Miriam to the students' section."

"But we are not students," Miriam said.

"It's okay. Akira can bring guests. It helps you wore school colors."

"Akira and Nyx took care of us," Rebekah said.

Akira took Miriam's hand. "I asked friends to save us seats."

Derrick watched the three girls trot toward the bleachers, where the students were seated. On either side of the students were teachers, although Derrick only knew a few by name.

Then he saw something unexpected. Mr. Jones stood and barreled out of the stands. Ms. Springfield in close pursuit. Miriam said Mr. Jones helped them escape. He had not cemented that as a reality in his mind. Mr. Jones ran to Miriam and hugged her tightly, Ms. Springfield hugged Rebekah. Then they switched. They seemed to know Akira. Derrick once believed his life was organized, compartmentalized, and predictable. Now, he recognized it was complete chaos. Part of him longed for predictable, but his heart told him mystery was best.

"Nyx, take Derrick to the team to warm up. I'll be over in a minute," Browning said.

"Let's go, Mr. King," Nyx said.

She had not called him Mr. King since they first met. But he sensed no hostility in her voice. Instead, she sounded playful.

As they walked toward the team, she said, "Hard as it may be, try to have fun today. There's no reason to torture ourselves with all the work if the event isn't fun."

"I'll try. I'm excited and scared at the same time," Derrick said.

"Then you're normal."

Derrick thought for a moment. "You're not scared. You've been doing this and you're so good."

"I'm scared as hell," Nyx said.

As they approached the team, each member glanced at them. Derrick could not read their expressions. Then he heard a familiar voice call his name.

"King! Mi amigo! Hold up!"

Derrick turned and saw Antonio Morales on crutches coming from the student section.

"I'll see you in a minute," Nyx said, continuing towards the team.

Antonio stopped, one leg in a brace held off the ground. "My friend you do make life interesting."

"Not on purpose," Derrick said.

"No, I suppose not. But interesting just the same. You're taking my place in a couple of events today, si?"

"That's what I understand."

"So, what are you running?" Antonio asked.

"One-hundred meters, four- hundred meters, and mile relay. I want to run cross-country if coach will let me," Derrick said.

Antonio whistled. "Dude, that's a lot. I can't believe you're running cross-country when you are a sprinter. Most cross-country runs aren't fast, so they go for endurance."

"Nyx runs both."

"You're not Nyx."

"True. She is exceptional."

"You think you're exceptional?" Antonio asked.

"No. Sorry."

"Don't be sorry, bro. You'd better start believing that you are exceptional. Otherwise, you'll fail miserably. Comprende?"

"I think so."

Antonio put his hand on Derrick's shoulder. "Good luck today, my friend. On everything."

Derrick watched Antonio hobble back to the stands. Akira helped him to the third row. He sat next to Rebekah. Derrick did not think his life could be more complicated. Yet, he knew that thinking was erroneous.

# 9

Derrick trotted towards his teammates. He wanted to stand next to Nyx, but the other girls surrounded her. Derrick stood outside the circle. Occasionally, one by one, people looked at him. He wished he could read their thoughts and then decided that would be a terrible idea. Browning joined the group, holding a clipboard, flipping through pages. The sun had reached its zenith; the warmth bathed Derrick's skin; it felt wonderful after being in the vast underground military complex. Taking a deep breath, he wished he had never seen the cave that turned out to be a tunnel. Maybe he could have escaped using other tactics; found Miriam and worked their way back to Potterville. Then that place would remain unknown. Images of dead bodies floated through his thoughts.

"Okay, listen up. I assume you've looked at the schedule. Everyone, except Derrick, knows how this works. Pay attention. I don't want anyone to miss an event because they're picking dandelions. Got it? Because it's Derrick's first meet, he'll be with me. However, should something pull me away, I'm expecting all of you to help him out." Browning flipped through pages on his clipboard, as if he were looking for something but couldn't find it. Finally, he said, "A lot of things have happened the past few days. You've probably heard things. I will confirm that Derrick's sister and her friend are here. They escaped from Pacific Edge. But that's all I'm going to say, and I don't want to hear anything about it. Savvy? Right now, we've got one thing and one thing only to focus on. Winning this event. If you can't deal with that, let me know now so I can scratch your name from the team. Any questions?"

After a few moments of silence, Browning said, "All in."

Everyone circled Browning, moved in close, and put one hand on the shoulder of the person in front. Derrick pressed in; Malcolm Cross stood in front of him. Derrick tried and failed to vanquish the dead bodies from his mind. Derrick put his hand on Malcom's shoulder. When he touched Malcom's shoulder, the rotted corpses morphed into his teammates. What he wanted would not change reality. That place existed; the evil of the place would never leave him; the forces behind it would hunt him; people around him could die. He fought back a tear. He already knew what he had to do. This would be his first and last track meet.

Coach Browning said, "Potterville, strength!"

The team yelled, "STRENGTH!"

Browning said, "Potterville, courage."

"COURAGE!"

"Potterville, fight!"

"FIGHT!"

Everyone raised their hands straight up in unison, pointing their index fingers. Derrick did the same, a little slower than the others. A cheer rose from the stands.

Derrick loved everything about this.

"Good luck today, bro, "Malcolm said.

"Thanks." Derrick said. "For everything. You've been good to me since the first day. I'll not forget that."

"Lighten up, bro. This is supposed to be fun. Now, let's kick ass."

"Right," Derrick said.

"King, walk with me," Browning said.

Derrick fell in beside Browning. "What's first, Coach?"

"Fifty-meters. We don't compete in that event. Then girls 100-meters followed by the boys. I thought you would want to watch Nyx."

Derrick wanted to watch Nyx, but he didn't say that.

Browning walked to the middle of the field. "I figured you'd want to watch her technique in the blocks. From here we can see her start and finish. And we're close to the starting line because you're next."

Derrick watched. Nyx was in her lane, behind the blocks. Other girls were getting into position. Nyx was not. She was loosening up. Light shake of her right hand and arm, light shake of her left hand and arm, stretch of her right leg, stretch of her left leg. The official said something to her and gave a hurry up hand signal. But Nyx was in no rush. All the time in the world. Derrick would not duplicate her strategy. She expected to win. He did not.

When Nyx moved to the blocks, she sped up. She got into position quickly, as if the official might start the race before she was ready; punishment for making everyone wait.

Which he did.

He failed.

Nyx rocketed from the blocks. In the lead within three steps. She never trailed. She pulled about three yards on the field; two girls maintained that gap to the finish line. Derrick realized Nyx won because of her start. And because she was smart. The week she worked with

Derrick; she emphasized the start. Made him do it over and over. Now, he wished he'd paid closer attention.

Browning headed towards the starting line at a fast walk. He waved to the official, indicating that Derrick was under his supervision. "Learn anything?"

"Yes. That I should have paid closer attention to Nyx last week."

Browning chuckled. "No one expects you to win this one. Antonio wouldn't have won it either. Just do your best. Every point counts. This is a good team we are up against."

"I'll try, coach."

"Don't try to do your best. Do your best."

"Yes, coach."

Derrick stood by the track near the start. Malcolm and Henry were there, as was Larry Kinkead.

Kinkead moved next to Derrick. He placed a hand on Derrick's shoulder, using him as a support as he stretched his quadriceps. "You might beat me on this one, but not in the 400."

"I'm just going to do my best," Derrick said.

"Relax. You're faster than me in the 100. I'm okay with that. But I have more experience in the 400. It's my specialty. I intend to set records this year."

Larry patted Derrick's shoulder and then stepped away. Derrick didn't know what to think of his comments. Maybe he'd ask Nyx about it later and then remembered it didn't matter. He hoped Larry set records. But today, Derrick planned to beat him.

The official called the boys 100-meter to the line. Derrick chose a lane, got into the blocks, and knelt waiting for the start sequence. Looking to his right, he saw no one. No one to his left either.

The official said, "Son, I assign the lanes."

Derrick looked over his shoulder. The official motioned for him back behind the starting area. Derrick stepped back. He lowered his eyes to the track. He had embarrassed himself, his coach, and team. He remembered how little he knew about life here. For no reason that he could understand, he thought about something Father said before Paul took him away from Potterville. Father said, "Maybe you can make a difference." Derrick wondered if Father knew about events here. He had made a difference all right. Everything he touched turned to shit.

"Bro, it's your first race. Don't worry about it. Just focus. See you at the other end," Malcolm Cross whispered.

The official motioned Derrick to a lane. He stepped inside and tried to loosen up like Nyx, but his arms felt like sticks. He scanned the bleachers, looking for Miriam, and found her. He waved, but she didn't see him.

"On your marks," the official said.

Derrick got into position. He worked his feet, ensuring they were snug against the starting blocks, and then raised up into position. He glanced left and saw that everyone else was still kneeling, conserving energy. He knelt. Although he tried to focus, nerves were getting the best of him. If he didn't get it together, he'd be last. He did not want to be last.

After what felt like hours, but was only a few moments, the official began the start sequence. Derrick rose, the gun fired. Running clicked in; the world clicked out. He got a decent start, better than his first attempt when he tried out, but he could see Malcolm led and runners in his peripheral vision just ahead of him. He focused on what Nyx taught him. Hands like blades, knees high, breathing, running. Halfway to the finish, running, gaining on those to each side. Three-quarters to the finish, bodies disappeared from his field of vision. Focusing on the finish line, he ran. At the finish, he pushed his chest forward, lunging through the line.

He did it. He ran his first race. He was not last. Despite not winning, he felt wonderful.

He trotted down the track and then turned with the others.

Malcolm gave him a high-five. "How did you do?"

"I don't know," Derrick said.

"That's good. If you knew, it would mean you were last." Malcolm laughed. "That would not be good."

When Derrick stepped onto the field, Nyx ran to greet him. Coach was right behind her. "I'm sure you were fourth. It was close. A kid from Fort Hill was second. Henry was third, but just barely. Malcolm was first."

"Sorry, coach," Derrick said.

"What on God's green earth are you sorry for now, King?"

Derrick puzzled a moment over Browning's phrase, and then said, "That I came in fourth."

"Fourth is two places better than I expected, King. I don't want to hear another sorry out of you unless you've done something wrong. Understand?"

Derrick smiled. "Yes, sir."

Browning cleared his throat, staring at Derrick.

"I mean, yes, coach."

"Better. It's going to be awhile before your next event. Go sit with your sister. I'll make sure someone gets you before your next race."

"Thanks, coach."

Derrick trotted across the field towards the stands. Miriam noticed his approach and scooted over, making room for him to sit between herself and Akira. Antonio stood, smiled, and then worked by a few people to the stairs. He met Derrick at the bottom.

"Good job, amigo," Antonio said.

"It wasn't great. But coach seemed okay with it," Derrick said.

"I would have finished fifth or sixth. You helped the team. That's what's important."

"I hope so. Are you leaving because I came over?"

"You are not running me off. I need to get around. Important business coming up." Antonio hobbled away but then turned and said, "Hey, I like your sister and her friend. Talk to you later."

With that Antonio left, moving quickly despite being on crutches. Derrick climbed the stairs to the row on which Miriam sat. He felt eyes following him, but he avoided making eye contact. The tension felt like electricity before a thunderstorm. Yet, he did not know what people were thinking; he understood those thoughts were his alone, just like he had assumed he understood the common world before he came. Now, he assumed he didn't understand anything. Better that way and more accurate.

Akira stood so Derrick could pass. "How did you do? It was too close to see from here."

"Fourth, I think."

"That's good. Isn't it?" Akira asked.

"Antonio said it was." Derrick sat.

"We've been catching Akira up on happenings in Pacific Edge," Miriam said.

Derrick wondered what that meant. Miriam had never been a social person in Pacific Edge. Rebekah, however, would know the latest gossip. When Miriam said, "we've been catching Akira up," it meant Rebekah had been doing the talking. Social things seemed important to girls, except for Miriam. However, he could not shake the feeling that catching Akira up meant more than gossip.

"Why are you not with Mr. Browning?" Akira asked.

Derrick shrugged. "He said it would be awhile until my next event. Told me to come sit with you guys."

Derrick searched the field. He could not see Browning with any of the runners, although he saw Coach Yates near the starting line. Yates held a clipboard like the one Browning carried. Or maybe it was Browning's clipboard. Maybe Browning had to use the restroom. But then he spotted Browning. Not with any runners but talking to Sheriff

Collins. Browning had his hand on his hips. It was too far to see them well, but Browning seemed angry.

Miriam leaned in and whispered. "I wonder what that's about?"

"What?" Derrick whispered.

"Browning and Collins. They've been arguing since after your race."

Derrick felt a knot form in his stomach. "I don't know. But we'll find out at some point."

"So, Akira is a computer whiz. And she has a contact who can help us with the Jane problem," Miriam whispered.

"How much did you tell her?"

"I didn't tell her anything. I asked questions. How much do you trust her?"

Derrick mulled the question for a few moments. "I don't know. About as much as I trust anyone here, I guess."

"Who else do you trust?"

"I don't know. Why are you asking me this?"

"I've been thinking."

"King!" Browning stood on the track below the stands, waving his arm in a frantic come-here sort of way.

"I have to go."

"Good luck," Miriam said. "Think about it."

Derrick started to say something but did not. He had spent his life doubting Miriam. He told himself he would stop doing that, but it turned out it wasn't as easy as he had hoped.

"Got to hustle, son. 400-meters is up next."

Derrick jogged behind Browning, wondering why Browning sent him to the bleachers for such a brief time. Then he remembered the heated conversation between Browning and Collins. He suspected that conversation was about him.

"Let's go, coach. Your runner is late," the start official said.

"My fault," Browning said. "It won't happen again."

"See that it doesn't. Next time I'm disqualifying your runner."

The official indicated Derrick's lane. The other runners glanced at him. Larry Kinkead gave him more of a glare than a look. Derrick had not warmed up or stretched.

*What race is this? Four-hundred meters. Must be.* Derrick took a deep breath, bent at the waist, and stretched. The official ordered the runners to the blocks. Derrick took a page from Nyx's book, taking his time, stretching each quad.

"Now, Mr. King," the official hissed from behind him.

He wasn't ready and this was a tough race. He twisted his neck and shook his arms as he lowered himself into the blocks, taking deep breaths, realizing this was how it might happen. When something bad came his way, he would not have time to prepare.

The gun sounded and Derrick shot from the blocks. Remembering Malcolm's advice, Derrick focused on running his pace. Nyx explained that the 400 was the most difficult pace to judge because of the staggered start. Derrick thought that was an advantage.

At the turn, Derrick decided he started too fast. His legs burned and he struggled for breath. He should have asked Browning where he needed to finish. In the 100-meters, fourth place was good enough. Then he remembered Browning said this was his most important event. Then he remembered he planned on beating Larry Kinkead.

Exiting the turn, Derrick felt sluggish, unsure of whether he should push harder or ease up.

Into the straight, he pushed harder. If he finished poorly, it wouldn't be for lack of effort. The straight felt like a mile. He did not know that every muscle could hurt this much.

Into the last turn, he ran harder. He might collapse before reaching the finish line.

When the staggered start evened up, Derrick was third place. Kinkead was in first. A kid from Fort Hill was second. Both looked fresh compared to how Derrick felt.

He pushed harder. Forcing every bit of speed, he could out of his weary legs. He lost track of who was around him. At the finish line, Derrick thrust his chest toward the finish at the last moment as Nyx had instructed.

He did not know what place he had finished.

He trotted down the track fifteen yards before turning off onto the football field. He came alongside Kinkead who stood with hands on his hips taking deep breaths.

"How did you finish?" Kinkead asked.

Derrick gasped for breath. "Not sure."

"I think you're second," Kinkead said.

"Why is that?" Derrick asked.

Kinkead pointed at the stands. "Because of that."

Derrick looked to where Larry pointed. Whether it was the oxygen deprivation to his brain or because he seemed so far removed from the implication, he did not know. Gradually, his mind accepted the sound, which he had shut out. In the stands, people stood, clapped, and cheered.

"We must have finished one-two," Kinkead said.

"They are cheering for you. You won the race."

"Sure. When we win, they cheer. But this crowd isn't typical for track and field. They came to watch you."

"Browning said that. I don't understand. Why would the come to watch me?"

"Not sure I can explain it either. Just remember, I plan to beat you every time we step onto the track. But if you do as well in the mile relay, we have a shot at winning this thing."

"I had not heard how we compared to Fort Hill. Browning just said they were the most competitive team we faced today."

"Understatement. They won state last year."

Browning waved. "Both of you over here."

Derrick trotted to Browning, Kinkead at his side.

"Get a drink, relax, stretch. Mile relay starts soon. They changed the schedule. Fort Hill pulled some strings. I can't prove it, but it will hurt us in the mile; you can bet on that, but you didn't hear me say that. Kinkead, stay with Derrick. Impart any wisdom you have about the relay strategy. I'll round up Malcolm and Henry. Meet me at the starting line in five minutes."

Browning turned and walked away. After five yards, he spun around. "Not official yet, but, Larry, you set a new track record. Derrick, you beat the old track record too. Well done. guys."

Derrick looked at Larry. Larry's face lit up with a smile. It occurred to Derrick that he saw Larry as an antagonist. Not quite an enemy, certainly not a friend. Worse, Derrick did not see him as a kid trying his best. Thrilled with victory; intoxicated with the challenge. Derrick had not seen Larry as a person; Derrick wondered how often he did that.

"Congratulations, Larry," Derrick said, sticking out his hand, not yet familiar enough with being a team member to give a pat on the back or a hug.

Larry hesitated, then took Derrick's hand.

"Thanks," Larry said. "Let's grab a drink. Important to stay hydrated."

They trotted over to the water, but it wasn't water. It was a strange lemon-lime flavored stuff. Light greenish yellow. It tasted okay, but it was not going to top a Coke or a milkshake.

Nyx joined them. "Fantastic job, guys. One-two, both of you beat the old track record."

"I owe Derrick thanks for that," Larry said.

"Huh? Why would you thank me?" Derrick asked.

"You've pushed me. I watched you running the 400 every morning. I timed your laps. I had to step up my game."

Nyx interrupted, "You guys better get to the starting line. Fort Hill screwed us in the mile relay. It's always our best event. If they can beat us, it ruins our chance to win."

Larry slapped Derrick on the back. "No pressure. Right, buddy?"

Derrick and Larry joined Malcolm, Henry, and Browning near the starting line.

"You're up next," Browning said.

"What's up with that. There were several events between the 400 and the mile relay," Malcolm said. "Henry and I just ran the 200 before Derrick and Larry ran the 400. They moved it up what? Two events?"

"Three," Browning said. "Fort Hill pulled two runners from the 200 and 400, so they are fresh. Apparently, they had an influx of sprinters this year."

"That sucks," Henry said.

"We'll be alright," Malcolm said.

"I'm changing the order." Henry, you run the first leg as always, I'm moving Malcolm to the second leg, Derrick to the third leg, and Larry to the last leg. Any questions?"

There were none. The boys started loosening up. Derrick copied them. He had been nervous about the first race. He proved that an appropriate condition because he made a fool of himself before they even got started. The second race was different. He would have been a nervous wreck, except Browning got him there late and he had no time to think. Now his hands were shaking, and he felt like he might throw up. He knew the relay was important. He also knew it was more difficult because of the baton pass, and now he couldn't remember how it was done. Adding that winning the meet came down to this race amplified his anxiety one hundred-fold.

Derrick felt a hand on his shoulder.

Henry Clark said, "Breathe. We got this."

Derrick nodded.

The official ordered the first runners into the blocks. Browning handed the baton to Henry.

Larry turned to Derrick and touched Malcolm on the shoulder. "Make sure we have a clean exchange. Don't let go of the baton until the next guy has a good hold. Better to have a slow handoff than to drop it."

Derrick understood that instruction was for him. He took no offense. "I'll be sure," Derrick said.

The starter shouted commands and the pistol fired. Derrick tried and failed to block the anxiety from his mind, could not drive out the thought that he would drop the baton and lose the match for the school in front of this crowd. He watched the runners as they rounded the track, but he mostly stared into space. As Henry came around the last turn, it appeared that the first three runners were close, but Henry was in the lead. Malcom readied himself on his mark. Derrick forced himself to focus on the handoff. Henry and Malcolm were experienced. Derrick just needed to duplicate their technique once today. Surely, he could do that. Malcom started to move forward as Henry approached, reaching his arm back to retrieve the baton, eyes focused on Henry's approach. Everything slowed down for Derrick. He had experienced this before but did not know how to control it. He watched as the baton touched Malcom's palm. Malcolm closed his hand on the baton, pulling it away from Henry. Derrick saw Henry's eyes go wide.

As Malcolm's hand move forward, the baton came loose and tumbled on the track. Malcolm scrambled to retrieve it, kicking it further away as he reached down. When Malcolm took off, he was twenty yards behind. Derrick looked at Larry. Larry shook his head in disbelief.

Derrick felt certain he *could* duplicate that technique.

# 10

Derrick heard a groan from the crowd as Malcolm set off in chase of the other runners. Larry Kinkead issued a steady stream of cursing under his breath. Derrick's baton-dropping anxiety escalated into a full panic. No doubt in his mind that he would do the same thing. Maybe worse. Then one of those typical Pacific-Edge-Derrick-King thoughts weaved into his consciousness. *At least Malcolm dropped the baton first.*

Derrick turned to Larry, and said, "If Malcolm and Henry can't do it, I sure as hell can't. I'm going to do the same thing. Maybe if you hand it to me while we're both standing still."

Larry grabbed Derrick's upper arms with both hands. "You won't drop it. We're handing it off clean and fast. And we are going to do our best to win this thing. It's up to us. Got it?"

"Okay," Derrick said with more conviction than he felt.

"Get into position, King," Browning shouted.

Derrick forgot what lane he was supposed to be in and then saw other the runners were lined up based on their teammate's position. That made it easy for Derrick. Malcom was still last, but he had made up five yards on the next runner.

Malcolm was coming fast, the baton a blur. Derrick desperately wanted the slowdown thing to happen, but he could not control it. Sometimes it happened, sometimes it didn't. He started to move as Malcolm approached, slowly and then faster. He concentrated on the baton, and then he saw the dirt flying up from Malcolm's shoes, as if it were suspended in air for a moment. Malcolm was holding the baton straight out; it seemed almost stationary.

Derrick accelerated; Malcolm's eyes grew wide.

Already near his top running speed, Derrick snatched the baton.

Derrick ran hard. Too hard. His grip on the baton too tight; his other hand clinched into a fist. He wasn't breathing like Nyx taught him. When he realized he was not following his training, it was too late. Recovery was impossible. His only option was to continue the lap running like the true amateur he was. Despite his poor technique, he passed two runners and was within ten yards of the first three runners.

Rounding the corner, he saw Larry Kinkead waiting.

Larry nodded.

Derrick focused, remembering Larry's confidence that their hand off would be clean. Derrick stretched his arm forward, trying to hold the baton steady. The first attempt he missed Larry's hand. The second attempt, Derrick slapped the baton in Larry's palm. Larry grabbed the baton and sped off. Derrick felt like crying. He had not been perfect. His chest ached. He could have done better had he used better form.

As Derrick watched Larry, a hand landed firmly on his shoulder. "Bro, I'm so sorry."

Derrick turned to see Malcolm Cross, tears streaming down his cheeks.

"I screwed up, man."

It would be easy to be mad at Malcolm at that moment. Then he remembered that when Henry Clark tripped him, it was Malcolm who first extended a helping hand. Malcolm saved him from his own stupidity when Derrick tried to befriend Jim Priest. Derrick did not know how to comfort people, nor did he know what was appropriate to say, so he said, "It's okay. We lose together, and we win together." And then he did something unexpected. He gave Malcolm a hug before turning to watch as Larry entered the last turn.

The crowd was on its feet, screaming. Derrick found himself screaming too. Larry had caught the first four runners, but he was in trouble, having spent his energy catching the pack. Pain etched in Larry's face; he fought hard the last few yards but could not pass the third-place runner.

The team finished fourth. Derrick knew that without the mishap, Potterville could have won. Fourth meant they weren't on the podium. He hated not winning, and he let the feeling soak in. Not that he enjoyed losing, but he wanted to never forget being on a team.

*Winning together, losing together.*

Henry Clark slapped Larry on the back. "Dude, you did the best you could."

Derrick felt small in the scheme of things. His voice was insignificant, but he said, "Great job, Larry."

Larry gave his head a slight shake and then threw his arms around Derrick. "Bro, you got me into position to get fourth. You ran a better lap than I did. And that handoff rocked."

Derrick felt hands slap him on the back. Henry Clark said, "Hell of an effort, King."

Although Derrick could not see Malcolm, he knew Malcolm stood back, not feeling worthy to join them in celebration. Derrick wanted to reach out but felt his words would not be meaningful.

When the noise fell away, Henry looked at Malcolm and said, "I screwed up on the handoff. That's on me."

Derrick watched the handoff as if in slow motion. It was Malcolm's fault. Derrick felt certain that Henry knew that.

That was the moment that Derrick understood why everyone accepted Henry Clark as the leader of the football team. Henry shouldered the responsibility even when he was not responsible.

*So, that's what leadership looks like,* Derrick mused.

Malcolm smiled. "It was my fault and you know it, Henry."

"Shake it off. We win together and we lose together. Like they say, it's not how many times you get knocked down, it's how many times you get up that counts."

Malcolm extended his hand, which Henry grabbed in an odd handshake grasp that seemed normal here. "It won't happen again."

That's when Derrick remembered the 400-relay remained, which left another opportunity for him to screw up.

"If the love fest is over, follow me," Browning hollered.

The four relay runners followed Browning to the far end of the field beyond the goal posts. No fans or runners were nearby, although Akira, Miriam, and Rebekah had gathered about twenty yards away.

When they stopped, Browning said, "It's clear what went wrong. It happens. We'll work on passes next week. Other than that, exceptional performances. If you all duplicate that without a drop, we'll set a new state record. Shake it off, so we don't have a repeat performance in the next relay."

"Coach, will you tell us our individual times?" Henry asked.

"You know that I won't. This is a team event. I'll just say that all of you had great laps."

"Get ready, the 400 relay is up soon."

"Coach, why did they screw up the schedule?" Henry asked.

"I think the Fort Hill coach finagled it, but you didn't hear that from me."

Everyone shook their heads.

"Derrick, the girls would like to talk privately with you. Be quick about it." Browning nodded towards the three girls.

Derrick trotted to the girls, something dark forming in his chest.

"What's up?" Derrick asked.

Akira smiled, "Good job."

"Thanks," Derrick said.

Rebekah shook her head, "Still amazes me that you're doing this, and how well you're doing it."

"Doesn't surprise me," Miriam said.

Derrick looked at Miriam. "Why do you say that?"

"I'll explain later," Miriam said.

Then Miriam looked at Akira. "Could Rebekah and I have a minute with Derrick alone?"

Akira looked a bit hurt and then said, "Sure."

Akira walked to the stands; shoulders hunched.

"Was that necessary?" Derrick said. "I think you hurt her feelings."

"Yes, it was necessary, and she'll get over it," Miriam said.

"According to Akira, things will happen fast. Probably some sort of hearing about our staying here after the track meet," Miriam said.

"She said that?" Rebekah asked.

"Not in so many words," Miriam said. "Sounds like the counsel is split. A third want us gone immediately, a third wants us gone but feel they should help us relocate, and a third wants us to stay."

"I did not hear any of that," Rebekah said.

"Not in those exact words," Miriam said.

"We knew it was coming. We just didn't know when. Two-thirds want us gone, so it sounds like we are moving. Besides, I don't want to put people here at risk, even though I want to stay," Derrick said.

"Right, but that's not the important part," Miriam said.

"What's more important than our future?" Rebekah asked.

"We must stay here a few days. Akira can help me fix Jane."

# 11

MIRIAM HAD A ONE-TRACK MIND. How she could think about fixing a robot baffled him. But she was stuck there, sure as could be. He had to get her unstuck and focused on their survival. He did not know how he could accomplish that. Changing her mind now would not be any easier than it had been when they were in Pacific Edge. The only difference was back then she was right, and he didn't realize it. Now, he was right, and she would not admit it. Or so he thought, and he had been wrong more than right, so this might prove to be no different.

"What's wrong with you?" Rebekah asked.

"Nothing's wrong with me," Miriam said.

The lack of emotion in Miriam's voice troubled Derrick a little.

"I made a promise, and I plan to keep that promise," Miriam said.

"To a robot," Rebekah said, raising her voice and then looking around to ensure no one was nearby.

"To Charlie, yes. But there's more to it than that."

"You're the most stubborn, irrational …"

Derrick held up his hands. "Stop. Fighting won't help. Rebekah has a point. We have more important things to worry about than that robot."

"Charlie," Miriam corrected.

"Okay. Charlie," Derrick said. "But that does not change our situation. We need to focus on us. It seems obvious we are not staying here. I'm not afraid to go somewhere else. We'll figure it out. I'll get a job, we'll manage somehow. But we need to focus. If they would help us even a little that would be most helpful."

Miriam rolled her eyes. "Derrick, you are still short sighted as ever. We can't just leave. There's still the problem with making sure Reactor One doesn't melt down. If you care about these people, making it safe should be your priority. Plus, it does not matter where we go; we won't be safe. They will still hunt us. No place will protect us or provide a place to hide. I don't want to live the rest of my life in that complex, but it's better than being dead."

"They won't kill us. The Chosen don't have a death penalty," Rebekah said, and then added, "and what about Anna? Have you forgotten about her?"

"I don't know what they will do to you. They might not kill you. They might drop you off in the Arctic without a coat and let you walk home. But for Derrick and me, just getting killed would be better than what they plan to do to us. And, no, I have not forgotten about Anna."

"What does that mean, better than what they plan to do to us?" Derrick asked.

"I'll tell you later," Miriam said.

"I wish I had been writing this I'll tell you later stuff down. I've lost track of it all."

"Don't worry. I remember it. I never forget," Miriam said.

Derrick looked up and saw Browning waving him over.

"I have to go. Anything else?"

"We have to stall leaving. That might mean we have to show someone part of the facility. Be thinking of who you trust most," Miriam said.

Derrick shook his head. "Okay." He turned and walked toward Browning.

# 12

Derrick trotted towards the starting line. Runners were getting in their starting positions. The order for this race was different. Malcolm, being the fastest sprinter, would go last.

As Derrick started towards the second-runner position, Henry arrived and said, "Coach wants you to run the third leg."

The change made no sense. Henry held third position; Henry was faster than Derrick. Maybe Coach didn't trust the handoff between Henry and Malcolm because of the previous drop. Maybe it was something else. Perhaps it would be better if the team could attribute failure to Derrick. That made sense. The others would be here for the season; he was not.

Derrick started to ask why coach changed the order and then decided it didn't matter. Truth be told, the thought of dropping the baton terrified him more than it did in the mile.

"Relax. You're going to be fine. Just focus like you did in the mile." Henry stared into Derrick's eyes. "With me?"

Derrick nodded.

"You're going to rock it again," Malcolm said, grabbing Derrick's hand.

"Let's win this one," Derrick said.

Malcom nodded.

Henry, Derrick, and Malcolm moved their respective position around the track. Coach Browning was waiting at Derrick's position.

"You okay?" Browning asked.

Derrick nodded, nervous, but an odd feeling of trust crept into his mind. It made little sense, but he trusted his teammates.

A shot rang out; Larry bolted from the blocks. He appeared to be in fourth place as he approached Henry. They completed the handoff smooth and fast. Even at this distance, Derrick studied their movements, locked them in his memory. As Henry approached, everything slowed down again to the point Derrick felt eager to go, as if Henry was taking too long to arrive. Derrick estimated they were still in fourth position, which wasn't good because he was not as fast as Henry. Malcolm couldn't win if he started in fourth place. Even the slightest delay in the exchange would cost them the race.

The baton smacked Derricks' palm. Then the slow motion stopped.

Derrick ran. It felt like the fastest he had ever covered 100 meters. He passed one runner and was within a yard of the other two. When he reached Malcolm, things slowed down like they had before. Derrick felt confident the hand off could go well.

It did.

Derrick ran across the football field toward the finish line. He saw Henry and Larry running toward the finish as well. The race was over when they got there. From the angle, Derrick could not see who won, but he did not need to see it to know. The look of Malcolm's face told the story. Henry threw his arms around Malcolm. When the embrace ended, Larry grabbed Malcolm's hand in the grasp Derrick had learned was traditional among the team members. Then something unexpected happened. The three team members turned to Derrick and for a moment he thought he had done something wrong.

Henry said, "Derrick, that was the fastest I've ever seen you run."

Malcolm threw his arm around Derrick. After a brief hug, Malcolm stepped back and said, "Bro, you made it easy for me. What did I tell you about Browning? He's got a sixth sense about things."

Derrick did not know how to respond, so he smiled. Words were unnecessary. He recalled Malcolm's comments about Browning but had not given it much thought at the time.

Browning arrived and said, "Fantastic! That keeps us in the hunt for the overall win. Derrick, Miriam wants to see you again." He pointed toward the stands. "Be quick and meet us at the goal posts." Browning pointed toward the south end zone.

Derrick jogged to Miriam. "What is it?"

"Go get Nyx," Miriam said.

"What?"

"No time to explain," Miriam said.

Derrick did as she asked. He wondered when there would be time for her to explain things to him. In this case, he would understand quickly enough.

Nyx watched as he ran her direction. She looked sad in a way he had never noticed before. Except maybe the time they met on the mountain, and he failed to be truthful. He had blocked the sadness of leaving so that it did not consume him. The look on Nyx's face brought him to the brink of a downward spiral into a dark depression.

"Miriam wants to talk to you," Derrick said as he reached Nyx.

"Can't it wait?" Nyx asked.

"I don't think so," Derrick said.

"What's it about?" Nyx asked.

Derrick shrugged. "I don't know."

Nyx rolled her eyes. "Better be important."

Derrick and Nyx ran to where Miriam stood. "What is it? We have to meet with Browning."

"How is the meet scored?"

"You called me over here for that?"

"I did. How is it scored?"

"It's complicated."

"Does that mean you don't know, or you don't understand?" Miriam asked.

"I understand it. But why do you want to know?"

"You said you don't have time, so stop wasting it and tell me," Miriam said.

Nyx looked at Derrick; frustration etched in her face.

Derrick shrugged.

Nyx explained the scoring. Derrick understood about half of it before she lost him.

When Nyx finished, Miriam looked at the ground for a moment and then said, "Is cross-country the only event left?"

"They are finishing the pole vault, but we don't have anyone competing," Nyx said.

"I can see that," Miriam said. "So, answer my question."

Nyx frowned. "Yes."

"Akira said you will win the girls' cross-country. How good are the Potterville runners in the boys' event?" Miriam asked.

"We don't have a runner in the boy's event."

"I'm going to run," Derrick said.

"Coach won't let you," Nyx said.

"Why not? I feel fine."

"Too dangerous given the Pacific Edge threat."

"How important is it for the team to win the event?" Miriam asked.

Nyx shrugged. "We always want to win. Why?"

"Because Potterville has to win both the girls and boys cross-country to win the overall," Miriam said.

"What makes you think so?" Nyx asked.

"You just told me," Miriam said.

"Huh?"

"You told me how they score the event; I calculated the score. Potterville needs first place in both the cross-country events to win," Miriam said.

"How did you calculate that?"

"I kept track of the events in my head," Miriam said.

"That's impossible. We have to go."

Miriam grabbed Nyx by the arm.

For a moment, Derrick thought Nyx might slap Miriam.

"You didn't answer my question. How import is it that the team win?"

"For god's sake. In the overall scheme of things, not important enough to risk Derrick's life."

"Well, it's important to my brother. Convince Browning to let him run."

Nyx said nothing. But somehow Derrick understood the girls exchanged a mystical girl-only transfer of information before Miriam released Nyx's arm.

They jogged toward the team grouped at the end zone. To Derrick's surprise, when they slowed to a walk, Nyx snaked her arm inside his as they approached Browning. Antonio stood next to Browning on one side, Sheriff Collins on the other. Derrick thought Collin's presence was a little strange. Antonio caught Derrick's eye, smiled, and winked.

Nyx pulled Derrick close. She stood on tiptoes and whispered, "Good job today. I'm proud of you."

Derrick never felt more confused.

"Listen up. One event left, cross-country. They are setting up spotters on the course. You've all done great. I've crunched the numbers. Assuming Nyx wins — sorry to put pressure on you Nyx — it looks like we will finish in second place. Fort Hill is in first place."

Nyx whispered, "I'll be damned, Miriam nailed it."

"What if we win the boys' cross-country," Derrick asked.

"We don't have a runner in boys' cross-country," Browning said.

"Yes, you do. I'm running it," Derrick said.

"I appreciate your spirit, son, but that's not possible," Browning said.

"Why isn't it possible. I feel fine," Derrick said.

"It's not about that," Browning said. "It's not safe. It was risky enough bringing you guys here. But we figured Pacific Edge wouldn't try anything in the stadium with this many people." Browning paused. "Sheriff Collins won't allow you out on the course."

Browning glanced at Collins.

Antonio nodded his head as if in sage agreement, as did Sheriff Collins.

"I can take care of myself," Derricks said, and without further understanding, knew he spoke the truth. "I'm running."

"King, I'm the coach. I say who runs."

"Sorry, coach. I didn't mean for it to sound like that. Let's be honest. This is likely my last event as a Potterville High student. Please, coach. Let me run." Tears streamed down his cheeks; Derrick did not care.

Browning looked at Collins.

Collins shook his head. "Damn it. We already discussed this."

"We go back a long way, Bill. I don't often ask for favors, but I'm asking for one now," Browning said.

Collins ran his hand over his head. "Shit. I can have a car follow him. No guarantees."

Browning looked at Derrick. "Son, if something happened to you, I don't know if I could forgive myself."

"Please, coach," Derrick said, sobbing.

"Let him run," Nyx said. "He deserves the chance."

"I don't like it. Not one bit. But I'll add your name to the cross-country," Browning said. Looking at Nyx, Browning added, "If you have any advice for him, now's the time to give it."

Derrick wiped his face.

Nyx pulled him away from the group and walked towards the starting line. "Things will happen fast after the event. I wanted to warn you. I realize the timing isn't great."

"I understand," Derrick said.

"I also need to tell you I'll be involved, but how I feel about — us — can't interfere. I'm sorry."

"It's okay. I don't want to put you or anyone else at risk. We are not your problem. Miriam and I will figure out what to do. Mostly, Miriam will figure it out."

"It's important you be honest."

"I won't lie. But there are things I can't talk about," Derrick said.

"Won't talk about," Nyx corrected.

"That too."

Nyx sighed. "I hoped you'd trust me."

"I trust you, but I won't put you at risk. So, do you have any advice for me?"

"Yes. Try to block this conversation from your mind." She winked and smiled weakly. "Run your own race and you'll be fine. Winning isn't everything. Doing your best is."

Derrick nodded.

Nyx stretched.

Derrick watched her and copied her routine. It occurred to him this would be their last run together. He wanted to run at her side, but he understood he had to run faster. He had no illusion he could win; although winning would be a fantastic way to end his brief track career.

But he would finish knowing he'd done his best. That was the only thing over which he had control.

The starter explained the route, how it would be marked and monitored. One lap around the track, outside to the course, and then two laps when they returned.

The race wasn't a sprint. No need to get into the blocks. Derrick lined up next to Nyx. "See you after the race."

Nyx said nothing; she gave him a slight nod.

When the gun fired, Derrick took off. He focused on his pace. He wished he had paid more attention to what his pace was for this distance and wondered how good the other boys in the race were. Did he have a chance or was he up against the best cross-country runner in the state of California? Derrick had no concept of what it meant to be competing against the best. That was good. It would have overwhelmed him. Last thing he needed was to be overwhelmed. He needed to focus on this one lap, followed by one block, followed by another until he was back at the school, and then two laps.

As they exited the track, Derrick trailed two other boys. The pace felt right. He did not have a strategy. That was a mistake. The closest thing to a strategy was what Henry Clark had told him about the 400-meters and how Larry would start too fast. He wondered if he was going too fast now.

A sheriff's deputy followed him. Derrick resisted the urge to watch the sky and analyze the faces he passed looking for someone from Pacific Edge. They would not come in the open, of that he was sure. Later he would remember how consistently he thought he knew such things.

At the half-way point, Derrick remained in third place. The first-place runner had separated himself from the second-place runner. Both runners were from Fort Hill. Derrick thought they might work together to ensure that one would win. It didn't matter. Derrick had to run his own race. He decided his own race meant he'd stay close enough to first place so he could try to pass him near the end. So far, that felt right. Running with ease, breathing steady, legs strong.

As they neared the school, Derrick had lost ground on the first-place runner but remained close to the second-place guy, but the effects of the previous races sapped his energy. His legs ached and breathing became difficult. He could not suck in enough air. It did not feel like he had total control of his muscles as fatigue grew with each step. That would prove to be the culprit.

When Derrick entered the track, the people in the stands stood and cheered. It was time to make his move. He picked up the pace. The runner in front of him did the same. It was good Derrick did not know the guy in second place won district last year. Derrick moved within a stride or two and matched his pace. They were reeling in the leader. The Fort Hill guys had a plan. The leader hoped to suck Derrick into a pace too fast, too soon. They failed. Derrick felt good about that.

That feeling would not last long.

Without warning, Derrick's left foot landed crooked.

His ankle collapsed.

In pain, he hit the track so fast he did not have time to catch himself.

He coiled up, grabbing at his leg, curling in a fetal position. He felt warm liquid on his face.

Then he heard a voice screaming. *"GET UP!"*

That voice was in his head.

Derrick struggled to his feet. He saw Browning running towards him. Derrick waved him off, taking a step. White-hot pain coursed through his ankle, and for a moment, he thought he would go down again.

Then Derrick saw the leader enter the first turn.

Derrick ran, wobbling as he staggered on his injured ankle.

Each step got a little stronger, although he felt like one leg was longer than the other. He gritted his teeth, forcing a faster pace. He caught the second-place runner, passing him. Derrick focused on the leader. Catching him would not be easy. The guy he passed was spent. That kid would be lucky to not get passed by more runners before he reached the finish. If he reached the finish.

Derrick had no guarantee of reaching the finish either. His ankle burned as if someone had poked a hot metal rod into the joint. His lungs ached and were incapable of supplying enough oxygen to his throbbing muscles. But what did that matter? This was the last lap of his brief Potterville High track experience. Derrick vowed one simple thing. At the finish, if he got there, he would have nothing left to give. Then, and only then, could he say he had done his best. His best is what he promised to give. That was a promise he intended to keep.

For the next twenty yards, Derrick matched the leader's pace, which under the circumstances was extraordinary, but that was not going to win this race.

He emptied his mind, focusing only on the finish line and him crossing it first.

Then Derrick ran faster.

As they started the last lap, Derrick had gained five yards on the leader.

Derrick ran faster.

Entering the last turn, Derrick had pulled within two yards. The leader glanced over his shoulder; eyes wide. The leader had nothing left to give. Derrick searched deep and found he had just a little more.

Derrick ran faster.

Had he glanced at the stands, he would have seen the crowd on its feet, the din deafening. But he neither saw nor heard them. He only saw the finish line. Ten yards to the finish, Derrick passed the leader.

Derrick won his first individual race, while running his last.

# 13

DERRICK HAD FORGOTTEN ABOUT HIS ANKLE. That changed. He limped onto the grass; his ankle felt as if someone had driven a hot metal spike into it, throbbing like an amplified heartbeat. Falling to his hands and knees, desperate to suck air; he felt certain that he would heave up anything remaining in his stomach. As his senses returned, he heard a loud roar. Looking up, he saw a horde of people running toward him. Miriam led the group. Officials attempted to keep people off the track as other runners were coming into the stadium.

Browning knelt beside Derrick. "Are you okay, son? My God, what a finish. Never seen anything like it."

"I'm okay," Derrick squeaked.

Browning helped Derrick to his feet; Derrick almost collapsed when he tried to put weight on his foot.

"Easy. We need a chair!" Browning shouted.

Opposite Coach Browning, Henry Clark put Derrick's arm around his shoulder. "Dude, you're an iron man."

"I don't feel like an iron man," Derrick said.

Rebekah arrived with a blue plastic chair.

With Browning and Henry Clark's help, Derrick eased into the chair.

A crowd formed around him, everyone talking at once. Derrick could not make out what anyone said. He heard amazing, congratulations, awesome, and wow. Lots of wows.

Miriam knelt in front of Derrick. "Proud of you, brother."

"Thanks, sis. That means a lot to me." Then Derrick said, "Where is Nyx?"

"She's on her last lap," Henry Clark said.

"Is she going to win?" Derrick asked.

"The second-place girl just entered the stadium," Henry said.

Derrick said nothing. But what he felt amazed him, thrilled more for Nyx than he was himself.

In a few minutes, Nyx made her way to Derrick, the crowd parting for her. Still out of breath, she said, "I take it you did okay."

"He did more than okay. The most fantastic finish I've ever seen," Henry said.

Nyx looked at Henry and then to Derrick. "Sorry I missed it."

"I recorded it," Akira said, squeezing in next to Nyx.

"Great," Nyx said.

Nyx sounded sad. Derrick admitted long ago he lacked the skill of reading others. And his lack of the skill amplified with Nyx. But he did not think he was wrong this time. His happiness faded.

He assumed the glory of victory did not last long, even under normal circumstances. But he felt sure it should last longer than this. But their situation was too grave to feel good.

As the runners entered and finished, the people filtered away from Derrick. Most left. A few went back to the stands. Most of those remaining looked like parents waiting for students.

"Henry, can you and Malcolm help Derrick inside? Go to my classroom. Keep everyone else out but those who need to attend," Browning said.

With Henry on one side and Malcom on the other, Derrick limped to the school. When they got inside, down the hallway next to the gym, they entered a classroom. Malcolm directed Derrick to sit on a table. Henry unlaced his shoe, pulling it off carefully. Derrick winced.

Rebekah pulled up a chair. "I'm going to pull your sock off. I'll be careful."

Derrick nodded. He wondered why Rebekah was doing this. Then remembered that she played soccer. Maybe she had experience with such injuries.

"Can someone bring ice?" Rebekah asked.

"Nyx is getting it," Henry said.

When the sock came off, Derrick looked down to see his ankle swollen, turning shades of blue and purple. It occurred to him that an injury was not good given their circumstances.

Nyx came in with the ice in a plastic bag. She stared at Rebekah for a moment, but Rebekah remained seated, hand outstretched, waiting for Nyx to handover the bag.

Rebekah held the ice to his ankle. "This will keep the swelling down. I've twisted my ankle plenty of time in soccer."

"Thanks," Derrick said. Otherwise the room was quiet. Too quiet for a bunch of kids who won a competition. This must be the council meeting. Nyx said it would happen soon, but this surprised him. He took inventory of the room. The table on which he sat was wooden and old, there were standard student desks — plastic chairs with a single plastic piece used to write on in the front, more of a torture device than a piece of furniture conducive to learning — and these desks seemed in worse condition than those in the other classrooms. At the front of the room was a board on which teachers wrote; Derrick had learned they called it a blackboard, but this was green like most of the ones in the other classrooms. He had not yet found an explanation of how they named things. On the blackboard were Xs and Os aligned across from each other. The drawing looked familiar, but pain and exhaustion robbed him of what meager analytical skills he normally possessed.

Henry Clark stood at the door. Others in the room, besides himself, Miriam, and Rebekah included Malcolm, Larry, Akira, and Nyx. A knock sounded at the door. Not a normal knock, but a distinctive pattern. Three fast raps, silence, followed by two slower raps. Henry unlocked the door, peering through a thin slat, shoulder braced as if he might have to force it shut.

Henry opened the door. Antonio entered on crutches. Derrick noticed that Akira wrote on a yellow pad. Henry scanned the hallway, closed, and locked the door.

Antonio came to where Derrick sat. He handed his crutches to Miriam, backed up to the table, and with both hands lifted himself next to Derrick. "Bro, you do keep life interesting."

"It's never my plan," Derrick said.

"Poor entrance, but fantastic finish." Antonio shook his head as he looked down at Derrick's ankle. "People speculated your ankle wasn't a bad injury to run like you did. I can see they were wrong. How did you manage that with a sprained ankle?"

Derrick shrugged. "I don't know. I did what I had to do."

A loud knock sounded at the door. Not like the knock Malcolm used. Two raps. Malcolm sprang out of a desk, sending it crashing on its side, and rushed to the door. Henry opened it a crack. Malcolm braced himself against the door.

Derrick looked at Antonio. Antonio stared at the door; his face as solemn as Derrick had ever seen it.

Henry said, "It's the doc."

Nyx said, "Let him in."

Henry said, "But …"

"It's okay. I knew he was coming," Nyx said.

Derrick wished he understood the dynamics of this group. Nyx, it seemed, was the leader. He now understood how badly he had bungled his time here. He wanted to tell Nyx the truth earlier, and he should have. She might have been able to convince the others to let them stay. According to Miriam, two-thirds want them gone. His chest tightened. He had hoped for one more trip to the bistro, one more hour with Nyx, one more chance to apologize; although he could never sincerely make it up to her.

Doctor Phillips walked to Derrick, pulled out a chair, and said, "Let's see what you've done to yourself."

A knock came at the door, same as Malcolm's.

Henry peered out and then let Coach Browning and Sheriff Collin's enter.

Doc Phillips motioned Rebekah to remove the ice. "Whose idea was it to put ice on it?"

Rebekah turned slightly red in the face. "I did."

"Well done. Exactly the right thing to do."

"I played soccer where I came from," Rebekah said, glancing at Browning.

Doc Phillips chuckled. "I'll wager you were good at it too."

"I still am," Rebekah said.

Phillips pressed on Derrick's ankle, moved his foot from side to side, back and forth. Derrick winced but made no sounds. After several minutes, Doc Phillips said, "A nasty sprain. I heard you ran the last two laps on this ankle. That true?"

"Yes," Derrick said.

Phillips looked at Antonio as if he did not believe Derrick.

"Never saw nothing like it, Doc," Antonio said.

"Son, you must have one hell of a pain tolerance," Doc said.

Derrick shrugged. "Team needed a win."

Browning put a hand on Derrick's shoulder. "Potterville won the event by one point."

Derrick heard a loud crack behind him. He turned to see Nyx standing in front of the blackboard in front of a dark brown lectern.

"A quorum of the student town council is present. At issue is the disposition of Derrick King, Miriam King, and Rebekah Ford."

Browning held up his hand. "Sorry to do this, but I'm pulling rank and cancelling this meeting."

"We talked about this earlier," Nyx said.

"I know. But it can wait. The team won. Let's take one day to enjoy that before we do this."

The room was silent for a moment.

"It's not a request," Browning said.

Antonio slid off the desk, grabbing his crutches from Miriam. "Works for me. Manana, amigos."

# 14

SHERIFF COLLINS AND COACH BROWNING WALKED with Derrick, Miriam, and Rebekah. Derrick limped, but his ankle felt better than he'd expected. Rebekah had taped it while Doc Phillips watched. Derrick hoped to spend time with Nyx, but Nyx said she had things to do. That changed Derrick's mood. Browning asked if they wanted to stop at the bistro for something to eat. Derrick didn't feel up to it, so he said they'd eat at his condo. Collins told Derrick if they wanted to go to the bistro later to call him, and he'd have someone escort them. There would be an officer patrolling the area anyway. It would not be a problem.

At the condo, Miriam went straight to the computer. Derrick wasn't hungry. Although it was midafternoon, the refrigerator had few options, so he cooked eggs, bacon, and pancakes. He served Rebekah a plate and the scent of bacon changed his mind and he cooked more for himself. After he finished eating, he had already cooked plenty of bacon for Miriam but cooked eggs and pancakes, and then went to get her.

Miriam sat staring at the computer monitor. She had the email program open. "What are you doing?" Derrick asked.

"Had to check some things. Now, I'm trying to decide what to do about these." Miriam pointed at three unopened emails. He recognized one as an advertisement for insurance he had also received. The other two he did not recognize. They were from an ajpatel@fastmail.com. The subject on one read "Trust me" the second read "It's about Anna."

"I know the first one. It's advertisement for insurance. What are the other two? Are they from the guy in Pacific Edge?" Derrick asked, leaning over her shoulder.

"Yes. And Not sure."

"Are you going to read them?" Derrick asked.

"No, could be a trap. If I open them, he'll know. Until then, he doesn't know if I've seen them, if he has reached me, or if I'm even alive," Miriam said.

"I cooked you some food," Derrick said.

"It smells wonderful. I have a couple of things to check, and then I'll be out," Miriam said.

"Okay. Don't be long, or it will be cold," Derrick said.

"I'll be done soon," Miriam said.

Derrick headed to the door.

"Derrick?"

He turned around. "Yeah?"

"Can you contact Akira?"

"I can," Derrick said.

Miriam said, "Ask her if she can come here. Alone."

Derrick wanted to ask why she had to come alone but decided he might not want to know. He did not want to know anything right now. He felt numb and wanted to stay that way. Numb felt like a luxury. He was correct about that. A luxury that would not last long.

"Okay," Derrick said.

Returning to the kitchen, Derrick fixed a coffee. He decided to text Akira rather than call. He didn't want to talk, nor did he want Rebekah to hear his conversation because Rebekah would ask questions. He didn't want to talk to Rebekah either.

Akira agreed to come and said she would be there in ten minutes. Derrick drank coffee alone in the kitchen. Rebekah seemed to sense that he wasn't up to conversation, or maybe she wasn't up to it. He didn't know. He didn't care.

Sensing ten minutes had passed, Derrick walked to the door, peaked through the peephole, and saw Akira approaching. He opened the door before she knocked. Derrick pointed and said, "Miriam is in there."

When Akira had left the room, Rebekah said, "What's that about?"

"I don't know. Miriam wanted to talk to her. She didn't tell me why. I didn't ask because I'm tired of hearing, 'no time to explain it now.'"

"Miriam has been more distracted than usual since we got here. I've wondered what's going on in her head, but I also don't want to know," Rebekah said.

Derrick nodded. "Agreed."

Miriam and Akira came out of the room he called a study. "Derrick, can you and Rebekah go get Nyx and bring her here?"

Derrick said, "She lives downstairs. I can get her myself."

"I want you to both go," Miriam said and then added, "safer that way. I'll eat while you get her."

Derrick shrugged. He didn't feel like arguing, not that it would have done any good. Apparently, Rebekah felt the same.

The door opened. Nyx had changed out of her track clothing. Derrick realized he had not and felt inappropriately dressed. Nyx wore pink sweatpants and a gray sweatshirt. Derrick tried to not smile. This was not a happy time. Smiling was inappropriate.

"What's up?" Nyx said. "I don't feel up to going out, if that's what you're here for."

"Miriam and Akira want you to come up to the condo," Derrick said.

"Why is Akira there?" Nyx asked.

"Miriam asked her to come," Derrick said.

Nyx took a deep breath and sighed. "Okay. Why is she here?" Nyx pointed at Rebekah.

"Miriam thought it would be safer if two of us came," Derrick said.

"Why didn't you just send me a text?" Nyx asked.

Derrick shrugged. "I don't know. I should have. Miriam asked me to get you, so I did."

They did not talk as they climbed the stairs. At his condo, Derrick held the door open for Rebekah and Nyx. The plate he fixed for Miriam sat uneaten on the kitchen counter. "They're probably in the study." Derrick pointed.

Nyx walked into the study and then came right back. "Not there."

Derrick felt the color drain from his face. He rushed to the bedroom. Not there either, and the bathroom door stood open.

Miriam and Akira were gone.

# 15

## Saturday, April 3, 4:25 p.m.

DERRICK RAN INTO HIS BEDROOM, GRABBED clothes, and changed. He suspected where Miriam went but found it hard to believe. Yet believing it was not difficult. She had been secretive since she found him in the mountains and distant all day, mind elsewhere. He knew she was capable of instant calculations, contemplated things he barely understood, and predicted events as if she saw the future. That she had been so preoccupied, scared him.

When Derrick exited his bedroom, Nyx said, "Where the hell did they go? Akira knows better."

"Maybe to the bistro?" Rebekah offered.

Derrick wasn't optimistic but said, "Maybe."

"I need to change," Nyx said. "Stay put and I'll be right back. Can you do that?"

"If you're fast about it," Derrick said.

"I'll be fast. Damn fast."

The door slammed shut.

"Do you think they went to the bistro?" Rebekah asked.

"No," Derrick said.

"Me neither," Rebekah agreed.

"See if she took that zapper thing," Derrick said.

Derrick considered leaving while Rebekah looked for the stun thing, but decided he needed her. He did not however need Nyx. Not that he didn't need Nyx, but he didn't want her exposed to the danger they were about to face. They had to leave before Nyx returned. Frantically, he looked around for anything he could use as a weapon. Nothing came to mind other than a pan, and all the pans here were lightweight. He had no heavy metal pans like Donna used at the bistro.

Rebekah raced back into the room. She tossed his jacket at him. She wore hers and had her bag slung over her shoulder. "It's gone. Also, her bag, flashlight, and other gear."

"Let's get out of here," Derrick said.

"What about Nyx?"

"We don't need her," Derrick said, opening the door.

Nyx stood in the hall; she tossed a silver bar thing, which Derrick caught.

"What's this?" Derrick asked.

"Baseball bat," Nyx said.

"Baseball?"

"It's a sport," Nyx said.

"I know what baseball is, what's the bat for?"

"Only weapon I could think of. Where do you think you're going?" Nyx asked.

"Just heading to the bistro. I thought we could meet there," Derrick said.

"Bullshit," Nyx said. "You were leaving without me."

"No, honest," Rebekah said.

"That's not true," Derrick admitted. "We were leaving without you." He looked down at his feet. "The part about the bistro was a lie, too. Sorry."

"Where are you going?"

"I can't tell you," Derrick said.

"You mean you won't tell me."

"That too."

"Well, guess what? I'm going and you can't stop me. Unless you think it's not important to look for Miriam."

Derrick wanted to argue. He even considered locking Nyx in the condo, but he could not think of a way to do that. All the locks were on the wrong side of the door. He could not outrun her. A bad thing about having feelings for a track star.

"I don't want you to go. It's too dangerous. Better if Rebekah and I go ourselves."

Nyx studied Derrick for a moment. "Is that the truth?"

Derrick felt a weight lift from his shoulders. She believed him, and he was telling the truth. Nyx had accepted that it was too dangerous for her to go. "Yes, I swear it is true. Thanks for understanding. If we don't come back, don't let anyone look for us."

"I said, I believe you. I didn't say I changed my mind. Three is better than two."

"There's more to it." Derrick paused, mind searching for how much to reveal. They might catch Miriam and Akira before they entered the passage to the hidden canyon.

"Promise that you won't tell anyone what you see."

"I can't promise that," Nyx said.

Derrick thought hard. The burden of the facility, which Miriam had tried to explain, weighed upon him now like the doomsday machine that it was. "Then, we can't go."

"Huh? You understand that Miriam is in danger?"

"I do," Derrick said, his shoulders slumping, the bat sliding through his hand, hitting the floor with a dull thud.

Nyx's eyes darted between Derrick and Rebekah. "Rebekah, can you talk sense into him?"

"The problem is, much as I hate to admit it, he's right. We didn't mean for this to happen. I wished it had not. I wish we'd taken our chances crossing the mountain."

"Shit," Nyx said. She crossed her arms and glared at Derrick. "Okay. I promise."

"Let's go then," Derrick said.

In the hall, Rebekah grabbed Derrick's arm. "You want this?" She held the stun gun.

"No. I'll use this." He held up the bat. "I'll look like the greatest threat. If you get a chance — if there's a problem, that is — perhaps you can sneak up while I distract them."

"There will be a problem of that much I'm certain. Miriam has a knack of finding trouble. It's fully charged and on the highest setting," Rebekah said, sticking the stun gun into her bag.

"Would that thing kill someone?" Nyx asked.

Rebekah shrugged. "I don't think so."

"Should you turn it down a little?" Nyx asked.

"I don't think so. Depends on the threat. I'll decide when the time comes."

Derrick did not pause at the bistro. He could not help but glance at the guitar shop to see if the old Martin still hung in the window. It did, which for no sensible reason, gave him a bit of comfort. Remembering that Rebekah played soccer and was probably in as good of physical condition as he and Nyx, he started running toward the river. He wobbled a bit on his ankle but blocked most of the discomfort from his mind. Miriam and Akira would have moved quickly, but they would not have been running, he was sure of that.

"You should not be running," Nyx said.

"I'm okay. It's not hurting much," Derrick said. If he could catch Miriam before she reached the hidden canyon, then Nyx wouldn't know about it. And not knowing was best. Nyx had a life and a future. She would set records, go to college, and eventually marry. To someone she wanted, not chosen from some list based on criteria set by a group of old men. He had no future. Not in Pacific Edge. Not in Potterville. Not with

Nyx. His future, if he lived that long, was playing chess with a robot named Charlie. Why Miriam would risk Akira's future baffled him. Perhaps the stress had become too much for Miriam. Derrick picked up the pace.

"Slow down. You'll make your injury worse," Nyx said.

"I'm okay," Derrick said, sprinting now. Something told him they were running out of time.

A slight glimmer of hope rose in his chest. Miriam's 1984 tracking chip no longer functioned after two jolts from the stun gun. The security cameras in the condo no longer worked. Paul checked them and found they had been disconnected. He could catch Miriam before the canyon. He felt certain of that.

Then something occurred to him. *Who installed the cameras?* Derrick had not suspected Paul. However, if Paul did it, then he could be lying about the camera's being disconnected, and if that were the case, Pacific Edge might have seen Miriam leave and then jumped at their chance to capture her.

Then something else occurred to him. *Akira still has a 1984 chip.*

They reached the river bridge. At the foot of the bridge, Derrick held his finger to his lips.

"Where are we going?" Nyx whispered.

"You'll know when you see it? It's important that we be quiet from here forward." Derrick looked at Rebekah. She nodded, held up the stun gun. Derrick repositioned his hands on the bat.

At the top of the bridge, Derrick saw no one on the path. He moved swiftly. The ground covered with soft leaves, slightly damp from rising moisture of the forest floor provided a path designed for stealth, perhaps nature's way of giving predators a chance. As they neared the meadow, he looked to the mountain ridge that concealed the enormous steel doors that protected the hidden canyon. Above the trees, the doors were visible, but only if you knew they were there.

Then the meadow came into view.

The situation, worse than he expected.

# 16

Derrick motioned the girls to be silent and stay put. Inching through the trees for a better view, his heard pounded in his chest. In the meadow, close to where Pacific Edge security officers captured him, sat a black aircraft on the path. On the other side of the craft, a black figure stood near Miriam and Akira. Miriam had sheltered Akira behind herself. Miriam's hand was in her bag, but she had not displayed the stun gun she carried.

The craft was not Pacific Edge Security. It was unlike any craft he had ever seen. Flat black, not an open platform like a hovercraft, but an angular-shaped machine that looked as if it could carry four or five people. No markings except for a single gray P on its side; a large rear door open.

Although the black figure was twenty-five yards away, Derrick could see that it was not a man. It was a robot, but not like Charlie the robot. Charlie looked more like a kid's idea of what a robot should look like. They built this machine like a man, except it was not a man. The machine and Miriam were in a discussion, but their voices were too low for Derrick to hear.

Miriam shook her head.

Because Derrick and Rebekah were absent, perhaps the machine would leave. Possibly, the machine meant no harm. But Derrick did not know. Because there were many other possible outcomes, he was unwilling to take the risk. He could not guarantee action would result in success. But he felt time was running out.

He motioned Rebekah to move behind him. He wished Nyx had stayed at the condo. None of them should be here; he should have recognized Miriam's distraction, sending him to get Nyx.

Derrick crouched and moved swiftly to the edge of the aircraft. Because the door was open, he could see through the window where the machine stood talking to Miriam. There were no additional robots in the craft. He motioned Rebekah to the other side of the craft. She nodded her understanding. He held his hand out to Nyx, indicating she should say. He mouthed, "I'll go first."

Rebekah nodded. The stun gun held in her hand, a green light glowing. Nyx pinched her lips together and shook her head.

Derrick eased around the craft. He wasn't sure he could sneak up on the thing. Maybe it had sensors that would detect his approach. If it recognized a threat coming, he was certain he'd have no chance.

He had less than ten yards to cross. Running at the machine, he pulled the bat back and hit it in the head as hard as he could.

The machine rocked slightly, and then the head spun backwards; its eyes turned from glowing green to blazing red.

Instinctively, Derrick fell to the ground.

A sizzling sound and a flash of red streaked above him filling the space he had occupied. With all his strength, he swept his legs at the machine's feet, sending the robot to the ground. The robot flailed for a moment before flipping over. Swinging the bat one-handed, Derrick smacked in again in the back of the head and then rolled and kicked it's arm out from under it causing it to topple back to the ground.

Rebekah leaped over his back, electricity already arcing between the gun's probes. She held the gun to the machine's head. An instant later, Miriam held her gun to the machine's back.

Arcs of electricity crawled up and down the machine for several seconds. When the girls withdrew their devices, it lay lifeless on the ground. Miriam jumped on its back, tossing her gun to the ground. She struggled with something and then pulled a black box from the machine, tossing the box to the side.

"Help me roll it over," Miriam said.

Derrick jumped up and grabbed a shoulder, Miriam pushed on its torso. Nyx helped, lifting on its leg. The machine flopped over and Miriam studied its chest. After a moment, she flipped four small levers. A black rectangular shape rose from what previously looked like solid metal. She removed a black box, walked to her bag, and placed it inside.

Nyx glared at Akira. "Why did you come out here and why didn't you contact me first?"

"There wasn't time," Akira said.

Before Nyx could speak, Derrick said, "What is that stuff?"

"I think that one is its power source." Miriam pointed towards the object she tossed on the ground. Lifting the bag, she said, "And this is its brain."

"It looked like you were having a conversation with it," Derrick said.

"I was," Miriam said.

"What about?" Derrick asked.

Nyx and Rebekah stood on either side of Derrick. Akira stepped to Miriam's side.

Miriam looked at Akira. Akira wiped tears from her eyes and gave her shoulders a slight shrug.

Finally, Miriam said, “It wanted Anna Ford.”

# 17

Rebekah dropped her stun gun. Miriam kicked the robot's head before walking to Rebekah where she threw her arms around her friend. Derrick looked at Nyx. Nyx seemed confused. Derrick shared the feeling. Rebekah had already expressed concern about Anna, and Derrick remained confused about Rebekah's true motive for being here. Rebekah said she just wanted out of Pacific Edge. That never settled with him as a solid explanation. She must have given leaving a lot of thought; yet, she did not factor in the impact of leaving her family, especially Anna.

Between sobs, Rebekah said, "Are you sure it asked for Anna? That makes little sense."

Nyx moved next to Derrick, stepping up on tiptoe, she whispered, "Who's Anna?"

"Rebekah's sister."

"Absolutely certain," Miriam said.

"But why?"

"They think Anna escaped with us," Miriam said.

Rebekah sobbed, her body heaving with each breath.

Seeing Rebekah in such pain hurt in Derrick's chest. He knew who Anna was, but he'd never paid attention to the girl. *What sort of person doesn't know the sister of a girl he might marry?* Beyond all that, Derrick did not like being confused. And he could not imagine feeling more confused than he did at this moment. In his state of bewilderment, he still managed one clear thought, which he shared. "Guys, I know this is important, but what are we going to do with these?" He pointed at the robot sprawled on the ground and the flying machine sitting in the meadow.

"I don't care about the damn things," Rebekah sobbed. "Where is Anna? I have to find her."

Miriam shook her head and whispered in Rebekah's ear. Rebekah nodded. Miriam whispered again.

Rebekah stood, took a deep breath, wiped her face with the sleeve of her jacket.

Miriam turned back to the others. "We can't help Anna if we're captured. I suspect they can track the aircraft, but not the robot, because the robot is dead. It won't take them long to figure out something is wrong. They might already have reinforcements on the way. If that is the case, then it might be too late already."

"We should make a run for it. Back to town where we can get help," Nyx said.

"No time," Rebekah said, suppressing a sob.

"Now she's doing it," Derrick said.

"Doing what?" Nyx said.

"Saying no time," Derrick said.

"That's what Akira said, too." Nyx threw up her hands.

"Exactly," Derrick said.

"I give up," Nyx said.

"Don't do that," Miriam said. "We don't have time."

Nyx grabbed her hair and groaned.

"Turn off your cell phones. Completely off," Miriam said.

"Why?" Nyx asked.

"So, they can't track us. Do it now, or we don't go any farther," Miriam said.

Nyx pulled out her phone and powered off. Akira did not reach for her phone; Miriam probably told her to turn it off earlier.

Miriam knelt by the robot, examining it. Then she stood and walked to the aircraft. Everyone followed her. Miriam sat in what appeared to be the pilot's seat. She touched the control panel in front of her and lights appeared. On the panel, a headset hung in a holder. She put the headset on.

With the strange-looking goggles on her head, she pushed at the control panel buttons, flipped some switches. After a few minutes, she took the goggles off and screamed, "RUN!"

Derrick made sure Akira, Rebekah, and Nyx were outside before he left. He was sure Miriam was right behind him; they ran for the trees. Miriam apparently pushed a wrong button and he expected an explosion at any moment. Halfway to the forest, he heard a sound but no explosion. Glancing over his shoulder, he did not see Miriam.

The aircraft door closed.

The aircraft rose ten feet off the ground, wobbling from side to side, and then crashed to the ground.

"What does she think …?" Akira shouted.

Derrick realized the sound was the motor of the aircraft, which did not sound like any machine he'd hear before.

"Stubborn girl thinks she can fly the damn thing," Rebekah said.

"Amazing," Nyx said, coming alongside Derrick. "You think she can do that?"

"I hope so," Derrick said.

The noise grew louder. They covered their ears.

Then the aircraft shot straight up. Hundreds of feet above them in an instant. It descended, drifting back towards the meadow. It wobbled from side to side, like a drunk weaving an unsteady path. When it was twenty feet above the ground, it darted towards the other side of the meadow and crashed into the trees.

Nyx grabbed Derrick's hand, squeezing it tight.

Rebekah said, "Dumbass."

The aircraft hung in the trees for a moment, smoke drifted from the branches underneath the machine. Derrick glanced at the meadow where the aircraft had been sitting. The grass was seared, leaving a blackened circle. He hoped no one happened down the trail because the black circle in the green meadow would be hard to explain. The black robot wouldn't be easily explained either.

A crack of breaking branches got his attention. The aircraft twisted free, turned, and then headed straight at them, bobbing and weaving. Nyx pulled Derrick to the ground, Rebekah and Akira tumbling next to them as the aircraft whizzed overhead, blasting them with hot air. Twisting his head, he grimaced, thinking it would crash into the trees again. This time the crash would be much worse because that side of the meadow was lined with gigantic pine trees that did not have the cushion of the smaller Aspens to the west.

Just before hitting the trees, the aircraft turned vertical and shot straight in the air.

Then it made a full loop before leveling off and speeding out of sight over the mountains.

Derrick stood and then collapsed on his butt. He stared at the black dot until it disappeared.

Nyx sat facing him. "I think she'll be okay."

"I hope so," Derrick said. His chin quivered.

"Miriam will be fine," Rebekah said.

When Derrick turned, he saw Akira on the ground. Rebekah held the stun gun in her hand.

Rushing to Akira, Nyx glared at Rebekah and said, "What have you done."

"Zapped her," Rebekah said.

Nyx ran at Rebekah. Derrick grabbed Nyx around the waist.

Nyx took a swing, but Rebekah was out of reach.

"Why would you do that?" Nyx screamed, fighting to free herself from Derrick's grip.

"Miriam told me to."

"For God's sake, why would you do such a thing. I'm going to kick your ass. Derrick, let go of me or I swear …"

"1984," Rebekah said. She pointed at Akira. "She led the robot here."

Nyx stopped squirming. "What are you talking about?"

"All of us in a Chosen Community had chips implanted in our backs. Me, Miriam, and Derrick had them. If they are activated, they can track us anywhere. They deactivate it when a person leaves the Community, but it can be reactivated. They must have reactivated Akira's chip."

Nyx relaxed but held on to Derrick's forearms. "So that thing," she pointed at the stun gun, "does something to the chip?"

"Yep. Disables it. Derrick, Miriam, and I have all been zapped. It's no fun but getting zapped by surprise is better than knowing it's coming."

"I still think it sucks," Nyx said.

Derrick released Nyx; but she remained pressed against him for a moment before walking to Akira.

Nyx knelt by Akira, stroking her hair.

Derrick glanced at the robot, fearful that it might rise if it detected that someone had stolen the aircraft. The robot did not move, but something else caught Derrick's attention. Miriam's bag laid on the ground. Her cellphone was in that bag. If something happened, she could not contact them.

Akira stirred. She groaned. Nyx helped her to sit.

"What happened?" Akira asked, rubbing her temples.

"Had to zap you. Sorry about that," Rebekah said.

"You did what? Why?"

"You're the reason that thing found you. You have a tracker implanted in your back. All Chosen have it. They deactivated it when they kick you out. They must have reactivated it. I'm surprised Miriam didn't think of it sooner."

"Miriam tricked us out of the aircraft so she could take it and Rebekah could zap me," Akira said.

"That's correct," Rebekah said.

"Speaking of tricks," Nyx stared at Akira. "Explain why you are here."

"Miriam won't tell me; she said Potterville was in danger. She was going to show me something to convince me."

"Why just you?"

Akira shrugged. "She trusts me."

"But not me," Nyx said.

"She asked me who she could trust here. I told her that if I was in her position, I would trust you. But she said she couldn't take you because it would cause a fight with Derrick. She said there wasn't time for arguing. Said it was urgent."

"Why does everyone keep saying that?" Nyx asked.

"Say what?" Akira asked.

"Stuff about me and Derrick?"

"Because she's right," Derrick said. "I don't want you involved."

"I don't get it," Nyx said.

"For a smart girl, you're pretty dense sometimes," Akira said.

"What does that mean?" Nyx said, the frustration clear in her voice.

Before Akira could answer, the aircraft flashed over the trees, made a sharp turn over the mountain that contained the hidden canyon and then slowed, gliding back to the meadow where it settled on the trail. The door slid open.

"Quick, drag that thing inside," Miriam said, pointing to the robot and grabbing her bag.

The robot was heavier than Derrick expected. Nyx grabbed an arm and grunting the two of them dragged it to the craft. Rebekah and Akira help get it inside by grabbing its feet.

"Get strapped in," Miriam said. "We're going for a ride."

Before Akira could strap in, Miriam zapped her in the back, catching her as she fell. "Strap her in."

Nyx started for Miriam.

"Sorry, it has to be done twice," Miriam said. "If you need to hit me or something, it can wait until we get this thing hidden. Get strapped in."

Miriam strapped herself into the pilot's seat and repositioned the goggles on her face. The machine rose and then flew towards the trees; feet before reaching the grove, it pointed straight up until only blue sky remained visible. Then it rocketed upward.

Derrick felt himself pushed back into the seat, struggled to breathe, and thought he might pass out. Nyx grabbed his arm, her fingernails digging into his skin.

Then the inside of the aircraft went black. The windshield that had been in front of the craft disappeared. Faint lights from the pilot's console provided dim light. Derrick sensed the craft level out, no longer accelerating, but they must have been far up; he had no concept of how high that might be.

"What happened," Rebekah said.

"Sorry. We need to take a slight detour. I think it's best that our guests don't see out until we land," Miriam said.

A few minutes passed.
Then the aircraft plummeted straight down.

# 18

In that split second, as they raced toward their death, Derrick wished for more time. Sure, he was only seventeen years old, and every kid wants more time on earth at 17, but he wasn't thinking about that. Not really. Like when he watched the baton before the handoff, time slowed down. He wanted time to tell Miriam how sorry he was for being a terrible brother. In time, maybe he could make those years up to her. Get to know her better. Maybe she could teach him things. Thanking Akira for being a friend entered his mind. Akira recognized him from Pacific Edge, knew he was lying, and still, she helped him. He could not understand that sort of friendship. He had never been concerned about anyone other than himself. And he wanted more time with Nyx. He wasn't sure what that would mean, but he wished he could have found out.

In a fraction of a second, they would hit the ground.

He wondered if any of them might survive. They were strapped into their seats. Perhaps the aircraft had some advanced protective systems that would save them.

When the world came back into focus, Derrick realized screams filled the aircraft.

But he also heard another sound.

Laughter.

The aircraft pivoted. The force smashing him into his seat. He felt the aircraft gain altitude, but they were not going straight up this time or accelerating.

"That is such a rush. Isn't it great?" Miriam asked, turning her head, still wearing the odd-looking goggles.

"Girl, I'm going to kick your ass," Rebekah said.

"I'll help," Akira whispered.

"Good luck," Miriam giggled, and then added. "Sorry about the second zap, Akira. Takes two to be sure the chip is nonfunctioning and we could not risk having them track us."

Nyx punched Derrick in the arm.

"What's that for?"

"She's your sister."

Miriam flew them around for fifteen minutes. The aircraft turned left and then right and then left again. He couldn't tell how fast they were going but thought they must have covered many miles during the flight, not to mention the high-speed run they'd made away from the meadow. Derrick thought certain Miriam had intended to take Akira to Engineering. However, they must be miles away from there by now. Perhaps in the desert where the Base is located. They certainly were not going to Engineering. Again, she had fooled him. He did not understand her.

The aircraft slowed and descended. In a few minutes, it settled to the ground. The sound of the propulsion system fell silent. The door slid open and the windshield became transparent.

They were, in fact, sitting just outside the Engineering facility, although not the front of the build where they exited before. In his exhaustion and sheer joy of being out of the facility, Derrick had not noticed much about the place. On the opposite side of the canyon from the door by which they exited, was a wall of rollup doors recessed into the canyon wall.

"What's this place?" Nyx stood and walked toward the front of the aircraft.

"They called it Engineering?" Miriam said.

"What is it?" Akira asked.

"No time. Let's get this thing inside. Then I'll explain. I promise."

Miriam pointed to a set of doors, big enough to drive a truck through. "See if you can open one of those. I'll fly it in." Then she threw her bag, hitting Derrick in the back. "You'll need this. Flashlight and such."

The door of the aircraft shut. He led Nyx, Akira, and Rebekah to the front of the building. The door Miriam had rigged to open was etched in his mind the day they left, which was just yesterday but seemed like months ago, but now he could not remember which one it was. He tried two before finding the third door open.

"I couldn't remember it either," Rebekah said.

"You left here yesterday. Right?" Nyx asked.

"It seems like a month," Derrick said.

Light poured in from the open door, spilling across the front lobby of the building. Above the long desk on the other side of the lobby, a sign read: Fort Hill Engineering Department. He didn't remember seeing the name before; he had not paid attention. But he must have seen the name elsewhere, which is why it sounded familiar when he learned Fort Hill was the name of a team in the track meet. He wondered what else he had missed. When the door shut, the room plunged into darkness.

Rebekah was ready. Her flashlight cast a dim light that the darkness consumed. Derrick fished around Mariam's bag for a moment before he felt the cold cylindrical shape. When Derrick turned on Miriam's flashlight, the beam, a dull yellow, provided little illumination.

"Great," Derrick said.

"We have batteries," Rebekah said. "But first, let's find the door so Miriam can get the aircraft inside.

Derrick walked towards where Miriam waited, but there were no doors going that direction.

Nyx went to a door behind the desk. "This one is locked."

"All the doors we tried were locked," Derrick said.

They moved behind the desk, trying each door, finding each door locked.

"If all the doors are locked, how did you get out?" Nyx asked.

"All the doors open from the other side," Rebekah said. After trying another door, finding it locked like the others, she added. "Some doors had a keypad. Miriam knows the code. But we didn't see any keypads here."

Akira had been silent. She was probably mad, and he couldn't blame her. And recovering from those jolts of electricity took a while. Still, he sensed there was more to it than just being mad. He walked to where she was standing, next to the long desk, or maybe it was called a counter. He wasn't sure. "I'm sorry about what Rebekah and Miriam did to you."

"You don't need to be sorry. You didn't do it."

"True, but I should have known what was going to happen. I'm not convinced being surprised makes it easier."

"Did they surprise you?"

"Yes. Both times."

"Did they get zapped twice?"

"Yes. I had to do Miriam. I hated doing it. But she made me." Derrick hung his head.

"Then she knows what it's like to get zapped when you know it's coming. I'll take her word for it."

"Okay," Derrick said. "I hope you will forgive her."

"You think I'm mad at Miriam?"

"Well, yes. I assumed because …"

"I'm not mad at her or Rebekah. I'm mad at myself. I led that thing to us. The question is will Miriam forgive me. Plus, it pisses me off knowing Pacific Edge put a chip in us. Like we were some sort of animal."

Rebekah walked up and Nyx joined her. Rebekah said, "Here's what I've been thinking. Derrick and I should have thought about Akira having a chip, but understandable we didn't. We are not genius material by any stretch of the imagination. But Miriam …"

Derrick held up his hand. "We need to find a way to those doors."

Akira walked to a door and touched the handle. "This requires a standard key. Like our homes in Potterville. You said Miriam knew the code to the keypads. How?"

"It was written on a piece of paper near the first door we came to," Derrick said.

"Then we need to search for a key. If they left the code for someone to find, they probably left a key," Akira said.

The counter had chairs, drawers, monitors, and keyboards. They jerked open drawers, many still contained paper and pens, notebooks, and notepads. But no keys. The panic crept into Derrick's chest. His heart thumbed. He was unsure why. Maybe it was because Anna Ford was missing, maybe it was because the aircraft and robot found them, maybe it was because Miriam sat outside in the strange aircraft, or maybe it was something else. Miriam was right about Nyx. He would have thrown a fit. Now, because of his predictable response, he was separated from his sister. Miriam could have been abducted had he been a moment later getting to the clearing. He would never let that happen again. The Pacific Edge Derrick King had no problem making decisions based on logic. In fact, he shunned emotions. Now, emotions seemed to drive most of this thinking. That had to change.

And then it did. He eased to a keyboard and nonchalantly turned it over. Taped to the bottom were the username, password, a yellow piece of paper neatly folded, and a key. "Found it."

Derrick pulled the key loose and slid the folded piece of paper into his pocket.

"We should have checked the keyboards in the first place. We must be brain-dead," Rebekah said.

"Why the keyboards?" Akira asked.

"Because that's where we found stuff before," Rebekah said.

"That's a security risk. We are always told, never write your username or password. They wanted to help whoever found this place," Akira said.

"That's what Miriam said too," Rebekah said.

Derrick stepped to the double doors in the center of the room. He inserted the key and tried to turn it. Nothing. The locking mechanism on the double doors appeared to extend into the top and bottom of the door frame because there was no center post. He pulled on the handle, trying the key again. If this was the only key, he needed to be careful he did not break it. And because he had little experience with keys, he did not know how much pressure he could safely apply. He twisted a little harder; the key turned, and the lock freed from the frame.

He opened the door; shining his light into the hallway, it only illuminated a few feet as the power faded. Rebekah stepped next to him. Her flashlight batteries were in better condition. The hallway extended farther than the flashlight's beam reached. In the wrong direction.

Leaving the double doors open, Derrick scurried to the door at the end of the lobby, beyond the lobby's long counter, closest to the side of the building where Miriam landed. He should have looked to see if there was another key on the last keyboard, but he did not. He stuck the key in the lock, wiggled it, pulled on the doorknob. It turned; the lock moved.

His light emitted a bleak yellow light, virtually useless, but Rebekah was right behind him. This hallway went straight for about ten yards and then turned ninety-degrees, which was the direction they needed to go. Derrick ran down the hall guided by Rebekah's light. He should have felt some relief, but he did not. At the end of the hall, they came to another door. This was a single door, yet oversized. Because it was leading out of the building, it had a crash bar. The lock was on the other side.

Derrick handed his bag and the flashlight to Nyx. "Sorry, the batteries are dead. You'll need to feel in the bag for fresh ones. Make sure this door is not locked or prop it open before you go through."

Derrick ran towards the middle door, weaving his way through junk in the enormous room, which was difficult because the light from Rebekah's flashlight bounced wildly as she ran behind him. He did not take time to understand what he was dodging. Some large vehicles, some machines secured in wooden boxes and with torn plastic coverings, some were oblong rectangles with rounded corners that were not unlike coffins.

When they reached the middle door, Derrick saw the construction was heavier than he had expected. Not that he was familiar with such doors. Only the one at the condo, which was metal but thin. He estimated this one to be at least three inches thick. Maybe more.

The operation was simple enough. A two-button switch on a rectangular metal box hung from the ceiling on a black cord. One button labeled up, the other down. An electric opener, but no electricity. He saw a chain loop hanging by the right side of the door. He pulled on one side. Nothing. Pulling the other side, the door raised half an inch, then stopped.

"Keep moving it up and down and I'll look for what's stopping it," Rebekah said.

Derrick did as she instructed. Up, then down, up, then down.

"I see it. Just a minute," Rebekah called.

Derrick heard a click from the left side of the door where Rebekah was. She came to his side, turned a brass-colored elongated knob, which retracted a thick bar that ran from the door through a slot in the rail that guided the door.

"Try it now," Rebekah said.

Derrick pulled the chain. The door raised. The aircraft sat outside the door. The engine started, sending dirt and debris into the air in a cloud that eclipsed the machine. Ten feet off the ground, the aircraft moved towards the opening. As it flew by, Derrick closed his eyes and ducked his head. He felt a wave of heat as the craft passed through the doorway. As the sound faded, he looked up to see it flying into the depth of the room. Bright lights had come on illuminating the cavernous space. He did not know what to call this place. The room was full of stuff, but there was an open lane in the center. He estimated the aircraft was 200 yards away when it settled to the ground. The engines fell silent and the lights with dark.

From deep in the room, Miriam said, "Some light down here would be nice."

Nyx and Rebekah were already running towards Miriam when Derrick got the door locked. He caught Rebekah and Nyx about 100 yards from the door.

As Miriam approached, she did something that surprised him.

With open arms, tears flowing down her cheeks, Miriam threw her arms around Akira. "I'm so sorry I had to do that. Seriously."

"Not your fault. I'm sorry too. You could have been captured because of me. I did not know I had a chip in my back. Honest. Can you forgive me?"

Miriam held Akira for a moment and then pushed her back, looked in her face, smoothed her hair. "You have nothing to be sorry about. You didn't know about the chip. I did."

"No one can blame you for not thinking about it," Akira said.

"I thought about it," Miriam said.

"You thought they might find you?" Derrick asked.

"Yes. Had to find out if 1984 was working. Pacific Edge is still out of commission. I had to know if someone could access 1984 from another place."

"That put you and Akira in jeopardy!" Nyx shouted.

"I did not expect a robot. I thought it would be regular security and that they wouldn't do anything to Akira. It's me they want."

"Pacific Edge used the computer in another community to find you?" Derrick asked.

"It wasn't Pacific Edge," Nyx said. "It was worse."

"Who was it?" Rebekah asked.

"Prime," Nyx said.

"What is Prime and why do they want Anna?" Rebekah asked, tears pooling in her eyes.

"You can cry if you want," Miriam said. "I'm proud of how you pulled yourself together earlier. You have permission to fall apart now."

"I'm not going to fall apart. We need to find Anna. I'll fall apart after we do."

"Wait. Who is Prime?" Derrick asked.

"We don't know. I thought Prime was just a myth. According to the myth, Prime controls everything." Akira said.

# 19

The brainwashing, as Derrick thought of it now, had been so complete he never considered himself a prisoner in Pacific Edge. Now the realization seeped into his mind, but he had not accepted it. Yet, it was true. The Chosen were captives. The walls, the guards, the patrols, were not there to protect them. They were there to keep them inside. He did not understand why, but he accepted it as fact. So, the Chosen were not the Creator's people as they had been taught. They were not even the top of the food chain.

"Why does this Prime person want Anna?" Rebekah asked, her voice more angry than fearful.

"Not sure, but now is not the time," Miriam said.

"Here we go again," Nyx said.

"Not really," Miriam said. "Follow me. I saw this brilliant spot as I flew over."

Miriam started for the door. Nyx looked at Derrick and shook her head. Derrick shrugged.

When they reached the lobby, Miriam went straight to the double doors. "Were these locked?"

"Yes," Derrick said.

"Where did you find the key?" Miriam asked.

"Derrick found it," Nyx said. "Last place we looked."

"Where?" Miriam asked.

"Under a keyboard," Derrick said.

"That was the last place you looked?" Miriam asked, turning to look at Derrick with a smile. "It should have been the first place."

"You weren't with us, and that was a mistake. We need to stay together," Derrick said.

"People should never write their username or password or hide things under their keyboard. That's poor security. It was like they wanted to help whoever found this place," Akira puzzled.

"Exactly," Miriam said.

Miriam turned left and then right. Twenty-five yards down the hall, light flooded through the windows. "That must be it," Miriam said, trotting toward the light.

Through a window, Derrick saw yet another unexpected marvel. A courtyard surrounded by the building. A lush area of trees and flowers, including a fountain in the middle. Covered tables were scattered through the area.

Miriam opened the door and used a little foot thing at the bottom to prop it open. "Isn't this fantastic? It's even better than it looked from above."

Derrick looked up. He did not see the sky, but rather a tall ceiling covered with a translucent material. "How did you see it? It's covered."

"You see things different through the goggles. I don't know the technology, but it's cool," Miriam said.

They selected a table near the fountain. Miriam beamed. Akira sat across from her.

Derrick sat next to Akira so he could face Miriam. Rebekah started to sit next to Derrick. Nyx cleared her throat. Rebekah moved next to Miriam. Nyx squeezed in next to Derrick. He accepted that he would never understand girls.

"Are you going to explain why we are here?" Nyx asked. "What is this place?"

"I don't know what this place is. Not exactly," Miriam said.

Nyx bumped Derrick with her elbow. "Does she always talk in riddles?

Before Derrick could respond, Miriam said, "Not a riddle. Not this time. I'm sorry I have not been straightforward. I hope in time, you'll understand. I don't know what this place is because we did not explore it. You've seen more of it than we did our first time here. I can tell you it's connected to a vast, unimaginable compound built beneath these mountains and abandoned decades ago."

"What kind of compound?" Akira asked.

"Military," Mariam said.

"I don't see how this affects us. You said it was abandoned long ago. We are just a small farming community trying to survive. I understand you're looking for a reason to stay in Potterville but finding this place won't change things." Nyx looked at Derrick. "I'm sorry, but I'm just being honest."

Miriam said, "The facility is self-contained. There is a nuclear reactor that generates power."

Nyx signed, "I'm sure it's all remarkably interesting, but we need to get back. Someone may have noticed us missing by now."

"Stop interrupting and listen," Miriam said.

"You've got five minutes," Nyx shot back.

"The reactor is still operational. Other parts of the complex have electricity. The reactor has been idling all these years, minimal power being used," Miriam said.

Akira said, "Nuclear power was done away with decades ago. There was a big accident in Washington. The government decided it was too dangerous. Plus, coal is cheaper."

"If you say so. But that's unimportant for now. Just after we entered the facility, a warning sounded. The reactor had reached a critical condition. Our presence, increasing the power demand, may have accelerated the problem."

"How far away is the reactor?" Akira asked.

"I don't know. But if it were to fail, the radiation would affect the area for miles, including rivers and water underground," Miriam said.

"Affect Potterville?" Nyx asked.

"Probably," Miriam said.

"Impact us how?" Nyx asked.

"Best case? Increased cancer and other health problems over time. Worse case? Kill everyone quickly," Miriam said.

"You're being dramatic," Nyx said.

"I am not," Miriam said.

"Is the reactor failing as we speak?" Akira asked.

"It could be. We fixed the problem that caused the alert, but the system showed many caution signs. The reactor needs to be maintained or shut down," Miriam said.

"Why didn't you just turn it off?" Nyx asked.

"Not that simple. The radioactive materials must be properly handled and stored. You can't just turn it off."

Nyx thought for a few minutes. "Okay. We know about it now. We can maintain it. That still doesn't change your situation. The student council meets tomorrow to decide." Nyx glanced at Akira and then continued. "I've talked to the council members. One person will vote for you to stay, one is undecided, the others are split between sending you away immediately with no help, the rest will vote to send you away but give you some support."

"What sort of support?" Derrick asked.

Miriam held up her hand. "How they vote is unimportant. We would just come here because this needs to be maintained. It's also the safest place for us. Besides, you still don't know how to get here."

"That's not an option. If you came here, they'd remove you by force," Akira said. "You won't be safe here. I'm sorry. Not my idea. I'm the one person who will vote for you to stay."

"Trying to use force would be a mistake," Miriam said.

"What does that mean?" Nyx asked.

"I said the complex was abandoned. I did not say it was empty."

# 20

The atmosphere in the courtyard grew uncomfortable, but Derrick trusted Miriam and thought it best to let her handle things. Still, her tone felt threatening even to him. Now hostility swirled in the air so thick it seemed visible. He did not see how this improved their situation. Making matters worse, just when he thought Nyx still had feelings for him, it appeared she would vote to send them away from Potterville. Send away is another way to say exile. He knew leaving Potterville was likely, and he had decided they had to leave to protect the people there. However, he did not anticipate Nyx would vote to exile him. *And where would they go?* Miriam said they would come back here, but what sort of life was that? Then there was Anna. Rebekah wouldn't agree to come here without Anna. The scales had fallen from his eyes. Although Pacific Edge was a prison, but a comfortable prison. Brainwashed Derrick King was happy, had a cushy life, and a bright future. Here he had nothing. For the first time in a long time, he regretted smacking Marcus Carver.

"What's that supposed to mean?" Nyx said.

"We'd be safe here. That's all," Miriam said.

The tone in Miriam's voice softened. Derrick felt relieved. Not his first mistake.

Nyx said, "You can't stay. They'd remove you by force."

"Not going to happen," Miriam said, "besides, what makes you think we are even close to Potterville?"

"Close enough that the nuclear reactor is a threat," Nyx fired back.

"Fair enough. But we are far from the reactor."

Rebekah stood. "Enough. I'm not coming back here. I must find Anna. I'll see you when I get back."

"Sit down, Rebekah. I understand you want to find Anna, but you have no chance of finding her and you know it. You're only hope to find Anna is to stick with us," Miriam said.

"You're not the boss of me here anymore than you were in Pacific …"

"Shut up and sit down!" Miriam snarled.

Derrick had never witnessed this side of Miriam. The tone in her voice scared him and she wasn't talking to him.

Rebekah folded her arms and sat.

"You're out of control," Nyx said, standing. "Now show us how to find the reactor thing and we'll leave. You can come back to Potterville with us or I'll send the sheriff to get you."

"That would be a mistake," Miriam said.

"Is that a threat?"

"Just being honest."

"I'm leaving. Come on Akira."

"I'm not leaving," Akira said.

Nyx glared at Akira. "You'd better get your priorities straight."

Derrick was not sure of many things, which was an understatement because right now he understood nothing. He would never understand girls; trying was a waste of time. A few minutes ago, they sounded like best friends. Now, he felt certain they were about to throw punches.

"This is out of control. All of you, calm down. Fighting is getting us nowhere," Derrick said.

"She started it," Miriam said, pointing at Nyx.

"Stop it! I'm serious," Derrick said.

Anger flushed Derrick's face; his chest rose and fell. Emotion poured through the air, thick like smoke from the emotional fire burning underneath the surface, and he was not immune to it.

"I'm sorry I raised my voice," Derrick said.

"I'm not wanting to fight, but I don't like the threats," Miriam said.

"You're the one doing the threats," Nyx said.

Akira intervened, "Guys, things are bad enough without fighting. Let's hear what Miriam's trying to tell us."

"Okay. I'll be quiet till you're finished," Nyx said.

Derrick noticed Nyx had scooted away from him. *So, this is the end for us,* he thought.

"This place has enough weaponry to destroy the entire West Coast, probably more. First, you don't know where it is; second, even if you found it, you couldn't get in, and third, if you tried to get in, we could defend ourselves. We would never attack Potterville, but if they attacked us, we could wipe it off the map and not even use a noticeable amount of the arsenal here."

Nyx began to say something.

Miriam held up her hand. "I'm just stating the facts. It's not meant as a threat; I'm trying to get you to understand how dangerous this place is."

"You're afraid of it falling into the wrong hands," Akira said.

"Thank you. That's exactly what I'm saying."

"Why didn't you just say that in the first place?" Nyx asked.

"Sorry. I'm not smart sometimes. This has not gone the way I intended," Miriam said.

The courtyard fell silent. Derrick hoped tempers would cool. Which they did, but he did not expect the rush of thoughts that replaced his anger. It was as if he had been aware of all the obstacles they faced, but he'd avoided adding them up. When he looked at the entire picture, he could not see any feasible solution. Miriam saw this before he did; because she was smarter than him. He hoped she had a plan that he could not envision. But if she had no plan, they were doomed.

"My God, I just realized something," Akira said, twisting her head.

Everyone turned to Akira.

"This place is immaculate. The building is spotless. The plants are perfect."

Nyx looked around as if she'd not seen the place before. "You're right. Someone is here."

"Robots do it," Miriam said.

"Robots?" Akira asked.

"We saw them polishing the floor at the place where we entered. We talked to one at another location," Miriam said.

"You talked to one?" Nyx asked; her voice higher pitched than normal.

"We did," Derrick confirmed.

Rebekah nodded.

"He is another reason I can't show you more," Miriam said.

"If I were not sitting here, seeing this, I wouldn't believe a word you've said," Akira said.

"Now you're starting to understand," Miriam said.

"So why can't we see this talking robot?" Nyx asked.

"I'm afraid he would not let us leave. He held us the first time, but I talked him in to letting us go. However, I made him a promise. If I go back without completing it, he won't be happy," Miriam said.

"You talk like it's a person," Akira said.

"He's not a person, but he's more than a robot. He has developed artificial intelligence. He thinks, and I suspect he has emotions. Maybe not just like us, but he's trying," Miriam said.

"What did you promise to do?" Nyx asked.

"Fix his friend. I have her back at the condo."

"I'm struggling to believe that. Sounds like a far-fetched story to avoid showing us more," Nyx said.

"It's true. I don't like calling it him, but it's not a simple machine, that much is certain. And Miriam's right. He would not let us leave," Derrick said.

"Maybe we should get out of here before the robots find us," Akira said.

"The robots here are not smart like Charlie. That's the robot's name. But we should go now. They might be looking for us. There's one more thing I want to show you, but I need you to promise me something," Miriam said.

"I can't make any promises," Nyx said.

"Then I can't tell you more. And I can't leave you with any idea where this place is. I can fly you back to the meadow, and then Derrick, Rebekah, and I will walk out."

"I promise not to tell," Akira said.

"Akira, you can't do that. You're a member of the student council. Potterville has to be your priority," Nyx said.

"Potterville is my priority, which is exactly why I can promise. Based on what I've seen and heard, this place presents a clear danger to Potterville. We can't let it fall into the wrong hands. I'm not even sure who the right hands would be, including us."

"Thanks, Akira," Miriam said. "I respect your decision, Nyx. And I appreciate you being honest. Let's go; I'll fly you back to the meadow."

They walked silently back towards the aircraft. Derrick felt he had lost something but wasn't sure what it was. He checked to see if Rebekah and Miriam had their bags. They did. He opened the door to the lobby; then froze.

Standing at the counter, was the black robot they disabled in the meadow.

# 21

MIRIAM PULLED THE BAG FROM her shoulder, setting it on the ground. She held the stun gun in her hand behind her back. Derrick put the bat behind his back too. He saw Rebekah set her bag on the floor, a stun gun also in her hand, hidden. The robot did not seem to notice them as it polished the counter with a blue cloth. Maybe the shock had scrambled its brain. Maybe it was a ploy. They could not get to the robot before it drilled them with those laser eyes; of that much, Derrick was certain.

Miriam stepped toward the counter. "Report."

The machine moved its head as if to look at Miriam. Derrick had not heard the robot in the meadow, so he did not know what to expect. However, he didn't expect the response. In an odd electronic voice, it said, "X series, 3000 model, unit 3145."

Miriam lowered the stun gun to her leg. "Status"

The machine turned its head as if pondering some profound problem.

Miriam said, "Condition."

The machine said, "Systems normal, battery 72%, 120 battery cycles remaining, current task 23% complete."

Miriam turned to the others. "Not the robot from the ship. It looks like the same machine, but this is a cleaning robot. I don't think it will bother us."

Derrick nodded, taking a shallow breath.

Miriam pulled two pieces of cloth from her bag. He recognized the strips as pieces of a shirt from his closet.

"Sorry, but to go farther, you'll need to wear these." Miriam held the cloth out to Nyx and Akira.

Akira accepted the cloth, placed it over her eyes, and tied it behind her head.

Miriam threw her hand up to Akira's face and then waved it in front of her eyes. "See anything?"

"Not a thing," Akira said.

Nyx said, "You said you'd fly me back to the meadow."

"I plan to, but first there's something else you need to see," Miriam said.

"You didn't say anything about seeing something else," Nyx said.

Miriam held the cloth in front of Nyx. "I changed my mind."

No way," Nyx said, shaking her head.

Nyx looked at Derrick and then to Miriam. "I'm not wearing it."

"Suit yourself. Stay here, we'll be back in about an hour," Miriam said, pausing and then added, "You'll probably be safe here."

Nyx looked at Derrick, her eyes pleading.

"I'll stay with Nyx," Derrick said.

Miriam frowned. "It's better if you are with us."

Derrick tried but failed to read Miriam's expression. She was trying to tell him something. He looked at Rebekah. Rebekah's expression indicated he should be smart enough to figure it out. Both girls apparently understood what he did not. No surprise there.

Akira held out her hand as a blind person might. "Nyx, it will be okay. Come with us. Derrick won't let anything happen to us. It's important you see this. If you don't, you can't make the right decision."

Nyx took Akira's hand, held it for a moment, and then let go. She turned to Derrick. "I don't like this."

Derrick was unsure what to say. He turned to Miriam. "Is this necessary?"

The look on Miriam's face made Derrick wished he'd left the question unasked. He felt sure a scolding was coming.

Before Miriam could speak, Nyx took the cloth from Miriam and held it out to Derrick. "I understand. I just don't like it."

Nyx stepped closer and turned her back. He put the cloth over her eyes and tied it behind her head. He sensed tears welling in his eyes. "I won't let anything happen to you," he said.

Nyx turned around and searched for his hand. Taking it, she said, "I trust you."

Miriam led them to the electric cart that would take them to the Circle. Derrick led Nyx and Miriam led Akira. Rebekah carried Nyx's bat, held doors, and scurried to the front again.

"This cart holds four. But Nyx, Akira, and I can squeeze into the back seat," Miriam said, "If that's okay with you, Nyx?"

"I'll survive," Nyx said.

Miriam guided Akira and Nyx into the back seat of the cart, positioning Akira was in the middle. Miriam squeezed in next to Akira. Rebekah got behind the steering wheel and Derrick unplugged the electric cord. He hoped the cord had electricity.

"We'd not fit if Derrick sat with us, that's for sure," Akira said.

"We could find another cart, or perhaps there are bigger ones. But that would take time. I thought it best if we did this as quickly as possible," Miriam said.

"How long are we in this thing?" Nyx asked.

Rebekah pulled away from the parking spot.

"Took us 27 minutes last trip. Might be a little faster this time because Rebekah knows how to drive now," Miriam said.

"Let's get this over with," Nyx said.

Rebekah floored the accelerator. Derrick felt they were going faster than the first trip. Perhaps Rebekah had driven slower, perhaps the vehicle's battery had recovered somehow, perhaps he was imagining it. Derrick looked over his shoulder at Miriam, motioning that perhaps Nyx and Akira could remove the blindfolds. Miriam shook her head, giving him an angry look.

He estimated they had been in the cart 25 minutes when they saw signs hanging over the tunnel. The signs were not visible traveling the opposite direction, so they did not notice them on the way out. He should have paid closer attention to such things the first time. On the sign, an arrow pointed left and read: Circle. Rebekah looked at him, giving her shoulders a slight shrug. He resisted the urge to look to Miriam for direction, and then said, "Let's check it out."

Rebekah slowed, taking the tunnel left, and then sped to what Derrick assumed was the vehicle's maximum speed. The tunnel curved left then right then left again, but Rebekah maintained the same speed. He wished she'd slow down. Then the tunnel descended. Within a few minutes, the descent grew steeper. The tunnel grew darker, the machine slowed, then Rebekah stopped. Derrick felt along the dashboard of the vehicle. He found a few switches and knobs, which he flipped or turned depending the type of control. With the flip of the fourth switch, the vehicle's lights came on illuminating the tunnel. Water seeped down the walls and covered the road.

"Now what?" Rebekah asked.

"We must be under the river," Miriam said, and then held her finger to her lips. She leaned out of the vehicle. "I can hear something, perhaps a pump."

"Looks like we have to go back," Derrick said.

"Would someone tell us what's going on? What river?" Nyx asked.

"I don't know what river. Take off your blindfolds," Miriam said.

Derrick glared at Miriam.

Miriam shrugged, "They won't know our location. Safer if we have to swim to the other side."

"I am not going in there?" Rebekah said.

"You have to; you're driving," Miriam said.

"Screw that, I'm turning around," Rebekah said.

"It doesn't look deep," Nyx said.

"I agree," Miriam said. "Unless the road is washed away. Then we could fall into a hole. Worst case, we get sucked into an underground river."

"The water looks still," Akira said. "I don't think there's a current."

"Spoilsport," Miriam said.

Derrick climbed out of the vehicle.

"What are you doing?" Miriam asked.

"I'll walk across first. You guys follow. If I disappear, you stop."

Miriam said, "Too dangerous. Get back in the vehicle."

"I'll be fine," Derrick said.

"Can you even swim?" Miriam asked, and then added, "I can swim. I'll do the walking."

Derrick turned to look at the girls. "I can swim."

"When did you ever swim?" Miriam asked.

Derrick thought hard, couldn't remember. "I swam in the ocean. Often. Give me your flashlight?" He held out his hand to Rebekah.

With Rebekah's flashlight in hand, he went to the water's edge. "The water is clear."

With that, he started in. Rebekah eased the cart forward. At first, the water was only two inches deep. Nothing to worry about. Then the water was halfway up to his knees. "Getting deeper," he called out.

When the water reached Derrick's knees, he stopped. He could see the other side; he estimated they were in the middle of the crossing. "How much water can the vehicle go through. And is it safe for it to be in the water? Seems like water and electricity don't mix. I'm not sure why I think that."

"You are not wrong," Miriam said. "I think we'll be okay."

Rebekah turned. "You three walk with Derrick. When you are out of the water, I'll drive through."

"Let's all walk. We'll leave the vehicle here. Safer that way," Miriam said.

"I don't feel like walking. You guys go. Wasting time. I'm getting hungry. And I want to get this over with," Rebekah said.

"I don't like it," Miriam said.

"No one asked for your opinion," Rebekah said.

"Let's just back the vehicle out of the water and we'll all walk," Miriam said.

"Get your ass out of my vehicle! Do it now," Rebekah screamed.

Miriam, Nyx, and Akira did as Rebekah said. They joined Derrick and worked their way to the other side. The water rose above Derrick's knees and then grew shallow as they neared the other side. When they stood on dry ground, Derrick called, "I think it's too deep. Just walk to us, Rebekah."

Rebekah said nothing, then started driving towards them. At the deepest point, the vehicle seemed to float, water churning beneath the wheels, drifting sideways. Then it caught traction and started moving again. When Rebekah stopped, water poured off and out of the vehicle. "Get in. And don't mess up my vehicle."

"That was brave of you," Akira said. "You could have been hurt. Or worse."

"Worse would have been best. Then my worries would be over. And I would not have to see what comes next."

"She's not brave. She's just stubborn and won't let anyone else drive," Miriam said.

"Shut up," Rebekah said.

"You shut up," Miriam said.

Nyx and Akira climbed into the back seat. Derrick started to the front seat.

"Get in the back, Derrick. I'm sure you won't mind being close to Nyx." Miriam climbed into the front and threw her arms around Rebekah. "Don't do shit like that."

Rebekah started driving. Slower at first, Miriam leaning against Rebekah's shoulder. When Miriam sat straight, Rebekah accelerated.

Nyx leaned into Derrick and whispered, "That was a little weird. Are they always like that?"

"You don't know the half of it," Derrick replied.

Akira said nothing. Derrick thought she looked sad. He was hopelessly lost and gave up understanding what just happened.

They came to a place with many vehicles like the one they drove; some had a third bench seat. Rebekah parked next to one of the larger ones; got out, snaked the black cord to the vehicle, and connected it. A green light appeared on the dash and at the pole that held the cord. Rebekah performed the task as if she'd been doing it for years.

"We're going to the silos, aren't we?" Rebekah asked.

"Just the last one," Miriam said.

"I don't want to see that again," Rebekah said.

Miriam put her arm around Rebekah's waist. "Neither do I, girlfriend. Grab your flashlight and stunner. Leave the rest, we'll be back."

Akira glanced at Derrick. He could not read her expression, other than something was troubling her. *You'll be more troubled soon,* Derrick thought.

"Where are we going?" Nyx asked.

"There's a second vehicle. It's not far. We must show you something for you to understand. Then we go back to Potterville," Miriam said, "Sorry, guys, but it's blindfold time again."

Akira put on her blindfold without argument. Nyx groaned and handed her blindfold to Derrick. He tied it on, thought about saying he was sorry, but was certain Nyx was tired of hearing him say that.

Miriam took Akira's hand and walked towards the tunnel that led to the Circle transports. Derrick took Nyx's hand, wondering if they would have to make the entire loop and hoped it would not be necessary.

Derrick assumed Charlie the robot was watching. If they went to the Base, perhaps Charlie could stop the Circle transport vehicle and imprison them. At Silo Number 8 laid the bodies of the final seven. When they first found them, he was so tired, scared, and desperate to find sunlight, the gravity of the murders had not fully embedded in his thinking. Seven people murdered. Three missiles launched. How many had they killed? Each time he thought he understood the magnitude of their situation, he realized he did not.

Although he knew the place was abandoned, he searched the shadows for threats. They had seen cleaning robots; perhaps they communicated with each other and Charlie. Perhaps there were killing robots that had not been unleashed. Derrick never thought about hurting anyone. Hitting Marcus Carver came as a complete surprise. For a guy who never thought about violence, now it was occupying far too much of his thinking. He didn't like it. That would not improve anytime soon.

All of it bothered him. Yet, what bothered him most, was a vague sense something, or someone, had prepared him for this sort of thing.

Strange time to be thinking about this, although it always on his mind. He wished he had told Nyx the truth sooner for many reasons, not the least of which was that he could have had more time with her without all the complications. Nothing could change that now. It was like dried concrete. The only way to change concrete was to destroy it. He forced the thought from his mind, afraid tears were not far away.

Derrick's thoughts drifted. He saw the Pacific Edge abduction attempt as an awful event. But if it had not happened, he would not have reunited with Miriam on the mountain. Had he not been on the mountain, Miriam would have found a different route to Potterville. She was there because of his 1984 tracking device. They would not have found this complex, and the people in Potterville might have died if not for those unrelated coincidences.

Rebekah's looked pale; her eyes dark. Stress emanated from her like a mystic aura one might see in an ad for a medicine promising everything short of eternal life. As they walked toward the Circle, Rebekah's strength impressed Derrick. He doubted he could hold it together if he were in her position. Rebekah, it seemed, grew stronger instead of falling apart.

As they walked, this revelation bounced around in his head. He applied it to things that had happened since his 17th birthday. He had grown as well. He tucked that away in a corner of his mind, certain he would need it.

Miriam mouthed something to Rebekah. He read her lips enough to understand. They were not going back to Potterville by way of the iron gate. He didn't understand. No matter how they went, Nyx and Akira would know how to return. It puzzled him.

When the got to the Circle, Miriam led them to a larger coach than the first one they took. Derrick had not noticed before that they looked the same on both ends. They climbed inside. This coach had a variety of seating arrangements. Some seats faced one direction; others faced the opposite; some were positioned along the windows facing inward.

Miriam sat in the front next to Akira, facing the direction that would take them straight to Silo Number 8 if the machine traveled either direction. Derrick wanted to shield Nyx from what they were about to see. But knew he could not. An aching started in his heart. He wanted to protect Nyx from everything ugly in the world. Searching his memory, he could not find another example of feeling that way. But he could not protect her from everything. He hoped he could protect her when it was necessary to do so. He tried to push the thought from his mind, but he knew the need to protect her would come.

"Silo Number 8," Miriam said.

As the Circle accelerated, Miriam said, "What you're about to see is disturbing; brace yourselves."

"Don't worry about us," Nyx said.

"Just warning you. I hope you'll understand how serious this entire situation is."

"Whatever," Nyx said.

Miriam's expression didn't change. "Does anyone else find it odd that a janitorial robot, decades old, is the same model as the one that intercepted us in the meadow?"

"I had not thought about it," Akira said.

"Doesn't seem odd to me. Pretty much like everything else," Nyx said.

"Explain," Miriam said.

"For example, take our computers and cell phones. Most kids have them, even though we don't have much money. It's because they are cheap. They are cheap because they haven't changed much in over 70 years. Before the great war, they used to cost a lot more because they changed all the time. Cars are the same way. You can buy a new one, but it's the same as an old one. One of the few good things that came from the stratocracy."

"Stratocracy?" Miriam puzzled.

"You know, after the Greatest War? The president, James Carver, declared martial law. When he retired, he turned the government over to the military. It's been that way ever since. Surely, they teach you about it in Pacific Edge," Nyx said.

"They do not. Never heard of it. What was the Greatest War?" Miriam asked.

"I can't believe then don't teach you about it. The Chosen originated after the stratocracy," Nyx said.

Akira said, "I never heard of it until I came to Potterville. I left Pacific Edge in grade school, so I assumed they didn't teach it until kids were older because of, well you know."

"I don't know. Because of what?" Miriam asked.

"Because so many people were killed so near to us," Akira said.

"That explains a lot," Miriam said.

"What's there to explain? We know all about it. North Korea launched a nuclear missile that hit California," Nyx said.

"Now things are becoming clear," Miriam said.

# 22

APPROACHING SILO NUMBER 8, THE CIRCLE slowed; Derrick recognized the stench drifting into the cabin. He knew about the bodies. Akira and Nyx did not. He wondered if the scent was real or if he was imagining it. Miriam turned, faced forward, and grew quiet. Maybe out of respect for the dead; maybe for some other reason.

"Something smells awful," Nyx said.

"It'll get worse," Miriam said. "Use your blindfolds to cover your mouth and nose."

Derrick heard Rebekah crying. He wished she did not have to see this again. He pulled his shirt up to cover his nose.

The odor seemed stronger than the first time. Possibly it was because Miriam disturbed the body of Jacob Truman, Charlie's supervisor.

The Circle transport stopped. They all exited. The roll-up door stood open. The bodies laid concealed in the darkness just beyond the opening. Derrick assumed Miriam would go first to the control panel as she did before, leaving the discovery of the bodies until they were on the way out. He was wrong.

"Follow me." Miriam led them to the roll-up door.

"My God, what is that smell?" Nyx said.

No one answered.

Although the tunnel was wide enough for trucks, they walked single file into the darkness. Derrick did not know why; it just happened that way. Akira walked behind Miriam. Nyx behind Akira. He knew they were near the first body when Miriam turned on her flashlight.

Akira moved her head to see around Miriam. "Oh, my God." Her hands flew to her face.

"What?" Nyx moved to the side to see passed Akira. "Holy shit."

Akira screamed. "Get us out of here!"

Miriam turned around. "Sorry. Can't. There's more to see."

"What happened here?" Nyx asked, her voice trembling.

"Someone murdered them," Miriam said, "decades ago."

"What is this place?" Nyx asked.

"An intercontinental missile silo. These people launched a nuclear missile from here. And then someone executed them." Miriam asked.

"The Greatest War," Nyx whispered.

"Three bombs?" Miriam asked.

"Yes. I thought you didn't know anything about the Greatest War," Nyx said.

"I don't," Miriam said.

"I don't understand," Nyx said.

"I know about three nuclear bombs: one in North Korea and one in Russia and one in California," Miriam said.

"That's right. The ones the United States launched hit North Korea and Russia but did not kill many people because they went off course, landing in remote areas. The first missile launched by North Korea hit Sacramento, California. Three hundred miles from Potterville," Nyx said.

"That's what you've been taught," Miriam said.

# 23

WITHOUT WARNING, WITH NOT A HINT of an illness or infection, Derrick felt he might vomit. Despite not being the smartest person in the world — not even the smartest person in this tunnel linking the giant instruments of mass destruction — the reality of the situation loomed in his mind as undeniable as the sun on a clear day: seven people launched three nuclear missiles from here, and then someone executed them. Those thoughts kept spinning through his head. He tried to make them stop and failed.

"Can we leave now? We've seen enough," Nyx said.

Rebekah stepped from behind Derrick and said, "Not yet. Show them, Miriam."

Miriam led them past the bodies, into the empty missile silo, and then to the other entrance. She stopped in front of the control panel.

"What's this?" Akira asked.

"It's an operation panel. or at least part of it." Miriam pointed to three brass keys and three keypads. "The launch sequence must require three people; each possessing a special key and passcode."

Miriam touched the panel, bringing it to life.

**MISSILE NUMBER EIGHT—STATUS: LAUNCHED**
**MISSILE NUMBER EIGHT—WARHEAD: THERMONUCLEAR-HYDROGEN**
**MISSILE NUMBER EIGHT—WARHEAD STATUS: ARMED**
**MISSILE NUMBER EIGHT—TARGET: SACRAMENTO, CALIFORNIA**
**BEGIN LAUNCH SEQUENCE Y=NULL N=NULL**

Akira stepped close to the screen; her fingers tracing down each line. In a voice barely audible, she said, "They destroyed Sacramento."

Nyx cried openly. "You're saying they killed a million of their own citizens?"

Nyx slumped. Derrick caught her from behind and then held her in his arms; her back to his chest; her body racked with sobs.

"It appears they did just that," Miriam said, tears now flowing down her cheeks as she put her arm around Akira.

"Are you starting to understand why we must keep this place secret?" Miriam asked.

"Shouldn't we tell someone? At least the sheriff," Nyx sobbed.

"You still don't understand. There are at least five more of these nuclear missiles here. Hundreds of smaller missiles and many other weapons. If the wrong people knew about it, millions more could die," Miriam said.

"But who are the right people?" Akira asked.

"No one, really. I wish we didn't know about it," Miriam said. "Promise you won't tell anyone. We must return to do repairs on the reactor, and we may need help, but we've got to trust the people we bring."

Nyx wiped her face on her sleeve.

"She's right," Akira said.

Derrick could not see Akira, but her voice didn't sound normal. It was scratchy and thick. He didn't need to see her to understand why she didn't sound her normal self. He did not cause this, yet he felt responsible. He could not have protected Miriam, Nyx, Rebekah, or Akira from this, but he felt he should have. None of them should have ever seen this or shouldered the responsibility of this place and the horrors it held. Yet, here they were, and it *was* his fault. It all started when he hit Marcus Carver. That single moment caused it all. He wondered how hard it was to aim and launch one of these missiles? Right now, if he knew how, he would launch one at Marcus Carver. Miriam was right, no one should have this much power.

"I understand. But I have responsibilities. I've taken an oath to protect Potterville," Nyx said.

"I promise," Akira said.

Derrick wished he understood what Nyx was saying. *An oath to what? What was she involved in that gave so much responsibility? And power?*

"You took an oath too, Akira. You can't make that promise." Nyx turned to Miriam. "Why did you bring us here and put us in this position?" Nyx asked.

Miriam positioned Akira next to Nyx, staring at them both for a moment. "Because I trust you."

"Trust us! You barely know us," Nyx said.

"I trust you because Derrick trusts you. That's all I need. I don't understand your positions in Potterville, but I believe that you will do what is best for the town. Keeping this place secret is best for everyone."

Nyx looked at Akira and then back to Miriam. "Can Akira and I have a few minutes in private?"

Miriam pointed. "This tunnel takes you back to the Circle transport. You two go ahead. We'll be out in five minutes."

After Akira and Nyx left, Rebekah said, "Do you think it's safe letting them see this? Do you think they can keep it a secret?"

"Time will tell. I could not see any other choice," Miriam said.

"No other choice? How about the three of us sticking together and figuring this out?" Rebekah said.

"Not enough time. I need to fix Jane and I need help to do it."

"Miriam, I trust you but what is the deal with you and that robot? I don't get it," Derrick said.

"Two things. First, we need to know what is in Level Two." Miriam stopped.

"And the second thing?" Derrick asked.

"Duh. I made a promise."

Rebekah rolled her eyes.

Miriam stepped to the control panel, removed each key, placing them in her pocket.

"Why are you taking those?" Derrick asked.

"There are more keys somewhere that fit the remaining missiles. I intend to find them," Miriam said.

"Why? We don't know the codes for the keypads," Rebekah said.

"You're not considering launching a missile. Are you?" Derrick asked.

"I'm considering many things. Nothing is off the table," Miriam said.

"How can you say that? Nothing's off the table," Rebekah demanded.

Miriam said, "Because we still don't understand what we are up against. We have a lot of work to do and little time. I'm going to blindfold Akira and Nyx again. And we are going to split up for a little while. Just trust me, okay?"

"Blindfolding them doesn't bother me, but what do you mean split up?" Rebekah asked.

Miriam said. "Rebekah, you go back to Engineering. Wait for us on the river bridge. You'll be okay. You'll beat us to the bridge. If you're not there when we get there, I'll find you."

"You want me to go by myself?" Rebekah asked, her hands planted on her hips.

"You can do it. I don't like separating, but it's best to return the Circle and the electric cart."

Rebekah looked unconvinced. "That doesn't make sense. We know the Circle runs when the vehicle is parked on the turnout." She pointed to the vehicle that carried the final seven, which remained there awaiting its passengers who would never return. "I don't want to be alone. What if one of those robots won't let me leave?"

Miriam glared at Rebekah. Rebekah glared back. Derrick, as was his custom, felt lost.

After a moment, Miriam said, "I don't think that will happen. We already encountered one of them. It didn't do anything. If one tries to stop you, be authoritative. Act like you own the place. And you have your stun thing, plus the bats are in the transport. Got it?"

"As if I can use two bats. And you have not explained anything," Rebekah said.

Miriam sighed. "I'll explain it later."

"When later?" Rebekah insisted.

"Someday — later," Miriam said. "Just do it, okay? If it were not important, I wouldn't ask you."

"Whatever. But you owe me."

"Girlfriend, I owe you more than you'll ever know, or I'll ever be able to repay." Miriam gave her a hug, then turned and walked toward the Circle transport.

Derrick felt confused. They were a long way from Potterville. He wondered if confusion had become a permanent condition.

As they walked, Miriam said, "Let me do all the talking. And don't say anything about where we are meeting Rebekah."

Akira and Nyx stood outside the machine, waiting.

"Did you have time for your conversation?" Miriam asked.

It pleased Derrick that she asked this question, at least giving the impression that she considered their feelings and the difficulty of their position, even if her empathy was insincere.

"We've discussed what was needed. For now," Nyx said.

Akira looked as if she wanted to add something but remained silent.

Rebekah climbed into the vehicle. "Staging."

Nothing happened.

"What's going on?" Nyx asked.

"Change of plan," Miriam said, "we're splitting up."

Miriam stepped just inside the door. "Control transfer." Nothing happened. She said, "Transfer command."

The disembodied voice said, "Command protocol open."

Miriam whispered, "Say: new command."

Rebekah said, "New Command."

"New command recognized."

Miriam stepped out. "See you soon."

"Whatever. Staging."

The door closed and the Circle transport moved back to the primary track and sped away. Derrick thought he detected a tear in Miriam's eye. He hoped they would see Rebekah again as Miriam said. He began to understand there was no guarantee that would happen and there was nothing he could do about it.

"Why is Rebekah leaving?" Nyx asked.

"We are going back another way," Miriam said.

Miriam said, "We can't take the flying machine back to the meadow and leave it there, so we must go another way."

"But why is Rebekah leaving?" Nyx repeated.

"We need to get this second transport back to Staging," Miriam said.

"Will Rebekah be waiting for us at staging?" Akira asked.

"She will not. She's leaving," Miriam said.

"Why?" Akira asked.

"She's mad at me," Miriam said.

"That makes little sense," Nyx said.

"Exactly," Miriam agreed.

"God, you're frustrating. I can see why she might be mad at you. Or are you worried we might find our way back?" Nyx asked.

"That too. Sorry, can't take that chance," Miriam said. "It's important you can't find your way back. We don't know what the student council will do. If we must come here, it's safer if no one can find us."

"I agree with Miriam," Akira said.

"I know. You told me," Nyx said.

Akira said, "We must convince the council to let them stay. At least for now. Potterville's safety is in our hands."

Derrick stood watching the tunnel, although the transport was out of sight. "I should have gone with Rebekah."

Nyx frowned at him.

Miriam said, "She'll be okay. Besides, I need you with me."

Derrick paused for a moment. "Why? You do know how to get back? Right?"

"Yep. I need you because I can't guide two blind people off the mountain."

Derrick thought he detected a quick wink. He wasn't sure, though. It reminded him of her slight gestures during communications when she was in Pacific Edge. That seemed like years ago. "Okay."

Nyx protested, "Blindfolded again?"

Miriam held up her hand. "Yes. Follow me." She walked to the second Circle vehicle. Once inside, Miriam pulled two pieces of navy fabric from her bag.

"You came prepared," Nyx said.

"I tried to be," Miriam said. "I didn't think you'd want to put the other blindfolds on, because of the stench back there."

"Thoughtful of you. Thanks," Akira said, taking a piece of cloth.

"Did you cut up another of my shirts?" Derrick asked.

"I did. I'll buy you one." Miriam climbed into the Circle transport.

Nyx and Akira followed her; Derrick entered last. When Nyx and Akira finished tying on their blindfolds, Miriam looked at Derrick, holding her finger to her lips and said, "Command protocol override, new commander, Silo Number 7."

The Circle transport door closed, and the machine eased onto the main track. Derrick wondered how the machine was powered and why it still operated after all these years. And how did Miriam know it would still work? Or did she? Perhaps that was just a guess. If it didn't work, they would have faced a long walk back to the parking facility were the electric carts were stored. When they arrived at Silo Number Seven, the vehicle pulled to the side and stopped.

"Where are we?" Nyx asked.

"Silo Number 7. I need to check something." Miriam winked at Derrick and held her finger to her lips again. Then she got out, but she just stood outside the machine.

"Where did she go?" Akira asked.

Derrick did not want to lie, but he did. "Just to where the missile is." Miriam waved to him from outside the window.

"What's she doing in there?" Nyx asked.

"I have no idea," Derrick said.

After ten minutes, Miriam stepped back inside the vehicle. "There. That should hold it till we get back. Staging."

The machine pulled back onto the main track and accelerated.

They talked little during the thirty-some minute ride back to the staging area, which gave Derrick mixed emotions. He did not want to think about the council and what they might decide. Akira said they needed to stay. Nyx had not committed to anything. Not even keeping the place secret. It surprised him that Miriam didn't demand that Nyx promise. He wondered what Miriam would do if Nyx refused.

When the Circle transport arrived at the destination, Miriam helped Akira off, and Derrick helped Nyx.

"We have quite a long walk ahead. I'll hold Akira's hand. Derrick, you help Nyx."

Derrick was okay with that; although he wondered if holding Nyx's hand for a long time would become awkward. Perhaps Nyx would want to trade places with Akira at some point. Derrick was starting to understand. He thought, but wasn't sure, that they were going back to Engineering, same as Rebekah, and going to Silo Number 7 was just a delay to ensure that Rebekah got out ahead of them; for what purpose, he did not know. He also did not know why they were taking a long way back, walking into the staging area where they had been before. Once inside the staging area, Miriam led them back to where she first got on the computer. She stopped just outside the door to the hallway.

"Akira, you stay here with Derrick and Nyx. I have to check something, and it will be faster if we don't take you where I need to go," Miriam said, pulling Akira next to Derrick and putting Akira's hand in his. "Be right back," she mouthed to Derrick.

"How long will she be gone?" Nyx asked.

"I don't know. Not long," Derrick said, hoping he was correct. He assumed Nyx and Akira were tired of the blindfolds. He would be.

Miriam returned ten minutes later. She gave a thumbs up to Derrick and took Akira's hand. "We can go now."

Miriam led them through the maze of vehicles. Making unnecessary turns at times, backtracking at times. At the elevator, she said, "We are in an elevator. Going up to the next level.

Then she led them to an electric vehicle parked in the tunnel. "We are at a vehicle like we first took from Engineering." She helped Akira into the back, careful that Akira didn't bump her head. Then she helped Nyx into the front, motioning Derrick to unplug the cord. "Derrick, can you drive this thing?"

"I think so. I watched Rebekah do it." Derrick climbed into the driver's seat next to Nyx and whispered, "You doing okay?"

"I'm surviving, but I'll be glad when I can see again. And try to drive straight. I don't want to get carsick."

Derrick nodded and then realized Nyx couldn't see him. "I'll do my best, but I've never driven before."

"How is that even possible," Nyx said and then added, "Oh, forgot. Chosen. Duh."

Derrick eased from the curb, drove slowly until he had a feel for the machine and then sped up.

"How much longer," Akira asked.

"About twenty-five minutes and then we walk," Miriam said.

"Can we take our blindfolds off?" Nyx asked.

"Sorry. You cannot," Miriam said.

After ten silent minutes, Nyx said, "You have not asked me to promise I'll keep this place a secret."

"I have not," Miriam agreed.

"Why?" Nyx asked.

"I didn't think it was necessary. You're smart." Miriam paused. "And Derrick trusts you. I said earlier, that's enough for me."

Derrick glanced at Nyx, but he could not read her expression behind the blindfold. He trusted Nyx, but he knew her commitment to Potterville ran much deeper than her feelings, whatever they might be, towards him. He hoped Miriam knew what she was doing. Glancing back at Miriam, he saw she was holding Akira's hand. That seemed unnecessary in the vehicle.

When they arrived at Engineering, Derrick saw the cart Rebekah had driven, but no Rebekah. Miriam gave him another thumbs up gesture. After helping their blindfolded companions out of the vehicle, Miriam led them to the enormous room where she parked the flying machine. Walking deep into the cavernous space, searching the area with her flashlight, she stopped at a coffin-shaped box. There were thousands of similar boxes stacked in the building, but this one sat by itself, the lid ajar.

"Great. I wanted to know what was in these." Miriam stopped. "I'm not leaving you, Akira. I'm right here. Okay?"

Miriam stepped to the box, worked the wooden lid free. It fell to the floor with a thud.

"What was that?" Akira reached out, searching for Miriam.

"Just the top of a wooden box I'm looking into," Miriam said, shining her light into the box.

Derrick stepped to her side.

"Just as I thought," Miriam said.

"What do you see?" Nyx said.

"I'll tell you later," Miriam said.

"When later?" Nyx asked.

"When it's the right time later," Miriam said.

"God, you're frustrating," Nyx said.

"Agreed," Derrick said.

"But she's good at it," Akira said.

"And consistent," Derrick added.

"Hilarious," Nyx said.

Miriam continued through the building, weaving her way among the stacks of wooden crates, some small, some huge, plus machines, some of which Derrick recognized like the machines back in the staging area with tracks, cannons, and missiles, and flying machines like the one Miriam flew here from the meadow, and some machines, unlike anything he'd ever seen. As she meandered, she searched the edges of the building with her flashlight. The light fell on a metal door, not unlike the roll-up doors at the silos. Miriam walked to a door with a keypad near the roll-up door. She touched the pad; the numbers glowed pale green. She punched the keys and Derrick heard the lock activate. He pulled the door open.

Inside was a hallway carved through stone, like the one that led to Reactor One. He remembered they were still under a mountain. At the end of the hall was a screen like those in the missile silos and another metal door and keypad. Miriam did not activate the screen; she punched the keypad.

Derrick pulled the door open when the lock released. Inside was another ICBM; dim lights lit the white missile. *How many of these things are there?*

Inside, Miriam pointed. "We're going up a ladder. I think you can do that blindfolded. Best that you don't see anything when we get outside. I'll go first and open the door. When Derrick sees the daylight, he'll send Akira and then Nyx. Derrick will come last. Once outside, Derrick and I will guide you out of here."

Miriam touched Akira's shoulders and said, "You okay?"

Akira nodded.

Derrick wondered why Miriam had not spoken to Nyx. He stepped in front of Nyx and said, "Ready?"

Nyx nodded.

Derrick noticed that her cheeks were flushed and a little wet.

Miriam said, "I don't think opening the door will be a problem."

"That's comforting," Nyx said.

"And if it is a problem," Akira asked.

"Then we implement Plan B," Miriam said, smiling and giving Derrick an obvious wink.

"And what is Plan B?" Nyx asked.

"I haven't thought about it yet," Miriam said, checking then strap of the bag slung over her shoulder, and then starting up the stairs.

"Someone should kick her ass," Nyx said.

Akira giggled softly.

*Girls are a mystery,* Derrick thought.

# 24

AS MIRIAM CLIMBED THE LADDER, DERRICK watched, giving Akira and Nyx updates, mostly because he could think of nothing else to do. He did not mention when Miriam was at the top and struggling to open the door.

"What's taking so long?" Nyx asked.

He could not lie. Not to Nyx. "She's having trouble with the door."

"Perfect," Nyx said.

"She'll figure it out," Akira said.

And figure it out she did. Although the silo had lighting, the sunlight provided a warm glow that contrasted with the cold light of the silo. "She's got it open."

"I can feel the warmth of the Sun," Akira said, looking upward.

Derrick helped Akira find the first rung. Up she went, hand over hand, appearing more confident with each step

"She's almost to the top. Up you go," Derrick helped Nyx find the rung and then boosted her up. Not that she needed help.

Derrick followed, keeping a close eye on Nyx, ready to catch her if she fell, not knowing how he'd do that while on the ladder himself, but determined to do so just the same. Halfway up the ladder, it occurred to him the silo had lights. How that was possible, he did not know.

As Nyx reached the top, Miriam reached down, taking her hand, and guiding her out. "You made it. Welcome to the outside world again."

"I would never have guessed how good it feels to be out of there," Nyx said.

"I understand, trust me," Miriam said

No one helped Derrick out. When he got outside, he could see why Nyx and Akira had to be blindfolded. The farms near Potterville were visible in the distance, Potterville itself must be just out of sight hidden behind a grove of trees. They stood on a high mesa overlooking the valley. Hard to believe people had lived so close to this place without knowing it existed. How was that even possible? Something told him it was not possible. Something told him they had to know the answer to how they did not know, and he was sure he didn't want to hear it.

Derrick pointed at the valley, pointed to Nyx and Akira, shrugged his shoulders, and silently mouthed, "How?"

Miriam held her finger to her lips. "We have to be careful getting off this mountain. Here's how we are going to do it. I'll lead Akira, and Derrick will lead Nyx. How's your ankle, Derrick? You did not seem to be limping."

"It's better, I guess. I haven't been thinking about it," Derrick said.

Miriam took Akira's hand. "Put your hand on my shoulder and stay in my footsteps and we'll make it. Any questions?" Miriam winked at Derrick.

"The lights worked in the silo," Derrick said. "I wonder why lights didn't work elsewhere in Engineering."

Miriam pointed. "Solar panels. They must use them as backup. Amazing they still work."

"Solar panels don't work. That's why they were abandoned decades ago. Coal works and is cheaper," Akira said.

"They lied to you about Sacramento," Miriam said. "Think about it."

Miriam closed the silo door and then started toward the valley, but in twenty yards, she turned left and walked 30 yards towards the trees. Then she made two right turns until they were walking back towards the silo. Miriam continued a zigzag march across the plateau, turning a mile walk into three. When they were next to the tree line, Miriam told Akira to bend her knees because she had to pass under some brush. Miriam bent and lowered her head. Akira's head grazed the trees. Akira took one hand off Miriam's shoulders to brush the pine needles from her hair.

"Stop! Stand completely still." Miriam turned around, putting her hand over her mouth, laughing silently.

Startled, Akira said, "What?"

"Did I not tell you this was dangerous?" Miriam struggled to not laugh out loud.

"Well, yes, but I just …"

"Do exactly what I say. I don't want you falling into the canyon."

"Okay."

Derrick felt Nyx's fingers dig into his shoulders. "Don't worry. I won't let anything happen to you." He wished that was true. Nyx was in no danger here, at least no danger of falling into a non-existent canyon. Beyond that, he was not confident he could protect anyone.

"Keep both hands on my shoulders and follow my exact footsteps," Miriam said.

"I'll try," Akira said.

"That's better." Miriam smiled at Derrick and gave him a thumbs-up.

Derrick shook his head. He did not understand why Miriam thought this was funny, and he did not care for tricking Nyx. However, when they reached the trees, he also ducked.

Instead of heading towards the valley, Miriam turned back towards the middle of the plateau where a rock outcropping stood. He understood the meandering, but why Miriam walked to this pile of rocks puzzled him. What happened next did not end his confusion.

Miriam stopped, standing before the pile of rocks, she turned to Akira. "This is the most difficult part of the trail. Derrick and I will have to help you across one at a time."

"Can't we take our blindfolds off for this part?" Nyx asked.

"No. Don't worry. We'll keep you safe. Trust us," Miriam said, winking at Derrick.

Miriam continued, "Nyx, you stand still and don't move. This will take us a few minutes."

"This is scaring me," Akira said.

Miriam looked at Derrick, sticking her lower lip out in an isn't that cute sort of look. "Don't you worry. I won't let anything happen to you. Trust me?"

Akira took a deep breath. "I trust you."

Miriam motioned Derrick in front of Akira.

"Just stand there. I'll be back," Derrick said to Nyx.

Nyx said nothing.

When Derrick was in front of Akira, Miriam said, "Derrick will hold your hands and I'll get behind you." Miriam pressed against Akira, although there was no reason to do so as she moved behind her. If anyone would have seen them, he would have thought they were crazy.

Derrick would have agreed with that assessment.

"Okay. Here we go," Miriam said. Miriam took Akira's leg, guiding her foot to the first stone.

Derrick pulled lightly as Akira stepped forward.

One-step and then another, Miriam patiently guiding as if Akira was a blind person trying to climb a mountain peak. Halfway across the mound, Miriam turned left so they would cross the top and then back down the other side.

After they had reached the other side, Miriam said, "I'll take Akira to a safe spot and then come back to help you with Nyx.

Derrick shook his head. Rather than retrace his steps, he walked around the rocks and rejoined Nyx.

"I'm back," Derrick said.

"How did you do that?" Nyx asked.

"Do what?"

"Come up behind me. I thought we were on a narrow trail on a mountainside."

*Damn, damn, damn.* He was so stupid it was amazing he could breathe. "Uh, I took a shortcut and jumped off a ledge." He hated it the instant the words came out of his mouth because that was another lie. He'd tell her the truth when it was safe to do so. If it ever became safe.

"I'm going to move to the front. Okay?"

"Sure. No problem," Nyx said.

Derrick placed his hands on Nyx's waist, held her close as he inched by. That part he did not mind. Nyx did not flinch or pull away. He assumed that was because she feared doing so might send her off a cliff. He wondered if she would remember this when he told her the truth.

Miriam, being smarter than he was, came over the rocks the same way as they had taken Akira. "I'm back. Ready?"

"Why didn't you take the shortcut?" Nyx asked.

"What shortcut?" Miriam asked.

Derrick shook his head, pointing he said, "I dropped off that ledge, which put me behind Nyx."

Miriam's face lit up. "Oh, I see. I'm too short to do that. Why are you in front?" Miriam looked at Derrick.

"I thought …"

"You thought wrong. Now get behind her where you belong." Miriam pointed, grinning.

Derrick repeated the process to move behind Nyx. This time he thought Nyx pressed closer as he passed, which probably did not happen. His imagination ran wild on him sometimes. Why it did so now, he had no clue.

They helped Nyx as they did Akira. Derrick guiding her feet and legs, holding her waist to ensure she did not topple off the imaginary cliff. While he felt the process was tedious as he and Miriam helped Akira, he felt it ended far too soon with Nyx. He looked back to see if the mound had shrunk. It had not.

As Derrick followed Miriam towards Akira, leading Nyx with her hands on his shoulders, Miriam danced, twirled, and spun circles hands, flying up in the air, smiling, and laughing silently.

She was playing.

He thought it impossible, yet another new sadness crept into his heart. Despite the danger and the death, and the threats before them, Miriam was still a young girl who wanted nothing more than to be just that. Full of life and fun. It dawned on him like a cold morning sunrise. He had never played with Miriam, not that he could remember. He had never played with anyone. Now that he thought about it, he could not remember doing anything in Pacific Edge other than eat, sleep, go to the Academy, and watch New America Media. And he could not remember seeing Miriam play or display so much happiness. How did he miss childhood? That's what he wanted to know. What he did know was that he'd never get a chance at childhood again. Too late for him. Maybe too late for Miriam. So, for now, he decided to smile, and enjoy, for just a moment, what he'd never known.

# 25

WHEN THEY NEARED THE FOREST, a game trail appeared on the edge of the mountain. It was not as steep as the trail Derrick was on when he ran into Nyx, the drop off not as extreme and the fall not nearly as far, but still dangerous if one of the girls stepped off the side. The game trail was narrow, but straight, at least for now. To the left, a ravine carved into the mountain; he could not see the bottom because of the brush, but he heard the babble of a small stream.

"Stay close," Derrick said.

Miriam stood next to Akira. Miriam said something, but Derrick could not hear what she said. Akira nodded.

They started down the trail. It was a steady and gradual descent at first; no trees or brush blocked the path. Then the descent grew steeper; rocks on the trail made footing tricky. Nyx slipped. Derrick stopped. He dared not look back for fear that if he shifted, she might lose her balance. "Are you okay?"

"I'm okay. The trail seems steeper here. Can we take our blindfolds off, at least until we get off this section?"

"Miriam, can they take their blindfolds off for this section?" Derrick asked.

"No, sorry. Just go slow and be careful. We'll be okay."

Derrick thought Miriam was being unreasonable. However, Miriam must have thought it was important because he did not think she would put Nyx or Akira at risk if it were unnecessary. He decided he could help Nyx if he described the trail as they went. Loose rocks here, larger rocks there.

Then they came to the worst section thus far. Straight below them to the right, water coursed swiftly through boulders. It was 20 feet to the creek, straight down. Derrick did not like the looks of this, not at all. One missed step would put Nyx on those rocks. It was far enough to break a leg, or worse.

Miriam had also stopped and studied the trail. "Looks like this only goes about 30 yards and then we are out. We need to take them down one at a time. Like we did before."

Derrick turned to face Nyx. A flat rock sat by the trail. "Would you like to sit? There's a rock here."

"That would be nice," Nyx said.

He felt bad that they had meandered around earlier. It was like lying. He guided Nyx to the rock; she sat. "You okay?"

"Yes."

"We'll be right back."

Miriam called out, "Don't take that blindfold off. I can see you all the way."

Nyx frowned but said nothing. Derrick did not know if the frown was because Miriam didn't trust her, or because Nyx planned on peaking."

"I'll go first this time," Miriam said. "Not safe trading places."

Derrick placed his hands on Akira's waist as they walked. Miriam called out the condition of the trail as they descended. It did not take long. He felt relieved when they reached the bottom.

"You doing okay?" Miriam asked.

"I'm okay," Akira said.

"Do you want to sit?"

"I'll be fine. You'll be back soon enough."

Miriam and Derrick helped Nyx down. The same routine; Miriam led; Derrick stayed behind Nyx. About halfway down, Nyx stepped too close to the edge and one foot slipped off the trail. Derrick gripped Nyx's waist, using a bit of force to get her back on the track.

"Damn it. I don't like this," Nyx said.

"I don't blame you," Miriam said over her shoulder. "I hope we don't have to do anything like this again."

Off the mountain, on a narrow, overgrown trail, they twisted along the creek until they came to a thick row of brush. The trail split off in either direction and then petered out into a pile of rocks in one direction and more brush in the other.

"One more problem, ladies," Miriam said. "This time we have a thicket of brush to go through. Derrick will go first and move branches out of the way. I'll guide you through one at a time."

This proved a time-consuming. Derrick fought to part brush, which consisted of scrawny reddish-brown twigs that were tough, tangled, and — covered with ants. A slight but annoying throbbing in his ankle became noticeable.

He pulled some branches apart, held them as best he could for Akira to step forward. He could feel ants crawling on his neck, hands, and arms.

"There are lots of ants on this brush," Derrick said.

"Crap," Akira said, "Let's make this fast."

Akira stepped into the opening Derrick created; Miriam right behind her. Now that both girls were in the brush, he needed to move back, which would mean letting go of what he held back, which meant that brush was going to close on Akira and Miriam. He had not thought this through. He thought about abandoning the bags and the bats but decided against it.

This swamp or march or bog, whatever it was, felt like his life. Stuck in the weeds. "I have to let go to move back. Try to move with me, but you're going to need to push limbs back as we go."

"This would be a lot easier if I could see," Akira said.

"I know. I'm sorry," Miriam said.

Now he knew why Nyx was tired of hearing him say he was sorry. Sorry didn't change the situation. Derrick pushed himself through the brush. The twigs dug into his shirt and skin. More ants. The ground was wet, muddy, and slick. "Careful. It's muddy."

"Great. I wish I'd worn old shoes," Akira said.

They moved like this, a few feet at a time, Akira occasionally catching her foot on a limb. Twice she stumbled forward, but Derrick caught her. At least Miriam wasn't smiling. She looked concerned, although there was no actual danger here.

They busted through the last of the brush into a meadow near the trail along the river. Now, Derrick understood why Miriam did not let them take the blindfolds off. It would be too easy to find their way back to this spot, and then not difficult to find the silo. If it were not for the way the brush grew here, someone would have explored the game trail they followed down.

Getting Nyx through the brush was a bit easier, but by the time they got to where Akira waited, Derrick and Miriam were both sweating. Miriam straightened the brush, making their path invisible.

Akira brushed at her arms and face, knocking ants from her skin and clothing. Miriam came to her aid, brushing her legs and back and grooming her hair with his fingers.

"Get these damn bugs off me," Nyx said, swiping both hands over her face.

Derrick stood behind her, his hands moving but hovering inches from her body as if she were too hot to touch.

"Is anyone there?" Nyx demanded.

"I'm here," Derrick said.

"Then help. I hate bugs."

"Uh, well, I'm not sure where is okay to touch you."

"It's not sex, for God's sake. Just help. I'll let you know if you're getting too personal."

Derrick did as Nyx asked. Brushing her shoulders and back seemed okay. He hesitated when he reached her backside. Nyx helped by brushing back there herself. He worked down her legs and then stood to comb his fingers through her hair.

When he could see no more ants on Nyx, he worked on himself. Miriam came over and brushed his back. He did the same for her. When they had done all they could, Miriam led them to the trail, which was only 25 yards away, but she meandered as much as was possible, doubling back a couple of times.

"Easy going now," Miriam said, taking Akira's hand, walking at her side.

Derrick took Nyx's hand, leading her along the river.

"We must be on the river path," Nyx said.

"Yes, I think so," Derrick said.

"I've been on the river path many times. When can we take the blindfolds off? It's not like we don't know where we are now," Nyx said.

"Soon," Miriam said.

Derrick did not know why Miriam didn't let them take the blindfolds off, but he did not complain. Without the blindfold, Nyx would not be holding his hand. She held his hand so he could lead her. It wasn't because she wanted to, but he liked it. Her fingers laced through his anchored him somehow; despite that it was an allusion to feelings that could not endure. Nyx would vote to send them away. Nyx had her priorities straight. He felt proud to know her. Even if his time in Potterville was extended, it was still limited, he felt certain that his feelings for Nyx would be with him forever. Although, his forever might not be exceptionally long. Had he not hit Marcus Carver, his life would have been long and safe in Pacific Edge. Now he understood life there was merely existing, not living.

He felt alive. He could envision no place he would rather be than right here, right now.

# 26

THE PATH TURNED AWAY FROM THE river and rose up the mountainside, following a gentle bend. For a moment, trees blocked the view on both sides. Then the trees to the right gave way and he could see the river forty yards distant, tumbling over the polished stones, glistening in the late day's sun. When they reached the crest of the rise, the river came into view. Rebekah stood in the middle of it, looking down into the water, her bag at her feet, two bats protruding out sat at her feet. As they descended, Rebekah looked up.

Miriam waved.

Rebekah waved back.

"Okay, 90-degree turn," Miriam said to Akira. "Almost there."

"Almost where?" Nyx asked.

Miriam glanced over her shoulder. "Almost to where you can take your blindfold off."

Derrick steered Nyx towards the bridge.

When they reached where Rebekah stood at the apex, Miriam said, "Okay, you can take them off now."

Nyx pulled the blindfold off. "I thought so."

"Thought so what?" Miriam asked.

"That we were on the bridge. I could tell when we left the path."

"The question is, could you find your way back?" Miriam asked. "Be honest."

"What if I could?"

"I'd have to toss you in the river," Miriam said.

"I'd like to see you try."

"I'm joking. But could you?" Miriam asked.

Nyx thought for a moment. "Maybe. But probably not. I don't think I could find my way back. I got confused several times. Why is that important?" Nyx asked.

"We've been over that. In case we have to make a run for it," Miriam said.

Everyone was quiet for a moment. Derrick hoped Nyx would provide some reassurance that making a run for it would not be necessary, but she did not.

After a few minutes, Miriam turned to Rebekah and said, "Any problems?"

"Nope. But I didn't like being alone." Rebekah turned back to the river, her forearms on the railing. "I love this river. It's peaceful. I felt better after being here for a few minutes."

"I'm sorry we had to split up." Miriam stood next to Rebekah, staring into the tumbling water. "It is beautiful. I'd come here every day if I could."

Akira forced her way between Rebekah and Miriam. "Enjoy it while you can."

"You think they're going to force us out soon?" Rebekah asked.

"Perhaps, but that's not what I meant. In a couple of months, this will be a trickle or completely dry," Akira said.

"Why?" Rebekah asked.

"The drought. They say this river used to flow all summer. But because of the new climate, there's not enough snow in the mountains."

"But Sheriff Collins said there was too much snow for us to cross the mountains," Miriam said.

"True, but still not enough. Don't they teach you about the new climate in Pacific Edge?" Nyx asked.

"They do not," Miriam said.

Akira sighed. "What do we do next?"

"I need a computer." Miriam turned to Akira. "I need your help with the robot brain thing."

"I need to call my mom," Akira said. She pulled out her phone and then said, "Uh, oh. She's called me like 10 times. I'm probably in trouble."

Nyx turned on her phone. "My mom is working." When her phone was on, several dings sounded. "Coach is looking for us. So is the Sheriff."

Both girls held the phones to their ears.

Akira said, "Hi, mom. —

"Yes, we're okay. —

"Just went for a walk in the woods. No cell phone service till we got back to town." Akira made a face as if she either hoped her mom believed her or did not start yelling.

"She's calling coach now. —

"I'm sorry. We have a lot to workout. Uh, would it be okay if I go to Nyx's house? —

"Yes, it's important. —

"I'll call you when we get there. —

"I won't. —

"Okay. Love you too." Akira gave a slight smile as she put her phone in her back pocket.

Then Nyx said, "Hi, Coach. You called? —

"Sorry. We're okay and together. We went for a walk across the river and had no cell service. —

"Yeah, we're back. By the river. Headed home next. —

"It can wait until tomorrow. —

Nyx closed her eyes and shook her head. "Can't be today. We need more time. —

"No. I'm serious. We won't come. We'll leave and you won't find us. —

"I'm dead serious. —

"Too early. Okay, seven will work. Yes, we'll be there." Nyx ended the call.

"Council meeting?" Akira asked.

"Yes. They wanted to move it up to this evening. I figured Miriam needed more time."

"Thanks," Miriam said.

"What about Anna?" Rebekah asked.

"Good question. Things don't make sense," Miriam said.

"Explain," Rebekah said. "And do not say later. I'm about to lose it."

Miriam touched Rebekah's arm. "I know. So, I've been thinking. Anna must have followed us the night we left. She waited outside Technical Services. When the system crashed, the door locks failed, and she went inside to find us. But we were already gone, and she left too."

"You can't know that," Rebekah said. Her chin quivered a little.

"It's the only thing that makes sense. The robot thought she is with us. Therefore, she escaped when we did."

Rebekah nodded. "I suppose you're right. What did the robot say?"

"It said, 'Leadership requires the return of the subject known as Anna Ford.'"

"And what did you say?" Derrick asked.

"I asked what was in it for me," Miriam said.

"You did what?" Rebekah asked, her face turning red.

"Best I could think of at the time. I wanted it, or whoever was listening, to think she was with us."

"Why would you want that?" Nyx asked.

"So, they wouldn't be looking for her someplace else, which is where she is."

The color faded from Rebekah's face. "So, what did it say?"

"It said the rest of us would be free to do whatever we wanted for the rest of our lives. No security patrols, no harassment, no restrictions."

"And you said?" Rebekah asked.

"I said that sounded good, but we'd need it in writing. That's when Derrick hit the bot with the bat."

"And you'd trusted them?" Rebekah asked.

"Of course not. But they don't know that. What they know is that we have their robot and their aircraft, and they think we have Anna. In my opinion, it has worked out for us thus far."

Derrick couldn't argue with her logic, although the entire episode didn't feel like a win. It amazed him how the feel of victory following the track meet had left him. He thought that feeling would last forever. It didn't last the afternoon. The sun, nearing the mountain horizon, cast a golden light on the ripples of the river. He had always felt at peace staring at the stream.

Now, he wondered if the water carried invisible and deadly radioactivity. "Should we have this water tested?"

"That would be a good idea," Miriam said.

"I know a place that can test it. We'll need to find the money for the test though," Akira said.

"I'll pay for it," Miriam said.

Derrick stared at her but did not ask how she could do that. He would wait until they could talk in private. "I'm hungry."

"How can you think about food?" Rebekah asked.

Derrick shrugged.

"Derrick is right. We need to eat," Miriam said.

"So, what's the plan?" Derrick asked.

"I need a shower. Let's go to the condo. Akira and I will freshen up. We'll have pizza delivered. We'll meet up at Derrick's and then discuss what's next," Nyx said.

"I need to do research," Miriam said.

Rebekah rolled her eyes. "I hope your research includes finding Anna."

"It does not. I'm still thinking about that," Miriam said.

"We need to do something. Just thinking won't help," Rebekah said, tears welling in her eyes.

Miriam stroked Rebekah's arm. Derrick never thought of Miriam as a warm person, which reminded him of how little he knew about his sister.

"I know how you feel. I felt the same way after Derrick was exiled. But thinking is the best thing we can do. Because that we are here shows a well-thought-out plan works. Here's what I don't understand. We assume the Prime tracked Akira and I to the meadow by activating Akira's 1984 chip. That means the Prime has access to 1984, even though Pacific Edge has not recovered from their computer crash. But they don't know where Anna is. They think we have her."

Rebekah wiped her eyes. "That is odd."

"It's more than odd. Someone disabled Anna's chip. If we can figure out who did that, perhaps we can find Anna," Miriam said.

"And what if we can't figure that out?" Rebekah asked.

"Then we may never find her," Miriam said.

# 27

THE GIRLS STARTED TOWARDS TOWN, Nyx and Akira led, walking side by side, but not touching; Miriam and Rebekah followed, walking arm and arm. Miriam and Rebekah had been through a lot the past few days, Derrick realized. Perhaps even longer because he didn't know what happened after he left Pacific Edge. Theirs still seemed an odd relationship. He could not shake the feeling that there was more to Rebekah coming here than she had admitted to. He circled back to it being about him, which caused him no small degree of anxiety for a variety of reasons.

Derrick stopped, scrutinizing the trees, the horizon, and the shadows. Peering into the forest, he thought there was movement, but he saw nothing. He did not need to be seeing ghosts, but he imagined within every shadow, he might see a black robot. Thinking how close the robot came to frying him with those laser eyes struck him fast and hard. He dodged death by a split second in the meadow. Had the robot killed him, his troubles would be over. Taking a deep breath, he felt more relief than anticipated. But it would also mean that he would not be here to protect Miriam, nor Akira, nor Rebekah.

Nor Nyx.

He trotted to catch the girls, who had now reached the street.

Nyx must have heard him. "Nice of you to join us." Turning her head, she winked and smiled.

Akira studied Nyx for a moment, then glanced at Derrick. He did not know what that meant, but he felt an unexplained warmth radiate from his chest.

Everything looked different. Long dark shadows, the colors muted. They were just five kids—four walking normally, one with a slight limp—carrying bags and baseball bats; that should not warrant the stares that greeted them. His limp was not that bad. Things had changed, of that much Derrick was certain, but he did not understand what the change entailed or why it happened so rapidly.

He scanned the sky and peered into the alleys and shadows. He saw nothing unusual. Jim Priest drove by, extending his middle finger. Derrick had seen him do that before; it was not unusual.

Akira yelled, "Grow up Jimmy."

Miriam let go of Rebekah's arm, spun around, walking backwards. "Here's another thing I don't understand. They abandoned that base decades ago, but people here should still know about it. Hundreds worked there. People must have known. You know, someone's friend's dad worked there or something. How could people not know about it?"

"That seems strange. But I have not lived here all my life," Akira said. "How about it, Nyx?"

"I've never heard anything about it. I agree it's weird but unimportant."

"It might be important," Miriam said.

"How so?" Nyx asked.

Miriam said, "I'm not sure. But if we learned how it was kept secret, we might understand why it's important."

Nyx shook her head. "More riddles. Spare me."

If that statement bothered Miriam, she didn't show it. "Who's the oldest person who has lived here his or her entire life?"

Akira looked to Nyx and then said, "That would be old man Fletcher."

Nyx nodded. "He must be ninety at least."

"Can we talk to him?" Miriam asked.

"I don't know. Maybe. Probably not," Nyx said.

"Riddles," Miriam said with a giggle.

"You're strange," Rebekah said.

"Thank you," Miriam said.

Derrick did not understand those two.

"We need to talk to him," Miriam said.

"I'll try to set it up. Maybe tomorrow," Nyx said.

"Not soon enough," Miriam said. "Has to be tonight."

"You don't understand," Nyx began.

"Is it really that important?" Akira asked.

"We'll know when we talk to him," Miriam said.

* * *

When they got to the condo, Miriam went straight to the computer, Rebekah went straight to the shower. Derrick wanted to order pizza, but he wasn't certain how it was done, and he no longer had a phone. Also, he had checked his wallet and found that he had $11. He did not know how much pizza cost but thought it likely more than he had. He inventoried the refrigerator and the cupboards. He had enough cereal and milk for five bowls if nobody wanted too much cereal and nobody wanted too much milk. Other than that, it looked bleak. He realized that even if they could stay; he had no food and no money. He could not risk working at the bistro. He could not risk leaving Miriam and Rebekah unprotected. He did not know how to protect them, but he had to try.

He sat in the window watching darkness fall on the town. In the distance, the fields disappeared and then the glow of streetlamps began to illuminate the streets. In the shadows, he kept envisioning black robots.

A knock came at the door. Derrick looked out the peephole, wondering why the person had not used the entry request bell. In the hallway stood Akira. He let her in.

"Nyx will be here in a minute. She's cleaning up. I ordered pizza already," Akira said.

"I don't think I have enough money," Derrick said.

"I'm buying this time. I owe you from the time we went to the bistro."

Derrick could not remember now if that was true, but it didn't matter. He only had $11.

"Where's Miriam?" Akira asked.

"She went straight to the computer," Derrick said. He pointed towards the study, which was just the second bedroom that he called a study based on Paul's suggestion.

"Do you know how to get into the crawl space above your condo?" Akira asked.

"Crawlspace?" Derrick asked.

"Yes, it's where the wiring and vents and stuff run. It's where the cameras would be hidden."

"I saw something that looked like an opening on the ceiling of the closet," Derrick said.

"That would be it. Go up there and look for cameras. If you see anything, make sure they no longer work," Akira said.

"But Paul said …"

Akira held up her hand. "I know what Paul said. Just do it, okay? And be quick because the pizza will be here soon."

Derrick went to the bedroom, tapped on the door. Rebekah did not respond. He eased the door open. He heard the shower running; felt the humidity. If the shower was running, he did not have to worry about Rebekah stepping out naked. He went to the closet, studied the opening into the crawlspace. A small metal ring hung at one end. In the corner of the closet, which was mostly empty, he saw a stick with a hook on the end. Using the stick, he pulled on the ring. The door opened and a ladder extended as it did.

He climbed the ladder, sticking his head into the opening. He felt cobwebs on his face, and he brushed at them, almost losing his balance. It was not entirely dark in the crawlspace as light leaked in here and there, but he could not see much other than a small green light. Something told him that wasn't right.

He should have grabbed Miriam's flashlight; he thought about retrieving it, but feared Rebekah would be out of the shower soon. Once he pulled himself into the crawlspace, which proved to make the name self-explanatory, he waited until his eyes adjusted and then worked his way towards the green light, staying on the narrow wooden boards because the panels in-between did not look strong enough to hold his weight.

The boards hurt his knees, so he raised up on his toes whenever possible. Before he reached the green light, he knew what he was looking at. He did not know how he knew, but he did.

It was a transmitter.

The box had two short antennas and a cord running to an electrical outlet. In other locations above the condo, he saw three additional pinpoints of green light. The closest one was over his bedroom, one over the living area, and one over the study.

The cameras were still on.

Paul did not disable them.

Or if he did, someone installed new ones.

# 28

DERRICK UNPLUGGED THE BLACK BOX AND then ripped it free from the wood. He worked his way to each camera and jerked them loose as well. One by one, he tossed them to the closet floor. When he finished, he descended the ladder, forgetting to listen for the shower, which apparently wasn't running because when he stepped from the closet, Rebekah stepped into the bedroom, hair wet, draped in a towel.

He turned his back, and said, "Sorry, I thought you were still in the shower."

With a quick glance over his shoulder, he saw that Rebekah had not moved. She rubbed her hair with one end of the towel, still mostly covered, but she did not seem concerned that he was there.

"Why would you think I was in the shower? Do you hear a shower running?"

"No. Well, yes, when I first came in, it was running."

"Why are you in here? It's inappropriate, don't you think?"

"Yes. I do think. I mean, I wasn't thinking. Well, I was thinking, but I got distracted."

"I see. And what distracted you?"

"These." Derrick pointed at the camera equipment at his feet.

"Are those cameras? I thought they were gone."

"That's what we were told."

"I've been on camera in the shower?"

"Not the shower. The bedrooms and the living room." Derrick bent, his back still to Rebekah, and gathered the equipment. Keeping his back to her, he shuffled to the door.

As he reached the door, he said, "Sorry."

"Knock next time," Rebekah said.

When Derrick opened the door, he saw Nyx had returned. He caught the door with his foot, trying to close it on his way out, but was sure that it did not fully close. Nyx and Akira stared as he walked to the table with the equipment in his arms. In unison, the two girls' eyes shifted from Derrick to the bedroom door. He tried to not look back but failed.

"I'll be right out," Rebekah said, standing in the door with the towel hanging in front of her.

Nyx glared at Derrick. "What's going on."

"My fault," Akira said, turning pink in the cheeks.

"How is that your fault?" Nyx demanded.

"I asked Derrick to check the crawl space for cameras. Rebekah was still in the shower when he went in. Apparently, she finished before he got out."

Nyx pursed her lips. "Apparently."

Gradually, Nyx turned back to the table. "This stuff was up there? In operation, I assume."

"It was all running," Derrick said. "This," he held up the main box with the antennas, "was plugged in, and this light was on. The cameras were also plugged in. I don't know anything about such things, but I think the electrical outlets were newly installed."

"Why do you think that?" Akira asked.

He said, "Because there were bits of wood and pieces of wire where the boxes had been installed."

Akira said, "That's good deductive reasoning, Derrick."

"This is bad," Nyx said. "Either Paul lied to us, or someone installed new equipment while we were out."

"How would they know we were gone?" Derrick asked.

"If the robot was broadcasting live, they could have seen us," Akira said.

"But they would have to send someone, do the install, and then get out. Unless they already had someone close by ready to do it. Still, it's a short time frame. The person would have to be good at such work," Nyx said.

"Like Paul," Akira said.

"Exactly like Paul," Nyx said.

"I find it hard to think Paul did this," Derrick said.

"I don't like it either. But how well do any of us know Paul?" Nyx asked.

"He was nice to me," Derrick said.

"He lied to us for money," Nyx said.

Derrick hung his head. It circled back to lying. Maybe it always would. "True."

The bedroom door opened. Rebekah joined them. Clothed. Hair still damp. Eyes red.

Nyx glared at her. "I see you got dressed."

"I don't wear clothing in the shower. Maybe the customs are different here."

The entry buzzer sounded. "That will be the pizza," Akira said, "I'll go get it."

"Go with her, Derrick, and take one of those stunner things," Nyx said.

Derrick and Akira returned moments later with pizza.

The smell of pizza must have reached Miriam because she entered the room as the pizza boxes opened. Derrick grabbed plates, forks, salt, and pepper.

"Do you have chili pepper flakes?" Akira asked.

"I don't think so," Derrick said.

Nyx came from the kitchen area carrying something. "Put this ice on your ankle. Your limp is getting worse."

Derrick pulled off his shoe and put the plastic bag of ice on his ankle. Nyx was right; he wondered why she bothered to extend this bit of kindness. Perhaps it was just her nature. Maybe it was one runner to another.

Miriam sat the Jane robot brain on the counter. "Akira, this is what I told you about. It contains six memory devices. I think they are called hard drives. One no longer functions."

"What is that?" Nyx asked.

Miriam hesitated and then said, "I guess you know enough to know more. It's the brain of a robot. Her friend led us hostage for a while deeper in the mountain."

"Her?" Nyx said.

"Charlie, the other robot, called her Jane. Both developed artificial intelligence. Charlie is the robot I told you about."

Akira said, "That's not how AI works. It's not developed. It's programmed. It has limits, which is why it is no longer used."

"It's true that Charlie and Jane were programmed with a limited artificial intelligence capability. But at some point — they evolved."

"I'm sorry, Miriam. But I find that difficult to believe. You might have misunderstood the machine's capacity. That is understandable because you did not have robots in Pacific Edge. Plus, you were tired," Akira said.

"She's right," Rebekah began.

"What would you know about it?" Nyx snapped.

"What's up with you?" Rebekah snapped back.

Nyx stood.

Rebekah stood.

"Guys! Calm down. I get it. I did not like Miriam calling that thing Charlie. But she's right. Charlie is intelligent, like us. How much like us I don't know. But Miriam is right." Something told Derrick that he did not get it.

Nyx sat.

Rebekah sat.

Miriam looked at them and then to Akira. "What just happened?

Akira patted Miriam's hand. "I'll explain later. I'm sorry I doubted you. So, why is fixing this important?" Akira picked the brain up, turning it in her hands. "We don't use hard drives anymore. That is an incredibly old technology. Everything now uses SSD."

"She's an old machine. What's an SSD?" Miriam said.

Akira said, "SSD stands for solid-state drive. No moving parts."

Nyx took a bite of pizza; with her mouth full, she mumbled, "Why do you need to fix it?"

"Her," Miriam corrected.

Nyx rolled her eyes and then waved her hand in a *come-on* gesture.

"I promised Charlie that I would," Miriam said.

"You promised the robot?" Nyx questioned.

"I did."

"We don't have time for this," Nyx said.

"You don't but I do. We need to get back there, and we can't go without fixing her."

"What if we can't fix her?" Akira asked.

"I'll figure that out if it becomes necessary," Miriam said.

"You didn't answer my question," Nyx said.

"I answered your question. You asked why it was important and I told you. Maybe a promise doesn't mean much here. But when I promise, it's important to me."

"That's true," Derrick said.

Nyx held up her hands. "Okay, okay. I'm sorry. I get it and promises are important. Still, I think there's more to it."

Miriam looked at Derrick. "She's cute and smart, too."

That startled Derrick and he did not know how to respond, but he agreed.

Miriam took a piece of pizza. After she swallowed her first bite, she said, "Two other things. One, if we go back without fixing Jane, I don't know how Charlie will react."

Nyx jumped in before Miriam could finish. "Simple. You tell him you tried. Couldn't fix it. End of story."

"Not that simple," Miriam said.

"How is it not that simple?" Nyx asked.

"Because I think Charlie loves Jane. His emotions might overcome his logic. He might become dangerous."

"Good grief." Nyx pulled off another slice of pizza.

"She's right," Derrick said. "I hate to admit it, but she'd right."

"Anything else?" Nyx asked, chewing.

"Yes," Miriam said.

"Well, out with it."

"In the facility where we found Charlie there's a section that only Charlie can access. He said that he and Jane perfected some projects."

"You've lost me," Nyx said.

"You mean there might be weapons there we can use to protect the town?" Akira said.

"Protect the town. Protect us," Miriam said.

# 29

WHILE DERRICK CLEANED UP THE PIZZA MESS, Nyx and Akira got on their phones. They moved to separate rooms, preventing Derrick from hearing the conversations. Miriam lead Akira to the study.

Rebekah stared out the window into the darkness. "Do you think we'll ever find her?"

"Find Anna?" Derrick asked.

"Yes," Rebekah said.

"Maybe. Probably. Yes, we'll find her. Or she'll find us," Derrick said.

"She doesn't know where to look for us," Rebekah said.

"But she's smart. We'll find her somehow." Derrick did not know what to say. He did not know Anna, although he felt that he should. Perhaps he did, but his mind wasn't working right. Too many things swirling around in there.

Rebekah said, "I'm not so sure. Who could have shut off her 1984 chip? Why do they want her? Too many things don't make sense."

Derrick had not thought about why Anna was important. He hadn't thought about many things. Reality became a blur and turned into a wave that surged upon him, tumbling him helplessly in a raging river of uncertainty. *Why was Anna important?*

* * *

Having finished her call, Nyx came to the living room and said, "We're set to talk with old man Fletcher. Sheriff Collins will pick us up in ten minutes. Where did Akira and Miriam go?"

Derrick pointed to the study. Nyx walked to the open door, "Akira! We need to leave."

Akira walked out, Miriam trailing. Akira said, "I don't see why we can't replace them with SSDs. I doubt those old hard drives are available anywhere."

"Maybe we can upgrade Jane and Charlie if this works. But I don't want to risk changing whatever makes Jane tick," Miriam said.

Akira said, "If you're sure, I'll make the call."

Nyx waved them towards the exit door, grabbing one of the cameras Derrick found above the condo before following them.

In the stairwell, Akira spoke into her phone. "Hi, Allen? It's Akira. —

"I'm alive. —

"No time to explain. I need a favor. Can you find six 3.5-inch, 7800 RPM, ten-gig hard drives? —

"I know. But we need hard drives with the exact specs. Seagate™ if possible. —

Akira whistled. "Wow. That's a lot."

She looked at Miriam and covered her phone with her hand. "He said he can get them, but they are rare and expensive. Ten times more than an SSD."

"How much is ten times more?" Miriam asked.

Akira said, "A thousand dollars each."

"An SSD is only a hundred dollars?" Miriam asked.

"Yes," Akira confirmed.

"Tell him we need seven hard drives and fifteen SSDs."

"That will be over twenty thousand dollars."

"More like twenty-two thousand," Miriam said.

"I don't have that kind of money," Akira said.

"I do. I just need to go to a bank."

"How can you have twenty thousand dollars?" Derrick asked, his voice raising an octave.

"Withdrew it from my savings account," Miriam said.

"What savings account?" Derrick asked.

"Too many questions." Miriam looked at Akira. "When can he bring them?"

Akira asked the question. Said she'd explain further when she saw him and tapped the screen on her phone.

"He'll be here tomorrow."

"Is there a bank open tomorrow?" Miriam asked.

"Maybe. I'm not sure," Akira said.

"Okay. We'll figure it out. This must be an incredibly good friend," Miriam said.

"Yes. He is my godfather."

They had just entered the condo parking garage when Sheriff Collins arrived. Derrick did not think about the fact he needed a code to get in the garage.

Nyx opened the passenger door. Before she slid inside, she grabbed Derrick's hand, pulling him into the front with her.

It was a tight fit, but he did not mind, yet he wondered why Nyx wanted him up front with her.

Nyx tossed the camera in Collins' lap.

"What's this?" Collins asked.

"What's it look like?"

"Looks like a camera. Where did it come from?"

"Derrick's apartment. Three of them plus the transmitter."

Collins said, "But Paul said they were disconnected."

"They were connected and turned on," Derrick said.

"But that doesn't make sense," Collins said.

"Paul is your responsibility; I have my hands full with these three." Nyx used her thumb to point at Derrick. "I suggest you have a council meeting of your own tomorrow regarding Paul. Derrick will be there if you need him to testify."

"I'd need to have a quorum to do anything," Collins said.

"You and Coach will be there; Donna never misses. Shouldn't be difficult to find one more. Not with all that's going on.

"Damn. I hate all of this," Collins said.

"I can't think of anyone who's enjoying themselves," Nyx said.

"What's up with old man Fletcher. He wasn't too enthused about talking to you," Collins said.

"Me personally or just talking in general?" Nyx asked.

"Not interested in talking to anyone. I told him he had to, or I'd take him to jail, not that I could, but he said yes. But he might change his mind when we get there."

"He'll talk," Miriam said from the back seat. Then she added, "I can be quite persuasive."

"I have no doubt," Collins said.

"You don't know the half of it," Nyx said.

Everyone laughed. Derrick felt surprised at how good it felt to laugh. It was like he had breathed for the first time since the race, which seemed like months ago rather than hours.

Collins parked in front of a small house set back to the alley. The front yard was planted with flowers and well maintained. The white house needed a coat of paint. Despite the flowers, something felt unwelcoming about the place. Derrick could not say why he felt that way but knew he would soon find out.

"Sheriff, I would appreciate it if you stayed out here," Nyx said, and then turned to the back seat and said, "I think it best if Derrick, Miriam, and I go in."

"I don't think that's wise," Collins said.

"Still, it's the way we are going to do it," Nyx said.

The tone of Nyx's voice had changed, and her words carried more authority than one would expect based on her age and size. Derrick marveled at the way she morphed into something different from time to time. She scared him when that happened. He assumed she scared others as well.

No argument came from the back.

"I'm leaving the windows down and the motor off. Scream if you need me," Collins said.

"We won't need you," Nyx said.

As Miriam got out of the back, Nyx said, "Leave your bag. We go in empty-handed."

"But …"

Nyx held up her hand. "You can stay out here if you want."

Miriam tossed her bag back to Rebekah. "Come running if you hear screaming."

As they walked to the front door, Derrick said, "Do you know Mr. Fletcher?"

"Not really. Know about him. My dad worked for him years ago. Mr. Fletcher came to my school once to tell us about his business."

"What did he do?" Derrick asked.

"He manufactures replacement parts for cars. Everything other than electronics. His parts are better than the originals."

Derrick had questions. *How long ago was that? What happened to her father? What happened to Mr. Fletcher's business? Surely, he did not still work*. But he dared not ask. Perhaps someday.

Nyx paused at the steps that led to the front door. The home had one entry but two doors, something Derrick had not seen before. Peeling pale-blue paint covered the thin wood of the first door, which also had a window that comprised the top half of the door, but instead of glass, the window was covered with transparent metal mesh. When Nyx rapped on the door, it shook loosely on its hinges as if the catch were not properly adjusted. After several minutes, a short, thin man, with hunched shoulders, pulled the second door open, but he did not open the door that separated him from them. Deep wrinkles carved his face; his hair steel-gray, long and pulled back into a ponytail. He looked well worn, as did his home.

"Hello, Mr. Fletcher. I'm Nyx Belos. My father worked for you."

"I know who you are. Sheriff told me. Only reason I agree to this is because of your father. Good man, despite what people say about him."

Mr. Fletcher did not open the outer door. He was not inviting them in.

"Go ahead. What's your question?"

"Could we come in?" Nyx asked.

"You can ask your question from right where you stand. I'm not prepared for guests."

Nyx took a deep breath. "This is Derrick King and his sister Miriam."

"I know who they are. I'm not stupid, you know. He's the troublemaker. She's the one who escaped from Pacific Edge." Fletcher glared at Derrick for a moment and then added, "I heard he's a hell of a runner though."

"Thank you, sir," Derrick said.

"No thanks needed. Stating facts isn't a complement."

"Yes, sir," Derrick said.

"Get on with it. What's your question? I have to get some sleep. I got work, you know."

As was his custom, Derrick's assumption that the man no longer worked proved to be wrong.

"Thanks for seeing us on such brief notice and at this hour," Nyx said.

Nyx's tone had changed from earlier. Now, she sounded shy and unassuming. Derrick realized that he was one-dimensional in comparison. It was no wonder she saw through his facade so quickly when they first met.

"I owe your father that much; God rest his soul. Don't read too much into it. Now, ask and be gone."

Nyx cleared her throat. "If it's okay, I'll let Miriam ask the question."

"I didn't agree to talk to those two." Fletcher gestured towards Miriam.

"I realize that you did not. However, Miriam understands the situation better than I do. I'd appreciate your cooperation on this one request. It would mean a lot to me."

"I guess it's just one question. Doesn't matter which of you ask it. Go ahead then."

Miriam took one step up, placing her on the entry with Nyx. Derrick hoped Miriam could alter her tone because her normal mode of asking questions was nothing like how Nyx spoke, and even Nyx's soft voice seemed to anger the man.

"You've lived here all your life."

"Yes. That's your question? You've wasted your time and mine." The man started back into his house.

"That wasn't a question," Miriam said.

Mr. Fletcher turned back, groaning a bit, and rolling his eyes. "Okay. I've lived here all my life. So, what? Lots of people have lived here all their lives."

"But not as many years as you. At least that's what I've been told."

"I'm old. So, what?"

"It means you are likely the only person in town who can tell us?"

"Tell you what? Damn it girl, get on with it; it's past my bedtime. I'm old and need my rest."

"Tell us about the hidden base in the mountains."

Fletcher glared at them. "I don't know nothing about any base in the mountain."

The man said he knew nothing.

But his eyes said something else.

# 30

FLETCHER TURNED AROUND, SHUTTING THE DOOR, but before it closed, Miriam stuck her foot in between the door and the jam. Fortunately, Fletcher had not slammed the door, Derrick thought that Fletcher was not the type of man who abused material things, perhaps out of respect because he built parts and others misused, broke, or wore out, or perhaps because the bones of his old home would not tolerate additional stress.

The door creaked as it rebounded from Miriam's foot. If it caused her any discomfort, she did not reveal it. Fletcher turned back to face Miriam. "I said I know nothing about it. Now, let me be."

Fletcher walked into the gloom of his home, not bothering to shut the door.

Miriam called out, "Did you know Jacob Truman?"

Derrick did not know why Miriam named Mr. Truman. There must have been hundreds, perhaps thousands of people working in the hidden complex. Fletcher would have been a boy, maybe a teen, when they abandoned the facility. Why would he know one man? It made little sense.

The house remained silent. Nyx said, "I guess we are done here."

Miriam held her finger to her lips.

After a few silent moments, Miriam hollered, "You have not answered my question."

They stood there for several minutes. Derrick became uncomfortable, having decided Mr. Fletcher had in fact gone to bed and they still stood on his front steps holding the door to his home open. But after what felt like an hour, but was probably a few minutes, Mr. Fletcher returned.

Fletcher's expression had softened. He looked at Miriam and said, "Why do you ask?"

"Because he was one of the last ones at the facility. Someone killed him. An execution. I suspect because he refused to do what he was ordered to do."

"How do you know this?" Fletcher asked.

"That's not important. And you're better off not knowing," Miriam said.

Fletcher stepped to the side, motioning them inside. "I have a few minutes. But that's all, mind you. Would you like some tea?"

"No, we are fine," Nyx said.

"We would love a cup of tea," Miriam said, rolling her eyes at Nyx.

As Derrick's eyes adjusted, he saw the home was not gloomy, but softly lit. Most of the ambient light came from small lamps mounted over pictures of transports, cars they called them here, none of which he recognized, yet the pictures drew him like a bug to a light, which reminded him of the experiment he and Akira were supposed to be working on and would likely never be completed. The vehicles were small, just two seats, one for the driver and one for a passenger. Many had no tops, all of them looked fast although they were sitting still and unoccupied.

Nyx and Miriam settled into seats. Derrick continued to move around the room, looking at one picture and then another.

"You like that one?" Mr. Fletcher asked.

"It's fantastic," Derrick said.

"It's my favorite," Mr. Fletcher said.

"What is it?" Derrick asked.

"1966 Shelby 427 Cobra. Come sit before your tea gets cold. Maybe someday you can come over and I'll show you my shop and collection."

Derrick joined them, marveling at how Mr. Fletcher was now so welcoming. It worried Derrick just a little. Yet, he could not think of any threat the man might pose. Miriam sat in an armchair situated closest to where Mr. Fletcher sat. Derrick sat on the couch next to Nyx. Mr. Fletcher poured tea and pointed out cream and sugar. Derrick had not been a tea drinker and did not know how he liked it. To be safe, he added cream and sugar.

Before Miriam could begin, Mr. Fletcher looked at Derrick and said, "My grandson knows you."

"Oh, from school?" Derrick asked.

"Yep. Football team. He helps me in the shop, can do most everything, weld, run the lathe, real natural machinist. But he wants to be an engineer. Needs to go to college for that. That's why I'm still hanging around. I got to keep the shop going to help him get through college. When he graduates, he can take over the business. Then I'm done."

"Who is your grandson," Derrick asked, taking a sip of his tea.

"Red Badowski. My daughter married a Badowski. Couldn't talk her out of it." Mr. Fletcher smiled and gave Derrick a wink.

"Mr. Fletcher, what can you tell us about the hidden facility?" Miriam asked.

"I've never told no one this story. Not nobody. Not even my late wife, God rest her soul, and I never kept anything from her, except this. Cause I feared for her safety and mine. Even now, I'd appreciate it if you'd keep this between us."

Miriam nodded.

"Jacob Truman was my best friend's dad. Heck of a nice guy. I was about fourteen, I guess, when it happened. Anyway, like I said, Jacob was a nice guy, but he liked to have a few drinks now and then. And one night when he'd had a few too many, he told Harry, that was his son, mind you, that he worked in a top-secret facility in the mountains. See, most folks at Fort Hill worked on the base there; but a few of them left every morning on buses to parts unknown. Jacob was one of those guys on the bus. So, Harry weren't no good at keeping a secret and he told me about the base. Made me promise to keep it hush-hush. I said I would, and I did, but I thought Harry was just being dramatic. In fact, I thought he was maybe pulling my leg, you know? Just seeing if I would repeat the story and then Harry would make fun of me. So, I never did."

"Did you ever hear anyone talk about there being a secret facility?" Miriam asked.

Fletcher poured more tea into his cup. "Nope. Never."

"The facility is real. We found it," Miriam said.

"Oh, I don't doubt it's real. Not after what happened."

"What happened?" Miriam asked.

"Well, they closed Fort Hill. Loaded everyone on busses to relocate them. Even though it happened fast, I knew about the base closure. Because of my friend, Harry, you see. I didn't know anything about how they did such things, of course. Just figured bussing everyone off at the same time was what they did. Any ways, I'd gone to see Harry off. He said he'd write when they got settled, but we met up in an alley near where they were loading busses. Happened that Harry and his mother were on the last bus to leave. But Harry didn't want to go because his father had not come home. He wanted to stay until his father got back. Harry argued with the soldiers. Then Harry ran straight back to the alley where I was watching. The soldiers chased Harry, but Harry was fast. I could see they weren't going to catch him. As the entered the alley, one of the soldiers shot Harry in the back."

Nyx gasp, throwing her hand to her mouth.

"That's terrible," Miriam said.

A tear formed in Fletcher's eye. "I ducked behind a big trash bin. Harry was lying on the ground, groaning as blood pooled around him.

The soldier walked up and said, 'same result, different day' and then he shot Harry in the head. They dragged him back to the bus and tossed him in the luggage area under the bus. I don't suspect anyone the bus saw what happened."

"You never told anyone? That seems strange that you'd watch them kill your best friend and say nothing," Miriam said.

Fletcher shrugged. "I was young and scared. I mean, these were soldiers after all. And what happened the next morning terrified me. I'm not a real smart guy, especially at fourteen, but I ain't braindead either."

"What happened?" Miriam asked.

"My mom told me they transported the all those folks from the Fort Hill Base to Sacramento, California. Next morning, at 5:12 a.m., about the time those buses arrived, a nuclear bomb killed everyone and everything in that city."

# 31

THEY SAT WITH MR. FLETCHER FOR A few minutes, sipping tea and trying to think of something to say that might be helpful. Derrick thought of nothing. Apparently, neither did Miriam nor Nyx. Finally, they thanked him. Miriam gave him a hug. Nyx shook his hand as did Derrick. Fletcher told them to come back sometime, if they could. No one asked what 'if they could' meant; that was unnecessary.

When they reached Collin's vehicle, they slid into the seats they had occupied on the way over.

No one spoke. Derrick was not certain that he could.

Collins started the car and said, "Well?"

Before anyone could say anything, Miriam said, "He couldn't tell us anything."

"You were in there a long time for nothing," Collins said.

"He made tea and wanted to chat about cars. Showed us pictures," Miriam said.

"He loves cars. No one, other than his grandson, knows what he has in that shop of his. It's better protected than a military base."

"He loved talking about cars," Miriam said.

"Did you learn what you wanted to know?" Collins asked.

"He knew nothing," Miriam repeated.

* * *

Akira spent the night at Nyx's place. Nyx said she'd get into the crawl space above her mom's condo first thing. Derrick did not expect to hear from Nyx and felt certain she would find the same surveillance cameras that he found.

Rebekah went straight to bed, Derrick slept on the couch, Miriam got on the computer.

Derrick woke in the night. Light from the study spilled into the living room. He tossed the blanket off and started toward the study to tell Miriam to get some sleep. When he stood, he saw Miriam sitting by the window, her knees pulled to her chest.

He sat facing Miriam. "Have you slept?"

"No. I got used to staying up at night and functioning on just a couple of hours sleep. I went to the Technical Services building at night."

"How did you get in there?" Derrick asked.

"Someone helped me. Long story."

"I have time."

Miriam thought for a moment. "It started months ago when my communication screen stopped working. I wanted to see how they fixed it or know if they just replaced it; so, I pretended to be sick that day. When the technician came, he was afraid to come in the house. I had to convince him it would be okay. The technician used a keyboard and mouse to work on the monitor. That's when I learned there was a computer system that we could not access."

Derrick shook his head, "Your curiosity is dangerous. But that doesn't explain how you got into Technical Services."

"I talked the technician into giving me a keyboard and mouse. When he logged into the system, I memorized his PIN. I used the same PIN to enter the Technical Services Building. That's how I got in."

"Didn't your monitor fail in December?"

"Yes. That's when I got the keyboard and mouse. I didn't go into Technical Services until after they exiled you. I could not learn much from the system that runs the home monitors. After your exile, I needed more information if I was going to help you."

Derrick shook his head. "I still can't see how you got into the Pacific Edge computer system. Getting in the door was one thing, but they must have usernames and passwords and other security."

"The same technician helped me. I found his office. He left the door unlocked. He left me a key so I could get back in and set up a fake account for myself in the computer system."

"Who was this man?"

"His name is AJ Patel," Miriam said.

"Why would he do all that? It doesn't make sense."

"I agree. I've been thinking about it since he first gave me the keyboard and mouse. At first, I thought he was just being nice to a curious young girl. A little careless letting me see his password and PIN, but he would not know that it was easy for me to retain such information. But when I went to Technical Services, found his office unlocked, and logged into his computer, I found a document written to me. He expected I would come," Miriam said.

"That's weird. How could he know that you'd go? Sounds suspicious."

Miriam nodded. "Agreed. But I had to use what he gave me. I think he was part of a test or a trap, but that was all I had. That's why I sent you that email telling you that I'd given up. I had to make them think that I'd quit."

"Is that why you went into the ocean?"

"Yes. That did not go as well as I'd hoped. Turns out security is not as efficient as one might think. In fact, if Rebekah wasn't watching me through a telescope when I went into the ocean, I would have been fish food."

"Rebekah. She still puzzles me. What if she's part of the trap?" Derrick asked.

Miriam stared at him for several minutes. "Damn. I'd never considered that. She puzzles me too. She started sitting with me at lunch just after your exile. I tried to ditch her, but she persisted. But she saved me. I don't think I'd have made it without her. I think we have become friends, but I still have not figured her out. I don't think she's one of them. Then there's Anna."

"What if Anna isn't missing? What if that's part of the trap?" Derrick asked.

"Crap. As if I don't have enough to think about. But she seems genuinely upset about Anna. Don't you think?"

"She does. Perhaps she's a good actor," Derrick said.

"You believe that?" Miriam asked

Derrick said, "Not really. But there are things that can't be explained. Not yet anyway."

"True. Now we need to be more careful than ever. Some things must keep just between us." Miriam stared at Derrick again. "You don't think I'm part of a trap, do you?"

"No of course not," Derrick said.

Miriam sighed, stared out the window.

After several minutes, Derrick said, "Your plans worked. You got out, which is amazing. I'm not sure I even want to know the details because it would prevent me from sleeping. So, you outsmarted them."

"So, I thought. But the more I think about it, the more I think I just did what they expected. Or that they monitored me all the way while I thought I'd hidden my tracks." She paused. "Patel was waiting outside of the Technical Building the night we escaped."

"He was waiting? What happened?"

"We zapped him. Wasn't sure why he was there. Perhaps he was there to help. But we couldn't risk it. If he was there to help, he probably is not interested in helping us now," Miriam said.

Derrick nodded. "Probably not. But he's not here, so he's not a problem. You said they set me up. I hit Marcus because they wanted me to, so they could exile me? I don't understand."

"They set this up, but everything has not happened as they predicted. You were not supposed to hit Marcus. They thought you would do nothing. Even if Marcus hit me. Sorry Derrick, but you failed their test."

"Oh. I don't know how I should feel about that," Derrick said.

"My plans were not as successful as I hoped either; there were things they did not anticipate. Those things allowed me to get here."

"What things?"

"Patel waiting for us, for example. He did not expect Rebekah. He did not expect that we would knock him out with a stun gun. Maybe he was trying to help; more likely he was there to ensure I did not escape. From what I can tell, Pacific Edge's computer system is still not operational. I don't think they saw that coming. They did not expect Anna Ford's escape. I'm certain they did not foresee we would find the hidden military base in the mountains. The more I think about it, I'm convinced that AJ Patel was part of a test, but whether he was an active participant or an unwitting accomplice, I do not know." Miriam pause. "Or perhaps I have it all wrong."

"Do you think Patel knows where we are?" Derrick asked.

"Probably, yes. He knew you came here. He knew your email address."

"Are you worried about him coming here?"

"No. He might be in trouble himself because he let us get away. Besides, they have sent Pacific Edge Security and Prime robots. He's just a computer technician."

"You must hate the guy."

Miriam said, "I suspect he had to do it. They may have threatened his family. His daughter was in my class in earlier years. We were told they moved to another Chosen community, but now we know that's not how it works. Hate is too strong a word. He's dangerous, though. I'm sure of that. I fear he's monitoring my computer use even now. But even if I'm wrong, he knows too much. He could ruin everything."

They sat for a few moments. Derrick sensed that something else troubled her. He wanted more details about how she got out. How she worked for weeks inside Technical Services without being caught. He struggled with reading people's emotions, but he felt sure Miriam's mood was darker than he'd ever seen before.

"I'm glad you didn't give up. I'm happy you're here, although it hasn't turned out like I'd hoped. But I think it will get better. If they let us stay, and the town supports us, I think Pacific Edge will give up. Things will get better," Derrick said.

Miriam gave him a weak smile. "I love your optimism. But things are not going to get better. Things will get worse."

"You can't know that," Derrick said.

Miriam pointed out the window. "Yes, I can. Because they already have."

Derrick twisted to see what she was pointing at.

On the corner, under a streetlamp, stood a black robot.

# 32

NOT THAT DERRICK FELT OPTIMISTIC, but he felt a duty to help Miriam feel better. Instinctual behavior, he would later conclude. Now, seeing a black robot like the one they had overcome in the woods, standing on the corner, caused the darkness he'd sensed in Miriam to flood into his chest.

"How long has it been there?" Derrick asked.

"They came about an hour ago," Miriam said.

"They? There's more of them?"

"I assume. A black aircraft landed and let two out. There were several more inside. The aircraft left, but it flew just inches over the street. It probably dropped others around town," Miriam said.

"Same aircraft as we saw in the woods?" Derrick asked.

"Yes. A capital P on each side. Same machine. Same robots."

"We need to call the sheriff before they hurt someone," Derrick said.

"No need. A deputy already saw it. He walked up to it with his gun drawn, but the machine must have said something. The deputy put his gun away and went back to his car. Sheriff Collins showed up a few minutes later and walked up to the machine. Nothing happened."

"Why are they here?"

"One reason that I can think of." Miriam said.

"Which is?"

"Looking for Anna Ford."

* * *

At 4:30 a.m., he convinced Miriam to get some sleep. Then he laid awake staring at the ceiling, thinking about robots, and wondering what to do about them. He came to no conclusions, expect that he, Miriam, and Rebekah needed to leave town. He would not put the people of Potterville at greater risk. They had not asked for any of this. Leaving was the only option. Beyond that, he found no solutions to anything.

* * *

**Sunday, April, 4, 6:42 a.m.**

Derrick woke to a sharp rap at the door. Light flooded through the window causing him to squint. He stumbled to the door, rubbing his eyes; his mouth as dry as desert sand. He peered through the peephole. Akira and Nyx stood in the hall. He opened the door; Nyx pushed past him.

"Have you seen them?" Nyx asked.

"The robots? Yes. Miriam and I saw them during the night."

"Why didn't you do something?" Nyx asked.

"Like what? What were we supposed to do?"

"Come tell us," Nyx said.

"And what good would that do?" Derrick said.

Derrick, Akira, and Nyx stood at the window. Sunday morning traffic was light. People approached the robot with trepidation steeped in curiosity. Some shook their heads. Others appeared to say something. The robot remained stationary. It caused no harm to any of the passersby.

"What do you think it's doing?" Nyx asked.

"Miriam thinks it's looking for Anna Ford."

"What is so fricking important about Anna Ford?" Nyx asked.

"I don't know," Derrick said.

"Let's go check it out," Nyx said.

"Give me a minute." Derrick went to the guest half-bath. He'd moved his essentials there. He brushed his teeth and dragged a comb through his hair; it was longer than he'd ever worn it, which drove him nuts at first, but he was starting to like it. He splashed water on his face before returning to the living room. Before leaving, Derrick pulled a stun gun from Miriam's bag.

As they walked down the stairs, Akira said, "At least they don't seem interested in you now?"

"Pacific Edge wanted Derrick. Prime wants Anna Ford," Nyx said.

"Maybe the Chosen and Prime are the same," Akira said.

"I don't think so," Nyx said.

On the sidewalk, they paused. The machine located just around the corner. "What's the plan?" Akira asked.

"I didn't know we needed a plan," Nyx said.

"We need a plan," Akira said.

Derrick held the stun gun out. "Nyx, you take this and go around behind it. Just in case."

"Why? Because it's too dangerous to be with you?" Nyx emphasized the word too.

"No. Well, maybe," Derrick said.

Nyx took the stun gun and then handed it to Akira. "You go around behind it."

Akira looked at the stun gun. Turned it on, sent an arc of electricity between its poles. "I'll zap it if it tries anything." Akira stabbed the stun gun out as if striking the machine in the back.

"Be careful. Don't do anything unless it's necessary," Derrick said.

Derrick and Nyx went one direction; Akira went the other. When Derrick turned the corner, the robot was visible at the end of the block. They moved slowly, waiting until Akira approached from behind the machine.

The machine seemed lifeless until they were within five yards. Then the machine's eyes lit green and it said, "I mean you no harm. I must locate subject three known as Anna Ford." Then the machine emitted a light clicking noise. "Greetings, Derrick King. Where is Miriam King? Prime issued an offer to Miriam King. Prime requires an answer."

"Miriam King is not with me," Derrick said.

"Unfortunate. When you see Miriam King, advise her Prime requires an answer to the offer."

"If I see her, I'll do that," Derrick said, walking past the machine.

As they walked away, the machine said, "Thank you, Derrick King."

Derrick and Nyx joined Akira. Once they got across the street, Derrick took a breath. "I'm sorry."

"What are you sorry for now?" Nyx asked.

"For causing this. We are putting the entire town at risk."

"The entire town was at risk before you came, and we didn't even know it. Isn't that true?" Akira asked.

"I guess," Derrick said. "I wish we had not found that place in the mountains. But I guess it would be there whether or not we found it."

"And if you had not found it, there would have been a nuclear accident, which could have poisoned the town," Akira said.

"I guess," Derrick said.

"Then you should not be sorry. You did not cause Anna Ford's escape. The Prime is here because of Anna," Akira said.

"Remind me to never argue with you," Nyx said.

"You have argued with me plenty of times and you've always lost," Akira said. Then Akira added, "Why did the robot call Anna subject three?"

"I have no clue. Perhaps they refer to Miriam as subject one and Rebekah as subject two. They think the three of them escaped together. What time is it?" Derrick asked.

"Perhaps you're right. Almost 8:30," Akira said.

"Now what?" Derrick asked.

"I'm hungry. Let's go to the bistro," Nyx said.

"I don't have any money," Derrick said.

"I'll buy," Akira said and then looked at Derrick. "Miriam can pay me back when she goes to the bank."

"I don't understand how she can have money," Derrick said.

Nyx shrugged. "I'll split the cost with you, Akira. Derrick can pay us back when he gets back to work."

"That will be a long wait," Derrick said.

"I'm more patient than you realize," Nyx said.

"What about Miriam and Rebekah?" Derrick asked.

Nyx said, "Let them sleep. If they wake up, they can find us or fend for themselves."

Outside, Nyx said, "You're not limping."

Derrick shrugged. "It feels fine this morning. Looks better too."

Nyx's brow wrinkled slightly. "You heal fast."

"I guess," Derrick said.

When they walked into the bistro, heads turned.

Donna stood at the counter. "Hi, guys. Glad to see you. You've seen the visitors, I assume."

"We have. We were just chatting with one of them. Seemed nice enough, but not much of a conversationalist. Are there more of them?" Nyx asked.

"Yep. Six is what I've heard. All downtown. There's a black aircraft sitting next to the school. No one has ever seen anything like the aircraft or the robots. A big P on the side. Some folks think Prime sent it."

"Some folks are probably correct. Are all the robots asking about Anna Ford?"

"Yep, like a broken record. They all repeat the same thing. What will you have this morning?"

"Coffees and three breakfast burritos," Nyx said.

Donna sat three mugs on the counter.

Nyx said loudly, "We'll sit outside so you all can get back to your breakfast."

They got their coffee and went outside. It was a pleasant morning under a clear sky, although a little cool. Derrick wore a t-shirt and wished he had worn more. Nyx and Akira both wore Potterville High sweatshirts. They were smarter than him. He already knew that. The sun would rise over the building in a few minutes. He'd survive till then but would shiver during the wait.

Before Donna arrived with plates, Akira nodded. "Look there."

Derrick turned his head to see Rebekah dragging her feet along the sidewalk. Hair combed, but not well. No makeup. Wearing his sweatshirt, which hung on her like an oversized tent.

"Thanks for waking me," Rebekah said as she plopped down in a chair between Akira and Nyx.

"You're welcome," Nyx said.

"You found us, so no harm done. Where is Miriam? I assume you saw the black robot on the corner?" Akira said.

"Miriam is on the computer, where else. I saw it. It nearly gave me a heart attack. Walking with my head down, I almost ran into the damn thing when it said, 'I mean you no harm.'"

"Did it say anything else?" Derrick asked.

"It said it was looking for Anna Ford and then called me by name and asked if I knew where Miriam was."

"Soon or later, they are going to figure out that Anna isn't here," Akira said.

"Then maybe they'll leave us alone," Nyx said.

"Maybe, but they will also start looking for Anna elsewhere," Derrick said.

"That will put Anna at greater risk and might place the town in danger too," Rebekah said.

"How so?" Nyx asked.

"Because they want Anna and they think we can help. So, they are not doing anything to harm us. Once they know we can't help, they'll have no use for us. They might do something to prove a point."

"Maybe we should give them their other robot and aircraft back. Miriam could fly it here." Akira said.

"She might be right. We should not start a fight with Prime, whatever that is. Prime has all the power, we have none. We should make peace," Derrick said.

"This is coming from the guy who got exiled for hitting a Carver?" Nyx asked.

"I reacted without thinking. Even Miriam said I shouldn't have hit Marcus," Derrick said.

Akira said, "Miriam said that? Doesn't sound like her."

"Not exactly. Someone, I'm not clear on who, set the entire thing up. Like a test. They did not think I would do anything." Derrick shrugged. "I failed the test."

"If you had not failed, you wouldn't have been exiled," Nyx said.

"That is correct," Derrick said.

"We would not have met," Nyx said.

Derrick hung his head. "I would not have put you at risk."

"Yet, you, Rebekah, and Miriam saved us," Akira said.

Derrick saw Akira give Nyx a look that wasn't quite angry but was close. "I just wish everything wasn't so difficult." He sipped his coffee and then added, "We should ask Miriam what she thinks about giving the other robot and aircraft back."

Nyx said, "Miriam doesn't make the decisions around here."

"Are you sure about that?" Rebekah asked.

Nyx's eyes narrowed, but before she could say anything, Donna arrived with burritos, a huge cylinder-shaped thing covered with red stuff, sliced avocados, and a dollop of sour cream. "Ah, your party has grown."

"Would you bring Rebekah a burrito and a coffee?" Nyx asked."

"Sure thing. I'll have it right out."

"Thanks," Rebekah said.

Derrick dug into the burrito. He was not sure of many things, but he was sure he'd miss Donna's cooking. The sun peeked over the edge of the building and warmth radiated over his body. As he chewed an oversized bite, he had a thought that should have occurred to him last night. *Why did someone want to test him? And why did they assume he would not hit Marcus Carver to protect Miriam? That made little sense. Perhaps Miriam was wrong.*

Donna returned, sitting a plate and mug in front of Rebekah. "Here you go, sweetheart. I put your order ahead of someone else. No fun watching everyone else eat." Donna turned to Nyx. "Coach called asking if you were here. He wants you to call him."

Nyx took a bite before she pulled out her phone. As she chewed, she tapped the screen several times and then placed the call.

"It's me, Coach," Nyx said.

"We are all at the bistro. —

"Sorry, I didn't have my phone on. —

"We saw one. Yes, we heard there are six of them. Wait, what? That's not fair. —

Nyx listened, nodded occasionally.

"Okay. I understand. We'll be there."

Nyx pushed her plate away. "They changed the counsel time."

"To when?" Akira asked.

"Noon," Nyx said.

"That doesn't give us much time," Akira said.

"It does not," Nyx agreed.

"But I told Allen 5 o'clock," Miriam said.

"Coach called Allen. He's serving as alternate on the counsel. He'll be here."

Akira said, "Serving as an alternate? That has never happened. I know they gave him that position to ensure his help with computer issues but letting him do it is something else entirely. Who can't come to the meeting?"

"Donna. Coach said she can't get away at noon," Nyx said.

"That doesn't sound like Donna. She's shut the doors to make a meeting in a pinch."

"I know. Actually, it's not Donna, it's Allen. Coach said Allen insisted. He threatened to end his relationship and report some of our — less than orthodox procurements."

"That doesn't sound like Allen," Akira said.

"Who is this, Allen?" Derrick asked.

"He's a tech guy who helps us here. He's bringing the hard drives that Miriam wants," Akira said.

Nyx said, "This doesn't feel right. But Coach made it clear that we don't have a choice. He's pulling rank on us."

"That doesn't sound like Browning either," Akira said.

"It does not," Nyx agreed.

# 33

THEY SAT A FEW MINUTES; NONE of them eating much. Derrick asked for aluminum foil to wrap his uneaten portion of burrito he would take to Miriam. Although worried about their future, he forced himself to sit without speaking, soaking in the moment. Sitting at the bistro table, sun warming his back, fragrance from trees, flowers, and ovens drifting through the air, seated with friends he would soon leave and miss. Hurting and yet thankful that he'd had this experience.

Derrick found Miriam still at the computer when he and Rebekah got back to the condo. "I brought you half a breakfast burrito. Want me to heat it?"

"Thanks. I'm starving." Miriam unwrapped one end and took a bite. "It's delicious and still warm. Close the door; we need to talk."

Derrick closed the door and sat on the floor at Miriam's feet. Before she could speak, Derrick said. "They changed the time of the council meeting. Something strange is happening."

"When is it?" Miriam asked.

"At noon."

Miriam said, "That's only two hours. What changed?"

"The tech guy, Allen, is making demands. He'll be here and is taking Donna's spot on the council. Allen is an alternative member, but this has never happened before. Coach is allowing it. Everyone is freaking out," Derrick said.

Miriam cocked her head. "Freaking out?"

Derrick smiled. "That's slang. Now that we're about to get booted out of here, I'm starting to understand some terms. It means scared, confused, stressed. Something like that."

Miriam turn off the computer. "That doesn't give us much time. I need to shower. You do too. We can't go there looking and smelling like bums. If we don't get some support from Porterville, it will make saving these people more difficult. And I need to go to a bank. There's one open just down the street."

Derrick said, "Rebekah is in the shower. What do you mean, saving them?"

"There's the threat of a malfunction in the reactor, but that's only part of it. Potterville is now on the most hated list of the Chosen and the Prime. There's no guarantee that there will not be retaliation whether or not we are here. These people are not safe," Miriam said.

"But staying here puts them at greater risk. It might be best if we disappear," Derrick said.

Miriam shoved the last of the burrito into her mouth, holding up her finger as she chewed. "Maybe. Maybe not. We are still of some value. If we are here, it might prevent something disastrous."

"You don't think they'll do something to the entire town do you?"

"You mean like Fort Hill and Sacramento? They killed over one million people instantly and another million died of complications and cancer within the following five years."

"But that was decades ago. The Chosen Communities were not even around then. The people that did that are gone," Derrick protested.

"Perhaps they are, but I'm not sure that matters," Miriam said.

"How could it not matter?" Derrick asked.

"I'm not sure yet," Miriam said.

"I don't understand …"

Miriam reached down, touching her finger to his lips. "We don't have time for this discussion and there are more important things I must tell you."

"Okay," Derrick said.

"First, I'm sorry."

"Sorry for what?" Derrick asked.

"For all of this. For the way I behaved in Pacific Edge. I was foolish."

"You don't …"

Miriam held her finger to his lips again. "Don't interrupt. What I'm going to say is difficult, even now. I saw things that others didn't, and I wanted them to see them too. I wanted you to see their lies. But now …" Miriam drifted off into some faraway place for a moment. "Now, I see what I could not see back then."

"I don't understand," Derrick said.

"It's so big, Derrick."

"What's so big?"

The entire thing. The Chosen. The Prime. Too big. I cannot envision a solution. I thought we could make a difference. If we only understood. Now that I understand more; I see I was wrong. There's no way out. There's no way to change this. No way back."

Derrick thought back to when Father said that perhaps Derrick could make a difference. It was such a strange thing to say. "Back to what?" Derrick asked.

"Back to normal. Back to freedom. Back to a better time. I should have just let it go. Fit in. Then none of this would have happened. You would have married Jana and been happy." A tear traced down Miriam's cheek.

"But if it had not happened, we would not have found the reactor. We saved the people here. And, … I'm glad to be here, even if I can't stay." He paused for a moment. "I'm happy to have met these people."

"Maybe we saved them. Maybe they would have been okay. Either way, it was not our problem to fix. We inserted ourselves into someplace that we didn't belong." Miriam folded the foil into a neat square before tossing it into the trash.

Derrick said, "I'm sorry I didn't listen to you when we were in Pacific Edge. I'm sorry that I wasn't a better brother."

"We are out of time. There are two things we must do. First, I must tell you something. I don't know how this council hearing will go, but I may say things that will hurt you. I wanted to wait and explain things to you in private, but I may have to say things in the meeting."

Miriam stood and held out her hand, helping Derrick to his feet.

"And the second thing?" he asked.

"We need to do an experiment with a robot."

# 34

MIRIAM HAMMERED ON THE BATHROOM DOOR, hollering to Rebekah, announcing that she was about to get company. A few minutes later, both girls emerged with wet hair and fresh clothing. The room filled with damp air and the smell of shampoo. Miriam pointed towards the shower and told Derrick to hurry. When Derrick returned a few minutes later, Nyx was seated at the kitchen table. Miriam explained her plan. She did not explain why it was important. The meeting would be at the school, and there was a robot nearby. That's where they would do the experiment. Miriam checked the stun guns. Both were at capacity. She set them both to high and gave one to Rebekah. Rebekah, Derrick, and Miriam would complete the experiment with the robot. Akira or Nyx could watch from a distance. For that much Derrick was grateful, but he said nothing.

On the way to the school, Miriam stopped at a bank, except they didn't call it a bank. The name on the door read: Potterville Credit Union. "You guys wait here. This won't take long. I started the process online."

"What process?" Derrick asked.

"Opening an account," Miriam said.

Only a few cars drove by and few people were on the street, but they all stared as they passed.

"I guess this is it then," Derrick said.

"Is what?" Nyx asked.

"I suspect the council will vote us out. We have no place to go except back to the mountain. Which is okay because we must stay there until we know that Potterville will be safe. Because we can't let anyone find the place, we might have to make a run for it," Derrick said.

"You're being a little dramatic," Akira said.

"Whatever," Derrick said; the corner of his mouth turning up just a little.

Nyx punched him on the arm. "Finally, you're talking like a human."

And then Nyx hugged him. When Nyx separated herself, she held him at arm's length and said, "Don't give up. This isn't over yet. It's not a sprint. Remember that."

Rebekah stood off to the side. Tears formed in her eyes. "Have you all forgotten about Anna?"

Miriam, having just exited the bank, went to her, taking her hand. "Girlfriend, I have not forgotten. I promise. I just don't have a plan yet. One step at a time and the next steps are right in front of us. You're the strongest person I know. I need you to be that person now."

Rebekah nodded, wiped her face with her sleeve. Derrick wondered why he had been so blind to Rebekah's nature when they were in Pacific Edge. Jana Somersworth seemed more like a caricature than an actual person to him now.

"Are we ready?" Mariam asked.

"I don't see why this robot thing is necessary?" Nyx said.

"Maybe it's not. But I'm afraid it is," Miriam said.

They walked toward the school. People stared at them. Most slowed their cars, staring as they passed. Some waved. A few gave them a thumbs up. Two gave them the middle finger that Jim Priest liked to deploy. Derrick was confused about Miriam's plan; he assumed the others were as well, perhaps more so. It made little sense. They knew what the robots said. And the robots had harmed no one in accordance with the opening statement they recited to each person. So, why did Miriam check the stun guns?

Two blocks from the school, they saw a robot standing at the corner. There were no people close to it. It was a suitable observation point for a machine looking for someone. Miriam and Rebekah separated from Derrick, Nyx, and Akira. The three of them waited until Miriam and Rebekah were in position.

"Any idea what this is about?" Akira asked.

"None," Derrick said.

"Seems like a waste of time. It's not as if we don't have enough going on already." Nyx checked her phone for the time. "We are going to be late for the council meeting."

Akira said, "We can't be late for the meeting because it can't start until you are there."

Nyx glared at Akira but said nothing.

Derrick said, "With Miriam, everything is done for a reason."

"I suspect that is true," Akira said.

"No use arguing with both of you," Nyx said and then pointed, "I see them."

With that, the three started towards the robot, but halfway down the block, Nyx and Akira slowed, separating themselves enough to observe Derrick's interaction with the robot without being too close. As Derrick approached, Miriam and Rebekah moved within five yards behind the machine.

The robot said, "I mean you no harm, Derrick King. Prime requires the location of subject three known as Anna Ford."

"I do not know where Anna is," Derrick said.

The machine issued a chime. Derrick stood still.

Nyx waved to Miriam, pointed to her own eyes, and then pointed at the robot.

"Derrick King. Engage."

Derrick said, "Engaged."

Miriam lunged forward, holding the arc of the stun gun at the robot's back. Rebekah joined her. They held the guns against the machine until they cycled off and then pulled the trigger again. After the second cycle ended, electric arcs continued to oscillate across the surface of the machine for a moment. When the iridescent blue slivers of electricity ceased, Miriam pulled a black box from the robot's back.

"Battery," Miriam said, holding the box up for the others to see before she stuffed it and the stun gun in her bag.

Rebekah turned the stun gun in her hand, studying it before switching it off. "These damn things have proven themselves quite useful."

Derrick stood motionless, staring forward.

"Derrick!" Miriam nudged him. "Derrick!" Then she slapped him. Derrick remained motionless. Miriam pulled the stun gun from her bag, adjusting it to its lowest setting. Then she placed it against his ribs and pulled the trigger.

Derrick jerked. "Ouch! Hey, what are you doing?"

"Sorry, brother."

"What just happened?" Nyx asked, running to Derrick's side.

"What did you see?" Miriam asked.

"The machine's eyes went weird, spiraling," Nyx said.

"Hypnosis," Akira said, rubbing Derrick's shoulder.

"Would someone tell me what you're talking about?" Derrick asked.

"Do you remember what the machine said?" Miriam asked.

"Huh, yes. It said, 'I mean you no harm, Derrick King. Prime requires the location of subject three known as Anna Ford.'"

"You remember nothing else?" Miriam asked.

"That's all it said," Derrick said, rubbing his side.

"It also said, Derrick King, engage," Miriam said.

"They must have hypnotized you before. Its swirling eyes were the predestined signal for you to engage in the previous trance," Akira said.

"I don't even know what hynosisis is," Derrick said.

"Hypnosis," Akira corrected. "It's a way of putting people in a trance-like state."

"I have never been in a trance," Derrick said.

"Apparently, you have. And at some point, we must discover what they told you to do, but right now we don't have time," Miriam said.

"I don't understand. Why would they do that?"

"Could be anything. But they programmed you to do something. Something you wouldn't normally do," Miriam said.

"You mean like steal something?" Derrick asked.

"I was thinking something much worse," Miriam said.

# 35

MIRIAM SLID THE STUN GUN'S SWITCH to high and looked at Rebekah. Rebekah nodded and checked the setting on her device. Miriam stuck the robot's power supply back into its receptacle and locked it into place. Nothing happened. She tapped the machine on the side of the head. Nothing.

Miriam shrugged. "I guess we broke it. Oh, well."

They walked away and then Derrick heard a whirring sound. "I think something's happening back there."

They eased back to the robot. Miriam and Akira stepped in front of it.

"Its eyes are glowing white," Miriam said.

"Is that bad?" Nyx asked.

"No clue," Miriam said. "Wait, they are green now."

"I mean you no harm. Hello, Miriam King. Prime requires and answer regarding your amnesty in exchange for subject three, known as Anna Ford."

"Do you have the written and notarized agreement?"

"The written agreement is available. However, Prime cannot provide a notarized signature."

"Why not?" Miriam asked.

Derrick marveled at her boldness, not to mention her creativity. He noticed that Rebekah's face had turned white, lips tightly drawn, jaw muscles working.

"Signature is not possible. The document can be delivered as soon as you produce Anna Ford."

"Sure thing, but not now. We have an appointment."

With that Miriam walked away. The machine remained silent. Derrick wondered if it could only see forward or if it was monitoring them as they walked across the school's front yard.

"Why does the robot call Anna subject three?" Nyx asked.

"Good question," Miriam said, casting Derrick a stern look.

When they arrived at the back of the school, Antonio was leaning against the door, holding it open. He smiled, shook Miriam's hand, gave

Rebekah a brief hug, and patted Derrick on the back, but he said nothing. Antonio nodded to Nyx and Akira. Inside a classroom that Derrick had not entered, Sheriff Collins and Coach Browning sat against the back wall. Both men looked comical and uncomfortable in the small desks. Jim Priest and another boy, who was unknown to Derrick, sat in front of Browning and Collins. Red Badowski sat in the back but separated from Priest and his friend by three rows of desks. Near the front sat Henry Clark, Larry Kinkead, and Malcolm Cross. Nyx walked to the front of the room.

Akira pointed at three chairs in the front facing the room. "Derrick, Miriam, and Rebekah, you sit there." Akira then sat next to Malcolm in the front row.

Antonio entered the room on crutches, making his way to a desk on the outside row about halfway back. "Mr. Allen is not yet here. He'll text me when he arrives."

"You should have had him text me," Henry said. "You move like an old lady."

"I'll smack you with my crutch when he gets here, and you can open the door for him speedball," Antonio said.

Derrick felt exposed sitting in a chair in front of the room. A desk would have been better, but not much. The desks gave him something to do with his hands. When he first sat in a desk at Potterville High, he could not bear touching the desktops. They were dirty, written on, and carved into. By the second day, he was studying the desktops, wondering who had written on them and what compelled them to engrave their thoughts for all to see. Mostly, the writing was to declare love and relationship. *TJ + AE. Jack loves Nancy.* He wondered if Jack and Nancy remained together, married, had children, lived in Potterville. Maybe more than having the symbolic barrier of protection that the desk offered, he wanted the illusion of permanence the carved writing provided.

Nyx slid a podium to the center of the room. "Where is the note taker?"

Derrick noticed a laptop computer on a desk turned sideways halfway along the edge of the room.

"Bathroom," Antonio said.

"We can't start until she gets back. I swear that girl is either way too early or late," Nyx said.

"We're still waiting on Allen," Henry said.

"We can start without Allen. The adults are not part of this unless they veto our decision," Nyx said and then added, "I don't anticipate that happening."

At that moment, a girl ran into the room, set her feet sideways, sliding toward the front row until she was almost stopped, then her feet found traction, and she took two awkward steps, arms flailing.

Derrick knew her.

L. Linda Maxton said, "I have arrived. But then you probably noticed that." She worked a wad of gum, caused it to pop in her mouth, and then tossed it in the trash.

L. Linda walked to Derrick and took his hand. "I don't get to vote, but if I did, I'd vote for you to stay." She turned to Miriam, still holding Derrick's hand. "This must be your sister. Hi, I'm L. Linda Maxton. Maybe Derrick has mentioned me." Then she looked at Rebekah. "I don't know who this one is." And then she turned and walked to the desk with the computer.

Nyx shook her head. "The Potterville Student Council is now called to order. Before the council is the case of Derrick King, Miriam King, and Rebekah Ford. Before we begin, some housekeeping."

Nyx looked to the back of the room. "Jim, why is Todd with you?"

"I get to bring one guest. That's what we agreed on," Jim Priest said.

"Then why is Red here?"

Red said, "I always come."

Nyx said, "You always come as Jim's guest. Jim said that Todd is his guest today."

"I always come," Red said, looking at the desktop.

"Let him stay. It wouldn't feel right without him," Antonio said.

Nyx frowned. "Do I hear any objections?"

There were none.

"You don't have a vote, and this does not mean that you are on the council. Understand?" Nyx said.

"I understand," Red said.

"In the case of Derrick King, Miriam King, and Rebekah Ford, do I hear motions for disposition?"

Larry Kinkead raised his hand.

"The chair recognizes Larry Kinkead," Nyx said.

"I motion that the three of them be removed from Potterville without delay following this proceeding."

"Does anyone second the motion?"

Henry Clark raised his hand.

"Motion seconded. Are there any other motions?"

Henry Clark raised his hand.

"The chair recognizes Henry Clark."

"I motion that the three of them be removed from Potterville as soon as possible, but that we offer reasonable assistance in their relocation."

"Does anyone second the motion?"

Malcolm Cross raised his hand.

Now Derrick knew who wanted them gone. Larry, Malcolm, and Henry had made their decisions and forged a pact that would likely not be swayed. Those three would vote to remove them; the only question was how soon it would happen.

"Are there any other motions?"

Akira raised her hand.

"The chair recognizes Akira Nakamura."

Unlike Larry and Henry, Akira stood and faced the room. "I motion that we allow Derrick, Miriam, and Rebekah to stay in Potterville and that we provide them with the full support of our council and community."

"Does anyone second the motion?"

Akira remained standing, searching the room with her eyes.

Nothing.

After several silent moments, Nyx raised her hand. "Let the record show that I second the motion."

Derrick saw confusion on the faces of Larry and Henry.

L. Linda squealed and raised her fist above her head.

"Are there any additional motions?"

There were none.

Derrick knew the three options. Miriam had been right again. If they had not taken Akira and Nyx to the facility, only Akira would help them. Although he did not think Nyx would vote with Akira, but she might vote to provide them some help. That did not bother Derrick. He had already decided they could not stay. However, some help made what remained ahead a little easier. Knowing people supported them would mean a lot.

Derrick had little insight into motives and emotions; certainly, he had no psychic abilities. Yet, something bothered him that he could not identify. It was as if an unknown darkness enveloped him. He pondered the black robots and the black aircraft and the missiles in the silos. None of those seemed right. He tried to dismiss it as emotion-fueled anxiety.

He failed.

Possibly it was the hypno-whatever the robot did to him outside. Although he had no memory of anything happening, maybe the fact that it did, and he was unaware, caused this haunted feeling. That was probably it. Identifying the source of his angst should help.

But it did not.

"The floor is open for discussion. Larry, you made the first motion and the floor is yours," Nyx said.

"There are two motions, but the result is the same for both. It's just a matter of whether or not we help them."

"Larry, there are three motions, L. Linda Maxton corrected."

"Yeah, sure, right. Whatever." Larry rolled his eyes. "Let me clarify. There are two viable motions. To be honest, I didn't like Derrick from the beginning. Lying to us like he did. But then, he grew on me. He did. His addition to the track team helped. But here are the cold, hard, honest facts. We have half a dozen robots from Prime, whatever in the hell that is, on our streets. From the Goddamn Prime, mind you. Not just from Pacific Edge, although they've plagued us as well. The entire purpose of the student council is to protect our community. Let's remember that what we have does not come easily …"

Jim Priest stood, interrupting Larry mid-sentence. "He hit a Carver! There should be no need for further discussion. They must be removed and with no help whatsoever."

"Sit down, Jim, and shut up. One more outburst and I'll have you removed," Nyx said.

Priest waved her off but sat as instructed.

The feeling of disaster intensified in Derrick's chest. Earlier, he was sure that he was ready for this proceeding; now, he was not sure he could sit here another minute.

Larry had turned to look at Priest. He turned back towards Nyx. "As I was saying, we've accomplished a lot in Potterville. We can't throw that away, despite how we might feel. I thought you of all people were on board with community first."

"My commitment has not changed," Nyx said.

"You appear to be letting your, uh, feelings affect your judgement," Henry said.

"My judgement is fine," Nyx snarled.

Derrick jumped to his feet. "Sorry. Can I have a moment to speak with Miriam in the hall?"

"Derrick, you are out of order," Nyx said. "Sit down."

"I can't. I need to speak with Miriam. Please. It will only take a moment."

"Maybe he wants to make a break for it," Henry said.

"You want them gone anyway, so if he makes a break for it, what would you care," Akira said standing, fist clinched at her sides.

Nyx stared at Derrick and then, oddly, she looked at Antonio. Antonio gave an almost imperceptible shrugged. Then Nyx turned back to Derrick. "Okay. No more than five minutes."

"Thank you," Derrick said, taking Miriam by the hand and leading her to the hallway.

He walked a few paces away from the door to the intersection with the main hall to ensure they were not overheard.

"What it is?" Miriam asked, the concern etched in her face.

"I don't know. I feel like something bad is about to happen. I don't mean the hearing. I mean, sure, that's bad, but this is something else. Something dark. Something dangerous. I'm not crazy. Maybe it's the hypno thing."

"Stop worrying about the hypnosis. I suspected they had done something like that and now that we know we'll fix it."

Derrick took a deep breath. Lifted his head; took another breath. "Okay, but that's not it. Maybe I am crazy."

Just then the door opened. Henry Clark came out.

"Has it been five minutes?" Derrick asked.

"It has not. Allen is here," Henry said.

When Henry had turned the corner, Miriam said, "You're not crazy. I feel it too."

"But this is not like me. I don't sense things like you do."

"Maybe you're sensing me," Miriam said.

"Is that possible?"

Miriam shrugged. "I don't know. Maybe."

"I'm sorry. I had to get out of there for a moment. This probably didn't help our case. Things can't get much worse."

"I fear they can get worse and will," Miriam said.

"I don't see how," Derrick said.

Henry Clark rounded the corner. A small, dark-skinned man carrying a bag walked at his side.

Miriam said, "I do."

The man smiled and said, "Hello, Miriam King."

Miriam said, "Hello, AJ Patel."

the end

Made in the USA
Middletown, DE
17 August 2020

15601930R00182